MW00782974

# EXTENDED
# CAPACITY

# EXTENDED CAPACITY

### ELENA GRAF

PURPLE HAND PRESS

Purple Hand Press
www.elenagraf.com
© 2023 by Elena Graf

This is a work of fiction. Names, characters, places, and incidents are the product
of the author's imagination or used fictitiously, and any resemblance to actual
persons, living or dead, businesses, institutions, companies, events, or locales is
entirely coincidental.

Trade Paperback Edition
ISBN-13 978-1-953195-22-7
ePub Edition
ISBN-13 978-1-953195-21-0

Cover photo © www.123rf.com/profile_3dart, used by license.

08.22.2023

*To the victims killed at Sandy Hook
Elementary School on December 14, 2012*

*The child who is not embraced by the village will burn it down to feel its warmth.*

—African proverb

# PART I

# Note

You can find a guide to the characters in this book on the author's website: www.elenagraf.com/hobbs-characters/

# Chapter 1

## 6:00 a.m.

*T*onight, thought Olivia Enright. *Tonight, I'll ask Amy to stay.*
They hadn't discussed it, but after giving Olivia the green light to have sex again, her cardiologist girlfriend should be expecting the invitation. Dr. Amy Hsu had put her on a strict diet, tweaked her medication, and prescribed yoga to reduce her stress. Last week, she'd pronounced her fit to resume all activities.

Olivia had already gone back to work full time, but today, her schedule was light—no appointments with her financial clients, no urgent business at the town hall except a meeting with the police chief about the new rules for concealed carry permits. She could enjoy a leisurely start to the day.

She poured another cup of *real* coffee, more progress since her last physical. She'd gleefully discarded all the bags of decaf despite their ridiculous cost. She'd bought them, hoping that premium mail-order brands would be an improvement, but they all tasted like dishwater. Her heart attack had taught her one important lesson—no amount of money could buy the pleasure she'd once enjoyed.

She could see the dark beach through the kitchen window and decided to take a walk. The weather had been unseasonably warm all winter. The snow from the big Christmas storm had melted by New Year's Day. At six a.m., the outside thermometer already read forty-six degrees.

The horizon was rosy by the time Olivia had put on her favorite walking shoes and stepped out onto the sand. Off season, only the dog walkers and a few hardy souls were out at that hour. Olivia often ran into Dr. Stolz and her wife, the Episcopal rector, but Lucy Bartlett had changed her morning routine. Olivia guessed she needed more practice now that her big comeback at the Met was only two months away. As soon as tickets had gone on sale, Olivia had reserved two seats, hoping Amy would want to come. Of course, that meant an overnight stay in New York and a debate over the hotel accommodations. Olivia wasn't looking forward to that conversation.

The excuses Amy offered to avoid sex sounded perfectly reasonable. Getting involved with a patient would cross an inviolable ethical line. The Thanksgiving heart attack, although not serious, was a wake-up call. Amy had described in frightening detail how the exertion during orgasm could trigger another attack. "I'm only telling you because I care." Without question, she did, but it also felt like she was keeping Olivia at arm's length.

Amy's resistance puzzled her. Olivia had never failed to maneuver a woman she fancied into bed, and this woman excited her like no other, not even Sam McKinnon, who was possibly the most thrilling sex partner she'd ever had. Amy was exotic, the first Asian woman to catch her eye, but it was less about her looks than her placid personality. After a lifetime of drama and high-stakes risk, Olivia found Amy's cool reserve oddly erotic.

Watching the sun emerge from an expanding puddle of incandescent pink, she imagined Amy standing beside her. Olivia preferred quiet in the morning, but she wouldn't have to assert the need because Amy listened more than she spoke. She never wasted words or tried to fill a silence with mindless chatter. Although Olivia loved a captive audience, she appreciated Amy's sincere attention. Unlike most of Olivia's lovers, who'd only been interested in her for her money, Amy seemed unfazed by her past as a powerful hedge fund manager or her many millions of dollars in assets. It was refreshing to have value beyond her portfolio, but Olivia sometimes wished Amy would be just a little more impressed.

The tide was coming in. Striding along the damp sand at the ocean's edge, Olivia dodged the lapping waves. Despite the warm winter, the water would be frigid. Getting it into her shoes would end the outing. Olivia hated wet feet.

The sun had finally risen. She zipped up her parka. It was cooler than she'd thought, and the wind off the ocean was brisk. She wished she'd brought her hat and thought about going back for it. Maybe if she picked up the pace, she could keep herself warm. She checked her pulse and heart rate on her smart watch and found it was within normal range.

*Good. Let's go for it!*

❋❋❋

The aria was winding to a close. *Perfect timing*, Liz thought. She'd reached the bottom of the blaze-orange thermal mug she'd gotten for spending fifty dollars at the Kittery Trading Post. With the shortages since COVID, it wasn't hard to spend that kind of money on ammunition. The students in her handgun class were supposed to supply their own, but someone always ran out.

Lucy came to the end of "Elsa's Dream," her character's signature aria. Thirty years ago, she debuted in *Lohengrin* at the Met. She was a lyric soprano, not specifically a Wagnerian, but she'd demanded a public apology for covering up her rape and suspected the casting was payback. Liz had tried to explain that the company wouldn't risk millions on a new production, only to do something so petty, but Lucy wasn't thinking rationally. The frenzy of preparing for this comeback performance had stolen her perspective.

"How was that? Better?" Lucy called to the back of the media room. Liz usually sat in the last row of home theater seats where she wouldn't be a distraction.

"Well…" Liz began, trying to buy herself some time. She didn't want to add to Lucy's anxiety, but she had to tell her the truth. "You're singing sharp again this morning. Can't you hear it?"

"Yes, especially here." Lucy sang the phrase again.

"Exactly."

Lucy raised her eyes toward heaven. "Gracious God, why did I have to marry a woman with perfect pitch?"

"Because it's useful. Lucy, you're not focusing. What's going on?"

"I'm meeting with the finance committee this morning about the bell tower renovations. Olivia keeps demanding more estimates."

"Oh, fuck Olivia," snarled Liz. "She doesn't own the place."

Lucy raised an auburn brow at the expletive. "In a way, she does. If not for her endowment, we couldn't even think of making these big repairs."

"So? You're the rector, aren't you?"

"Yes, but I'm only an honorary member of these committees. I don't actually have a vote."

Liz finished the last swallow of coffee and looked at her watch. "You've been at this for more than an hour. Your mind's not on singing. Let's go for a walk."

"I don't think we have time this morning."

"All right, we'll walk at lunchtime. But you need to take a break. Doctor's orders. Come on. I'll make you some breakfast."

In the kitchen, Liz took out a skillet and tossed in a lump of butter. "Rye toast this morning? Or cinnamon-raisin?" Lucy's green eyes smiled her answer. She might be approaching sixty, a therapist, and the rector of a church, but deep down, she was still a little girl who loved cinnamon-raisin toast.

"What are you doing on your day off?" Lucy asked, filling a coffee pod for herself and one for Liz.

"Working in my shop till it warms up. After I meet you for lunch, I'll go over to the range to practice. I'm teaching that handgun safety class on Saturday." She looked out the kitchen window at the bare ground. "We've had so little snow this winter the outdoor range will probably be open."

"I envy you, being outside. It looks like it will be a beautiful day."

On the way to the refrigerator, Liz kissed the crown of Lucy's head, where her red hair was fading. "But you hate guns, so you won't miss that part."

\*\*\*

Courtney looked around to make sure no one was watching before leaning closer to accept Melissa's kiss. At that obscene hour, everyone at the train station was half asleep, and if someone saw, did it really matter? Courtney tried to tell herself that Hobbs was a tolerant place. They accepted a lesbian rector at the Episcopal Church, a lesbian town manager, a lesbian doctor, and a lesbian police chief. Why wouldn't they tolerate a bisexual school principal? But she worked with children, and when it came to their kids, people could lose their minds.

"Promise to be back by Thursday," said Courtney, gazing intently into Melissa's blue eyes. Her impressive mass of curly, dark hair was still damp from the shower.

"I can't promise, but I'll definitely be home by the weekend. Once I get this trust signed, Mike will get off my back. The deal will make my quota for the first quarter, which means I won't have to go into the office for a while."

"That's good. I always miss you when you're in Boston."

"I know. I miss you too. I'm lucky I can still work from home. The other partners are all back in the office. Mike only lets me work remotely because I bring in so much money."

Melissa gulped down the last of her coffee and put the thermal mug in the cup holder. "You make the best coffee," she said with a smile. "I always miss it when I'm away."

"You miss *my coffee*?" asked Courtney incredulously. "With all those trendy coffee bars near your office!"

Courtney secretly suspected that their quiet life in Maine couldn't compete with the exciting lifestyle Melissa had once lived in Boston. Whenever Melissa had to work in the firm's downtown office, Courtney worried that her girlfriend would be tempted to move back to the city. Melissa seemed to sense her concerns and often reiterated her reasons for living in Hobbs. She *loved* Courtney and their life together. Her family was living nearby, now that her mother was a full-year resident and her sister had moved to Portland. Her job as a successful trust attorney wasn't as exciting or satisfying as it used to be. Melissa insisted that, at forty-three, she wanted more out of life. Harriet Keene, the town lawyer, had invited her to join her practice, but Courtney couldn't see a woman of Melissa's ambition and talent doing wills and real estate transactions for the rest of her life. But who knew?

"What's on your agenda today?" Melissa glanced at the dashboard clock. They were both keenly aware the train would arrive soon.

"Nothing special except a faculty meeting to review last week's active shooter drill. Brenda said we didn't do well."

"Those drills must be a nightmare for the kids."

"And for the teachers, but the superintendent says we have to have them, so we do."

"Say hi to Brenda for me when you see her." Melissa reached for Courtney's hand. They sat holding hands, watching the dashboard clock tick down the minutes. "I'm sorry, babe, but the train will be here any minute. Give me another kiss, and I'll let you go."

### 6:30 a.m.

Brenda suspected that her wife was secretly laughing at her, but she didn't want bacon spatter on her uniform. The floral apron had once belonged to Cherie's mother. The worn cotton grew thinner with every washing, but Cherie believed in using the things passed down from family, not locking them away. She insisted she'd wear the apron until it fell apart.

When the bacon was done, Brenda fished it out and cracked eggs into the pan. Before the kids moved in, Cherie usually made breakfast. Out of necessity, Brenda had become more domestic. It surprised her because she'd never expected to be a mother. Unlike most women of her generation, her childhood dream had never been a big wedding and smiling babies. Brenda had always wanted to be a cop like her dad and big brothers. Yet, here she was, cooking breakfast, as she did most mornings after packing everyone's lunch and lining up the brown lunch bags on the counter like her mother used to do.

Since they'd adopted the kids, Brenda had finally cut her hair short to grow out the blond. The monthly ritual of dyeing it took up too much time, and at her age, she wasn't kidding anyone. Cherie insisted that she liked her new "butch" haircut. Eventually, she'd grow it out because long hair required less attention.

"Hey, lover, what are you thinking about so hard?" asked Cherie, opening a yogurt for her youngest.

"Hair."

"Hair?"

"Yes, I'm deciding to grow mine again once this mousy blond is gone. Maggie Fitzgerald rocks a white braid, and I've been learning some new tricks from doing Megan's hair. Will you mind?"

Cherie's blue-green eyes were full of love. She was a natural blonde—unusual coloring for a biracial woman, but a stunning combination. "Sweetie pie, you are the most beautiful woman in the world, no matter how you wear your hair."

"You don't think the gray makes me look old? That's the only reason I ever dyed it. So those smart-ass new recruits don't think I'm an old lady."

"Brenda, you've been the police chief in this town for so long, I don't think anyone would dare. Besides, you could just give them your death stare. It makes even my blood run cold."

"It does? Really?" Brenda kind of liked the idea of being scary.

Cherie giggled. "No, but I think women should enjoy being the age they are. You worked hard for those grays."

"I did, but I still have twelve years till retirement. Liz says my heart is almost back to normal. I think I can make it."

"So do I. You're doing great. And now that we have two kids to send to college, we'll need the money. Doesn't look like tuition is going down anytime soon."

"They're just babies," said Brenda, gazing at Keith and Megan contentedly munching their Cheerios.

"I know, but it will go by faster than we think." Cherie finished peeling an orange for her daughter and broke it into segments. The girl smiled and popped one into her mouth.

Brenda served Cherie's eggs and her own. Try as she might, she couldn't interest the kids in an old-fashioned breakfast like the meals her mother used to make. They were content with cereal and yogurt. Brenda decided she should be happy because it made her life easier, and they could all get out the door on time.

***

"I'm glad you're not one of those backward healthcare people who think eggs are bad for you," said Susan as Bobbie put a plate in front of her.

Bobbie laughed. "For an old lady, I like to think I'm open-minded and keep up with the research. So many primary care providers don't. My boss insists on it. She quizzes us at staff meetings."

"That sounds like Liz," said Susan, breaking the egg yolk with her fork.

"I bet she had to do a lot of teaching when she was surgical chief at Yale," Bobbie said, sitting down with her plate. "She's good at it. I always learn something I never thought of."

"Not everyone can be a good teacher. When I was in the convent, other nuns were going into social work, prison reform, legal action. I decided to stick with teaching because I love it. Plus, it pays better." Susan sighed. "I just wish it weren't so fraught with politics. The kids don't care. We're not harming them by telling them the truth. What's hurting them is all this hate!"

"I could never do what you're doing," said Bobbie. "It's hard enough to keep my mouth shut." She glanced at the baby monitor beside her plate. "Eat up, honey. I'll need to deal with Joyce soon."

Bobbie looked up from her plate to see the warmth in Susan's blue eyes. She looked so kind and saintly. Bobbie almost expected to see a halo floating around her sleekly-styled, gray hair. She'd discovered that Susan was no saint, especially not in bed. Getting there had been so worth the wait. Bobbie hadn't known what to expect from a woman who'd been a nun and now a priest, but Susan was a tender lover, generous and attentive. Joyce had always had the upper hand. With Susan, there was an equitable balance, a give and take that boded well for the future.

*The future.* Bobbie was afraid to think about that. They were still sneaking around, hoping no one noticed when Susan stayed the night. Bobbie had been picking her up and dropping her off so Susan's car would remain in the rectory parking lot. But a small town was like a fishbowl.

"I can see you're hatching a scheme over there," said Susan. "You're so deep in thought."

"I'm thinking about coming out."

"What? Why now?"

"Joyce always insisted we stay in the closet, but she won't even know, and I'm sick and tired of hiding."

Susan looked worried. "I understand...and sympathize, of course, being in the same place. What do you plan to do?"

"Nothing, for now. I need to think about it and how it will impact you. People are going to judge us when they find out what's really going on."

"And what's really going on? You're loyal enough to take care of your partner who has dementia. Someone else would have written her off and stuck her in a home."

"I do have legal responsibilities. She made me her guardian, turned over this house to me. She has no other family."

"Yes, but it's out of kindness and love that you keep her in her home and created this clever scheme for her care, bringing in your student boarders, inviting a refugee nurse to live with you. People shouldn't judge."

Bobbie shook her head. "But they always do. They have romantic ideas about 'until death do us part.' What happens when the person doesn't even remember you?"

"I think Joyce still remembers you. I'm glad she's calmed down now that she's realized I'm no real threat."

"For now..." said Bobbie philosophically. "This disease is so quirky. Who knows what's next?" She smiled to indicate she wanted to change the subject. "What are you doing after school today?"

"I have a meeting about the active shooter drill we had last week. We didn't do as well as we'd hoped. The police chief is coming to review our performance and tell us what we can do better."

"That school is a fortress. What are they so worried about?"

"I don't know, but the district requires the drills. I hate them."

"Are you afraid?"

Susan's penetrating eyes engaged Bobbie's. "Yes. Anything can happen. There are so many guns around. People who own them aren't careful. They leave guns in places children can find them. Believe me, children see everything. If you don't want a child to get something, you need to lock it up."

Bobbie nodded in agreement. She was no expert on children, but Susan had been teaching for decades, so she should know.

✳✳✳

Sam put on the old sweatshirt that she wore around the house and a pair of flattened moccasins. She needed to get back to her tiling job, which would have been finished by now if she hadn't fired that stupid kid. She scratched the little patch of skin in the small of her back that got dry in the winter because she let the hot shower beat on it. That spot got sore from lifting forty-pound bags of thin set and mortar, which was why she'd hired Peter Langdon.

Maggie stirred and turned in Sam's direction. "Thought you could sneak out, did you?"

"Good morning, gorgeous," said Sam, sitting down on the bed beside her. "You don't have an early class this morning. You can sleep in."

"I know, but I want to make you some breakfast. That's why you keep me, isn't it?"

Sam idly arranged Maggie's long, white braid on the pillow. "I 'keep' you because you're beautiful and sexy, and...I love you."

Maggie's hazel eyes lit up. No matter how often Sam told her how beautiful and loved she was, it was never enough. At first, Sam couldn't understand why a woman like Maggie, who'd been on the stage and admired all her life, needed to hear so many compliments. Then one day, she got it.

Sam had excelled as an architect and won a slew of prestigious awards, but her mother never even mentioned her success. She'd wanted her daughter to wear fashionable clothes, marry a wealthy man, and take her place in society. Sam couldn't think of anything worse. Clearly, Maggie had old wounds too, but their solutions had been completely opposite. Maggie became a glamorous actress to get the adulation she craved; Sam hid behind her competence. Despite their differences, they seemed to fit together just right, like two pieces of a puzzle.

After a tight-lipped kiss because Maggie was self-conscious about morning breath, Sam said, "If you insist on getting up and making me breakfast, I won't turn it down."

"Hmm. How about eggs Florentine? I have some spinach." Sam imagined Maggie flipping through the recipe box she carried around in her mind.

"Sounds good. I'll start the coffee." Sam was glad Maggie had insisted she put away her single-serve coffee maker and make pots of coffee. Before Maggie had moved in, Sam gulped down her morning coffee out of a thermal mug in her truck. The old-fashioned method meant relaxed breakfasts while they finished the pot together.

By the time Sam finished her first cup, Maggie had showered and put on her makeup. She'd left her white hair loose to dry and wore a colorful caftan with fancy sandals that highlighted her sexy nail polish. Sam went out to the living room to load the hopper of the pellet stove so her girlfriend's feet wouldn't get cold. By the time she returned, Maggie was whipping up a gourmet breakfast. Watching from the doorway, Sam felt overwhelmingly grateful for this fantasy come true.

"What's the matter?" asked Maggie, turning around.

"Nothing. Just admiring you." Her reward was a radiant smile.

"Get yourself another cup of coffee. Breakfast will be ready in a minute."

As Sam refilled her cup, she remembered a question she'd been meaning to ask. "I heard you talking to Liz last night. Everything okay?"

Maggie dramatically raised a brow. "Not eavesdropping, were you?"

"No, you didn't close the door, and it was impossible not to hear. I hope there's nothing wrong...with your health, I mean."

"Actually, I'm fine," said Maggie, turning back to the stove. "Liz was kind enough to tell me my tumor marker results. When the report is negative, my regular doctor doesn't always call. Meanwhile, I'm crawling the walls until I know I'm in the clear."

"I can't imagine having something like that hanging over my head for the rest of my life."

"That's how it is when you've had cancer and a gene mutation. It's always there, like a ticking bomb." Maggie cracked the eggs and carefully eased them into the simmering pan. "Liz checks the markers every time and calls me with the results."

"Did you know she was keeping track?" asked Sam, bringing her coffee to the table.

"Yes, but I didn't ask her to do it. She just does."

"Don't you feel like it's an invasion of your privacy? I mean, you're not married anymore."

"No, I appreciate that she cares."

"Don't take this wrong, Maggie, but I think Liz still loves you." Sam waited while Maggie figured out what to say.

"I know, but we can't be married. I need what she can't give. She needs what I can't give."

Sam nodded, wondering if she was giving Maggie what she needed. She certainly hoped so. She liked this arrangement.

"Are you jealous?" Maggie asked. Her narrowed eyes made Sam think she wanted her to be.

"Maybe a little."

"Don't be. I'm your woman now." The phrase was old-fashioned, but Sam liked the possession it implied. What they said and did in bed probably wasn't politically correct either, but that was no one's business. "Her woman" knew exactly how to get her going.

Maggie brought the plates to the table. Sam valued good visual design, and Maggie's plating was always a feast for the eyes. This breakfast, garnished and arranged to perfection, was no exception.

"How much longer will you be working at the school?" asked Maggie, reaching for the fancy butter from Ireland that came in a brick.

"I'm grouting today. I would have been done by now if I didn't have to fire that kid."

"You've been complaining about him for months. I'm surprised it took so long."

"When Peter's focused, he works hard, but he's not consistent. I don't have many people working for me, but I need to be able to count on the ones I have."

"Was he having personal problems?"

"Yeah, his girlfriend threw him out a couple of weeks ago, and he had to move back to his mother's house. After that, I could always smell pot on him. I wouldn't be surprised if he's doing harder stuff."

Maggie sighed. "Some boys just can't seem to find their place in the world, or if they do, how to keep it. I see them at the college. They start out okay and then something happens. It's like they have no resilience."

"Believe me, Maggie. I really tried with him."

"I know you did. I remember when Liz got you involved."

Maggie was there when Liz had told Sam about a kid with problems looking for a job. "I wasn't sure about him at first, but he turned out to be a good tiler. He has a great eye for design." Sam got up to get another cup of coffee. "I can't wait for this project to be over. It's kind of boring. I only took it because I was getting antsy waiting to hear about the museum project."

"I knew that. But it's good to stay busy. I know I'm glad to be teaching again, especially now that my baby-sitting services are no longer required." Maggie put up a brave front, but Sam knew she was hurt by how quickly her daughter and grandchildren had adjusted to her leaving. "How often will you have to be in California?" Maggie asked.

"Maybe a week or two a month. More in the beginning...and at the end when the finish materials are being installed. Will you be okay with that?"

Maggie shrugged. "Do I have a choice? I want you to be a success."

"Maybe you can come with me sometimes. I could show you off. My arm candy." Sam was just teasing, but Maggie's eyes grew large.

"Is that how you see me?"

"No! Of course not," protested Sam anxiously.

"Just pulling your leg, Sam. I know I'm more than that. But it's flattering to hear you think I'm still attractive."

"You had me going for a while."

"Well, I hope so. I'm an actress, remember?" Maggie gave Sam a sexy wink.

### 7:30 a.m.

Amy Hsu enjoyed listening to the soft murmur of the assistants and nurses as they prepared for the day. She liked being part of this community of women who looked after the health of the town. Raised in a close-knit ethnic circle, she'd never felt completely comfortable with white women. When she was growing up, Amy's parents did most of their socializing in the Chinese community. Friendships with Caucasians were discouraged. As if Amy would have time for friends between her studies and all the after-school activities carefully chosen to help her get into the right college.

When the time came to look for a mate, she'd been encouraged to choose one of her own kind. Her parents weren't overjoyed to learn that Amy was a lesbian, but when they met Jill Chen, a brilliant neurosurgeon who even spoke Mandarin, she instantly became the approved choice. While Jill looked perfect on paper, she had a dark side. Surgeons needed strong egos and overdeveloped confidence to do their jobs, but Jill took pleasure in putting Amy in her place, reminding her that she was "just" a cardiologist. Raised to be unfailingly respectful and dutiful, Amy had endured the constant put downs until she couldn't anymore.

When she'd finally complained about the abuse, her friends didn't believe her. She had no bruises, so she must be exaggerating. Her parents, especially her mother, expected her to turn a blind eye and make the marriage work. With everyone questioning her choices, no wonder she'd begun doubting herself, but there was one thing she was very sure about. Even though she missed the intimacy, sex especially, she was in no hurry to get involved again.

Amy decided to make another cup of tea. As she dispensed hot water from the instant hot faucet in the break room, she wondered if her cultural heritage had determined her choice of morning beverage. Teresa Gai, the newest medical assistant, came in to make tea, waiting respectfully while Amy filled her cup.

"And how are you on this fine day, Dr. Amy?" Teresa asked. "I am told that it is very warm for this time of year." Her English accent implied that her preference for tea was probably also an ethnic choice. She was a recent refugee from a part of war-torn Sudan that had once been a British colony.

"I was here last winter," said Amy. "It seemed colder than New York, but according to the national weather service, it was the warmest winter on record."

"But it's always refreshing!" When Teresa smiled, which was often, her teeth contrasted brilliantly against her dark skin. Being a recent transplant from the old world, she wasn't mixed blood like most African Americans. Amy found it comforting to have another woman of color in the practice. Cherie Harrison was biracial, but with her blond hair and light skin, she could pass for white. Everyone assumed she was, no matter how often she asserted that she was black.

Amy wondered why she was thinking so much about race this morning. Her friends in Hobbs treated her like anyone else. Olivia said that she didn't even consider Asians another race, but she'd said she found Amy's eyes "exotic." *Can't have it both ways*, thought Amy. *Make up your mind!* In some ways, Olivia was as overbearing as her ex, except she was direct, whereas Jill was passive aggressive. She always denied pressuring Amy.

"Teresa, it seems you've become the queen of blood draws," said Amy, to be sociable.

"Dr. Amy, I am glad to be able to use my training in any useful way. And Dr. Liz is kind to be flexible about my hours so I can go to school." In her own country, Teresa had been a certified nurse, but her credentials had been lost, along with her husband, her parents, and her home. She and her daughter had barely escaped with their lives. But to practice her profession in her new country, she must retrain and be licensed all over again.

"We're glad to get good people with all the labor shortages. How does Grace like her new school?"

"Very much. I feel lucky that we can live in one of the best school districts in the state. Miss Bobbie is encouraging her to study science."

"That's good. We need more girls in STEM disciplines."

"A woman must get a good education and be prepared to make her own way in the world. One never knows where she will land. Look at me!"

**7:46 a.m.**

Riding shotgun in Liz's big F-150 always made Lucy feel like a real Mainer. As they passed their neighbors out walking or jogging, Lucy waved to them, and they waved back. The friendliness of a small town in Maine was so different from the Massachusetts suburb of Springfield, where Lucy had grown up, or Boston, where she'd been a curate, or New York, where she'd attended Juilliard and made her home when she was a principal soprano at the Met. Hobbs felt like home in a way no other place had.

Since she'd been going back and forth to New York for her doctorate and the surprise opportunity to return to singing, Lucy had been spending more time away from Hobbs. No wonder she clung so fiercely to her new wife, her friends, and her congregation. She wanted to sing again, but she was trying to find a balance. It felt like the preparation for the new production of *Lohengrin* had taken over her life.

Studying Liz's strong profile, Lucy envied her freedom to do whatever she liked today. Because Liz didn't have to see patients, she wore no makeup and had barely pulled a brush through her unruly, gray hair. It didn't matter. Her deliberately messy grunge style looked the same whatever she did.

A hand reached across the console and rooted around in Lucy's lap until it found hers. Somehow, Liz always sensed when she was struggling. Even before they'd become involved, whenever there was trouble, Liz showed up to help. She'd come into the church where Lucy was praying and quietly sit beside her or appear at the rectory office with coffee from Awakened Brews. As a priest, Lucy couldn't officially believe in reincarnation, but she often wondered if they'd been together before. She'd never told Liz, who openly ridiculed new age religions. "No, things don't happen for a reason. No, there isn't a lesson to learn in every disaster," she'd say in her most disparaging tone. Liz always said things like that, but Lucy knew she was more spiritual than she let on.

Liz's hand was warm and squeezed Lucy's gently. "Honey, you need to stop worrying. That bell tower was falling apart decades before you came to Hobbs. It's still standing, and you don't have to fix it today."

"I try to remember that God is leading me and to live in the moment."

"Look at Erika. When she woke up that morning and headed up to Colby to teach her class, she had no idea she'd be dead by nightfall." Lucy couldn't forget that awful night. She wondered what would have happened if she hadn't fallen asleep in front of the TV downstairs and discovered Erika sooner. Liz said that aneurysms were often silent killers. In an otherwise healthy woman in her sixties, a doctor wouldn't necessarily consider a headache serious. "I shouldn't have brought up Erika," said Liz. "You have enough on your mind."

"No, I'm glad you did. Life is short and things can change quickly. Erika popped into your thoughts to remind me." Lucy could only get away with saying such things because she knew that Liz believed in spirits. She'd even admitted to having posthumous conversations with her dead friend.

Liz parked in front of the rectory door and yanked up the hand brake. "I'll pick you up at twelve-thirty and bring you a sandwich. Tuna okay?" Lucy happily agreed. Liz never made tuna salad from a can or foil pouches, only from fish left over from dinner. "We can eat in the truck before we go for our walk. It's warm today, but not that warm." Liz leaned over to offer a goodbye kiss. Lucy caught her arm and held on tight.

"I love you," she said more fervently than usual. Those words had been accompanied with all sorts of feelings—passion, playfulness, lust, joy, relief. This morning, they sounded desperate.

"I love you too," said Liz, looking curious. Her reassuring smile, along with another gentle kiss, made Lucy feel better. "See you later."

Lucy stood on the rectory steps and watched Liz drive off, missing her already. At the start of a marriage, wanting to be together every minute wasn't unusual, but they weren't kids anymore, and they both had responsibilities. Lucy trudged up the rectory stairs and opened the door.

Jodi, the admin, looked sleepy when Lucy passed her desk. She had two toddlers at home and getting them off to day care must be challenging. Ironically, work was probably the only place she felt off duty. "Oh, Lucy," Jodi called as Lucy reached her office door. "Reshma was just here, looking for you. Should I call her and let her know you're here?"

"Sure. Thanks."

Lucy unpacked her laptop. She was reading her emails when she heard a familiar voice.

"Mother Lucy, do you have time for me now?" asked Reshma, standing in the doorway with two cups from Awakened Brews. Lucy motioned for her to come in.

Reshma settled into one of the visitors' chairs. She was wearing a linen collar this morning, so she must have done her laundry recently. Before Liz had installed a washer and dryer in the rectory, Lucy had to wash her clothes at the laundromat in town. By comparison, Reshma had it easy.

"Thanks for the coffee," said Lucy, prying the plastic lid off her cup. She'd already had plenty of coffee, but she didn't want to hurt her curate's feelings. "Tell me what's going on."

"Mother Lucy, I promise you that I am doing my best to get this Sunday school project off the ground, but I can't find any teachers, and there's only a handful of children signed up. People tell me the Sunday school was struggling even before the pandemic."

"It was. The parish had fewer young families with children, so we had to cut back on the number of classes."

The young woman emitted a deep sigh. "Mother Lucy, maybe this isn't a good assignment for me. I know nothing about education or what children need."

"Think back to your own childhood and what you needed."

"At Sunday school age, I was in a refugee camp in Sudan."

Reminded of Reshma's difficult path to where she was today, Lucy erased her smile. "I wish I could help you, but the only formal teaching I've done was in graduate school. Okay. I gave voice lessons to Denise, but that doesn't count."

"But at least you're a mother."

"But my child was sixteen when she came back, well past the age for Sunday school." Lucy studied Reshma's frown and realized she was genuinely perplexed. "I'm sorry, Reshma, but I really don't know how to advise you. Susan is a teacher. Maybe she can help you. Or Simone. She used to be an elementary school principal."

"Good idea. I'll ask them, but I thought you should know why I haven't made more progress."

"I appreciate your keeping me informed. Let's bring it up in the vestry meeting again and see if anyone has any suggestions. Meanwhile, reach out to Susan and Simone to see if they have some ideas."

Reshma nodded, but now she seemed even more discouraged. "I was looking forward to this project. I like children."

"That helps," said Lucy. "I know you can do this. I'm counting on you!"

"I'll do my best," said Reshma without an ounce of enthusiasm.

After the young woman left, Lucy finished the coffee she'd brought and discovered she'd wanted it after all.

❋❋❋

Sam groaned as she lifted the forty-pound bag of grout powder. This was the reason she hired young men. For a woman in her sixties, she was strong, but why break her back when a kid less than half her age could easily lift these bags? She was annoyed with herself for letting Peter Langdon go in a fit of temper, but she'd warned him about smoking pot at work. It didn't matter that cannabis was legal in Maine now. She'd have done the same if he'd been drinking alcohol on the job.

She couldn't blame Liz. She'd been up front about the boy's problems. He'd been living with his single mother and couldn't hold down a job. Lucy, who'd been counseling his mother, told Liz about his stash of guns. That's when Liz made him her project and tried to straighten him out. She'd talked Sam into giving him a job. "On a trial basis, of course. If it doesn't work out, I'll figure something else out. I know a lot of people in the chamber of commerce." Liz often used her connections to fix things quietly, like getting Erika's father a place in senior housing. People complained about "old boys" networks. In Hobbs, the hidden power structure was a bunch of old girls.

Sam was willing to take a chance on the kid. Sometimes, the only thing a misfit needed was a chance to feel useful, but Peter was a strange one, all right. Barely legal, he was tall and gangly, but he had powerful arms and a strong back. Sam saw intelligence in his intense blue eyes—one reason she had been willing to give him a chance. His friends called him "Pete," but he'd asked his new boss to call him "Peter." Sam guessed it was his way of asking for her respect.

Sam brought in the last of her buckets and the mixer. She set them down and surveyed Peter's work. He had talent as a tiler, but lately, his mind hadn't been on the job. He'd volunteered that he'd been fighting with his girlfriend and asked Sam's advice. She didn't know what to say. Her own track record with women had been spotty at best.

Peter brought the girl around to show off some of his work. He'd grinned like a fool when she complimented him. Before they broke up, the fighting had gotten ugly, but he swore he'd never laid a hand on her. He had a temper, so Sam would not be surprised if he did. There was so much domestic violence in Maine, especially during the long winters.

When the girlfriend finally threw Peter out, he'd crawled back to his mother's. Not long after, Sam had met Renee at the supermarket and asked how it was going with Peter home again. Renee didn't say much, but from her hangdog look, it was obvious she wasn't happy about having him back.

Sam put on a mask and added grout to the bucket. She was glad she was still strong enough to keep the industrial-size mixer from dislocating her elbow or ripping her shoulder out of the socket, but this was a job she would have happily left for a male helper. She wondered how much longer she could do tile work if she couldn't find a replacement for Peter. After she put on her knee pads, she spread some grout to test the consistency. Just right. Usually, she enjoyed the mindless work of spreading grout because it gave her time to think. This morning, her thoughts annoyed her.

She was angry that Peter had let her down after all she'd invested in mentoring him. She'd shared the design secrets she'd learned from a master tiler in Rome, where she'd gone in her fifties to study art history. She'd taught Peter the theory behind what they did along with the mechanics, explaining how modern decoupling membranes were based on the same principles the Romans used in mosaic floors that lasted thousands of years. He'd sucked up the knowledge like a sponge, always prompting her to tell him more. Before she'd fired him, she'd started teaching him drafting.

*So much wasted talent and potential. What a crying shame.*

### 8:00 a.m.

Courtney always waited outside while the buses arrived. When she was in elementary school, the principal used to greet the students at the door. Now that she was a principal, she hoped her students felt as welcomed as she had all those years ago. Elementary school had been the best time of her life. Her parents were still together and weren't constantly fighting. She'd adored her teacher, Mrs. Murphy, and had a perfect circle of girlfriends. She'd wished it would never end, probably why she'd chosen teaching as a profession.

She watched Brenda Harrison get out of her car and help her youngest, who still needed a booster seat. She set her campaign hat on the roof while she lifted her down, then carefully replaced it. She'd said she always wore full uniform around town because a chief needed to set an example. She always looked buttoned down, her shirts pressed with perfect creases, the cuffs never crushed. Courtney guessed her wife did the ironing in that family, but maybe not. Brenda looked more than competent. Courtney was glad that Melissa's dress blouses were "no iron." Expensive, but worth every penny.

Brenda herded her children toward the school entrance. She touched two fingers to the brim of her hat in a little salute. "Morning, Ms. Barnes." She always addressed Courtney formally when the children were nearby. Courtney supposed that was also to set a good example. The chief's careful manners and courtly, old-school respect had a certain charm. No doubt, the world could use more courtesy.

Brenda bent to give each child a goodbye kiss and a hug. The girl always clung to her mother, but Brenda gave her a little nudge forward. Her eyes followed them carefully as they went through the front doors, opened wide when the buses arrived, but carefully locked when school was in session. At this point, Brenda would usually tip her hat again and depart. Courtney guessed that she wanted to talk about the meeting that afternoon.

"I'll let you take the lead," said Brenda. "You'll know how to frame it with your teachers. I'll just give the details of how they fell short."

"Okay, but try not to be too hard on them. Morale is low lately. We're short-staffed as it is, and there's all the background noise."

Of course, Brenda would understand the code Courtney was using to refer to the political controversy over library books and the history curriculum. The school board regularly requested a police presence at their meetings in case things got out of hand.

"I understand, Courtney. I won't pound your staff, but these drills are important to their safety. It's my job to protect people, but there are so many threats. Sometimes, I don't know how."

Courtney felt Brenda's frustration. She reached out and touched her arm. "Thank you. We appreciate your efforts."

"Glad you do. Not everyone thinks police are the good guys anymore. It's hard on department morale. Like you, we're having trouble hiring. Used to be that young men dreamed of being cops. Some young women too." Brenda grinned affably. "And I was one of them."

For a moment, Courtney could look past the jowls and the crow's feet and picture an eager young police rookie, looking sharp in her new uniform.

### 8:17 a.m.

Olivia wasn't sure she liked Brenda with short hair, but she admired her for growing out the blond and going gray. The idea of doing such a thing was alarming to Olivia, who'd carefully observed how signs of aging triggered unforgivable judgements. As soon as a female news anchor looked old, she got kicked out the door. Olivia had decided that physical decline must be suppressed at all costs, surgically, if necessary. She'd had work done on her eyes and a chin lift. She continued to dye her hair the dark brunette of her youth. The contrast made her blue eyes even more compelling, which people said was attractive, especially Amy, whose naturally dark hair was as sleek as a crow's wing.

Hair color was a conundrum. Suddenly, even younger women were going gray, and they could because their young faces set against the gray revealed it was just another costume, another fad. Olivia listened to them in the salon while the stylist stripped all the color out of their hair. They had no idea how it felt to get old, to be pushed out, to be a has been. Worst of all, to become invisible. When Olivia walked down a Manhattan street at thirty, she hated the wolf whistles. At sixty-four, she'd consider it a compliment.

She gave Brenda another critical look. She had a handsome face with a strong chin. Her blue eyes were resolute, but not aggressive. They understood each other, which was why they made a good team.

There was a time they didn't get along. At first, Brenda had sided with the townies and saw Olivia as an adversary. Olivia had only run for town manager to head off financial and ecological disaster. A beach town lived or died by its natural resources, and Hobbs' greatest assets were miles of sandy beaches and verdant marshes filled with waterfowl. The board of selectmen (and they were all men) wanted to build on every patch of land, including the marshes.

Olivia had yet to win over the board completely, but she knew she had Brenda on her side. Keeping her on the job after COVID weakened her heart had been the right decision. Brenda was an experienced officer and had many productive years ahead of her. She was something of a role model when it came to heart trouble. If she could fully recover, so could Olivia.

Today, Brenda had come with a proposal that had the power to disturb the town ecology, but not in the salt marsh. As the chief of police, Brenda oversaw issuing gun permits. Now, she wanted to change the rules. Olivia wanted to be re-elected, so she needed to make sure this new regulation wouldn't offend the Second Amendment people.

"Okay, Brenda, I've read your new rules, but not being a gun owner, I don't really understand. Give me the high points." Olivia always believed in cutting to the chase. Her time was valuable.

"In Maine, we have what's called 'constitutional carry,' which means that anyone can carry a handgun. The only people who still bother to get a permit are those required to carry a weapon for their jobs, law-abiding types, or gun safety advocates like Liz Stolz."

"In other words, out of necessity or a conviction that some regulation is good. But if those are the only people who apply for a permit, why change the rules?"

"That's a good question, and honestly, it's my small way of doing something about the gun problem."

Olivia liked the honest answer, but she could always count on Brenda to be candid.

"How will your new rules help?"

"The state only requires a recent photo of the applicant. By asking people to come in so we can take their official photograph and review their paperwork, we can look them over and see if they look sane enough to carry a gun. It won't be an extensive interview, but a trained officer can pick up a lot of information from a casual conversation. It's amazing what people will reveal when they feel relaxed. It will give us the chance to look the people in the eye who own guns in our town and know what we're dealing with."

"It does stick out Hobbs as being different from surrounding towns."

"That could be a good thing. Maybe it would set an example."

The change could bring some valuable publicity to Hobbs, but also negative coverage. Olivia needed to weigh the political harm from each, but she felt inclined to approve the new regulations.

"Okay, Brenda, write it up, and I'll send the proposal to the board of selectmen for discussion at the next meeting. Will you come and explain it to them like you just explained it to me?"

"Of course, I'd be happy to do it. And I'll bring along Officer Girard. This was his project, and he can answer any questions."

# Chapter 2

Maggie glanced up at the clock over the window, a mid-century modern classic that perfectly fit Sam's design sensibilities. Her first class wasn't until one and the content was essentially unchanged since she'd taught it at NYU. Although it was still the same course, successive generations of students reacted to it differently. Maggie had seen many youth crazes in her time—from hippies and preppies to yuppies and goths and punks and emos. A recent crop had dumped ice water buckets on their heads and eaten pods of laundry detergent. Ironically, her students at the community college were more serious and thoughtful than the university students she taught. Maybe the extra effort to get an education had given them more respect for it.

She was still in her nightgown, but she'd exchanged her sexy sandals for fleece-lined slippers. The dampness from Jimson Pond seeped into the living space in every season, but in the winter, the floors were frigid. Sam always filled the hopper of the pellet stove before she left, but eventually, the pellets ran out. Maggie found the galvanized livestock pails Sam filled with pellets too heavy to lift. Since her double mastectomy, which had prophylactically removed both breasts, she was extra cautious about lifting heavy things.

Now that she no longer had to get up to wake her granddaughters and get them off to school, she often lounged around in the mornings. Maggie missed the girls, but she didn't miss being tied down to their schedule, meeting the bus every morning and afternoon, preparing their afternoon snack, or feeding them when their mother was late at her job as a senior news producer at the TV station. She didn't miss their demand to sit with them while they watched their favorite TV shows. Maggie was sure she'd seen every episode of *Young Sheldon*.

She decided to make another cup of coffee, mildly scolding herself for procrastinating when she had things to do, like reviewing the students' suggestions for the spring musical. The classic Broadway hits from the past didn't seem to resonate with this generation. They wanted to believe they could perform *Hamilton*, but their youthful ambition exceeded their talent. As usual, Maggie would have to choose the play.

When she finally put her cup in the dishwasher, she noticed some ducks floating idly on the pond. This winter had been so warm that the waterfowl seemed to think it was still fall. When she'd lived with Liz, Maggie could see the ocean from her bedroom window, but this beautiful view was not the consolation prize. Neither was Sam.

**9:22 a.m.**

The school was always overheated, and the bathroom was sweltering. A dark V of sweat in Sam's T-shirt showed how much she was perspiring. The humidity building up in the bathroom had fogged the mirrors over the bank of sinks, leaving a slick sheen on the tile. Moisture was good because it slowed the grout cure rate, which meant a stronger bond and less cracking. In hot, dry weather, Sam misted the grout with a spray bottle to keep it damp.

Working her way to the door, Sam smiled, thinking of the first bathroom floor she'd tiled. She'd forgotten the old maxim, "never paint yourself into a corner." When she'd finally decided against standing in the bathtub all day, she'd discovered that stepping on a newly grouted floor didn't really matter.

Sam gazed over the expanse of boring beige tile. She'd begun to hate this job. She'd assumed a bathroom in a school should be educational and had designed a colorful mural depicting some of Maine's small mammals. She'd relished the challenge of executing a mosaic depicting porcupines, beavers, and fisher cats, but the school board had rejected the design for budgetary reasons. Even after Sam had decided to eat some of the costs and lowered her estimate, the school had opted for something uninspiring and vanilla. "We don't want the kids hanging out in the bathroom, admiring your work," one sour-faced board member had said to grunts of agreement. "We want them to do their business and get out!"

Sam knew the importance of exposing children to art. Her parents, stiff, old-school WASPs, had made many mistakes raising her, but they'd brought her to some of the world's greatest art museums—the Louvre, the Vatican Museum, and the national galleries of so many countries. She'd seen color and space put together in ways she would have never imagined, and learned that light made all the difference.

When she looked over this project, both her eyes and her soul were bored. Any apprentice could have laid this tile, which is why she'd left it to Peter. He'd done exacting work, precise cuts and evenly set tile. She suddenly wished that she hadn't fired him so impulsively, but it was too late now.

Sam quickly washed up in the janitor's sink, but catalytic-cure grout could block the pipes, so she'd have to dump the rinse water outside. *Good thing it's a warm day for January*, she told herself as she opened the back door. After being in the overheated school, the cold air smacking her face made her choke on her words. She imagined ice crystals forming on her wet arms like in nature videos depicting a quick change of seasons.

She quickly positioned the brick they'd been using to keep the door open and hurried around the corner of the building to the lone spigot. It never made any sense to her that the water access was so far from the door. Whoever had designed that school was an idiot. Unlike Sam, who'd deliberately spent time in the trades, many architects ignored practical considerations. Sam's lone female professor at Princeton used to say that men needed to get out of their heads and think with their hands and feet. Professor Shannon had supposedly been an affirmative action hire. Sam's detractors had hurled the same accusation at her. They said she'd only gotten the big commissions and awards because she was a woman, which had taken all the sweetness out of her success.

*Why am I thinking about this old shit when I'm freezing to death?* Sam wondered as she blasted the trowels and floats with frigid water from the spigot. She carried the heavy bucket to the curb and poured the water and sludge down the storm drain. By now, her hands were tingling from the cold. As she cleaned the blades of the mixer, she had a strange feeling that she was being watched. She banged the metal beater against the side of the bucket to dislodge most of the water. The floats and trowels were mostly clean, but she rinsed them again. As she dumped the wash water, she eyed the trees on the other side of the parking lot. There was no motion. The only sound was the light wind rattling the branches.

As Sam carried her buckets and tools to her truck, her fingers were so numb she couldn't even feel her fingertips. She remembered that she had an old, zippered hoodie in the back seat and put it on. Before she opened the door of the truck, she gave the little forest behind the school a last suspicious look.

### 9:49 a.m.

"Ms. Gedney, I don't feel good," said a small voice.

Susan gently raised the boy's chin. His eyes weren't glassy or gluey from a cold, or, God forbid, COVID. Susan was instantly suspicious. This wasn't the first time Keith had faked an illness to get out of class. She felt his forehead with the back of her hand. Maybe it was her imagination, but he seemed to lean into her touch, like he wanted the contact. But he didn't feel feverish. His skin felt dry and cool.

Susan bent to meet his eyes. "Keith Harrison, tell me the truth. Are you really sick?" she asked in a firm, but kind, tone.

"Yes, Ms. Gedney. My stomach hurts." He rubbed it for emphasis.

Over the forty years she'd been a teacher, Susan had seen dozens of children fake illnesses to get out of class. Many boys found sitting still in class a challenge, but most of them looked forward to gym. Susan debated whether to send Keith to the nurse. The boy's mother was a physician's assistant. If her son were really sick, she wouldn't have sent him to school.

Susan looked up and noticed that the classroom volunteer, Simone Ballou, Keith's great aunt by adoption, listening attentively.

"Would you like me to take him to the nurse, Ms. Gedney?" she asked.

Susan peered at the boy. "Keith, do you need Mrs. Ballou to take you to the nurse?"

"No, I know how to get there." He should. He'd been there often enough.

"All right, but I want you to go straight to her office. No stopping to go to the bathroom or anywhere else, do you understand?"

The boy nodded gravely. "Yes, Ms. Gedney."

"I'll check to see how you are after gym class, okay?"

He smiled and took off with an enthusiasm that only increased Susan's doubts.

Simone looked concerned. "Maybe I should have gone with him."

"No, he needs to know we trust him." Why was she telling Simone, who'd been a teacher and a school principal for years? She wondered if she knew some reason not to trust the boy. Was he getting into mischief at home? She studied Simone for more clues, but the older woman had already turned her attention to the girl she was helping with the math lesson.

After Keith left, Susan picked up his notebook. His handwriting was awful, but that was common among young boys. The margins were full of doodles, mostly cartoon characters rendered with remarkable accuracy for a boy his age. She'd noticed before that he had artistic talent. The math symbols were copied more neatly than the words on the facing page, and every problem Susan had put on the board had been solved correctly.

She knew the basics of the boy's sad history. His parents had died in a murder-suicide. How would a life-changing trauma like that impact such an intelligent and sensitive mind? Fortunately, one of the women who'd adopted him was a licensed therapist in addition to being a PA. His other mother was the police chief, which couldn't be easy on the boy, as if he didn't have enough troubles.

Susan carefully closed the notebook and moved on to the desk of the next student. This poor girl's hair smelled greasy and looked unkempt, but there was no sign of nits. Twice this year, Susan had needed to email the parent and alert the school nurse. Susan knew little about the child except that her mother had abandoned the family. The father did what he could despite working three jobs. His mother, who lived in the same trailer park, tried to help, but she was working too. The girl's clothes often smelled of cigarette smoke, and sometimes, marijuana.

Susan went down the row, checking the students' work until the bell rang.

"Ms. Gedney, would you like me to take the boys to gym class?" asked Simone.

"No, please take the girls to Mrs. Martel for health class. I can drop off the boys on my way to my meeting with Ms. Barnes."

"Sounds good to me," said Simone brightly. Susan liked her cheerfulness and listening to her warm Southern accent.

### 10:02 a.m.

Courtney closed her door, although the administrative assistants were all on break except for their newest hire. It was probably better that fewer eyes witnessed the meeting. Susan's project had been a covert mission from the start. Courtney had asked her to find a subtle way to mentor two new teachers. So far, neither had caught on, but their classroom management had shown a noticeable improvement.

After much wrangling, the school board had agreed to give Susan an extra-duty bonus for her efforts. Her gratitude for four hundred dollars seemed a little over the top, but Courtney understood. When she'd first come to Hobbs and her ex-husband was behind in his child-support payments, she'd struggled too.

They reviewed the progress of the new teachers before moving on to a more complicated topic—expanding the mentorship program to include some of the old timers. Positioning the arrangement in a way that wouldn't offend anyone was tricky, especially because both Courtney and Susan were new to the district.

"I talked to Keith Harrison's mother this morning," Courtney said. "How's he doing?"

"I had to send him to the nurse again. He claimed to have a bellyache."

Courtney felt comfortable enough with Susan to make a face. "I bet he did."

"I know. I thought the same, but he could have a bug. There's that stomach virus going around."

Courtney let out a long sigh. "After the pandemic, these little bugs the kids pass around seem so insignificant, but they can be so awful when you have them."

"Considering what that boy has gone through, I think his symptoms are psychological, but I'll call his mother after school. She'll want to know."

"Can't be easy for Cherie and Brenda, suddenly becoming the parents of two kids. They're not young."

"Careful, Courtney," said Susan with the barest hint of a smile. "You're talking to an old lady."

Courtney still hadn't gotten used to Susan's dry sense of humor. It took her a moment to realize she was teasing. "I'm sorry. I didn't mean anything by it."

"I know."

"You're older, but I think of you as a peer. I hope that's okay."

"It's more than okay." Susan's smile was full of warmth.

"I meant to tell you how much I enjoyed your sermon yesterday.

It's a little weird to see you in your other role, but Kaylee is suddenly going through a religious phase and wants to go to church."

"Good for you for letting her explore her faith. Because of the sexual abuse, some parents won't let their kids go near a church."

"It feels good coming to your church. Melissa is a Jew, but she comes along to support us. I think she likes being there, too."

"Lucy has created a welcoming atmosphere at St. Margaret's, and it seems to be working. You should bring Kaylee to our youth bake-off. We give the kids the ingredients and they need to come up with a creative cake. Should be fun."

"Sounds like fun. I'll mention it to her." Courtney glanced at the clock over the door. "We have a few minutes. Want to go down to the faculty lounge and see what the others are up to?"

"Yes, let's," said Susan, gathering her papers.

Courtney heard a sharp crack. "What's that?" she asked in a loud whisper.

"Sounded like a gun."

"I thought hunting season ended in November. Could be kids shooting in the old sand pit."

"No, it was closer than that," said Susan, glancing anxiously at the door.

Another sharp crack sounded, then another, followed by a long stream of shots. Courtney's breath caught. The moment they'd all feared had come.

She ran into the open office outside her door and snatched up the microphone from the admin's desk. "Lock down! Lock down! Active shooter in the school. All teachers return to your classrooms and lock your doors. This is NOT a drill!"

She turned to Susan, whose face was gray. "I need to get my class. My boys are in gym. The girls have health."

"Let those teachers handle it. You stay here," said Courtney. The young admin was visibly shaking. "Lock the door," Courtney ordered. She had to say it twice before the young woman got up and fiddled with the lock. Courtney suddenly remembered that the administrative office was still on the list to be reinforced. "Hardened," they called it in military terms. "Both of you come into my office. We'll be safer in there."

### 10:07 a.m.

Sam had spent enough time at the range with Liz to recognize the sound of gunfire. She slammed shut the door of her truck and ran to the back of the school. As she turned the corner, she saw the door swinging in the wind.

"My God!" she murmured under her breath as more shots sounded. She whipped out her phone, but her hands were shaking, and it took two tries to pull up the keypad to dial 911. Her head swam as she waited for the operator to answer. Finally, a female voice came on the line. "Please state your name and the address you're calling from."

"This is Sam McKinnon. I'm at Hobbs Elementary. Someone is shooting inside." She tried to answer the dispatcher's questions while hurrying to the open door. She cautiously peered down the dark hallway. "Please!" Sam begged. "Please, just tell them to come!"

"Yes, Ms. McKinnon, please be calm. The chief is being informed. Officers will be on the way soon. How many shots did you hear?"

"How the hell should I know? Please! Just come. Now!"

Against her better judgment, Sam went down the short corridor. She tried the door and found it locked from the inside.

### 10:10 a.m.

Brenda leaned on the lectern while Officer Meehan struggled to get out his question. She admired him for getting over a childhood stutter, but sometimes it tried her patience. She couldn't understand why a simple change to the permitting process was drawing so many questions. She looked over her shoulder and reread the wording projected on the whiteboard.

The door flew open. "Chief, active shooter at Hobbs Elementary."

The dispatch supervisor's eyes were wide. All faces turned in her direction, then back to Brenda, whose mind suddenly went blank. She tried to remember which officers she'd assigned to the active shooter response squad. Fortunately, they identified themselves by jumping to their feet. That woke her up, and she did a mental review of the patrol schedule. Most of her officers were in that room for the weekly meeting. Only two cars were out on the road. Dispatch would have already called them to the scene. She just hoped that the trained team got there before they did. One of those patrol officers was a rookie.

"Make sure you wear protective gear," Brenda called after the officers leaving the room. "Second squad, head out to direct traffic. Third squad, block the roads to the school." The room emptied quickly as the officers headed to their assigned locations. On the way to the parking lot, Brenda called the number of the state police commander.

"We're heading down there," he assured her. "Your dispatcher already called."

"I can't believe it," said Brenda, getting into her squad car. "How can it happen here?"

"It's our turn," he said with a sigh.

### 10:13 a.m.

The workshop lights flashed. Focused as she was on making an incredibly precise cut, Liz didn't notice at first. She pushed the piece of wood through the blade and turned off the motor. The relay that flashed the lights when Liz had a phone call had been Sam's suggestion, but now, Liz had to figure out where she'd left her phone. She patted her workshop apron and found it in the usual pocket. The call had already gone into voicemail, but Brenda had left a message: "There's an active shooter at the Elementary School. Heading down there now. We could use your help."

Liz stripped off her shop apron. Without even bothering to brush off the sawdust, she turned off the shop lights and slammed the door behind her. Her knee was a little stiff this morning, but she sprinted up the path to the house. She paused for a moment to think about what to bring. Obviously, she might need her medical bag and the emergency surgical kit. The first aid kit on the wall of the garage was full of bandages. She was glad she'd had it during the big fire at Cliff Manor that had almost canceled her wedding. For the second time in less than a year, she yanked the metal box off the wall.

She looked over her shoulder to back out from the garage and noticed the tactical bag she'd packed for her afternoon target practice. It held two of her favorite pistols and plenty of 9mm and .380 target ammunition. Both guns were loaded with hollow points in their extended capacity magazines. *Why am I even thinking about defense ammunition?* she wondered. *I'm going to this scene as a doctor.*

### 10:19 a.m.

While Olivia hammered on about the estimates, Lucy noticed a green bubble floating across her phone screen. When she saw it was from Liz, she leaned forward to read it. *Active shooter at Hobbs Elementary. Heading there now.*

"Excuse me, Olivia," said Lucy. The woman gave her a filthy look. She never hesitated to interrupt others, but when she was talking, she expected respectful silence. "You and everyone here need to know this," said Lucy with a firm look. "There's an active shooter at the elementary school."

There was a collective gasp around the table. Olivia jumped to her feet. "I need to go," she said. She threw her papers into her bag and hurried out.

"Obviously, this meeting is adjourned," said Lucy. "Abbie, can you discuss with the senior members of the vestry how we can help in this situation?"

"Absolutely, Mother Lucy, but where are you going?"

"To the school. Once the news gets out, there will be frantic parents needing trained people to keep them calm."

The meeting room door opened, and Jodi stuck her head inside. "Mother Lucy, there's a shooter at the elementary school."

"Thank you, Jodi. We know. Please call Mother Reshma back from her home visits. She'll be needed here."

Lucy heard herself giving orders like a pro. A few years ago, she would have suggested they all pray, but this situation called for action, not spiritual guidance. She wished Tom were here. "Jodi, please call Father Simmons in Florida and tell him what's happening."

Lucy glanced around at all the worried faces. Maybe she was wrong. Prayer was exactly what they needed. "Please join me in praying for the safety of our children, the teachers and staff at the school, and all our first responders."

They all bowed their heads.

### 10:22 a.m.

After Maggie showered and dressed, she settled into the little office that Sam had created for her in a small room off the den. She located the electronic copy of *Suddenly Last Summer* on her laptop. She was lecturing on the play in her American drama class tomorrow. She preferred to perform a scene instead of reading the text because the students always seemed more engaged. It wasn't much extra effort. For an experienced actress, it was easy to learn her lines.

As she searched for the passage, a message popped up on her screen. She was surprised to see it was from Laura Maglione, who'd worked with her in the theater department at NYU. She'd recently retired and gone on an extended cruise of the Greek islands with her new boyfriend. Maggie leaned closer to read her text.

"Turn on the TV! Your little town is about to hit the national news!!!"

# Chapter 3

The patrol cars were already on the scene when Brenda and the active shooter squad arrived. Brenda was pleased to see that everyone was following orders, just like in the drills. They were all wearing their protective vests and SWAT helmets. When she got out of the car, she put on hers.

A truck suddenly screeched to a halt, and a tall woman jumped out. "He went in the back door!" Sam shouted from twenty paces. "The back!" She pointed emphatically.

"Sam, get down!" Brenda hissed, patting the air to demonstrate that she should take cover. Sam finally reached her and leaned on her knees to catch her breath.

"I left the back door open when I cleaned my tools."

"How long was it open?"

"Maybe four, five minutes at most."

"Long enough for someone to slip in if they were waiting."

"I felt someone watching me from the woods. Oh, my God! I'm so sorry."

"You can tell me all about it later. We need to get in there."

"The inner door is locked. You'll need to break it down."

Brenda redirected the active shooter team to the back of the school and ordered the van with the battering ram nicknamed "the enforcer" to follow them.

"Sam, you need to take cover," Brenda called. "If you want to help, go to the middle school parking lot and direct traffic. We need to keep civilians away from the scene."

"Yes, right away." She started to walk back to her truck, then turned around. "I'm so sorry. I know your kids are in there."

The statement hit Brenda like a gut punch. Since the dispatcher had burst into the meeting, Brenda had been on autopilot. "Yes, they are, but we all have a job to do, and I can't think about that now. Now, get over to the parking lot and help keep people out. If you meet up with Cherie, please tell her that I love her." To her surprise, Brenda choked up on the last words. She blinked to clear the tears in her eyes. She didn't have time for that. She needed to be strong and alert because this was promising to be one of the ugliest days of her life.

### 10:27 a.m.

Liz knew where to find the staging area because she did tactical training for the Hobbs police. She'd never expected to get so involved, but she'd gone from giving up her hunting license, because she couldn't stand killing animals, to a handgun enthusiast and safety training officer. Her attitude about guns had changed abruptly after some angry young men flying patriotic flags from the back of their truck had followed her right to the door of the supermarket. Instead of intimidating her, they'd created a badass who'd trained hundreds of other women to use guns. Many of them had been abused by their boyfriends or husbands, even raped. They listened with strained ears to the faintest sound they heard in the dark. She'd taught them to defend themselves. That was the little secret the right didn't talk about. The "libs" had guns too.

Liz shook her head at the angry political thoughts as she drove into the parking lot on the side of the school. Because she'd been in on the drills, she knew it had been chosen for the command post because it was at a lower elevation than the school, tucked into a hillside that provided a natural barrier. A shooter wouldn't have a clear shot, even from the school roof.

Brenda was leaning on the door of her squad car, barking orders on the secured radio signal, when Liz pulled up behind her. "Good to see the general behind enemy lines instead of being a hero," said Liz, sliding out of her truck.

"Brought you a vest. It's in the backseat."

"Are they inside yet?"

"No, breaking down the inside door. Sam left the outside door open by mistake. The shooter locked himself in. I'm assuming it's a he. They usually are."

"Shit. I hope it's not Peter Langdon. Sam had to fire him the other day."

"That messed up kid? The pot head?" Brenda looked surprised, then seemed to see the sense of it. "I thought you two had straightened him out."

"I thought so too, but Sam caught him smoking pot on the job."

The radio began to squawk. "We're inside, Chief."

"Proceed with all caution according to plan."

"Yes, ma'am."

Liz opened the back door of Brenda's car to get the vest. After she put it on, she attached the Velcro holster of her 9mm underneath. "Your vest stinks," said Liz, wrinkling her nose. "Jesus. You could wash it once in a while."

"Can't be washed. It compromises its integrity."

Brenda watched her friend smile as she processed the information. Liz was a sponge for explanations of how things worked.

There was a loud cry from the radio. "Oh, for God's sake! Oh, shit! We're in the gym. There are dead kids in here. Lots of them. The teacher's down. Blood everywhere."

"Any sign of the shooter?"

"No, and the shooting's stopped."

Brenda became alert, and Liz strained her ears to listen. It was quiet.

"Keep looking," ordered Brenda. "Keep your head down."

Liz waited until Brenda switched off the radio to ask, "Can we go in and help the survivors?"

"Not yet. They need to secure the scene."

"Time is critical," Liz reminded her. "Every minute counts."

"Don't you think I know it?" asked Brenda, turning around.

**10:37 a.m.**

Lucy was following the directions of the police officer into the middle-school driveway when her Bluetooth flashed Tom Simmons' name on the caller ID screen. Lucy opened the call from her steering wheel while she looked for a place to park.

"Oh, Lucy, I'm so sorry," said Tom. The sympathetic warmth in his voice made her want to reach through the speaker and hug him. "We're coming back to Maine. Jeff is on the phone with the airlines, trying to get the next flight into Boston."

"Oh, Tom. That is so kind!"

"I love Hobbs, and my friends. I promised you that when I left that you could always reach out to me, and I would be there."

His words brought tears to Lucy's eyes, but she was trying to navigate through the crowd without hitting anyone, so she had to pay attention. "Tom, I can't stay on the phone. There are so many people here. Parents will be anxious while they wait for word about their children. I need to see what I can do to help." Lucy finally saw an empty spot and pulled into it.

"Is Liz there?"

"Of course. Brenda called her."

"They make a good team. Okay, Lucy. I'll call later when I know what our travel plans are."

When Lucy signed off, she saw Cherie approaching the car and opened the door. Cherie fell into her arms. "Are you okay?" asked Lucy soothingly.

"Lucy, my kids and my aunt are in that school!"

"I know, Cherie. We need to pray and hope for the best."

"Thoughts and prayers. That's all we ever get," said Cherie bitterly, pulling away.

Lucy looked directly into Cherie's blue-green eyes. "I know you're upset, but I need you to help me keep these people calm."

Cherie swallowed so hard that Lucy could hear it. "I see what you're trying to do. You think helping others cope will keep my mind off the worst."

Lucy smiled. "Shame on me trying to manipulate another therapist, but I do need your help. Not everyone responds to someone wearing a collar."

"You could take it off."

"I could, but to some people it gives a special kind of comfort, like a doctor wearing a white coat. We'll work as a team like we always do."

Cherie's sad chuckle sounded almost like a muffled sob. "At least we're out of harm's way, unlike our crazy spouses."

"Oh, neither one of them is crazy. But that hero complex can be dangerous." Lucy took Cherie's arm and led her towards the staging area the police had set up. "Come on, let's see what we can do to help these terrified people. God knows you can sympathize from direct experience."

### 10:52 a.m.

Liz had seen gory scenes in the ED and at road accidents, but she had never seen anything like this. The gym of Hobbs Elementary School looked like a battlefield. The polished wooden floors were covered with blood and body parts. Before releasing anyone, the police had marked out where the victims had lain. So far, nine were dead, including the gym teacher. Six kids were wounded, three in critical condition. The shooter had used an assault rifle, so the flesh of the victims looked like hamburger. Some victims had been shot in the face and were unrecognizable. The coroner would need DNA from the families to identify them. Hardly anything made Liz queasy anymore but looking at a bloody hole where a child's face used to be turned her stomach. Moving quickly from one small body to the next, she managed to keep down the bitter vomitus rising in her throat.

A surprising number of kids had survived by playing dead. "That trick of playing possum worked. We made it a game in the drill," called Brenda from across the room. "Glad they remembered it."

"I'm not sure this shooter was in it to kill kids," said Liz, closing the staring eyes of a dark-haired boy. He'd been shot in the thigh and bled out slowly.

"What makes you say that?" asked Brenda, walking over to where Liz stood.

"If he wanted to kill them, he would have been more efficient. He just shot a straight path through the gym. He skipped many of the kids. That's why there aren't more dead."

"He made sure to take the teacher out. She was shot in the head execution style with one 9mm round."

"That's what I mean. I don't think this was about shooting up kids to get attention. He stopped shooting and went directly to the principal's office. He was after the adults."

"Hmm. You'd make a good detective, Liz."

"Bullshit. I just notice details." Liz pointed to the child at her feet. "This boy might have survived if we'd gotten to him sooner. If we'd gotten a tourniquet on him five minutes ago, he might still be alive."

"A shame, and I know how it must be killing you to think you could have saved him, but we had to make sure the shooter was contained."

"I haven't heard any more shots. Are you sure he's done?"

"No, but there's no more gunfire."

Someone had figured out that the dead boys belonged to the third-grade gym class, but they hadn't found Keith Harrison among the dead or the wounded.

"Did you find your kids? Are they safe?"

"Megan's fine. Keith was locked in with the nurse the whole time. He went to her office before gym class with one of his fake stomach aches."

"Brenda, I told you. He's not faking it. Psychological problems can cause real gastro issues. The kid has been through a lot."

"He would have been in this gym class," said Brenda, looking stricken at the thought. "Thank God for a fake stomach ache."

"Where are they now?"

"They're taking them to Cherie, but she's trying to help your wife keep the crowd calm." Liz could see the anxiety in Brenda's eyes and touched her shoulder.

"It's hard when your role in the community needs to come before your family," she said, "but you're doing a great job."

Brenda looked like she might cry, but she just nodded.

Liz watched the officer taping off the places where the ambulance staff had removed wounded victims. "Is there anything else I can do here?" she asked. "I've double checked for survivors."

"Maybe you could give Peter Langdon a call and see if your suspicions are correct."

### 11:03 a.m.

The town manager's voice, magnified by the mobile public address system, sounded scratchy and much too loud, but it got everyone's attention. Olivia scanned the crowd. Lucy Bartlett stood in the front row, beaming a smile of encouragement. She didn't need her priest to tell her that delivering the right message was critical at a time like this.

Olivia had experienced firsthand what these parents feared most. Gazing at their stunned faces, she could imagine how she'd looked when the policeman had come to tell her that her son had taken his life. Fortunately, he was a seasoned officer, probably used to breaking bad news, and he'd spared her the gruesome details. Only later did she learn that Jason had put a pistol in his mouth and pulled the trigger.

People thought she was cold, but she had loved that boy with all her heart. She remembered cradling his tiny body, his sweet smell and baby warmth. He was the only one she had ever truly loved. Maybe her mother too. She'd loved her before she began to drink herself to death. She'd even tried to save her. Then she gave up on all of them and left them behind for her own sanity.

She'd tried so hard to protect her son from becoming his father, a calculating, unscrupulous financier. Ultimately, all the private schooling and psychiatric counseling meant nothing. Jason had stolen money from his own family, embezzling from the hedge fund his mother had created. That was bad enough, but when she found out he'd molested his daughters, he became a monster in her eyes.

A dark-haired woman with a muff-covered microphone was standing below the dais to capture the speeches. Behind her was a man with a video camera. Olivia recognized the reporter as Maggie Fitzgerald's daughter, Alina, a senior news producer at the local TV station.

Olivia cleared her throat and tried again to get the attention of the crowd. "Thank you for remaining calm. I know this is a frightening day, a day we'd hoped would never come. The police are in the school. They have the shooter surrounded. He's barricaded in the principal's office, where he is holding three hostages. I'm sorry to tell you there have been some fatalities."

There was a sharp moan, like the cry of a wounded dog, but many of the faces in the crowd seemed calmer. Even the barest amount of information was better than none.

"The paramedics are treating the wounded," Olivia continued. "The students, who were not affected by the shooting, are being evacuated from the school through the back door. We will announce where you can meet them shortly. Chief Harrison will now give you further details."

Olivia stepped aside so Brenda could take her place at the microphone. "As Ms. Enright said, we appreciate the calm and restraint you've shown. Many of us have kids in that school, but right now, the best thing we can do for them is to let the first responders do their jobs. Unfortunately, we do have one confirmed adult fatality, Mrs. Lavoie, the gym teacher. Identifying the children will be more difficult because kids don't carry ID. If your child doesn't show up at the designated meeting place, it doesn't mean the worst. We are transporting the injured to Southern Med as fast as we can get them out safely. Unfortunately, this is a crime scene, so only those who can benefit from medical attention are being removed from the school at this time."

Olivia saw that Brenda's usual straightforward approach to information was effective. While she'd been speaking, the crowd had relaxed by degrees. A hand shot up.

"Chief Harrison, what are you going to do about the hostages?"

"As you know, the protocol is to rush an active shooter and try to take him down. The shooting has stopped, so we will proceed as we would in any hostage situation. We'll do our best to protect the people he's holding and take the suspect alive."

### 11:08 a.m.

"Mom! Can you please just do what I ask for a change?" said Melissa, finally giving in to her frustration. "Pick me up at the transportation center at two-thirty-two. That's all I ask!"

She couldn't believe she had to plead with her mother to do something so simple, but Ruth Morgenstern had never liked Courtney. Melissa knew that her mother secretly considered her girlfriend trailer trash. It hadn't helped that she was living in an actual trailer when they'd first met, but she'd gotten the job as assistant principal late in the summer when there were no apartments anywhere and she had to take the first place she could find. Living in a trailer was bad enough, but Courtney was a shiksa. It had taken Ruth a long time to adjust to having two lesbian daughters, but she had no problem with her sister's wife, a devout Jew straight from Israel. If Courtney were Jewish, her mother probably wouldn't be so hard on her.

"Are you sure your boss is okay with you coming home?" asked Ruth doubtfully. Her Queens accent always sounded stronger on the phone.

"Of course he is. My partner is being held hostage by a shooter! That's a good excuse, don't you think?" Mike had personally interrupted the meeting with Melissa's clients and called her out into the hall. His face was ashen when he told her the terrifying news. "Go home," he'd said. "Take care of your family."

She'd been running late that morning, so she'd skipped checking into the hotel and came to the office with her luggage. That meant she could go directly to the station. She'd need a ride when she got home. She could have taken an Uber, or a taxi, but she felt a strong need to be with family.

"Okay, Lissa," Ruth finally said, "I'll meet you at the station, but what do you think you're going to do for her when you get here?"

Melissa wanted to scream. "I can be there for her. If Jack were a hostage, wouldn't you be there for him?" Melissa knew Ruth would hate the comparison to her relationship with Jack. Despite her mother's grudging acceptance, in her estimation, being with a woman would never be equal to being with a man.

"Yes, of course I'd want to be there," said Ruth, sounding insulted. "But you have no idea how crazy it is here. Fire trucks and police cars everywhere. The Post Road has been shut down. The TV people flew in from New York in a helicopter and landed in Harbor Park. The news people are coming from everywhere!"

"Mom, I don't care. I have to get home. If you can't come to the station, I'll get a taxi or Uber."

"Oh, for God's sake, your sister is calling me! I'll see you at the station."

"My train comes in at two thirty-two."

"Melissa, I remember! I'm not senile yet! I need to talk to your sister. Bye." Ruth hung up.

In frustration, Melissa threw her phone into her bag. For the first time since Mike had come to her office, she became aware of her surroundings. The platform stank of dirt, urine, and diesel exhaust. In the distance, she could see the headlights of her train. At least, it was on time.

### 11:12 a.m.

One of the cops had given Sam a vest with a fluorescent green stripe, showing she had the authority to direct traffic. Olivia had issued an order to keep the news people away. The vans with broadcast antennas on top were backed up outside the school entrance. Sam wasn't letting them in, so they parked any place they could find, knocking down the post and rail fence around the soccer field and crushing the beach rose hedge. Like crazed insects, they destroyed everything in their path.

Sam's phone rang, and she dug under the vest to get to her pocket. "Sam!" Maggie's voice. "Are you all right?"

"I'm fine. I was outside packing up my truck when I heard the shots." Sam waved on a bus and spoke into her shoulder in a low voice. "I put a brick in the door while I cleaned my tools. The fucking spigot is on the other side of the building. I think it's Peter."

"Oh, my God. You really think it's him?"

"I'm pretty sure. I felt someone watching me when I went outside. Peter would have known I was cleaning my tools with water from the outside spigot. We've been cleaning our tools out back since we started the job."

"Sam! Keep your voice down. When people find out that's how he got in, they'll be after you!"

"Maggie, I was filthy, and I wasn't going to tramp through the school to the front, dripping grout water everywhere. We'd been putting a brick in the door to keep it open."

"You mean you've been leaving the door open?" Maggie asked incredulously.

"It was only for a few minutes."

"Sam! I'm sorry to say this, but that was incredibly stupid."

"How should I know I'd end up letting him go?"

"You've been complaining about him since you started this job. For weeks!" Maggie lowered her voice as if the people around Sam could hear her. "Sam, just shut up about this. Don't tell *anyone*. I know you're a straight arrow and always tell the truth, but don't volunteer any information."

Sam felt a chill that had nothing to do with the January temperature. "Too late, Maggie. I already told Brenda."

In the silence that followed, Sam could hear Maggie's worry.

# Chapter 4

Maggie was getting ready to leave for class when Reshma John called. "Mother Lucy asked me to prepare a place for the children to wait for the parents who couldn't come to the school. We can use the Sunday school classrooms, but we need adults to supervise. I'm calling you because you might know people who can help."

"Leave it to me," said Maggie. After she called the dean's office to cancel her class, she called the woman in charge of notifying the choir if practice had to be canceled. Once Maggie explained the situation, she offered to call the people on her list. A retired high school teacher Maggie knew from when she was moderator of the drama club said that she'd be happy to make some calls. Soon, Maggie had assembled a crew of mostly senior women who'd agreed to meet her at the church.

As she drove into town, she thought about her conversation with Sam. She loved Sam's impulsive need to blurt out the truth, but sometimes she was just too honest. The town would certainly turn on her once they learned how the shooter had gotten into the school.

Maggie knew all too well how people in a small town could behave. When Barry ran off with his assistant at the engineering firm, all their couple friends shunned her. Even the woman she thought of as her best friend made excuses when Maggie invited her to go shopping or out to lunch.

The car behind her honked. The light had changed, and she hadn't moved fast enough. State police cars whizzed past with sirens blasting and all their lights flashing. When Maggie tried to move off to the shoulder, a car cut her off from the right. Hobbs was suddenly a very dangerous place. Maggie's daughter, at the scene as a reporter, had warned her to stay away from the school. Alina had always been fearful and overprotective of her mother, but in this case, she had reason to be.

Reshma greeted Maggie at the rectory door when she arrived. The young priest, ordained barely a month ago, made it clear that she was on duty by wearing a clerical collar under her colorful sweater. The intriguing geometric pattern suggested her African heritage. Her lithe figure carried clothes like a model. Although her ebony skin was flawless, she wore a little makeup to accent her natural gifts.

"Thank you so much for coming, Dr. Fitzgerald," Reshma said. Despite Maggie's multiple requests to call her by her first name, the curate always addressed her formally. Maggie often wished more young people would adopt her respect for their elders.

"Some of your friends have already arrived," said Reshma, leading her down the stairs to the lower church. "I thought we could have a quick meeting to discuss what we need to do."

The retired teachers looked far more relaxed than when Maggie had known them in their professional guise. Their edges had softened into a grandmotherly affability, perfect for reassuring terrified children. Reshma assigned each of them to classrooms, where there were toys and old-fashioned blackboards, perfect for word games. Maggie went into hers and found the bulletin boards covered with Bible verses in colored letters and illustrations of Jesus with children. Everything was a little dusty because the classroom hadn't been used since the lockdown. Stray Christmas decorations poked out of odd places.

The first bus arrived. The children filed noisily through the hall, directed by Maggie and Reshma into classrooms. "Thank you so much for finding all these women to look after the children. I know next to nothing about children. I don't know what I would have done without your help."

"I'm happy to help, but Reshma, just go with your instincts. From what I've seen, you're a natural when it comes to children."

"I'm doing the best I can, but it's all an act."

"*Everything's* an act," Maggie reminded her with a firm look.

Reshma glanced at her watch. "It's almost lunchtime. How do we feed these kids?"

"Order pizza and ask to have it delivered." Maggie dug her wallet out of her bag and handed Reshma a credit card.

"How many?" Reshma asked, looking baffled.

"Oh, two pies per classroom should do it. That makes ten. Round it up to a dozen. Plain only. Kids like basic food."

"Good to know," said Reshma. She raised the credit card. "And thank you for your generosity."

"Not exactly multiplying loaves and fishes, but it should feed your young crowd and the volunteers." Maggie patted Reshma's arm. "Don't worry, *Mother* Reshma. You're doing just fine."

### 11:38 a.m.

Praying with a group of women, Lucy wanted to think what she was offering was more than "thoughts and prayers." The right's lame sentiment after every mass shooting made her cringe, but as a priest and a therapist, she believed in giving anxious people what they needed to regain their balance. The harsh reality of what had happened would hit them soon enough. Liz's face after she'd returned from doing triage in the school said it all. "You don't want to know," she'd said before Lucy could ask.

The ambulances with the injured children drove away with a wail of sirens. Some of the emergency vehicles parked around the school continued flashing their lights. Lucy wished they'd turn them off. People's emotions were already at such a high pitch.

She ended the prayer with a blessing and touched the shoulder of each of the women. Out of the corner of her eye, she saw Cherie approaching with her children.

"Lucy, I'm sorry, but I need to take my kids home. They've already survived gun violence, and this is bringing up so many bad memories."

Megan, who'd been clinging to her mother, released her and captured Lucy's leg. "L-u-u-u-cy," she crooned.

Lucy reached down to stroke the girl's hair. "It's okay, Megan. Mama C's going to take you home. No more school today." Megan only clung tighter.

"I hate to leave you all alone here," said Cherie, frowning as she looked around. "To say this crowd is getting restless is no understatement."

"Don't worry about me. I can manage. You need to do what's best for your family."

"It was Keith's gym class. All the victims were his classmates. I don't know how that will affect him, but it can't be good. I know from experience that the survivors often have terrible guilt. We need to plan, Lucy. Our work is just beginning."

Cherie was saying something obvious, but Lucy was too focused on dealing with the present crisis to think that far ahead. "Go home. Take care of your kids. I'll call you later."

"Thank you," Cherie said. Her eyes filled. "Thank God for you." She put her arms around Lucy and squeezed her tight. "Good luck. Please call me. Promise."

Lucy promised. She watched Cherie thread her way through the crowd with her kids attached to her hips. Those poor kids had now witnessed two devastating incidents of gun violence. They were so common now, almost everyone was touched by these tragedies, if only by hearing about mass shootings on the news almost every day.

Loud voices from the other side of the parking lot drew Lucy's attention. She excused herself from the group of women who'd been praying with her. They'd remained huddled around her as if she were a talisman that could keep them safe.

Lucy walked down the driveway to see two men arguing with a female police officer, who looked straight ahead while the men screamed into her face. As she got closer, Lucy heard what they said. "Why aren't they telling us anything? We want to know! They're our kids!"

Lucy knew they were being told, but quietly. She'd seen people in the crowd answering their phones and then reporting to an area roped off with police tape. As the victims were identified, a social worker from the state broke the news. Lucy was glad that someone specially trained for this work would be handling the communication. As someone wearing a collar, Lucy would be expected to explain why God had allowed this horror, which, of course, she couldn't.

She decided to intervene in the loud argument at the barricade, but a tiny older woman got there first. Lucy watched Gloria Parrish, her friend and fellow therapist, skillfully ease herself into the conversation. The rigidity in the men's faces began to relax, almost as if Gloria were a fairy godmother who'd put them under a benevolent spell. One of the men answered his phone and looked toward the area where the families of the victims were being told their condition. Lucy's heart broke for the poor man. He'd wanted to know what was going on. Now he was about to get the worst news of his life.

While Gloria continued to listen to the complaints of the anxious father, she smiled a greeting in Lucy's direction. The man finally moved away, and Lucy slipped in beside Gloria.

"Thank you for coming," she whispered.

Gloria reached for Lucy's hand. "Once I heard, I knew I had to be here."

"We're going to need you in the coming days."

"I know," said Gloria. "I'm here for you."

# Chapter 5

Brenda was relieved to get a text from Cherie saying they were home. Now, she could finally put her worry about her family aside and concentrate on her duty to the people of Hobbs. Her father had always said a cop shouldn't live in his own precinct. "If you live where you work, the perps know where to find you and your family," but avoiding conflict of interest was the real reason. It was hard to arrest your own neighbors or watch their tragedies play out before your eyes.

Brenda had been going into the third grade when her father had given her that piece of advice. He'd just turned down the opportunity to join the local precinct. The Harrisons were living in the small house in Brooklyn, where they'd lived since Brenda had been born.

That summer, the city streets were bristling with tension. Blacks and island people had been moving into neighborhoods that used to be almost completely Irish. The newcomers were supposed to be dangerous. Although Brenda's parents couldn't afford it, they enrolled her and her brother in a Catholic school, supposedly to protect them.

Most of the whites were fleeing to the outer boroughs or to the suburbs. There was official pressure on cops and firemen to live in the city, but the Harrisons had no other choice. A botched hysterectomy had disabled Brenda's mother after her last pregnancy, and she'd had to quit working. Brenda's oldest brother was still in the academy. He'd promised that once he got his badge, he'd contribute to the mortgage so they could all move to a better place. Then he got into a fight with his father and moved out, so it never happened.

Decades later, when Brenda had been hired by the Hobbs PD and found an affordable raised ranch right in town, her father's words came back to her. She'd dismissed them because she thought her family would be safe in this idyllic place with its white beaches and small-town ethos. Then her first wife was T-boned at an intersection by a drunken tourist. Her children's biological parents had died in a domestic dispute. Now, a class of little boys had been gunned down while playing volleyball in their school gym.

Danger wasn't about color or the neighborhood where you lived. Danger was everywhere. When Brenda was growing up, only cops and criminals had handguns. Now, everyone had them, and your kids could be shot by a nut who'd grown up right next door.

"Brenda?" Brenda turned and saw Sam. "The troopers said they'd take over directing traffic. Is there anything else I can do? I want to help. I feel so bad about what happened."

Brenda leaned closer so she could speak into Sam's ear. "Thanks for your help, but if I were you, I'd get the hell out of here."

"What?" Sam's mouth opened a little. Clearly, that wasn't what she'd expected to hear.

"I know you didn't intend any harm, but when people find out you left the door open, they'll be screaming for your head."

Sam's brown eyes narrowed, and she pulled into her shoulders, like a dog expecting a beating. "You're not going to tell them, are you?"

"I'm not going to make a public announcement, but it will come out in the investigation." Sam stared at the ground, no doubt considering the implications. Brenda put a hand on her shoulder. "Sam, I know it wasn't intentional, just carelessness, but even stupid things can have big consequences."

Sam stared at the school building, now surrounded by police and emergency vehicles. "Do you really need to tell people what happened?"

"I'm sorry, Sam, but I do. I can't cover it up."

"Will I be charged with a crime?"

"Probably not. You didn't do anything illegal. Maybe some slick lawyer could argue you were negligent, but it's hard to prove."

Sam's eyes blazed with agitation and anger. "If they hadn't put the fucking spigot around the corner, I would have seen someone trying to get in. I felt like I was being watched. It was creepy."

"That's when you should have trusted your instincts and called me." Brenda was a little shorter, maybe an inch, but she looked Sam right in the eye. "Go home and stay out of sight. We'll need a statement from you. I'll call you."

"But I haven't finished the bathroom."

Brenda looked at Sam and wondered how a smart woman could be so fucking stupid. "Sam, no one is going to be using that bathroom for a long time."

Sam nodded, finally comprehending.

"Where's Maggie?" Brenda asked.

"Helping at the church with the kids whose parents aren't here."

"We'll have everyone hooked up soon, and we'll send her back to you. Now get the hell out of here!"

Brenda watched Sam hurry away until she was lost in the crowd. One thing she knew for sure. She wouldn't want to be Sam today. It was bad enough being herself, responsible for dealing with this crisis and worrying about her kids.

"Chief?"

Brenda turned around and saw Officer Vachon waiting politely. The young woman had come a long way since they'd found her puking outside her squad car on the night Keith and Megan had been orphaned. Now she looked steady and composed. Good for her. To succeed, a female officer always needed to be tougher than the guys.

"Yes, Vachon. What's up?"

"Langdon isn't answering Dr. Stolz's calls. She's called him repeatedly. No answer."

"Maybe he doesn't have his phone."

"Maybe not, but we've called the principal's office, the admin's desk, and the main number for the school. No one's answering."

Brenda didn't like the sound of that. She hoped the perp hadn't hurt the hostages. Resisting communication wasn't a good sign, not that she was an expert in hostage negotiation. Good thing the FBI was sending someone up from Boston.

"The mother's here. We sent a car for her like you said."

"Did she try to call the kid?"

Vachon shook her head. "She wants to talk to you first to find out what you want her to say."

"Okay, so let's go talk to her." She gestured ahead. "Lead the way."

They returned to the table set up as a command center. Liz was sitting on the rail of the fence, scrolling through her phone.

"I heard you tried to call him," said Brenda. "He's not answering."

Liz didn't look up. "I did, but maybe he doesn't have me in his address book, so he might not know it's me. I did send him a couple of text messages. No reply."

"What are you doing now?"

"Messaging with Ginny to close the practice and send the staff over here to help."

"Sounds like a good idea."

Liz grunted, as she often did when she was involved in something.

"Here's Mrs. Landon," said Vachon, bringing the woman forward. Brenda scrutinized Renee Langdon. She'd aged so much since she'd last talked to her before the pandemic. The isolation had stolen years from everyone. She was letting her hair grow out to gray, but it was an improvement over the dark brunette that just made her look pale. Her face was pinched, understandable given the fact that her son was the prime suspect. Brenda remembered her saying how much Lucy had helped her get through her seasonal affective disorder. Could winter depression have contributed to her son's sudden breakdown?

"Hello, Renee. How are you holding up?" Brenda had been taught to make small talk to help witnesses calm down, but the question sounded lame.

"I'm upset. Wouldn't you be?" the woman snapped.

"Of course," Brenda said in a soothing voice. "It must be so hard even thinking Peter could do something like this."

"Are you sure it's him?"

"No, but we have strong reason to believe he's the one. We're doing a search of his social media posts to see if there are clues. When did you last see him?"

"He came home late, after I went to bed, but I heard him come in. When I got up this morning, I saw the dinner I'd put aside for him had been eaten. Usually, he puts his plate in the dishwasher after he finishes eating, but he just left it in the sink without even rinsing it. That's not like him."

"Hmm" intoned Brenda, looking up from the pad where she'd been scribbling notes in her own shorthand. She still carried an old-fashioned, leather-bound police pad like the one she'd been issued as a rookie.

"So you didn't actually see him come in last night?"

"No, but his bed had been slept in. I'd done his laundry and changed the sheets. He's been a mess since his girlfriend threw him out. I never cared for her, but she seemed to make him happy. After he'd moved into that dump of a trailer with her, things were going pretty good for him. He liked his job. When he came home, he was pleasant to his brother and sister instead of snapping at them all the time."

Brenda finished writing and flipped closed her pad. "Okay. I want to hear more later, but now let's see if he'll answer your call. I want you to turn your phone on speaker so we can hear and record your conversation. Any clue might help us find a way to end this situation. We don't want him to know we are listening. Even though you're stressed, I want you to talk as naturally as you can. Ask him where he is. How he is. What he wants. How we can help him. Can you do that?"

Renee nodded. "I can try."

Brenda signaled the technician to come closer with the recording device and for Vachon and another officer to stand within hearing distance as witnesses.

"Okay, Renee. Please call Peter."

The woman's hands were trembling, but she located her son's number in the favorites and tapped open the call.

"Speaker!" Brenda reminded her in a loud whisper.

Renee fumbled, but got it on. Brenda prayed while the phone rang and rang, knowing it would soon go into voicemail. Then someone spoke. "Mom?" asked a shaky male voice. "Mom, is that you?"

Renee looked like she was going to cry. "Yes, honey, it's me. Are you all right?"

There was a long silence. "Are the police there?"

Brenda shook her head. Renee hesitated, but then said, "Yes." Brenda understood. It would be hard to lie to her kid, too. "Pete, I need to know you're okay," said Renee. "Where are you?"

"In the principal's office. Hasn't changed. Just like I remember it."

Vachon scribbled on her pad: *Ask who's with him.*

"Are you alone?" asked Renee.

"No, there are some ladies here. One is the principal. The other is a teacher, and the young one is the secretary, I think."

Brenda breathed a sigh of relief. Usually, there were half a dozen administrative people in the main office. They must have been on break. After this conversation, she'd ask the evacuation team to confirm that the others had been removed from the school.

"Are the ladies all right?" Renee asked. Her hand, holding her phone, was still shaking, but she was handling herself well.

"They're fine. They're just sitting here, looking at me."

"Maybe they want to leave. Why don't you let them leave?"

"No, I can't do that," said Peter with an audible sigh.

"Why?"

"If I let them leave, the cops will shoot me."

Brenda realized she had to intervene. "Peter, it's Brenda Harrison, the police chief. I promise, if you release the ladies without harm and surrender, no one will shoot you. We just want to talk to you."

"You found the kids, right?"

"We did."

"Then you'll shoot me."

The call went dead.

### 12:12 p.m.

After Renee's conversation with her son abruptly ended, she looked shaky. Lucy went over to talk to her. Renee instantly brightened at seeing a familiar face.

"How about a chair for Mrs. Langdon?" called Lucy, and a young paramedic brought a sling chair. When Renee sat down, her eyes were full of relief. She managed a weak smile. "Mother Lucy, I'm so glad to see you. If I'd known you'd be here, I would have brought you a peanut butter and jelly sandwich." Her counseling sessions with Lucy had always been at lunchtime, and she'd brought a sandwich for Lucy too.

"If you're hungry, Dr. Bartlett," said the helpful paramedic, who'd brought the chair, "the Webhanet Deli sent up sandwiches and bottled water for the emergency squad."

"Thanks, but I'm not hungry. It's an inside joke between Mrs. Langdon and me. I will take some water. How about you, Renee?"

The woman nodded wearily. After the paramedic brought the water, Lucy gratefully glugged down half the bottle.

Liz had noticed them talking. She jumped down from the fence rail and came over. Lucy could see why. Renee looked pale. "How are you doing, Mrs. Langdon? Feeling okay?" Liz asked, her fingers seeking the woman's wrist.

"I'm fine, Dr. Stolz. Well, not fine, of course. But I feel okay... physically, I mean."

"I tried to call Peter," said Liz, "but he didn't answer."

"You probably don't have his new number. He wasn't paying his phone bills, so they cut him off. He has a burner phone now."

"Do you mind giving me his number?" Liz asked.

"No, of course I don't mind. Do you think he'll talk to you?"

"I don't know. Let's find out."

Renee handed Liz her phone so Liz could get the number. "I could call Peter again, if the police think it will help."

Liz waved to Brenda to join them and explained about the burner phone and calling the wrong number. "Which do you think would be better? Mrs. Langdon trying to call him again or me?"

"Hanging up on your mother is a pretty clear message," said Brenda. "Why don't you try, Liz?"

"Can you get everyone together, and we'll give it a try?" said Liz. "Let me text him to expect my call." She began typing out a message.

"Liz, it would be easier if you came back to the table where we have all the equipment set up. Mrs. Langdon, you're welcome to join us or stay here with Lucy. Your choice."

"I want to hear his voice," said his mother, struggling to get to her feet like she was eighty instead of in her forties. Brenda offered her arm, and Liz brought along the chair.

"Okay, Brenda, I wasn't there when you had Mrs. Langdon call Peter. What do you want me to say?"

"Just get him talking first. Our main objective is to get him to release his hostages. Find out what he wants in exchange."

"Why do you assume he wants something?"

Brenda looked impatient, but Lucy knew that knowing the rationale would help Liz figure out what to say.

"Most hostage takers try to get something in exchange for releasing the hostages, like a means to escape, or money."

"Realistically, do you think he wants money?"

"How the hell should I know?" snapped Brenda. "It's what they teach us to do in a hostage situation. Maybe we should wait for that negotiator to come up from Boston."

"Those hostages might be dead by then," said Liz bluntly. "Who's in there with him?"

"The principal. One of the admins, and one of the teachers. The teacher whose class had gym that period. Do we know who that is yet?" Brenda turned to the officers nearby, looking for answers.

"It was Ms. Gedney's third grade," an older female officer reported efficiently.

At the sound of Susan's name, Lucy gasped, which made everyone turn in her direction.

"Sorry, Lucy," said Brenda. "I know you're friends. We'll do our best to keep everyone safe." She turned to Liz. "Well, are you ready?" Liz nodded. Brenda raised her hand like she was going to flag the start of a race. "Go!"

Liz called the number Renee had given her and activated the speaker.

"Is this you, Dr. Liz?" he asked in a surprisingly young voice.

"Yes, Pete, it's me. I'm calling to see how you are. I have your mother here, and she's really worried about you."

"Please tell her I'm fine."

"What about the women with you? Are they okay?"

"Yes, they're okay."

"Let me speak to them."

"Why? Don't you believe me?"

Brenda looked anxious, hearing the implied challenge, but Liz smoothly replied, "Of course I do. But I'm a doctor. I learn a lot from how people sound. When you come to see me in the office, you don't ask someone else to tell me how you feel, do you?" Lucy was impressed. She never knew Liz could be so sly.

"No, I don't," said the voice on the phone cautiously.

There was dead air on the phone for a minute before a familiar and very welcome voice came through the phone. "Dr. Stolz, it's Courtney Barnes. Everyone is okay. He hasn't hurt us."

"Glad to hear it, Courtney. Thanks. How about Susan?"

Susan's voice was more distant. "I'm fine, Liz."

"The young one is shaking her head," interjected the male voice. "She looks like she's about to piss herself."

"Well, maybe you should let her go to the bathroom," said Liz in a practical tone.

"I guess I could. I don't really need her for anything. If I let her go, will they get the cops off the roof?"

"Hold on. I'll ask." Liz muted the phone and looked at Brenda for an explanation.

She shrugged. "We put some snipers up there in case we got a shot."

Renee emitted a sharp yelp like a hurt puppy.

"It's only as a last resort," Brenda said quickly. "Our hope is he'll surrender. Anyway, we can't shoot because he's got the women parked in front of the window. He's using them as a shield."

Liz turned the sound back on. "Peter, why are you holding those women? What do you want?"

"They need to pay."

"Why? Has any of these women hurt you?" Liz exchanged a look with Brenda and then her eyes sought Lucy's.

"Doc, if you want to hear my story, then come in and talk to me. Tell them to take the snipers off the roof, and I'll release the girl."

Again, the call went dead.

Lucy watched Liz's face. The permanent lines between her brows were deeper when she was stressed. She took Liz's arm and led her away. Underfoot, the tiny, rounded stones sieved from the ocean crunched under each step.

"Liz," said Lucy, once they were out of earshot. "I know you. You always want to be the hero. You think you're the one who's supposed to save everyone. When you were a surgeon, I'm sure that gave you an enormous adrenalin rush. But this is a very dangerous situation. You could be killed."

"Don't I know it! I'm fucking scared. It's one thing to play tactical games at the range, pretending to dodge bullets and take cover. It's another thing to face an angry kid shooting live ammunition. Someone who already shot a woman and a dozen kids."

"You don't have to accept this challenge, Liz. You can say no."

"Yes, I could. But he's willing to talk to me. If I let him tell me his story, maybe he'll let the women go."

"Maybe you'll be killed. Liz, I've already been widowed once. I can't take another death. I just can't."

"I'm not going in there to be killed. I'm going in to talk. You're a shrink. How did he sound to you?" Lucy had asked Liz to stop calling her a shrink so many times she didn't bother anymore. She paused for a moment to gather her impressions.

"He's desperate and not thinking straight. He wants people to see him. He wants to be heard and believed. Maybe something happened in that school when he was a student, and he's never forgotten it. I'm speculating."

The light wind played in Liz's hair. "We've all been hurt in childhood. When I was in school, the nuns were always ridiculing kids, beating them. I watched one bash a kid's head against a blackboard so hard it cracked. Can you imagine what that did to his brain?"

Lucy wondered about his psyche. "That's so wrong. Hopefully, he got help for that trauma."

"I tried to help Peter. In the end, it didn't fucking matter." Liz turned away in anger and frustration.

"It did matter," said Lucy, pulling on her arm so she would face her. "He almost made it. You don't know what happened to him before you met. Some wounds are so deep they can never be healed in this life."

Liz's blue eyes were filling up. She gazed at the sky. The light reflecting in her tears made them even bluer.

"What are you going to do?" Lucy asked, although she already knew.

"I'm scared, Lucy."

"I know."

"But I need to do this."

**12:22 p.m.**

Olivia watched in silence while the officer in charge of communications positioned the microphone so they could hear Liz's conversation with the shooter. Olivia had always considered herself fearless, but she didn't know if she could do what Liz was doing, walking right into a place where someone was waiting for her with loaded guns. Brenda wanted Liz to go in unarmed. "If he frisks you and finds weapons, he might shoot you on the spot," she said.

"First of all, he's not going to frisk me. Rooting around under my boobs would be like frisking his own mother. Second, I'm not going in there defenseless. And if he finds the guns, he'll just take them away." It sounded logical and deliberate, but that's how Liz operated and why she and Olivia got along. They both knew when to take a considered risk.

When Olivia had told her friends on Wall Street that she was going to start her own hedge fund, people laughed. Women didn't start hedge funds, at least not before Olivia founded the Enright Fund. It killed her to put her married name, her husband's name on it, but people could barely pronounce her Polish maiden name and something so ethnic wouldn't be good for the brand. People felt better about investing money in something recognizable and familiar, something thoroughly WASP. Her husband used to say it was all marketing. Michael had been born to wealth, attended the best boarding schools, went to Harvard for both undergrad and business school, which was where they'd met. He was a total ass, but smart about product positioning.

Liz took out the gun from under her vest and pulled back the top part until there was a click and let it slide back slowly. Olivia knew nothing about guns, but she sensed Liz was getting it ready to fire.

"This extended capacity magazine holds twenty-one rounds, but I feel like I should take another magazine, just in case."

Brenda grinned. "According to my favorite safety instructor, if you need that much ammo, you're probably already dead."

Liz returned the smile. Obviously, it was an inside joke, a form of gallows humor. Olivia was amazed these two could be so calm, considering what Liz was about to do. Of course, their choice of profession required nerves of steel, something Olivia had aspired to but had never quite achieved. She could do it in public, but in private, she always broke down.

"Are you sure your old smelly vest will do the job?" Liz asked.

"It should. Besides the aroma, there's nothing wrong with it. Do you want to change to a new one?"

"If you have one. Not that I don't trust you, but I want to go in there with the best protection. Chalk it up to my anal attention to detail."

"You wouldn't be Liz without it." Brenda signaled to one of her officers. "Bring Dr. Stolz a new vest."

Liz exchanged vests. They repositioned the wire. Olivia wondered if it was just a delaying tactic, but if she were on this mission, she wouldn't rush in either. She'd want to be prepared.

"Hey, maybe you should take along some sandwiches and water," Brenda suggested. "When I was working homicide, we always brought coffee or food to interrogations. Shows you care even though you don't."

Liz gave Brenda a sharp look. "I do care, or I wouldn't be doing this. Okay. Give me some sandwiches."

While they waited for the food, Lucy and Liz took a moment together. In front of everyone, they kissed passionately. Some people looked away. They could be embarrassed by the sight of two women kissing, but maybe they just wanted to give them privacy for what might be their last moment together.

Liz finally got into the squad car, and it headed up to the back door of the school. Brenda tested the connection to the microphone. "You doing okay, Liz?"

"Never better," Liz quipped. Her sarcasm sounded oddly cheerful, like she was looking forward to the challenge.

Olivia's eyes followed the police car up the hill. Brenda's radio barked a message from the SWAT team. "Chief! You can tell the perp the snipers are off the roof."

"Did you hear that, Liz?"

"Copy." Olivia smiled at the thought that she was living in a TV police show.

Liz opened a call to the shooter and reported the information about the snipers. "So, Pete, show us you mean business by letting the admin go."

The dead air on the communication line hissed with anticipation. There was the distant sound of a male voice shouting. "Get out of here, you bitch! Get out! Now!"

A few moments later, the squad outside the principal's door reported in. "Ms. Denton is out. We have her, and she's safe."

"Get her to a bus so the paramedics can check her out."

"Copy that, Chief. She says she needs to pee."

"Well, let her do that," Brenda replied dryly. "Get her to a safe place first."

"Yes, Chief. We're escorting her to the bathroom now. Davis is going in with her."

Olivia felt a surge of pride watching the Hobbs police in action. They were as professional as any she'd find in a big city, maybe more so.

Liz's voice came on the speaker. "It's Stolz. I'm in the school. Can you hear me all right?"

"Loud and clear," answered Brenda. "You know the way to the principal's office."

"Heading there now."

A short man with a shaved head pushed his way through the crowd and headed to Brenda. "Are you the officer in charge?"

"Yes, I'm Chief Harrison." Brenda extended her hand, but the young man looked at it like it was dirty before he took it. "Are you the negotiator?" she asked.

"Dylan Crosby, Boston FBI."

"You're not wearing a vest."

"Do I need one? The office said the perimeter has been secured and the command post is out of range."

Brenda nodded, indicating he had the right idea. "But if I were you, I'd put on a vest, just in case." She motioned to one of her officers to get him one.

"Give me a status update," Crosby ordered impatiently.

"The shooter asked to talk to Dr. Stolz. He knows her. She volunteered to talk to him. Sounds like a potential hostage swap."

"You sent in a civilian to talk to him?" demanded the man in an incredulous tone. "I can't believe it!"

"Look, Mr. Crosby, you weren't here. And for your information, Dr. Stolz has a connection to this kid. She and a bunch of townspeople were trying to turn him around. He trusts her. Isn't that the first rule of hostage negotiation, gain the subject's trust?"

He exhaled a long sigh, but he nodded.

"Don't worry. Liz Stolz does the department firearms training, and she was chief of surgery at Yale New Haven. She had to deal with a gun incident there."

"I hope she's not armed."

"She took her 9mm with her."

"Oh, for god's sake!" The man leaned on the table and shook his head.

Brenda's face darkened. Olivia could imagine her biting ridges into her tongue. It was time for her to intervene. "Mr. Crosby!" Olivia said, addressing him in her most authoritative voice, "I am Olivia Enright, the town manager. It's nice of you to come, but we have all been doing the best we can. Now, instead of criticizing Chief Harrison, maybe you could give Dr. Stolz advice before she enters the lion's den?"

The man perked up at the suggestion. "Good idea. Can you open the channel?"

"Stolz," answered Liz.

"Dr. Stolz, are you aware that we are basically talking about making yourself a hostage?"

"Who's this?" asked Liz impatiently.

"Dylan Crosby, Boston FBI."

"Yes, of course I know I'm making myself a hostage. Do you have a better idea?"

"You should get something in exchange. Ask him to release the others. How are you communicating with him?"

"On my cell phone. Do you want me to call him now?"

"Yes, right away. We have to get them out before you go in."

They all listened while the call rang on the other end. "Hello?" asked a cautious male voice.

"Hey, Pete. It's Liz Stolz. I'm in the school. I want to make a deal. If you release the women, you can keep me in there as long as you want."

"Are you armed?"

Fortunately, Liz didn't hesitate for a second. "With sandwiches and water. It's lunchtime. I thought you might be hungry. I know I am. How about letting the ladies go?"

"Maybe the young one, but I'm keeping the one with the gray hair."

"Why? What's she to you? Do you know her?"

"I'll tell you when you get here."

The sound obviously changed. He'd ended the call.

"Well?" asked Liz. "Is that good enough, or should I push harder?"

"If you're comfortable with that, Dr. Stolz," said Crosby. "One for one is not a bad swap. I'd rather get them both."

"Me too, but I'll take what I can get. Any last words of wisdom before I go in there?"

"Stay calm and keep him talking. Find out as much as you can. Don't argue with him. Don't talk except to ask questions. *Listen.*"

"Will you let me know when I'm doing something wrong?"

"I'll do my best, but once you're in there, you're mostly on your own."

"I was afraid of that."

Olivia was distracted by the arrival of Amy Hsu, wearing a white coat covered by an L.L. Bean parka. The stethoscope around her neck indicated she'd come to help. As a new arrival in Hobbs, Amy really didn't owe the community her support, but she had come anyway.

Olivia kissed her on the cheek. "Thank you so much for coming."

Amy quickly explained that Liz had closed the office and suggested the staff join the support effort at the school. Many of the patients were involved in the crisis and had canceled their appointments. "After that, it hardly seemed worth keeping the practice open," Amy said. "Where's Liz?"

Olivia gestured in the direction of the school. "Starting a new career as a hostage negotiator. She just went into the school to talk to the shooter."

"Oh, my God! Is she crazy?"

Olivia laughed softly. She'd wondered that herself. "Actually, she got one of the hostages released, maybe a second one, when she goes in to talk to the shooter."

"Leave it to her to be in the thick of things," said Amy, shaking her head. She looked around. "I should probably ask how I can help instead of standing here admiring you."

As much as Olivia liked that idea, she knew Amy was right. "That woman there is apparently a therapist who came up to help." Olivia pointed to Gloria Parrish. "I'd ask her what you can do." She reached down and covertly squeezed Amy's hand. "Thank you for coming."

"Of course, I would. I belong here."

### 12:36 p.m.

Liz entered the corridor leading to the administrative office. The SWAT team was positioned behind barricades on both sides. The leader indicated with a wave that she should hug the wall. She crouched into the defensive position, even though it was hard on her knees. It was easier to speculate about when she might need to have them replaced than contemplate the possibility of her death by gunfire that day. She was determined to come out of this alive.

On the way in, she'd passed the young woman who'd drawn the worst duty that day, being the admin who stayed behind while others went on their break. The paramedics were giving her the once-over. From where Liz stood, she looked shaken, but otherwise okay.

In a solemn but affectionate greeting, the SWAT members patted Liz's shoulders as she passed. She wondered if they were offering encouragement or commending her for being brave. She didn't feel brave. In fact, she had never been more frightened in her life. She'd faced a gunman once before, in the emergency room at Yale New Haven, when she'd responded to a request for a surgeon. Wrong place, wrong time. Then, she could let the police handle the situation. This time, she'd be on the front line.

What would she say when she got in there? The hastily shared instructions from the FBI negotiator had already flown out of her head. Her mind had been racing, and he'd talked so fast. A few things had stuck, but they were obvious things she would have thought of on her own.

She mentally reviewed the geography of the administrative office, trying to think of places to take cover if things went wrong. The interior of the school was metal framed with a drywall skin that couldn't stop assault rifle fire. The overturned desks set up by the SWAT were no guarantee of safety either. Once inside, she'd have to survive on her wits, like when something went wrong in surgery and there was no protocol. She'd just have to make it up as she went along.

"Once the shooter brings the hostage to the door, position yourself between them," said the SWAT leader. "Push her as hard as you can in my direction. I'll be there to catch her fall. I know it sounds hard, but try to do it without any quick motion. You know why."

Hearing a familiar voice, Liz looked into his eyes and realized he'd been one of the rookies who'd gone through her training class.

"Wish me luck, Matt. This is my first time putting theory into action."

The brown eyes through the face shield looked surprised to be recognized. He smiled. "Mine too, Dr. Liz. I guess we'll figure out if it works." He handed his rifle to the officer standing behind him and turned to Liz. "Ready?"

Liz nodded and called Peter. She tapped her foot while she waited for him to answer. Each successive ring heightened her anxiety. Finally, his voice came through the speaker.

"Hello?" he asked, as if he was answering a casual call.

"Peter, it's Liz Stolz. I'm outside the main door. Let Ms. Barnes come to the door, and I'll come in. I'm bringing in a bag with water and sandwiches. Don't shoot."

"All right, but tell the cops out there not to try anything, or I'll shoot the old one."

"They promise not to harm you if you let the principal go and let me come in."

He agreed, but his voice sounded different, more distracted. Liz wondered what had changed.

The door of the office at the end of the hall finally opened, and Courtney came out. "She's coming. Get ready," said Liz. One of the SWAT officers pushed open the door in front of Liz. She grabbed Courtney's wrist and yanked her through the doorway, flinging her into Matt's open arms. Liz looked over her shoulder to make sure that Courtney landed safely and saw that the back of her skirt was wet. At some point, her bladder had let go.

"Get in here," ordered Peter, with a wave of his rifle.

Hands held high, the supermarket bag dangling, Liz walked slowly toward the principal's office. "Hey, Pete," she said when she reached the door.

"Get in and sit down," he said coldly.

"My knees are bothering me today. Mind if I stand?"

Pete waved his agreement with the rifle barrel. Once Liz stepped inside, he slammed shut the door and locked it. The pot smoke in the air was so thick she could probably get high just breathing. Susan's lips were moving silently. She raised her eyes for a moment to acknowledge Liz's arrival, then went back to praying.

Peter's eyes were glassy, and the pupils were dilated. His hair was matted like he hadn't washed it in a week. He was wearing military fatigues and the kind of cheap protective vest found online or in army navy stores. The militia people were snapping them up like crazy. Liz wondered if they could really stop a bullet. The fact that he wore a vest meant her options were limited if she needed to take a shot.

"Can I put my hands down?" she asked, dangling the shopping bag in his direction. He grabbed it and threw it on the round conference table by the door.

"Okay. Put 'em down," he said. His voice had lost the angry edge and sounded almost kind.

Slowly, Liz lowered her hands. "Smells good in here," she said with a grin. "But aren't you worried about smoking with all these cops everywhere?"

"It's legal now," said Pete. "Fuck them."

"Thanks, but I'll pass," quipped Liz. "I'm not into uniforms."

A voice broke into her earphone. "Be careful with the humor, Dr. Stolz. You never know what might set him off." Liz resented the advice, even though she knew he was right. She wished Brenda was calling the shots instead of the useless FBI negotiator.

"Do you mind if I see what kind of sandwiches they sent us?" Liz asked. "They're from the Webhanet Deli. Nice of them to think of us."

His pistol still pointed at Susan, Pete upended the shopping bag, dumping its contents on the table by the door. A bottle of water rolled onto the floor. "Leave it!" he ordered.

"Okay," said Liz in a friendly tone. "Oh, look. They marked the sandwiches. Made it easy for us. Let's see. We have two chicken salad sandwiches. Mind if I take one? Their chicken salad is the best. We also have a ham and cheese, and a 'real Italian.' Always makes me laugh when I see that. I grew up in New York. When I went to college, I'd bike down to Arthur Avenue to get a sub. The bread was crusty and always fresh. The provolone stank like dirty feet. The roasted peppers tasted smoky. Now, that was a 'real Italian.'"

Peter stared at her as if she were insane, babbling over sandwiches with an assault rifle pointed at her chest. It made no sense to aim at her body mass, which was protected by her vest. Probably an idle threat to show he was paying attention.

"If you're smoking, I bet you're hungry," Liz ventured. "I know I am. Which sandwich would you like?"

"I'll take ham and cheese."

"Susan?" asked Liz.

She looked up and shook her head.

"How about water?"

That got her a nod. Liz looked into Pete's eyes. "I'm going to open your sandwich and put it on the desk. Okay? And I'm going to give her some water."

He motioned his approval of the plan with a wag of his gun.

While Liz unwrapped his sandwich, she continued the conversation in a casual tone. "So, tell me, Pete. What brought you here today? Sam told me she had to let you go. That's a shame. I heard you liked your job."

"I did," he said in a surly tone.

"I bet it made you mad to lose it."

"You bet it did." He took a big bite out of the sandwich Liz had positioned on the desk.

"Come on, Pete. You invited me in here to tell me your story. I'm all ears." She opened a bottle of water for Susan and put it within her reach.

"Are you angry with Sam? Is that why you came here today?"

"No. She warned me twice about smoking on the job. I deserved to be fired."

"So, not Sam. Then what?"

Lucy's voice came into her earpiece. "You're doing a great job, Liz. I love you." The sound was so welcome that Liz's eyes filled.

"Last night..." Peter began, looking dazed. "Last night...I was in bed at Mom's. A guy I know gave me some really good pot. I was thinking...you know, going back to the beginning."

"And what happened at the beginning?" Liz took a bite of her sandwich to encourage him to eat, too. She chewed, but the normally delicious chicken salad tasted like wet sawdust in her mouth.

"It was the fat gym teacher," said Peter, his eyes unfocused, staring at Liz but not seeing her. She realized he was imagining a scene from the past. "She used to make fun of me. I was skinny because Dad didn't have a job and we couldn't buy enough food. Mom tried, but that was before she worked at the bank. You could see my ribs when I took off my shirt."

"I'm sorry you didn't have enough to eat."

"The fat gym teacher looked like she ate plenty. She called me 'puny.' I didn't even know what it meant. I had to ask my mother. It made me mad because I couldn't help being skinny. And I was hungry."

"That was mean to make fun of someone for not having enough to eat," said Liz, sounding angry in sympathy.

"Yes!" Peter agreed adamantly. "It was."

"She saw my dick when I changed. She called that 'puny' too. I was just a little kid. Of course, I had a little dick. When no one was looking, she'd touch it and hold it. If it was so puny, why did she want to hold it?"

A cold clamminess crept over Liz's skin, and the hair rose on the back of her neck as she absorbed the horror. "Touching you like that was wrong."

"She said it wasn't. She said she wanted to make me feel good."

"Did it?"

"No!"

"How did you feel?"

"Ashamed. I kept pushing her hand away, but she kept touching me. I'd try to hide after gym or go to the nurse to get out of it, but she kept finding me."

"Did you tell your parents?"

"No."

"How about your teacher?"

"I told her. She said I was lying and just wanted to get out of gym. I kept telling her, but she still said I was lying. Then she called my father and told him I was a liar. She asked what he was going to do about it. And do you know what he did?"

"No, tell me." Liz wrapped up her sandwich. At this point, she couldn't even fake an appetite.

"He took me outside and threw me around. He told me to get out and never come back. I had a little place in the woods where I used to hide. I'd made a lean-to out of some pine branches and leaves. I went there and waited until my father left the next day. He always told Mom he was looking for work, but when the school bus passed the convenience store, I'd see him coming out with a six-pack. He was never looking for work."

Liz wished Lucy were here asking the questions. She'd know exactly what to say.

"I am so sad to hear you went through this, Pete. Did you finally come home?"

"I did, and Mom told me to stay away from Dad. It wasn't hard. He never noticed me unless he was mad. He was drunk most of the time. Then he'd go outside and piss against the house. He told me that's what real men did, and I should try it sometime."

"Didn't your toilet work?"

"It got blocked up a lot. The septic needed pumping, but we didn't have the money."

Liz nodded. "It's sad that your father didn't listen. And telling you that real men piss against the house is bullshit. You know that, right?"

"When I saw his big dick, I knew the teacher was right. Mine was puny. But why did she want to touch it?"

"I don't know. Some adults abuse children because they think they can't get love from adults. Kids are an easy target because they're small and can't push back."

"My girlfriend told me I should take my little dick and get the fuck out of her house."

Liz instantly perceived the causal loop that had sent Pete to the school that day. Now, if she could only figure out how to break it. "That was a really mean thing to say."

"And it's not even true. Doc, you've seen my dick. You know it's not little."

Liz suppressed a smile. Men were so obsessed with the size of their penises. "You're right. It's not little. It's exactly as big as it should be."

Peter grimaced, and Liz realized that was as close to a smile as she was going to get.

"Well, that story helps me understand why you'd want to shoot the gym teacher. But Peter, the woman wasn't the same person who made fun of you. How did that help you get back at the one who really hurt you?"

He shrugged.

"And what about Ms. Gedney? What do you have against her?"

"She looks just like my third-grade teacher, Mrs. Hanrahan, tall, skinny like the witches in the kid's books. Gray hair just like that. She was the one who told Dad I was a liar." He glared at Susan.

All at once, Liz saw the whole picture, but she had no idea what to do next.

# Chapter 6

**12:43 p.m.**

Lucy and Gloria exchanged a look. Liz was doing an excellent job of getting the subject to trust her and drawing out his story, but now she'd reminded him why he was holding Susan hostage. Lucy grabbed the microphone away from the negotiator. "Liz, try to distract him. Ask him something else to get the focus away from Susan."

She knew Liz understood the message when she heard her ask, "Hey, Pete. What ever happened to that gym teacher who assaulted you? Is she retired now?"

"I heard she died a couple of years ago. Pancreatic cancer. According to my friend, whose mother knew her, she really suffered in the end."

"See? You don't have to punish people. The universe takes care of it."

"Maybe. But if I do it, I can make sure it gets done."

There was a long pause. Then Liz said, "So if the gym teacher hurt you, why did you kill the kids?"

"I was their age when that bitch touched me. I didn't want them to get hurt, too."

"So you were trying to save them?"

"Yes."

"Their parents will be sad. Your mother would be sad if something happened to you."

"Maybe, but she didn't do anything when Dad hit me. She didn't come after me when he threw me out."

"Maybe she couldn't. Maybe she was afraid of him, too. Did he hit her?" Lucy could see how uncomfortable Renee looked at this question. She pulled into her shoulders and stared at her feet.

"Mom was black and blue a lot. She hid it with makeup."

90

"If he beat her too, she was probably too afraid to help you, but wished she could."

"I don't know. I never asked her. She was different after Dad finally left. She perked right up after she got a job at the bank. Things were better after that. We had food because Dad wasn't spending all the money on beer and cigarettes. They're expensive now. Over eight dollars a pack!"

"Hah. When I was smoking, they cost fifty-five cents a pack."

"You smoked? I don't believe it. You're a doctor."

"Lots of doctors smoked back then. Do now too. Sometimes you just need something to take the edge off. Life sucks sometimes."

"That's why I smoke weed. Damn! This stuff Kyle gave me is great. Want to try some?"

"Thanks, but no. I've done enough damage to my lungs with tobacco."

"You sure? This shit is great."

Lucy imagined Liz shaking her head, declining a toke.

"You know, I saw your mother out there. She's really worried about you. Want to talk to her? I can get her on the phone."

"I can call her if I want. I don't want to talk to her. She'll just make me feel bad about what I've done."

"What have you done to make her feel bad?"

"I killed those kids."

"Yes, you did. Are you sorry?"

There was a long pause. "Maybe, but they died fast, instead of dying a little bit at a time...like me."

### 12:52 p.m.

Brenda knew that Liz was smart, but she was impressed with how she was handling the perp. The FBI guy obviously thought the same. He just stood there, leaning on his hands, listening. What the hell did he know about the people in this town? People from away never understood Hobbs like the people who lived there.

When Brenda and Marcie had first found the town on the Maine Atlas and reserved a cabin for a week, they'd only seen the beaches and tourist attractions on the Post Road. They had no idea people lived on the other side of the turnpike. They didn't see how hard the year-round residents worked to keep Hobbs going. The townies stocked the supermarket shelves. They fixed the roads and plowed the snow. They had the grit to survive the winter. Mrs. Langdon was one of those tough Mainers whose people had come down from French Canada. Watching from the command post, Brenda wondered what she could do for her.

She nudged Lucy and gave her a side nod. Lucy was quick. She always picked up on cues. They walked a few paces away. "Do you think I should have an officer take Mrs. Langdon home?"

Lucy looked back to where the poor woman sat, staring vacantly into space. "I doubt she'll leave. She wants to see what happens to her son."

"She was pretty upset about the snipers. You know I was just doing my job."

"Of course, but imagine if Peter were your son. You'd be upset to find out the police were trying to shoot him."

"We always try to take them alive, but in this situation, after he killed all those kids, and he's holding two people hostage, if we got the shot..." Brenda deliberately let her voice trail off, knowing Lucy would draw her own conclusions.

"You can ask Mrs. Langdon if she wants to go home. She has other kids. They're old enough to pay attention to the news."

Brenda tried to charm Lucy with a smile. "Would you ask her?"

"Sure, I'll talk to her," said Lucy with a sigh that made Brenda think she'd seen that trick before.

Brenda left Lucy to deal with Mrs. Langdon while she went back to the command table to see what was going on. As she passed the asshole from the FBI, she gave him a dirty look. He was sitting with his chin in his two hands, scowling. This was not going the way he planned. Maybe she should put the snipers back on the roof and try to get a shot. If they stayed out of sight, the perp would never know.

### 1:06 p.m.

Paradoxically, the anxiety made Liz ravenous, so she wolfed down the rest of her sandwich. Peter had finished his, too. He burped contentedly. Except for the fact that Susan hadn't touched her sandwich, it felt like they were all sitting at a lunch counter, waiting for the waitress to return. Susan hadn't said a word either, which was probably a good idea. Peter kept staring at her, which meant he still hadn't decided what to do with her.

Standing was hard on her knees, so Liz locked them to maintain her stance. If she sat down and needed to take a shot, she'd be fumbling to get back into position. She hadn't heard anything from the command post for a while, but she could use guidance on how to resolve this situation. Early on, the negotiator had suggested asking for the shooter's weapons. Liz already knew Peter wasn't going to give them up, so why even bother? But the FBI guy was the expert. Maybe he was right.

"Hey, Pete. You know, if you put down your guns, we can all get out of here."

Pete barked out a single chuckle. He threw his joint on the floor and ground it out on the carpet. "Did they tell you to say that?"

"Yes," Liz answered honestly. "I figured I'd give it a try. Come on. Isn't this getting old?"

"Not really. I've never held hostages before." He grinned. "It's all new to me."

"You know, Pete...eventually, we're all going to have to pee."

"I can hold it a long time."

"Me too. Sometimes, I'd be in surgery for seven, eight hours, and I had to hold it. My max is about ten. If I knew I was going to be in the OR longer, I'd wear one of those adult diapers, just in case."

"That's a good idea. I should have thought of that." Peter ground the carpet with the sole of his boot where he'd thrown the marijuana butt. Liz wondered if he'd seen it smoldering. "Did you like being a surgeon?" he asked.

"I did. I liked it a lot. Sometimes I miss it."

"So, why did you quit?"

"That's a long story, but here's the short version. Some movie star came to me with breast cancer. She didn't want me to remove her breast, so I did a lumpectomy. You know, I took out just the cancer. It was a big lesion for a lumpectomy, but within the guidelines. I warned her that she'd need radiation afterward, but when they set up the treatments, she skipped out. No explanation. Then she came down with cancer again and blamed me."

"Women can be such bitches," said Peter, lighting another joint.

"They can," said Liz, trying to sound sympathetic. She thought of Lucy out there listening and wondered what she was thinking.

"That teacher who called my father was a bitch." Pete glared at Susan again. "I can't believe how much she looks like her."

Liz unlocked her knees and flexed them a little. This conversation was taking a wrong turn. "But Susan isn't your teacher. She wasn't even living in Maine when you were in school. She was in New York, studying to be a priest."

"How do you know all this?" asked Peter, still trying to get his joint lit. Liz didn't like the idea that he was getting more stoned than he already was, but it indicated he'd relaxed a little.

"My wife, the rector of the Episcopal church, went to seminary with her."

"No kidding." He took a long drag. "My mother goes to that church."

"I think I knew that."

"Your Mom probably knows Mother Susan. You should ask her."

Peter shook his head. "Nah, I don't want to talk to her. She'll just start crying."

A male voice spoke into Liz's ear, "Good job trying to distinguish his target from the person he associates her with. Keep that going if you can."

"My wife is so happy that Mother Susan is working in the parish. Being a priest is her real job. She just teaches to make extra money."

Liz could feel Susan's eyes on the side of her face, but she didn't look in her direction. She kept her gaze focused on Peter's glassy eyes as he pondered the information.

"You mean she's not really a teacher?"

"Yes, she's a teacher, but her real job, what they call a vocation, is being a priest. You haven't seen her around town in her collar? She visits the old people after school sometimes."

He nodded thoughtfully.

"The people of the church love her. She gives great sermons. You should come and listen to her preach some time."

"I hate church. Mom used to make me go. It was sooooo boring!" He looked at Susan again. "She sure looks like Mrs. Hanrahan, those blue eyes and that stuck out chin. They could be sisters."

"But sisters, even twins who look alike, aren't the same person."

With narrowed eyes, Peter scrutinized Susan.

"Do you know what happened to Mrs. Hanrahan, Peter?" asked Liz, trying to divert his attention from Susan. "Did she die like your gym teacher?"

Peter shrugged. "Dunno. She moved out of town, and I never saw her again." He walked over to Susan. "So you're a priest." He took a long toke on his joint and blew smoke into her face. "Ever smoke pot?"

Watching anxiously, Liz moved her hand closer to the pistol holster attached to the inside of her vest.

"Leave her alone, Pete. She's not bothering you."

"Sure she is. Just by being here, she bothers me."

"Then let her go, and you won't have to look at her."

"There's no way I'm letting her go." He pointed his pistol at Susan's temple.

"Stop, Pete," said Liz, watching his finger move into position. She saw the tiny movements of the muscles, his finger bending slowly. She always taught her students to squeeze, not yank the trigger.

Instinctively, Liz dropped into the defensive position and fired. Something sprayed onto her face, and she blinked. A scarlet fountain spurted from Peter's arm where Liz's bullet had hit an artery. Susan screamed when blood spattered onto her face and clothes.

Peter's eyes widened, then pure rage filled them. He turned the barrel of his AR-15. Liz felt a sharp pain in her shoulder before firing two rounds into his throat.

His eyes rolled back in his head, and he fell backwards with a thud. His left carotid pumped out bright blood. Liz dropped her gun, ran to him, and dug into the wound with her fingers, pressing on the artery to stop the flow. His brachial continued to gush. She clamped her free hand on his arm. Then she saw that one of her shots had gone straight through his throat into his spine.

### 1:12 p.m.

Lucy suppressed a scream when she'd heard the first shot, but a strange feral sound, half groan and half cry, had emerged from her throat. Gloria's arm around her gripped tight as the next shots sounded.

"Liz! Liz! Are you all right?" Brenda barked through the radio.

When there wasn't an instant reply, Lucy felt she might jump out of her skin, but Gloria held her tight. Finally, Liz's voice, sounding defeated and weary, spoke. "I'm okay. Susan's okay. Pete is dead."

Lucy sent a stream of prayers toward heaven. Gloria released her, apparently realizing she'd found solace from another source. Brenda rushed through the crowd and grabbed Lucy's hand. "Come with me. I'll take you to her." Brenda pulled Lucy in the direction of a waiting squad car.

On their way to the school, the SWAT leader radioed Brenda to report on the scene. "Looks like she tried to stop the perp by shooting him in the arm. What a shot! Too bad he didn't give up. Looks like he got mad and fired his assault rifle, but he was too stoned to shoot straight. You should smell the pot in the air! I could get high just standing here. Dr. Stolz hit him twice in the throat. Either shot would have killed him."

"How is Dr. Stolz?" asked Brenda.

"She's bleeding from the arm. We wrapped it up, but she won't leave the scene."

"I'm bringing the wife up to the school. We'll be there in a minute."

"Copy that."

When they arrived at the front door of the school, two officers came out to meet the car. One opened the door for Lucy.

"Are you sure you're ready for this, Lucy?" asked Brenda as they ran up the stairs to the administrative offices. "There will be a lot of blood."

"Just bring me to Liz."

Brenda turned to one of the officers escorting them. "Where's the teacher? Do the EMTs have her?"

"She won't leave Dr. Stolz. She's dazed and shocky, but she won't let the medics touch her until they take care of Dr. Stolz."

"Come on, Lucy. Looks like you're on duty." Brenda pulled her through the hall leading to the administrative office. She pushed a path through the throng of police and paramedics blocking the door. "Make way!" An officer opened the door to the principal's office.

Blood spatter covered the walls. Peter's crumpled body lay in an ocean of blood that was beginning to congeal at the edges. Doubled over in front of Peter's body, Liz was on her knees, sobbing.

"Liz, it's not your fault," Susan was saying, gently stroking her back. Susan's hair, face and the sleeve of her sweater were stained with blood. "You tried, but you had no other choice." She looked up and saw Lucy standing there and moved aside. "Please talk to her, Lucy. She won't listen to anyone."

Lucy took Susan's place and touched Liz's shoulder. "Sweetie, I'm here."

Liz sat up. Her hands were red with blood. On each cheek was a bloody handprint. There was a spray of perfectly round red dots on her forehead and eyelids. Lucy's stomach roiled, but she forced down the rising gorge. "Sweetie, I'm here," she repeated. "Please let the paramedics help you. You're hurt."

"It's nothing," said Liz, sounding almost normal. "Just a surface wound. Nothing to worry about."

"But it's bleeding," Lucy said. Liz turned to look at her shoulder, where an awkwardly tied bandage showed a spreading red stain. "Please let them help you," Lucy begged. "Please."

Liz struggled to get to her feet. Lucy could see that her knees were hurting from kneeling so long. Brenda reached out to help steady her. Lucy took her other arm.

The SWAT team in the hall parted for them and stood by like an honor guard.

### 1:20 p.m.

Olivia had been listening to the privileged communication among the command team and knew the shooter was dead. According to the chatter of the officers on the scene, it had been quite a feat of marksmanship. One kept going on about how amazing it was that at her age, Liz had the reflexes and aim to take down a shooter without harming the hostage. The ageist talk infuriated Olivia, so she walked away.

She watched Lucy's friend, the therapist, head to the barricaded section reserved for Renee Langdon. She'd been kept away from the other parents for her safety and protection. Olivia couldn't hear what they were saying, but she could see the exact moment Gloria delivered the bad news. The poor woman sobbed like her heart would come out of her throat. After that, she stared vacantly. The therapist stayed with her, rubbing her shoulder and speaking softly.

Losing a child was bad enough, but losing one that people considered a villain meant being despised and isolated. Sympathy was thin, if there were any. Everyone assumed the dead man had gotten what he deserved. The guilt by association made the parent a pariah. When the Feds had uncovered the kiddie porn on Jason's computer, Olivia had done everything she could to suppress the story and protect her granddaughters. She'd paid off people in the press and used whatever leverage she had in the city government to shut people up.

Peter Langdon's mother didn't have Olivia's resources. The carnage her son had caused was already national news. There was nowhere she could hide. Olivia wondered what to do with her in the short term. She couldn't send her home without support. Fortunately, her other children were probably still in school and, hopefully, ignorant of their brother's death. When Brenda got back, they'd talk about how to protect the family.

"How's it going?" asked a familiar voice.

Olivia looked into Amy's calm eyes and nodded in the direction of Renee Langdon, who was now nodding in response to whatever Gloria was saying. "I'm trying to figure out how to help the mother."

Amy gazed in her direction. "I brought some tranquilizers from the drug safe in the office in case anyone needed them. She looks okay, but shocky. Should I ask?"

"That friend of Lucy's seems to have the situation under control...for the moment."

"Is it over now?" asked Amy.

"The shooting is. Your boss is a hero."

"Knowing Liz, that's the only role she could play. Perfect for a surgeon. They're all cowboys."

Olivia gave Amy a sharp look. "I know your ex was a surgeon, but they're not all the same. Liz Stolz risked her life to save those hostages. Have some respect!" The little smile on Amy's face vanished, and she took a step back, which made Olivia realize her tone had been too harsh. "Sorry," she muttered.

"I have nothing but respect for Liz," Amy protested. "What she did today was incredibly brave."

Olivia was glad Amy had so easily conceded. She was relieved that the crisis was over, but the resolution had shaken her. The last thing she wanted was an argument.

"I knew it would end this way," Olivia said.

"You did? How?"

"Once the shooter started talking about being molested, there was no other way for this to end."

### 1:42 p.m.

After Bobbie had learned the office was closing, she came to the school with the others to see how she could help. Ginny had come through the office to deliver Liz's message, but now that Bobbie had arrived at the scene, she was too distracted to be of much use.

Frantic with worry, Bobbie had repeatedly tried to call Susan even though she knew cell phones had to be turned off during school hours. She told herself that Susan might not be able to get to her phone during the evacuation of the school. At least, she knew she wasn't dead. The news report said there had been only one faculty fatality, the gym teacher. All the other victims had been children.

Bobbie stood behind the police line with the others awaiting updates about their family members. Everyone was getting their information from their phones. Things were happening so quickly that official statements couldn't keep up with the online news feed.

The recent sound of gunshots had sent a ripple of anxiety through the crowd, and people had pressed closer to the barricade, trying to see what was happening. Someone pushed Bobbie from behind. She turned around and gave the woman a dirty look.

Then someone shouted, "They got the shooter!"

"Look! Look! Someone's coming out."

Bobbie instantly recognized the gray-haired woman huddled under a Hobbs Emergency Services blanket. "Susan!" she called.

"Susan!" She ducked under the barrier. Two police officers chased her right to the ambulance door.

"Let her pass. She's my partner," said Susan in an authoritative voice that made her pursuers stop short.

Bobbie huddled around Susan protectively as she tried to find the source of all the blood. It was everywhere—on her face, in her hair, all over her sweater. "Oh, my poor, dear girl! What's happened to you?"

"He locked us in the office. Me, Courtney, and one of the admins. He said I reminded him of his teacher."

"Are you telling me you were a hostage?" asked Bobbie, trying for Susan's sake to be calm, but not completely succeeding.

"Excuse me, ma'am, but I need to make sure she's okay," said a paramedic, trying to insinuate himself between them.

Bobbie refused to budge. "I'm a nurse practitioner. I can examine her."

"Please, ma'am, just let me do my job." The earnest young man couldn't be more than twenty.

Bobbie suddenly remembered how much she resented family interference in a patient's care and moved aside. "Go ahead," she said, but she watched his every move. He attached leads for a heart monitor and shyly moved aside the blanket to take Susan's pressure. All her numbers, except her heartbeat, were in the normal range. With so much blood on her clothes, it made sense to look for sources of bleeding, but Bobbie hadn't thought of looking in her hair. The paramedic carefully, almost tenderly, combed through it, searching for shrapnel.

"You look okay," he said, removing the leads from the heart monitor. "Do you feel okay?"

Susan reached for his hand. "Yes, thank you for your kindness. Can I leave with my friend?"

"If you feel well enough, but the police will want to talk to you."

"Don't worry, I'm not leaving Dodge," quipped Susan. The young man looked puzzled by the reference, but Bobbie was relieved to see Susan's dry wit was still intact.

As they headed to where Bobbie had left her car, Susan pulled the blanket off her shoulder. "I should have returned this." She walked back to where the paramedic stood.

"No," he said, pushing it into her hands. "It's cold. Keep it. We have lots more."

"Are you sure?" Susan asked. In answer, he gently arranged it around her shoulders. A few tears came to Bobbie's eyes. She couldn't tell if they'd been brought on by his kindness or her overwhelming sense of relief.

Bobbie clicked open the door locks of her car. "I'm bringing you home to pick up some clothes, and then you're coming back to my place."

"No, Bobbie. Lucy will need me."

"Never mind. Lucy will manage. You need to be looked after, and I'm going to make sure you are. You're coming home with me."

Fortunately, Susan didn't argue. Bobbie didn't have the energy for it.

### 2:12 p.m.

"Ms. Fitzgerald, I love you," declared Maggie's young admirer, who barely came to her hip.

"I love you too, Ethan." Maggie tousled the boy's hair. "I really enjoyed singing with you. Maybe you'd like to join our youth choir. It meets after school, and the school bus can drop you off right here." She glanced at the boy's mother, who smiled.

"Can I, Mom? Can I?" asked the boy, pulling on his mother's parka.

"We'll see," the woman said and mouthed the word 'thanks' to Maggie.

Maggie enjoyed being with young children, but she was glad their parents had come for them. Dealing with the little ones took so much energy. Attempting to put the classroom back in order, she went around collecting crayons and picking up stray toys. The toys hadn't been used in a long time. The Sunday school and the nursery had been closed since the lockdown. When people couldn't come to church, they fell out of the habit and hadn't returned after in-person services resumed. Maggie wondered if the young families had left for good.

"Does every little boy fall in love with you?" said a familiar voice.

Maggie looked up and saw Sam standing in the doorway. "I don't know. I never thought about it."

"You're every little boy's fantasy of what a woman should be," Sam said, stepping into the room.

Maggie mugged a glamor pose reminiscent of a 1940s movie star. "What about every little girl's?"

"Well, mine certainly." Despite the humorous exchange, Sam's face was grim, and her shoulders drooped. Maggie opened her arms. Sam rested her head on Maggie's shoulder and leaned heavily against her like a weary child.

"It will be all right, Sam," said Maggie, making circles on her back. You'll see."

Sam finally let her go. "Brenda told me to get out of sight, but I thought I'd come here first and see if you were ready to go home."

"I'm ready. Let's get out of here." Maggie grabbed her bag and coat.

The other classrooms were dark as they passed, except one, where Maggie's friend from the high school was reading to the few remaining children. Maggie stopped to wave goodbye and mouthed, "Thanks."

They found Reshma at the door to the parking lot. She put her hand on Maggie's arm to stop her from leaving while she wound down her conversation with a mother who'd come for her child. After the woman left, Reshma opened her arms to Maggie.

"Thank you so much for rescuing me!"

"I didn't do much, just made a few calls. Believe me, I enjoyed it more than teaching my class. When my kids were young, I used to do a lot of children's theater. It's always fun acting out the old fairy tales."

"I was watching from the doorway. The children loved it, and so did I. I never saw anything like it when I was their age." She turned to give Sam a hug, but it was awkward. Sam wasn't big on social affection. "We have so much pizza in the refrigerator, and all those sandwiches the deli sent," said Reshma. "Would you like to take some home?"

"Maybe you can give the food to people who need it more than we do."

"We sent sandwiches home with the kids. For many, that school lunch is the big meal of the day. But I don't know what to do with the rest. I'll have to figure out how to get it to the right people." Now that Reshma had executed the task her rector had assigned, she looked less confident. "Whether or not I want to be, I'm in charge now. Mother Lucy is on her way to the hospital with her wife."

"Oh, my God! Is Liz all right?"

"Yes, she was injured in the shooting, but apparently not seriously."

"What happened?" Maggie asked, anxiously gripping Reshma's arm.

"She went in to negotiate with the shooter. When he threatened to kill Mother Susan, she shot him dead. Everyone is saying she's a hero."

Maggie doubted Liz would agree. She hated killing. She'd mourned for days after shooting the chipmunk that had been eating her tomatoes.

"When you talk to Lucy again, please ask her to call me," Maggie said. "I want to know that Liz is okay."

"I certainly will. And if I hear any updates to the contrary, I'll call you right away."

"Thank you, Reshma," said Maggie, although the thought that

something might happen to Liz terrified her. She drew on her acting skills to maintain the appearance of calm. "Are you okay here by yourself? Is there anything else I can do?"

"Monsignor O'Brien called. He's trying to organize a prayer vigil tonight at Harbor Park. Could you get the choir together and think about some hymns we could sing?"

"Of course. When is this event?"

"Seven o'clock."

"I'll call you later with details once I talk to the choir. We'll be there," said Maggie. Sam looked at her, but before she could even open her mouth, Maggie said, "*You'd* better stay home."

Reshma looked curious, but Maggie had no intention of explaining.

# Chapter 7

Susan hadn't felt so helpless since she was a child. When Bobbie had asked for her keys, she'd handed them over without question. While she waited for Bobbie to open the rectory door, she saw the blood spatter on her face reflected in the glass. She remembered a warm spray hitting her face. When she'd screamed, her voice had been unrecognizable. She never knew her throat could even produce such a sound, like something out of a grade-B horror movie.

"Susan? Are you okay?" asked Bobbie. She'd been holding the door open, expecting Susan to walk through, but she hadn't been able to move.

She glanced at Bobbie. "Yes, I'm fine."

"You sure? You look pale." Apparently worried that Susan might faint, Bobbie took her arm as they walked down the hall.

"I'm okay," Susan insisted. "Do you mind if I take a shower and wash off the blood before we go?"

"I'm here for you, Susan. Whatever you need."

Reshma came out of the office she shared with Susan. "Thank God! I'm so happy to see you!" Halfway down the hall, she stopped short, blatantly staring, before she averted her eyes.

"Yes, I know...I'm a sight," said Susan with a sigh. "I can't wait to get out of these clothes."

"If you give me that sweater, I'll wash it for you," Reshma said, reaching out.

"Thanks, dear, but I'm going to throw it away. I bought it secondhand in a thrift shop."

"The police might need it for evidence," said Bobbie. "Maybe we should wrap it up until we ask them." Susan hadn't thought of that, but Bobbie was right. "Excuse us," Bobbie said to Reshma, gently tugging on Susan's arm. "She's been through a lot."

"Can I help?"

"Not right now. She wants a hot shower. Once she gets her things together, I'm taking her home with me."

"Are you sure that's a good idea?" Reshma had been an unwilling witness at the Sudanese feast when Bobbie's partner had screamed out their secret. "I mean, wouldn't Mother Susan be more comfortable at home?" added Reshma, apparently realizing she was treading on sensitive ground. "I could look after her here."

Bobbie scrutinized the young woman with savvy eyes. "I know what you're thinking, Reshma, but things have settled down since that awful night. Joyce seems to have adjusted to having Susan around."

"That's good. I mean, I'm glad that Joyce is okay with Susan there. But I want to help. Please let me know if there's anything I can do."

"I will," said Bobbie over her shoulder, leading Susan toward the stairs.

After Bobbie unlocked the door to the rector's apartment, Susan headed straight to her bedroom to take off her bloody clothes. The colorful quilt that Lucy had bought to brighten the dark room suddenly hurt her eyes. Seeking relief from its obscene cheerfulness, Susan focused on the wall paneling.

"Come here, honey. Let me unbutton your sweater." Being undressed by Bobbie would ordinarily be a sweet, sexy gesture, but Susan felt like she was releasing her from unbearable filth. Bobbie carefully rolled up the cardigan. "I'll wrap it up in case the police need it."

Bobbie turned on the shower before going into the kitchen to find a plastic bag for the sweater. Susan had taken off all her clothes by the time Bobbie returned. When her eyes swept over her naked body, Susan felt shy and dirty. Other than that, she felt nothing. She felt completely hollow inside, like someone had reamed out her soul with an apple corer.

Bobbie gently steered her toward the bathroom. "Wash your hair. It's full of blood."

Susan reached up and felt the sticky strands clumped together. It felt like when she was ten and got gum in her hair. Her mother had tried to harden it with ice to make it easier to remove. It hadn't worked and Susan needed to have her hair cut short for the first time.

The bathroom was full of steam. When Susan was alone, she usually left the door open to vent it. She was glad the mirror over the sink was fogged, sparing her another look at her bloody face.

Bobbie pulled back her sleeve and reached behind the shower curtain to check the water temperature. "Want me to bathe you?" she asked. "I can get undressed and get into the shower with you."

"Thank you, but I can manage."

Bobbie closed the door, which made the steam in the room swirl in the air. For a moment, Susan stared at it in wonder. It looked magical, like tiny fairies dancing in the air.

The hot water beating on her face was a relief. Susan leaned into it to rinse her hair. When she looked down, she saw that the water pooling at her feet had turned pink, like when she'd started going into menopause and her periods had become heavy. After she scrubbed everywhere with soap, she finally felt clean.

The towel felt warm when she picked it up. Bobbie had put it on the rack by the old-fashioned cast iron radiator. After spending only a few nights in the rectory, she'd already learned most of Susan's self-care habits.

Bobbie was sitting on the bed, scanning her phone, when Susan came out in her terry-cloth robe. "Feeling better?" she asked, looking up.

"Almost normal."

"Amazing what a hot shower can do."

Susan took out clean underwear from her dresser, including some extras. "How long do you expect to keep me?" she asked, counting out the panties.

"Forever," said Bobbie without hesitation.

"I mean, seriously," said Susan, turning around.

"Seriously, you're staying with me as long as it takes. Pack a week's worth of everything to be sure. We can always come back for more."

Susan kept her bath robe on while she pulled on her underpants. She hated how her breasts hung when she bent over. Although her old body repulsed her, she could feel Bobbie's admiring eyes when she took off the robe to put on her bra. It went both ways. In bed, Susan never thought about Bobbie's little belly and full hips, except to appreciate how much their soft abundance excited her. *How can I be thinking of sex at a time like this?*

She remembered a passage from Lucy's book on sex: "In times of grief, the desire for sex is more than the wish to blot out the pain of loss with the ecstasy of pleasure. It is the impulse to affirm life in the face of death, the urge of the life force to reassert itself."

After Susan put on her bra and slip, Bobbie became less interested in being a voyeur. Her eyes returned to her phone.

"Let's see what's going on at the school."

### 2:28 p.m.

The paramedic glanced at Lucy, looking embarrassed that she couldn't get her patient under control. After an argument, Liz had finally allowed her to replace the bandage because the blood had soaked through the first one, but she snarled when the woman tried to take her blood pressure. Not surprisingly, it was through the roof.

In a way, Lucy was relieved that Liz was being difficult. If she'd been passive and acquiesced to the examination, it would have been out of character. When she'd seen Liz weeping so bitterly over Peter's bloody body, the possibility of a psychotic break had crossed her mind. Liz almost never cried, not even over her mother's death.

"Dr. Stolz, please lie down," begged the paramedic. "Please, Doctor. You know how dangerous shock can be." Deliberately deaf, Liz wouldn't even look at her.

Lucy saw it was time to intervene. "Liz, stop this nonsense and lie down," she ordered firmly. To her surprise, Liz swung her legs up on the stretcher.

The paramedic raised Liz's shirt and looked under her bra to inspect the bruise where the vest had stopped a bullet. She glanced anxiously at Lucy, probably concerned about violating privacy rules. "It's all right," Lucy assured her. "We're married."

"She sees me naked all the time," Liz boasted with a proud grin. If Liz was thinking about sex under these circumstances, she'd be just fine.

"That's quite a bruise," said the paramedic, pulling down Liz's shirt. "You're lucky it wasn't a direct hit."

"I don't know why he shot me in the chest. He saw I was wearing a vest, but he was stoned and shooting with his right hand. He's a lefty."

"I'm amazed you can remember it all so clearly," said Lucy.

"It was like when you're in a car accident. Time seems to slow, and you experience it in slow motion." Lucy had never been in a major car accident. Obviously, Liz had—another thing Lucy hadn't known about her.

Liz still had two bloody handprints on her cheeks. "Do you have any wet wipes?" Lucy asked the paramedic.

"Sure thing," she said, jumping up to find them. It was a new package, and Liz rolled her eyes impatiently while the woman struggled to open it.

For all her resistance to the paramedic's efforts to help her, Liz turned up her face like a child while Lucy wiped it. "Close your eyes, sweetie. It's even on your eyelids." There was only so much Lucy could do in the moving ambulance, which was top-heavy and swayed with every curve in the road. Afraid the alcohol would sting, she stopped working around her eyes and started wiping the blood off her hands.

"I can do that," Liz protested, snatching away the wipe. Lucy knew better than to insist. She ripped a few more wipes out of the pack and left them on Liz's jeans. "Blood really sticks," said Liz, meticulously cleaning between her fingers. "The clotting proteins and hemoglobin bond to organic surfaces, especially skin." The pedantic lecture was further proof that Liz was mentally sound.

"What if they keep you at the hospital?" asked Lucy.

"They won't. They'll be too busy with real patients. Compared to them, I'm fine. Thanks for coming with me."

"Of course, I'd come with you."

Lucy reached for Liz's hand. Rust-colored stains had lodged deeply under her fingernails and cuticles and stuck in the creases of her knuckles. Lucy felt a little strange, knowing the blood belonged to the man Liz had killed.

### 2:35 p.m.

"Olivia, are you sure you want to go in there?" asked Brenda. "It's still a mess."

Olivia hated to be coddled like she was a fragile female. "How can I report to the town what I haven't seen for myself?"

"Can't you wait until CSI is done? Once they get their photos, we'll move the bodies to the medical examiner's office. Trust me. It's not pretty in there." Brenda exchanged a look with Amy. Olivia could sense their unspoken pact to dampen her enthusiasm for viewing the scene.

"Olivia, Brenda is right," Amy said. "You should wait until the bodies are removed. It's already been a difficult day. The sight of those dead children could be too much for your heart."

Olivia bristled with indignation. "Not you too!" She was horrified to think that Amy saw her as one of those weak women who need protection from upsetting sights. Despite Olivia's feminine appearance, she was tougher than she looked.

An officer approached Brenda and whispered something into her ear. "The medical examiner's people are nearly done," Brenda said after the officer walked away. "Let's give them another five minutes, and then we'll go in."

Two black vans drove by. Olivia followed them with her eyes, sensing they were carrying away the bodies of the dead children. Suddenly, she was grateful that time had made the decision for her. Amy was always hard to read, but she looked relieved too. As a doctor, she'd probably seen her share of grisly sights, and the frequency of school shootings had numbed many people. Olivia was glad to know that Amy wasn't one of them.

After another van drove by, an officer came out of the school and waved them in. Brenda peered at Olivia. "You're sure?"

"Brenda! I know you're trying to protect me, but please give me some credit!"

No one spoke as they entered the school atrium. The only sound as they headed down the hall was the echo of their footsteps. A state trooper, stationed at the door of the gymnasium, opened it and touched the brim of his hat.

Olivia took a deep breath as she stepped onto the polished wood floor. Beside her, Amy gasped. Around the gym, outlined with chalk or tape, were the shapes of small boys, legs splayed, arms akimbo. Near each was a sticky pool of blood. Small yellow signs with numbers indicated where a bullet had landed. A trail of shiny brass cartridges led to the other door of the gym. Bullet holes riddled the aluminum bleachers. Beneath them was more blood.

"My God," Olivia murmured under her breath.

### 2:48 p.m.

"Mom, can't you drive any faster?" asked Melissa, sitting rigidly upright. If not for the seat belt restraining her, she'd literally be on the edge of her seat.

"Honey, I'm already driving over the speed limit. We're almost there. Take it easy."

Since the identities of the hostages had been released, Melissa couldn't sit still. Courtney had called to say she was all right, and the ambulance people were bringing her home. She'd sounded so shaky and shouldn't be alone. She'd said she'd been so scared when the shooter broke into the office that she'd wet herself. Courtney could be unnecessarily nervous, but this detail proved how truly terrified she'd been.

Melissa was sure that if she ever faced a shooter, she'd do the same. Guns had always frightened her, but especially since her Uncle Ben had died after being held up at gunpoint. He was locking up the bank he managed in Floral Park when a small-time crook stuck a gun in his face. The old man had collapsed and died on the spot. The doctors said he'd had a heart condition, but the family was sure his terror had killed him.

Ruth finally pulled up in front of the beach house. Melissa barely waited for the car to stop before opening the door. She took the porch steps by twos.

Downstairs, it was all dark. "Courtney! Courtney," Melissa called frantically.

"In the bedroom!" As Melissa ran up the stairs, she heard her mother coming into the house.

Courtney was sitting in bed, bundled under a pile of quilts and throws. The heat was cranked up to a tropical temperature, so it clearly wasn't for warmth. She had the hood of her polar fleece over her head. All she needed to complete the picture of a frightened child was a menagerie of stuffed animals. Melissa wondered if she should borrow some from Kaylee's bed.

She scooped Courtney into her arms. "Thank God! Thank God, you're okay!" Courtney instantly began to sob. Melissa held her tighter. "You're okay," she soothed. "You're okay."

"No, I'm not! I'm a fucking mess! And I need to get myself together. Kaylee will be home any minute now."

Courtney's face was wet with tears. Melissa wasn't an expert, but she'd spent enough time in therapy to know that tears were a good sign. Otherwise, the repressed emotions would show up later.

"Melissa!" called Ruth from downstairs.

"You can come up, Mom." Melissa could imagine her mother grumbling that she had to climb the stairs with her bad knees. Jack kept trying to talk her into replacements, but she ignored his advice because he was a surgeon. "All they want to do is cut," she said dismissively.

Ruth was winded when she appeared at the bedroom door. "How are you, Courtney? Okay?"

"Not really," Courtney admitted honestly. "But I need to keep it together. My daughter will be home soon."

"Yes, it's important to be strong for your child," Ruth agreed.

Courtney turned to Melissa. "Are you going to be in trouble at your job?"

"No, Mike can be a bastard, but he volunteered to take care of my clients. He may take a cut of my fee, but he'll land the deal."

"That's such a relief. You need to keep this job until we save up enough money to buy a house."

"You're buying a house?" asked Ruth, her eyebrows shooting up.

"Not yet, Mom," said Melissa. "We're still saving for the down payment. The real estate prices keep going up along with the mortgage rates. We can't keep up."

"It's *meshugge*. Jack says it was giving away all that money during the pandemic."

"Jack is a Republican. What does he know?" said Melissa.

"He knows a lot. Maybe more than you," said Ruth, defending her boyfriend. Given the choice, she always sided with men. "Let's talk about it later. Courtney doesn't need to hear us arguing about politics. I'm sure she has enough on her mind." Conceding a debate to her daughter was something new for Ruth. Melissa stared at her.

"I don't want to be rude," said Courtney, "but could you both get out of here so I can get dressed? Kaylee will be here soon. I don't know how much they told them at school."

"I heard on the news that they were letting all the schools out early," said Ruth.

"Well, that's a stupid move. All those kids will be heading home with no supervision when they get there." Obviously, Courtney was thinking with her principal's brain, but Melissa took that as a good sign. She guided her mother out of the room and shut the door.

"She seems okay," her mother whispered on the stairs.

"It will hit her later. I'll go out and get my luggage out of your car."

Her mother put her hand on her arm. "It can wait."

Melissa led Ruth into the kitchen. "Want something to drink? Tea? Coffee?"

"I wouldn't mind something stronger, but you don't have to entertain me. I'm not here as a guest."

"How about a glass of wine?" asked Melissa, opening the refrigerator to look for the bottle of chardonnay they'd opened the night before. "Thanks for coming to get me at the station. I'm sorry I was so short with you on the phone."

"We're all jumpy with this shooting." Ruth shook her head. "I don't understand. How can anyone shoot children?"

"According to statistics, it's disturbed young men."

"But children, how can anyone kill them? They're just babies. It's so wrong. Those poor parents."

Feet pounded up the porch steps, and the front door swung open. Kaylee threw her backpack on the sofa. "Mom!" she called at the top of her lungs.

Melissa caught her in her arms and held her tight. "She's fine, Kaylee. She's getting dressed, and she'll be right down."

Kaylee struggled to get free. "Mom!" she called frantically.

"I'm here, sweetie," said Courtney, running down the stairs. "I'm here."

"You're okay?"

"I'm fine. Just fine."

Kaylee threw herself into her mother's arms. "Oh, Mom. Mom! I'm so glad you weren't hurt."

Courtney's eyes filled as she hugged her daughter.

"Girls, I think you should come home with me," said Ruth, "all of you." Melissa turned around. Was this the same mother who'd refused to let Courtney move in when she was about to be homeless?

"What did you say?" Melissa had heard correctly, but she wanted Ruth to repeat it because she didn't believe her ears.

"Come home with me. It's the best thing. Pack a bag, Courtney. You too, Kaylee. We'll take care of you. Jack's a doctor. He's good at that. I'll make a big dinner. Rebecca is coming for the vigil tonight."

"Mom, are you sure about this?" asked Melissa, still skeptical.

"Yes, I'm sure. This is a time when a family needs to be together."

Melissa realized her mouth was open and closed it.

### 3:05 p.m.

Bobbie settled Susan in the sitting room of her apartment. Outwardly, she looked calm, but Bobbie could see in her eyes that she was shaken. Bobbie draped a polar fleece throw around her shoulders and turned on the electric fireplace.

"Will you be all right for a few minutes while I see what's going on here?" asked Bobbie, looking directly into her eyes.

"Apart from desperately wanting a drink, I'm fine."

After what Susan had gone through, it was no surprise that she was craving a drink. Since Susan had been spending the night, Bobbie had removed the most obvious temptation, but she mentally located the alcohol in the house. She'd moved the wine from the rack in the sitting room—mostly gifts from guests—into the basement of the main house. The cabinet over the stove had once held a collection of whiskey. She'd stored that, too.

"Maybe you should call your sponsor," Bobbie suggested.

"A good idea. I should have thought of that sooner."

"I'm sure you had enough to think about." Bobbie leaned down to give Susan a kiss. "I won't be long. Teresa's on duty today. Joyce always behaves for her. She's a lot tougher than I am."

"I find that hard to believe," said Susan, reaching for her bag. Bobbie watched her take out her phone. If experience served, Susan would be on with her sponsor for a while. Bobbie took the opportunity to slip out. She crossed the hall into the main house.

When she opened the door to the TV room, Teresa looked up and smiled. Her skin was so dark it reflected light, which always made her seem to glow. She was not naturally attractive like her friend Reshma, who'd introduced them, but the pure kindness in her face had its own kind of beauty. Many people who'd experienced hardship became hard and bitter. Teresa had lost nearly everything, yet she was always smiling. While she worked, she sang the bewitching women's chants of her homeland. They were responsive and sometimes, her daughter, Grace, sang the antiphon. Joyce's eyes lit up whenever she heard them singing.

In those moments, Bobbie caught a glimpse of Joyce's former beauty. She still had the perfect bone structure that came from what Bobbie's mother used to call "good breeding," the match of well-heeled, attractive men to equally attractive, socially prominent women. Joyce's brilliant mind was gone now. Her vocabulary had shrunk to a dozen words essential to expressing her needs. Fortunately, the loss no longer seemed to bother her. The days of anger and frustration were gone, and she had achieved a kind of serenity. Her face, despite the lines and sagging jowls, had become beautiful again.

"How is she today?" Bobbie asked, giving Joyce a hard look.

Teresa smiled in the direction of her charge. "We listened to the 'Golden Oldies' station and danced." Joyce could no longer walk, so 'dancing' meant swaying in her wheelchair to the rhythm of the music. "They say that music binds memories like nothing else," Teresa said. Her British English had a pleasant African cadence that was song-like. "That's why our stories are set to music. It helps us remember."

"Music and smells." Bobbie, who'd specialized in geriatric

nursing, knew there was a scientific basis for the observation. Teresa, who'd been well-educated in her home country, probably knew it too.

"I saw you brought Mother Susan home. The news report said that she was one of the hostages."

Bobbie glanced at the television, which was off. "How did you know?"

"I've been following the story on my phone. I kept the TV off because it might upset Joyce. News about the shooting is all that's on." Teresa sighed. "Miss Bobbie, I can't believe that I left Sudan to escape violence, only to find it here in this little town in Maine. Today, I thanked God that my Grace is past the age for primary school. They say they might close the schools for a few days." Teresa's shy daughter had finally settled into her new school and made some friends. Bobbie hoped this trauma wouldn't be a setback. The girl was bright and had so much potential.

"I need to get back to Susan," said Bobbie apologetically. "Will you be okay for a while?"

"This is my shift. If not for the shooting, you would still be at the practice, seeing patients." She was right, but after the morning's dramatic events, the normal routine felt like life in a parallel universe. "Go back to Mother Susan," urged Teresa. "I have studying to do. I'll turn on the music station for Joyce. We'll be just fine."

When Bobbie returned, the distracted look in Susan's eyes reminded her uncomfortably of Joyce's vacant stare, but shock could also disrupt cognitive function. Bobbie gently rubbed Susan's shoulder to bring her back to the present.

Susan's blue eyes looked up to engage hers. "Greater love hath no man than this, that a man lay down his life for his friends." Bobbie wondered how she could look so confused, yet be quoting a Bible verse.

"You're talking about the first responders?"

"No, Liz Stolz."

Bobbie doubted Liz's behavior was motivated by any religious belief. "Isn't Liz an atheist?"

Susan stared at her. "As they say, there are no atheists in foxholes. We all pray when faced with the ultimate. And if she wasn't praying for herself, I was praying for her."

"I'm sure she appreciates it," said Bobbie, only being agreeable because it had become a habit from dealing with Joyce.

"She risked her life to save mine. I always thought she hated me." That surprised Bobbie. She knew her boss had strong opinions, but she didn't seem like the hating kind. Indifference was more her style.

"Why would she hate you?"

"When I came to Hobbs, Lucy was seeing Liz. I tried to break them up."

"Why?"

"Lucy and I were together in New York and Boston. I'd hoped that after her first wife died, we might have another chance..." Susan's eyes focused on Bobbie's face. "I'm sorry. I should have told you sooner."

"It doesn't matter," said Bobbie, but as the facts came together in her mind, she turned away to absorb them.

### 3:15 p.m.

Sam took Maggie up on her offer to clean up after lunch because she could barely move. Brenda's advice was finally sinking in. Once people figured out what had happened, they'd hate her. All the effort she'd put into building a business in this town would be wasted, and all for doing one stupid thing. If only she'd gone around instead of leaving the back door open.

Maggie came out of the kitchen and saw her staring into the fire. "Sam, stop thinking about it!"

"How did you know?"

"Because I know you, Sam. You're a ruminator, like Liz. Your mind is always working."

"I can't help it. That's how I am."

"Think of something positive. When will you hear from the museum board?"

Sam shrugged. "People tell me it's a done deed. They just need to meet to formalize the decision." She wasn't sure this was a positive change of subject. She was anxious just talking about it. It had been years since she'd worked on anything bigger than a strip mall. It would be exciting to be building something important again, but she wondered if she still had the edge to oversee a major project. The thought of leaving Maggie behind in Hobbs and how much she'd miss her made her feel even worse.

"I wish I could take you to California with me."

"Well, I can't leave until the semester is over. I'm under contract for this term."

"Will you stay here or go back to Scarborough?"

Maggie frowned as she considered the question. "I don't think Alina wants me back." Her daughter's boyfriend, the news director, had moved in full time. Understandably, they didn't want Alina's mother living right downstairs.

"But it's your house," Sam pointed out. "You own it."

"I know, but now that they're talking about getting married, they might buy me out."

"You don't sound happy about the idea."

"Well, her first marriage was a disaster. Her ex lost all their money, their savings, the house. I just don't want her to make another big mistake. Liz isn't here to bail her out again." Sam stared at Maggie. Was that how she saw Liz? As a bank account? With her trust fund, Sam probably had more personal wealth than Liz. Obviously, Maggie didn't see her new partner as offering the same level of security. "When I sold my co-op in New York, I gave up my home," Maggie said with a sigh. "If I sell to Alina and her boyfriend, I'll be homeless again."

"You're not homeless. You live here now."

"Maybe you'll go to California and decide you don't want me here anymore. What if you meet someone out there? Someone your own age."

"Maggie, today has been hard enough. Do we really need to talk about this now?"

She shook her head and said, "I'm sorry, Sam. No, of course not."

"I want you to stay here while I'm gone and come out to see me on weekends."

Maggie moved closer to Sam. "Of course I'll visit, but not every weekend. It's a long trip."

"On school breaks, you can stay longer. It will be fun." Sam liked the idea of planning weekends with Maggie in California. She desperately needed something to look forward to, something beyond this terrible day.

### 5:12 p.m.

When Liz awoke from her nap, it was already dark. The respite had been welcome, even though she'd had crazy dreams about bullets moving in slow motion. Opioids always made her sleepy, and after she'd gotten into bed, she'd gone out cold.

She lay in bed for a few minutes, trying to get her bearings. She reminded herself that the events of the day had been real, not just a wild, opioid dream. Peter Langdon was dead. The boys and the gym teacher were dead. But Courtney and Susan and that girl in the office were alive. Liz's throbbing shoulder and aching chest reminded her that she was alive, too.

She thought of Lucy bathing her, tenderly washing her face with a warm cloth. She'd been patient when Liz had insisted on inspecting her injuries. The vest had stopped a bullet headed to the side of her chest. From a slightly different angle, it would have broken the rib. The other round had passed through her shoulder just beneath the dermis. That would heal quickly, but now it ached because the percocet had worn off. She debated whether to take another, then decided to be conservative and take Ibuprofen instead.

In the winter, the water straight from the bathroom tap was cold enough to make her teeth hurt. Her mouth was dry from the drugs, so it tasted good. She drank the entire glass and refilled it. Then she was chilled, but she often was after getting up from a nap, so it wasn't necessarily a symptom of shock.

Liz completed her auto-diagnosis as she zipped up her sweat-shirt. Even without the post-nap drop in body temperature, the house felt chilly. Lucy didn't always remember to put wood on the fire, so Liz went downstairs to check. She discovered that the fire had burned down to ash and stirred the remains. The glowing embers looked encouraging. She threw in some kindling on them and sat down to wait for it to catch.

"You're awake!" said Lucy, coming into the living room. "I thought I heard you coming down the stairs. How do you feel?"

"Sore, but the nap helped." Liz noticed that Lucy had a white smudge on her chin. "What are you doing?"

"Making dinner," she said proudly. "I'm cooking one of the recipes Olivia taught me. Chicken Francese." The egg wash explained the flour on Lucy's chin. "It's more complicated than I remembered."

Liz didn't dare smile. Lucy was sensitive about her cooking. "Want help?"

"No, I can do it."

The kindling was blazing, so Liz added wood to the fire and followed Lucy. The kitchen looked like a bomb had gone off—egg-shells in the sink, flour all over the counter and the floor, measuring cups, and utensils strewn everywhere. Liz struggled to keep the disapproval out of her face. She'd been taught to clean up while she cooked. "Why don't you get your pasta going while I tidy up here a little?"

"No, you sit down. You're hurt. Why aren't you wearing your sling?"

"There's nothing broken. It's only to remind me not to use my arm too much." Liz could tell Lucy wasn't impressed by the explanation. "Really, I don't need it," Liz insisted, picking the eggshells out of the sink. She ran water to soak the flour-encrusted plate.

"You're disappointed," Lucy said, watching her face.

"No, I'm grateful that you're making dinner, but you should have gotten me up. I would have done it."

"Now, you're making me feel worse."

"I'm sure it will be a great dinner. I'll just clear a path for you to work." Liz congratulated herself on coming up with a diplomatic way to express why she was intervening, but Lucy clearly wasn't taken in. She stood there, chewing on her lower lip, which she only did when she was holding back tears. Liz decided that reacting would only confirm there was something wrong. Instead, she opened a cabinet and took out her favorite sauté pan. "Use this one. It works best for this recipe." She set it on the burner and started cleaning up the counters.

Despite the mess, Lucy's meal was delicious. Olivia was a gourmet cook, and Liz wasn't surprised that she was a good teacher. "This is great, Lucy. You should cook more often."

"Thank you, but you like to cook. I only cook when I have to."

"If you cooked more often, maybe you'd enjoy it more," said Liz, helping herself to another tasty cutlet.

Lucy looked up from her plate. "Is that a hint?"

"Maybe. What if something happened to me today, and I wasn't able to cook?"

Lucy frowned, evidently contemplating that possibility. "Then, of course, I'd cook."

Liz wondered if she would. When Erika died, Lucy had fallen apart. Rather than feed herself, she'd wasted away. Finally, Emily had called Liz to rescue them from takeout food and pizza. Liz could understand becoming depressed after losing a spouse, but Lucy wasn't even able to feed her child. Granted, Emily had been a teenager and could mostly fend for herself, and their relationship wasn't the usual bond between mother and daughter. Emily had burst into Lucy's life as an emancipated minor, searching for her birth mother. Parenting a virtual stranger who was on the spectrum wasn't easy.

"Maybe I should insist you cook more often," said Liz. "Aren't you the one who always says, 'it's good to mix it up a little?"

"I do say that, don't I?" Lucy reflectively chewed a mouthful. "It is good, isn't it?"

"As good as Olivia's."

"You're not just saying that?"

Liz studied her wife and saw she wasn't just fishing for more compliments. "You know I don't do flattery, Lucy."

"No, that's one thing I can count on, Liz. You never hold back. You always tell the truth."

Liz crossed her fork and knife on her plate. Since her surgical residency, when she'd often had to gulp down a meal before her beeper went off, Liz ate faster than anyone at the table. She always finished before Lucy.

"I should really go to that vigil tonight," said Lucy. "I don't want to go, but I think I need to show my face."

"So finish eating, and I'll start cleaning up," said Liz, heading to the sink with her plate. "I'll go with you."

"Are you sure, Liz? You've been through a lot today."

"I have, but I'll go to support you. It's important for the town to see I'm okay."

"Good point." Lucy smiled. Obviously, she wanted company.

"Better dress warmly," said Liz, opening the dishwasher. "It's going to be cold tonight."

The parking lot was full when they arrived at Harbor Park. Flickering luminaria lined the driveway leading to the Gazebo. Students from the high school were handing out candles and discs of paper to catch the wax. The stiff breeze from the ocean made the survival of any flame an iffy proposition. They'd held a vigil for Ukraine at the start of the war, and the wind had extinguished almost every candle. This time, Liz remembered to bring tea lights in vigil holders. An electric candle would have worked even better, but it didn't have the same significance as a real flame.

They found seats near the front. Although Lucy was wearing her collar, she'd said she was only coming to support Reshma. She tucked into her down coat to avoid drawing attention.

Monsignor O'Brien stepped up to the microphone and spotted Lucy in the crowd. "And there's Dr. Bartlett," he announced happily. "Come up here and pray with us, Mother Lucy."

Liz watched Lucy struggle between her role as a faith leader in Hobbs and her intention to let her curate shine. She turned to Liz, obviously looking for advice. "You're the boss," said Liz with a shrug. "It's your job to represent St. Margaret's."

"And bring Dr. Stolz up with you," said Monsignor O'Brien, his voice echoing through the park. "Bring her up here so we can thank her for her bravery."

Someone began clapping. Then more people. Finally, everyone was clapping. The sound of all those hands smacking together made Liz's ears ring. *Why are they clapping?* she wondered. It sounded so wrong. She'd tried to talk a young man into releasing his hostages and ended up shooting him. Were they applauding her for killing him? The applause grew louder until it became a roar. They were cheering and calling her name.

Liz climbed over the people next to her to get to the center aisle. Once she'd pushed her way through the crowd, she ran down the path to the parking area as fast as her bad knee would allow. By the time she reached her truck, she was limping.

# PART II

# Chapter 8

Usually, Lucy didn't have trouble dozing off, but Liz was sleeping fitfully because she couldn't lie on her bad arm. Fortunately, the house, designed to accommodate summer guests, offered many alternatives to their third-floor bedroom. Lucy's favorite was the "seashore" room, one floor below, that doubled as her office. It held Erika's desk and the bed Liz had built for her as a wedding gift. After Erika's death, Lucy had found sleeping in the bed difficult. Since building a prie-dieu with Liz's help, she'd realized how much effort and love had gone into making the bed. Now, it was Lucy's special retreat when she was sick or couldn't sleep.

She crept downstairs and got under the thick duvet. She shivered, waiting for her body heat to warm up the bed. Eventually, she felt drowsy, but as soon as she closed her eyes, her mind churned up horrible images. She saw the young victims lying still and cold in the coroner's office. She imagined the boys' souls running through the school, looking for their teachers or any adult who could help them find their way home. She heard their cries as they searched for their missing bodies.

Unnerved, Lucy got up and lit a vigil candle. She clasped her hands and closed her eyes. Her mind reached out to the young souls. She prayed for them, determined to keep watch so they wouldn't be alone.

The funeral director had told her the bodies would be released soon. The police had held them until they could all be positively identified. Many had been so mangled by the spray of high-velocity bullets that only their DNA could prove who they were. When Liz tried to explain why that kind of ammunition shredded human flesh beyond recognition, Lucy couldn't listen.

She wondered how they would all get through this. Some of the families, including people who'd left the Church long ago, had already approached her to make funeral arrangements. While she'd held the hands of the weeping mothers, she'd tried to keep back her own tears, but sometimes, she simply couldn't. Then she'd hold the grieving mother, and they would cry together.

Lucy's theological studies for her doctorate had shaken her rock-solid faith. What had replaced it was less certain, but more complex and nuanced.

God had never promised to solve all of humanity's ills, only to be present. "I am with you always, even until the end of time." As the candle burned down, Lucy felt less alone. She kept the vigil until the first light of morning brightened the horizon.

*** 

The stuffed animals looked ratty after the ice storm. The mountains of flowers, mostly bouquets in plastic sleeves straight out of the supermarket, had become brown and brittle in the icy air. Cemetery vigil lights, covered against the elements, flickered behind colored glass tubes. The unsheltered candles had gone out; only their burnt-out stumps remained. Someone had made angel lawn ornaments to represent each of the dead children. Photos tacked to the painted wood showed the kids in happier times—getting a sports trophy, dressed in their Easter best, blowing out candles on a cake. The last was especially poignant because none of those boys would ever see another birthday.

Olivia had heard that things were piling up in front of the elementary school. On her way into town, she'd deliberately gone by to see for herself. She'd seen news photos of the kind of things people left after a mass shooting, but having the candles, stuffed animals, and lawn signs in her hometown was disturbing. Most of the items had been sent anonymously, but some bore signatures and return addresses. Many came from far away, out of state, even out of the country. The sentiments were mostly maudlin, but Olivia understood the impulse to offer sympathy. The grief of the parents who'd lost children was unimaginable to many. Having buried a child, Olivia was one of the few who could understand.

The parents who'd shown up at the vigil had clutched their living children closer, as if they were suddenly more valuable. But as time passed, they'd go back to their routines and forget. Their child's loud music or the smelly sneakers under the bed would annoy them again. But for a parent who has lost a child, there is no forgetting.

At the vigil, Maggie Fitzgerald had sung "Amazing Grace." No one sang it better than she did, with a little warble and strategic breaks in tone. She had a much better voice than the woman who'd sung it at Jason's funeral. Then, Olivia couldn't cry, but at the vigil, a few tears came to her eyes. She hated to show weakness in public, but in that context, it felt right. Maybe now people would see she was human too.

With an ache in her heart that wouldn't quit and numb from the cold, Olivia returned to her car and headed to her office at the town hall. Everyone in Hobbs still called the municipal building the town hall, and for a change, she went along with the locals. The new name was too modern for a town that had been incorporated in 1653.

"Ms. Enright!" called the admin as Olivia passed her desk. The woman struggled to her feet. She was well past retirement age, but had been hanging on for a bigger pension. "Ms. Enright, someone left enormous boxes on the front steps this morning. They're full of blankets."

"Blankets?"

"Yes, very nice, high-quality, fleece blankets, half with teddy bears, half with bunnies. There are hundreds of them. The note said there should be enough for all the children at the elementary school."

"Did it say who sent them?"

The admin shook her head. Olivia frowned, wondering why any-one would send hundreds of blankets to one of the wealthiest towns in Maine. Why not donate to help war refugees? Or give money to a disaster area? Then she realized that Hobbs *was* a disaster area.

"Ask Kristen to take a couple of photos of the blankets and write up a notice that parents of school-age children can claim them during business hours. Post it on the Hobbs website and our Facebook page. On second thought, add the actual hours to the posts. People never read!"

"Yes, Ms. Enright," said the woman. She walked away, looking pleased. Olivia knew people liked to have clear instructions, the more specific, the better.

She opened her laptop to check her email. The counter showed over a hundred. On an average day, she got ten. She skimmed through them. Many were from mayors or town managers expressing their condolences and offering their support. Olivia would never think of asking for help, but she responded to everyone who wrote to her about the shooting. She'd written a stock message for this purpose, but she wrote original replies to the mayor of Uvalde and the town manager of Newtown. Having been through this nightmare, only they could truthfully say they knew how she felt.

For years, Olivia had been a regular donor to Sandy Hook Promise. She'd cheered on the parents who'd won the lawsuit against Alex Jones, who'd claimed the shooting was a fraud. Then she read how he was transferring assets to protect himself from bankruptcy. Men always seemed to avoid consequences. Many public figures had been guilty of insider trading, but only Martha Stuart had gone to jail. Jason's shady dealings had forced Olivia to give up her controlling interest in the Enright Fund, while her equally guilty male colleagues skated free.

The admin popped her head into the doorway. "Ms. Enright, Chief Duvaney is here to see you."

"Give me a minute. Then show him in," said Olivia and typed a closing to the email she'd been writing.

She wondered what Duvaney wanted. When she'd first become

town manager, she hadn't known what to make of the gruff, over-weight fire chief and pegged him as a typical misogynist like many blue-collar men. Then she'd heard him defend Brenda Harrison and her wife when they were trying to adopt their kids. Olivia had since decided that Paul Duvaney's crusty exterior was mostly male posturing to keep his troops in line. Well, maybe some of it was real, but he was basically a decent guy.

Duvaney gave Olivia a little salute. "How's your day going, boss?"

"Busier than usual for this time of year. I bet it's been that way for you too."

"Hell, yeah," he said. Before he sat down, he pulled up his trousers a little so they wouldn't bag in the knees.

"What can I do for you, Paul?"

"Those news people keep blocking the entrance to the firehouse with their vans. I'm thinking about pulling out some of the trucks to form a barricade."

"Can't you just put up some sawhorses and police tape?"

"We tried that. They just move them. Their vehicles are parked everywhere—along the road, in the parking lots of the supermarket, the library, the church. They've taken over the whole town! Don't they have somewhere else to be?"

"When there's another mass shooting, they'll leave," Olivia replied bluntly.

Duvaney sighed. "We probably won't have to wait long for that." Unfortunately, he was right.

"All right, Paul. Proceed with your plan. You're the expert on readiness. You need to get those trucks out if there's a fire."

Duvaney took out his phone and sent a quick text message. Olivia expected him to leave, but he didn't.

"Is there more?" asked Olivia, peering at him.

"No, just checking to see how you're holding up. Can't be fun to have your job right now." His eyes gave her an obvious professional once-over, reminding her that he was also a paramedic. "We really need you now, but pacing yourself is important. Heart conditions can be tricky." Olivia wondered if people would ever get past the heart attack that had sidelined her for months.

"Really, Paul, thanks for your concern. My doctor assured me that, health-wise, I'm fine. But how are your first responders doing?"

"It hit some hard. Two EMTs took leave. It's not every day you see a bunch of eight-year-olds blown to bits." Her stomach churned as she remembered the school gym after the shooting.

"This is something that happens in other towns," she said, shaking her head. "Not here."

"I bet that's what every town says...until it does." He grimaced. "Well, I'm sure you're busy, so I'll get out of your hair." He leaned heavily on the chair arms to launch himself to his feet. After he stood, he adjusted his belt under his belly. "Take care, Liv. You know where I am if you need me, and I mean that. Professionally and personally."

"Thank you, Paul." Olivia felt like they'd really connected today, which was good. To get through this crisis, Hobbs needed to stick together.

Olivia went back to answering her emails. She'd almost gotten through half when there was a knock at the door. "Steve Caron is here for you, Ms. Enright."

Olivia struggled to connect the name with a face. Some of her heart meds gave her brain fog. Finally, it clicked that Caron was the head of the transportation department. They were predicting a big storm, but the selectman in charge of public works usually approved the snow removal plan.

She got up and shook Caron's hand because his visit was so unusual. When he took the same seat that Duvaney had vacated, Olivia wondered if it was still warm. "Are you coming about the storm?" she asked.

"Yes, it could be a big one. We've gotten off easy this winter. Hope my guys remember how to plow."

"Yes, it's been a strange winter," Olivia agreed.

"Isn't that the truth? And now the thing at the school. Glad my kids are in high school."

Olivia looked at him. It wasn't wrong to be glad your own kids had been spared, but what about the victims? Survivor's gratitude was a strange thing.

"Are you prepared for the storm?" asked Olivia, trying to keep the conversation moving. The pace at which some Mainers talked made her want to pinch them to hurry them up.

"All set. We've been spraying the saline in advance. Really helps. The plows are on, greased, and ready to go. But that's not why I'm here."

"Okay," Olivia leaned forward, hoping to encourage him to get to the point.

"That stuff in front of the school is going to get wrecked by the storm. Do you want us to move it?"

It was a good question. Olivia frowned as she considered it. She needed to think about the town. She might think the sympathy "gifts" were tacky, but the people of Hobbs deserved to see how much other people cared.

"I'll call the superintendent's office to see if we can get someone to open the school," Olivia said. "Let's move everything into the atrium. Extinguish all the live candles first and discard the dead flowers."

"Of course, Ms. Enright." He got to his feet and Olivia could see that his coat looked old and thin. Olivia wondered how much they paid him. After he left, she'd look it up.

"Thanks for thinking of that, Steve. People will appreciate it."

"You're welcome, ma'am. Glad I thought to ask." When he smiled, she saw that one of his front teeth was missing.

***

Sam answered the question for what seemed like the hundredth time. No, she did not see anyone. She just had a weird sense that someone was there in the woods, watching while she cleaned her tools.

She guessed Brenda was probably listening to the interview from behind the two-way mirror. She'd offered her silent support by sitting in the room until Sam's lawyer had arrived, a few minutes late. Melissa had advised Sam to get an attorney and had recommended Naomi Gold, a criminal defense lawyer from Boston.

When they'd first met, Sam had told her she'd been raised to believe that honesty was the best policy. Naomi's response was sobering. "In a perfect world, maybe, but it's the job of the police to find someone to charge and build a case." Whenever the detective pushed too hard, Naomi nudged Sam and said, "Don't answer that." Sam was glad to have her there. She'd explained the purpose of the repetitive questioning. They were trying to expose any inconsistencies in her story, hoping to wear her down until she said something she didn't mean or blurted out details that would make her look bad.

"Why did you think it might be Peter Langdon?" asked the investigator, despite Sam's five previous explanations.

She took a deep breath and explained as patiently as she could. "He knew I was working on the school bathroom. He knew I was using the back door to come in and out."

"But you had no reason to think he had any malicious intent."

"No, he didn't even seem mad when I fired him. He just shrugged when I told him, collected his tools, and left."

Sam didn't understand why they kept going over and over this. Peter was on tape, telling Liz that he deserved to be fired.

The door opened and Brenda came in. "Okay, Bates, that's enough."

The man went to the door to consult his boss, the head of the state investigations unit.

"Aren't they done yet?" asked Sam in a low whisper, but Naomi raised her hand to silence her. She was focused on the conversation going on behind them.

Brenda came in. "All right, Ms. McKinnon, you can go." The formality sounded so alien coming out of her mouth that it took a moment for Sam to realize Brenda was talking to her.

Naomi tapped her arm, and they got up. "Will you require Ms. McKinnon for further questioning?"

"No, we're satisfied she's answered all our questions," Brenda said despite the investigator's frown. He obviously wanted to keep hammering on her.

"I don't understand why you've put her through so many rounds of questioning," Naomi said. "Ms. McKinnon's story has been consistent, and your subject is dead."

"We want to make sure that everyone is clear about what happened, and there was no deliberate negligence."

"So there will be no criminal charges?" pressed Naomi.

"Not that we can see. She's free to go."

"You're sure? She has an important architectural commission waiting for her in California. Returning from the project could cause delays and be costly." She was cleverly hinting at possible damages if the police continued to restrict Sam's travel.

Obviously, Brenda would pick up on the implications, but she deadpanned. "She can leave the state if she wishes. If something comes up, we'll be in touch." Brenda left without saying another word.

Sam understood why she was keeping her distance. Even the hint that she was giving her friend preferential treatment could taint the investigation, but Brenda had been acting like she didn't even know her. When they'd bumped into each other in the hardware store, Brenda hadn't even said hello. Sam had felt other people withdrawing too, but not everyone. Liz had called twice to see how she was doing. She sounded like she was having a hard time herself, so Sam didn't feel like she could unload on her. Maggie kept urging her to stay strong and let the whole thing pass. She didn't like to dwell on unpleasant subjects and would start talking about something else. Only Amy had been willing to hear Same tell her side of the story. She'd called to check in and listened to Sam for almost an hour before saying, "We should have this conversation in person. I'm off on Friday. Come over, and I'll make you lunch."

When Sam had accepted the invitation, she hadn't known she'd be called for another interview. Now, she needed to find a polite way to ditch Naomi, who hadn't been happy about coming up from Boston for another day of interrogation.

"I'd invite you for coffee, Naomi," Sam said in the parking lot behind the police station, "but I have a lunch date."

"That's fine. I need to get back to the office. Maybe another time. Tell Melissa I said hi and call me if you need me." She beeped open her car door.

As Sam watched her drive away, she wondered if she'd ever see her again. Of course, she hoped the case was closed, but it was strange to be so closely tied to someone, and then suddenly they were gone. Sam knew it happened all the time in professional relationships. She'd get close to a construction team, go out for beers with them, but once the project was done, everyone moved on. In some cases, Sam had tried to keep those contacts alive past their shelf life. Her persistence had led to a few long-term friendships. The same with her relationships. Unless the end was nasty, she kept in touch.

After Sam ended her volatile relationship with Olivia, Amy's cool, even-keeled personality helped her regain her balance, but it never went anywhere. Sam began to wonder if she was losing her touch. Then Amy admitted she wasn't ready for another relationship. They agreed to remain friends, but Amy put far more effort into the friendship than Sam. If they hadn't talked in a while, Amy would text or call. A "buddy check," she called it, "like in summer camp." Sam liked the association with one of the few good memories from her childhood.

Savory smells greeted Sam when Amy opened the door to her apartment. She was wearing a clingy yoga ensemble that showed off her good figure, reminding Sam that she was a damn good-looking woman. Too bad it hadn't worked out. In some ways, they were too much alike—keen observers, who analyzed everything but said little. Someone in a relationship needs to be a talker.

"Thanks for being flexible about the time," Sam said, accepting a kiss on the cheek.

"Thanks for giving me fair warning, but I'm making red-braised chicken, which is pretty forgiving. It doesn't mind waiting."

"That sounds exotic."

"Not your usual Chinese restaurant fare. It's my mother's recipe from her grandmother, so it's authentic. I'm trying to up my game now because Olivia's such a gourmet."

"I'm surprised she lets you cook for her. She wouldn't let me near her kitchen."

"I don't give her much choice," said Amy, hanging up Sam's parka in the closet. "If she wants to spend time with me, we both need to agree on the terms."

"Good for you," said Sam in a genuinely admiring voice. "Mostly, I ignored Olivia when she was bossy. Maggie says I'm passive aggressive."

"Well, you are, but at least you know it." Amy tugged on Sam's arm. "Come in and sit down. Tell me about the hearing while I get lunch on the table."

"Brenda said I'm off the hook. I can leave the state, which means I can go to California to sign the contract for the commission."

"Well, that's good news," said Amy, dishing out their lunch. She put a plate in front of Sam, who leaned closer to inhale the delicious aroma. For some reason, the hearing had left her ravenous. As soon as Amy sat down, Sam dug in. She noticed Amy fluffing out her napkin. Sam's was still at the side of her plate, so she stealthily slipped it into her lap.

"When are you leaving?" asked Amy.

"I have a few loose ends to tie up here, so probably not until next week. I'd really like to finish up the job at the school."

"You're not serious," said Amy, her eyes wide for effect.

"Yes, I am. I stand by my work."

"Oh, Sam, stay as far away from that school as you can. You don't want people associating you with that place or what happened there."

Sam sat back and pouted. "That's what Maggie says."

"And she's absolutely right."

Sam let out a long, frustrated sigh. "Will I ever be able to work in this town again?"

Amy focused on her plate. "I don't know, Sam. Maybe not."

Suddenly, Amy's delicious meal didn't taste as good, but it had nothing to do with her cooking. Sam put down her fork.

"Don't you like it?" asked Amy anxiously.

"It's delicious. Just give me a minute. That's a lot to absorb. I've worked so hard to build my renovation business. It was really beginning to feel like I belonged in this town. When Liz talked me into winterizing the house on the pond, I wasn't sure about living here full time, but now I feel like Hobbs is home, like I have family here."

"Your friends will stand by you, and you can still live here. Look, you just got an important commission. Maybe that's a sign you should practice the profession you studied for instead of setting tile."

"But I like doing tile installations."

"You could still do them, just not in Hobbs. I would think you'd be happy to go back to architecture. Vincent tells me your style is coming back in a big way." Amy's brother, a prominent architect in the Bay Area, was a big admirer of Sam's work. "This might be the opportunity you've been waiting for."

"I don't know, Amy. It's just one project."

"But it's an important project, and it's a start." Amy looked directly into her eyes. "I believe in you, Sam, but you need to believe in yourself. Those judges for the museum project chose you because your design was the best. Vincent said it's brilliant."

Sam stared at her plate. Everyone was telling her the same thing. This commission was her opportunity for a comeback, and she needed to seize the opportunity.

"Eat your lunch," said Amy, "or I'll think you don't like it."

"I do like it. Here, watch." Sam smiled and picked up her fork.

❖❖❖

Lucy was pleased to see Susan looking so well after spending the week with Bobbie, almost as if she'd returned from a restful vacation at one of Maine's idyllic lakes. Lucy wasn't surprised that Bobbie had taken good care of her, but it was encouraging to see that Susan had allowed it. After bringing Lucy back from her depression as her opera career faded, Susan wouldn't even allow her to nurse her through a cold. Lucy was a smidgen jealous that Bobbie had succeeded where she couldn't. *That's ridiculous*, she told herself. *Be grateful someone can help her.*

"Looks like Bobbie took good care of you," Lucy said warmly.

"She did, and I feel rested and refreshed. Maybe it will hit me later." Considering how the mind protected itself against traumatic memories, she could probably count on it. "It wasn't easy being at Bobbie's. She drinks wine with dinner and keeps it in the refrigerator."

"Have you asked her to put it out of sight?"

"We discussed it. I told her I'm glad she respects me enough not to manage my addiction."

"But Susan, you haven't been sober long. Maybe she could give you a little consideration?"

Susan shook her head. "I live in the real world, where people drink. But I admit I was on the phone with Sally...often." Lucy had never met Susan's AA sponsor, but from Susan's stories, she'd decided she would like the sassy hair stylist.

"Sounds like you're getting good support from your sponsor," said Lucy. "I'm glad."

"Me too, and I thank God every day I came back to Hobbs, where I have you and other people who care about me." Susan gave Lucy one of those beguiling smiles that made her think she still hoped for more than a friendship.

Lucy deliberately spoke in a professional tone. "A good support network is important."

"Lucy, I think getting back into my routine will help me feel normal again. The school is still closed, but I'd like to resume my church duties."

"I'm glad you want to come back, but Tom has agreed to take your nine o'clock worship for the next couple of weeks."

"Ouch," said Susan with an exaggerated flinch. "Replaced so soon?"

"You haven't been *replaced*, Susan. It's only temporary. We're overwhelmed with requests for counseling. I know that's not your forte. Tom has volunteered to pitch in. Gloria Parrish is holding free therapy sessions for anyone affected by the shooting. I can use the help, especially since I have things to deal with at home." Lucy let the statement trail off there, knowing Susan would draw the correct conclusions.

Her blue eyes were instantly sympathetic. "I'm sorry, Lucy. I should have asked. How is Liz?"

"Honestly, I don't know. I always thought we had such good communication, but now she won't talk to me."

"Probably because she's used to processing her issues alone. I do that too." Susan smiled weakly. Lucy only returned the smile because she'd been thinking the same. She wondered how much to share, given their history and Susan's attempts to disrupt her relationship with Liz. "Don't worry" said Susan, studying her face. "I know we're not getting back together."

"I certainly hope so. I can't deal with any more drama."

"Lucy, I'm happy in my relationship with Bobbie, even if we do have to keep it under wraps. I still hate the idea of sneaking around behind poor Joyce's back."

"You could have waited," Lucy said cautiously.

"According to Bobbie, Joyce is healthy, and her body could go on for a long time. Yes, we could have waited, but what purpose would it serve?"

"You wouldn't feel guilty."

"Should I feel guilty?" Susan challenged. "You're the expert on sexual ethics. Do you think what I'm doing is wrong?"

Lucy had given Susan's situation serious thought, but still hadn't decided. This was one of the many gray areas where church guidance seemed rigid and unloving. "Honestly, Susan, I don't know what to think. They never married, even when they could. From what you've told me, that relationship had changed even before Joyce's Alzheimer's diagnosis. Liz says I should keep an open mind."

"You've discussed this with Liz?" asked Susan, her brows shooting up.

"Of course, I discussed it with Liz," said Lucy indignantly. "She's my wife and my sounding board. I talk to her about everything."

"It's okay, Lucy. I'd expect you to talk to your wife, but I'm sad that she won't open up about her trauma. I know it's a long shot, but maybe she'll talk to me. We share the bond of having a gun pointed at us and facing death. Maybe we can help one another."

Susan didn't enjoy counseling, but her instincts were usually good. Her willingness to talk to Liz was something new. Usually, those two tried to stay as far away from one another as they could.

Lucy weighed the suggestion. Liz hated when anyone tried to "shrink" her, as she called it. "I can say you want to talk to her and see what she says."

"It's not a lie. I do want to talk to her, if for no other reason than to thank her for saving my life. Maybe more will come out of it. If you say that I need to talk about what happened for my own mental health, I bet she'll agree without question." That sounded so obviously manipulative, but Susan was right. Liz would never refuse what she would consider a professional duty. "Devious intentions aside, Liz and I share an experience no one else can understand. I *do* need to talk to her."

***

Cherie tried to get up from the kitchen chair, but Megan refused to let her go. "Honey bear, Mama C needs to check on dinner. You want to eat, don't you?" That only caused Megan to tighten her grip. Cherie knew she was supposed to teach her kids to stand on their own two feet, but mostly, she didn't mind when they clung to her. It proved that, even though she hadn't borne them, they were hers.

"What do you need to do, hon?" asked Brenda, watching. "Tell me. I'll do it."

"Just peek in the oven and see if those chops are brown enough. If they are, take them out." Cherie could tell when they were done from the pop and sizzle of the fat under the broiler better than any timer, but she liked visual confirmation.

Brenda bent to look. "Yup. They're done." She grabbed a pot holder and pulled the pan out of the oven.

Cherie kissed Megan and finally forced her off her lap because she needed to drain the beans. "Go tell your brother to wash his hands. We're going to eat." The steam from the bean pot fogged the window over the sink. It was damn cold outside, and the snow was still coming down. Cherie hoped Brenda wouldn't be called out tonight.

She finished mashing the potatoes while Brenda set the table. They made an efficient team because they had to be. Adopting the kids had upended their lives.

Keith and Megan came into the kitchen and held up their hands for inspection without Brenda needing to ask. Once they were all seated, everyone clasped their hands, and Cherie said the old Catholic grace she'd grown up with as a child in Louisiana. "Bless us, O Lord, and these thy gifts, which we are about to receive through thy bounty..." While she was praying, Cherie imagined them in an updated Norman Rockwell painting showing a mixed-race woman, her graying wife, and their two pretty children, heads bowed in a ritual that few families practiced anymore.

After what her children had gone through, Cherie was trying to give them an extra-normal childhood, but how could their life be normal, when guns just wouldn't leave them alone? They were all around them—in their school, on her wife's hip all day, secured in the gun safe bolted to the wall of the hall closet at night. Guns had terrified Cherie since a trooper had shot and killed her half-sister who was obviously black. Cherie had always suspected that was the only reason he'd stopped her. His bullet went right through her sister and hit Cherie. She still had a little scar on her thigh.

Cherie looked up and saw Brenda studying her with a frown. "You look upset. What's on your mind?"

The children appeared occupied with their pork chops, tearing the meat from the bone with their sharp little teeth. They looked like they weren't paying attention, but Cherie spelled it out, anyway. "G-U-N-S."

Keith looked up. "Mama C, I know what that spells," he said with a grin.

"You do?" asked Cherie, trying to look surprised and proud, although her stomach had twisted at the thought.

Keith made a pistol out of his hand by pointing his index finger and cocking his thumb. His imitation of gunfire was uncomfortably realistic. Although his parents wouldn't let him play violent video games, they couldn't prevent him from playing them with his friends. Brenda looked at Cherie across the table before resuming her meal.

The kids made quick work of their dinner so they could finish their homework in time to watch their TV shows. Cherie wasn't a fan of TV for children, but she didn't mind the extra time alone with Brenda.

"Have you wrapped up your investigation?" she asked.

"We questioned Sam again this morning. The state investigators were there too, going over the same ground. Of course, there won't be any charges. It was just a dumbass thing to do, especially since she knew the kid was a druggie and owned guns. All of them were legal, of course. He had no record. He kept getting off on the marijuana offenses in high school."

"Does that mean Sam's in the clear?"

"Legally, anyway." Brenda took a sip of milk, which she'd gone back to drinking to set a good example for the children. "Doesn't mean people won't blame her."

"When I hear them muttering about it in the office. I say, 'Don't judge. She didn't intend for anyone to get hurt,' but they say, 'Doesn't matter. Those kids and that teacher are still dead.' And you know, they're right."

"It was bad judgment on Sam's part, but not criminal negligence. I'm glad she got a smart lawyer. You know how Sam is. She'll tell you anything."

Brenda scooped the remaining mashed potatoes onto her plate and dribbled on the last of the gravy. She licked the spoon and grinned like a kid before she enthusiastically dug into the potatoes. "Thanks for another great meal, sweetheart." Brenda's obvious enjoyment was all the thanks Cherie needed. "I heard you picked up some of those blankets for the kids."

"You people in the town offices are so gossipy. Olivia brought a pile to the practice to give out to the patients with elementary school kids. They're nice blankets. I got the one with a teddy bear for Keith and a bunny for Megan."

"Sex-role stereotyping." Brenda pursed her lips. "We have plenty of blankets. We didn't need more."

"No, we didn't, but if our kids don't have them and their friends do, they'll stick out."

"Peer pressure over a teddy-bear throw? Like wearing the right designer jeans?"

"That was our era, Brenda. I don't think the label on jeans means much anymore, but I'm decades out of high school, so what do I know?"

Brenda crossed her arms. "Having one of those blankets is like getting a participation prize for being in a school shooting. Why would anyone want a reminder?"

"You know how they give out those little cards at funeral homes? You put them in your Bible or prayer book and when you see them, it reminds you of the person who's gone."

"I just think it's cheesy. What kind of people would send this crap?"

"Good people, Brenda. People who care."

"It's a hazard. Lit candles. Wet stuffed animals. Wooden crosses pinned with photos of dead kids. You should see all that shit piled up in the school atrium. Olivia had it moved inside because of the storm."

"I'm surprised. That was a sensitive thing to do."

"I know you're not an Olivia fan, but she has her moments. Did you know she lost a child too? I mean, he was grown. He killed himself when he was caught with kiddie porn on his computer."

"Actually, I did know. It's her baby, no matter what he did. And I don't think it matters how old your children are when you lose them. It's not natural for a child to die before the parents."

"Olivia said her sad experience is helping her figure out how to deal with the parents of the victims. She's been meeting with each family personally. So far, she's doing all the right things. The question is, can she deal with how this will change the town?"

Cherie sighed. She'd been pondering that question, too.

❋❋❋

From the kitchen window, Lucy could see the light on in the porch. Technically, it was a three-season room, but Liz used it in the winter by running the propane stove at full blast. They'd gone back to their normal routine of Liz making dinner, so Lucy was tidying the kitchen. They'd both stopped watching the TV news, because there was nothing on but nonstop coverage of the shooting and the investigation.

The reporters were desperately looking for new angles on the story. Maggie's daughter wanted to interview Liz, but she wouldn't talk to her or anyone in the press and refused to be photographed. In news stories, they used her photo from the Hobbs Family Practice website, which showed a smiling doctor in a polo shirt with a stethoscope around her neck. It was a strangely incongruous image to represent the heroic "good guy with a gun."

Her silence on the subject even extended to Lucy. After dinner, Liz would take her bottle of single-malt scotch and retreat to the porch. She never got obviously drunk, but she snored when she had too much to drink. Lucy was already having enough trouble sleeping.

She squeezed the water out of the sponge. After a quick look around the kitchen, she decided it was tidy enough and poured herself a glass of wine. She eyed Liz through the kitchen window and decided to join her.

When she opened the porch door, a comforting blast of warm air greeted her. Liz patted the seat cushion and moved over a little. The wicker couch creaked softly when Lucy sat down.

"Thanks for cleaning up," said Liz. Lucy liked their practice of thanking one another for doing household chores. She put her hand on Liz's thigh, relieved that unlike last night, she didn't nudge it away. That had been the final straw. Of course, she understood why Liz might not be interested in sex after such a horrendous experience, but she wouldn't even hold her. "Okay, Liz, I get why you

might not want to make love, but I'm hurting, too. I need hugs!"
After a long sigh, Liz had taken her in her arms. The comfort of her
wife's warm body had released Lucy's tears. She'd cried until she
had none left, but the weeping jag had been cleansing. For the first
time since the shooting, Lucy had slept through the night.

The memory of feeling Liz close encouraged Lucy to set aside
her wine and lean into her body. "How are you doing?"

"Okay. I'm watching the snow and enjoying the quiet." Lucy
wondered if that was a subtle hint that she'd invaded Liz's privacy.
She sat up to give her more space.

Liz didn't even seem to notice. She appeared mesmerized by the
dance of the snowflakes in the spotlights over the deck. "I should
shovel, but maybe I'll wait until morning."

"Won't it hurt your bad shoulder?"

"It's mostly healed."

"You could ask one of the kids from Awakened Brews to shovel
the snow."

"That's a good idea. I'll decide in the morning. I'm home, so it
can wait."

"I'm glad you're taking some time to recover. You need it."

"I did, but I'm thinking about going back to work. I'm getting
bored, and it feels weird not being at the office." Lucy knew that was
why Liz hadn't retired, even after she'd passed her full retirement
age last year. She could talk all she wanted about the shortage of
doctors in Maine, but Lucy knew the real reason she continued to
practice—it was part of her identity.

"Are you sure you're ready to go back to work?"

"No, I'm not sure, but I won't really know until I get there, will
I?"

"Do you mind if I give you some advice?"

Liz raised a brow. "Do I have a choice?"

"Of course not."

Liz grunted. "Didn't think so."

"Give yourself more time. After that trauma, you're still in shock. It hasn't all hit you yet."

"I'm fine," Liz said flatly.

"No, you're not. You're not yourself. You sit out here brooding every night. You won't talk to me…"

"I talk to you," Liz protested and poured herself another drink.

"No, you don't. You just sit out here in the dark with that nasty whiskey."

"I like watching the fire. It calms me."

There was no winning with Liz. She had an answer for everything. "Liz, I know you think you're indispensable, but if you care about your patients, stay away from the practice for another couple of weeks."

"In a couple of weeks, I need to take leave because you're singing at the Met."

Lucy took a sip of wine as fortification for what she was about to say. "Well, I'm rethinking that."

"What?" Liz sat forward and stared at her. "Lucy, you've waited years for this. It's the most important performance since your debut. You *must* sing."

Lucy shook her head. "No, not if you don't take care of yourself."

"Lucy, you've worked so hard. You can't just throw it away. Don't be crazy."

"I'll sing *if* I think you and this town are in good enough shape to leave for a couple of weeks. That means you need to do something to help yourself."

"Like what?"

"Talk to someone."

"Lucy, I'm fine."

"You're not fine. I know you Liz. You are NOT fine. You need help. Tom is back. He helped you after your mother died."

Liz finished her whiskey in one gulp. Then she sat there, watching the snow fall like she'd never seen anything like it before. "I suppose I owe Tom a visit, since he came all the way from Florida to help you. I'll call him in the morning to see when he's free."

"He's helping me counsel families of the victims in the morning. Call after lunch."

Liz put the cork in her whiskey bottle, which made Lucy happy.

"And Susan wants to talk to you."

"That's nice, but I don't want to talk to her."

"She wants to thank you for saving her life."

"I don't want to be thanked!" Liz snapped.

Lucy spoke in the kind, patient tone that always made Liz listen. "Sweetheart, Susan needs to talk to you. She said only you know what really happened to her. You'd be supporting her."

"Nice try, Lucy." Liz jumped up and started to pace, reminding Lucy of a tiger in a cage.

"Liz, I think you should talk to Susan. Let her thank you. To her, you're a hero."

Liz stopped pacing and turned sharply. "Don't you get it? I don't want thanks! I don't want applause. And I'm not a fucking hero!" Liz's voice had increased in volume until she was nearly shouting. *"Can't you understand?"*

For the first time, Lucy did understand. She waited until Liz sat down again to say, "Talk to Tom. You need help, Liz, and I can't give it to you. Promise me you'll call him."

Liz let out a long, frustrated sigh. "All right. I'll call him if it makes you happy." She took her bottle of whiskey and headed toward the kitchen.

# Chapter 9

Lucy reviewed the schedule while she half-listened to Reshma catch up with Tom. Just back from Florida, he sported a perfect tan that contrasted vibrantly with his white beard and crew cut. His blue eyes were merry despite the tragic event that had brought him back to Hobbs. Today, Lucy desperately needed his cheerfulness. Worry about Liz and the thought of all the upcoming funerals had dampened her spirits.

Fortunately, everyone at St. Margaret's had stepped up to help. Reshma had taken on a share of pastoral counseling in addition to her regular duties. Even Susan, who'd been in danger herself, was doing the hospital and home visits to allow Lucy and the other clergy to focus on helping the families.

"I'm sorry," Susan murmured as she slipped into Lucy's office and closed the door. She was only a few minutes late, but for someone so compulsively punctual, it was odd. She took the empty chair at the table. "Hello, Tom," she whispered when she sat down. "Glad you're back."

"Okay, let's get started," said Lucy. "We have a lot to cover." She noticed that Susan was hugging herself, even though she was wearing a heavy sweater. She'd been complaining of the cold, so they'd raised the thermostats in the rectory. Lucy had already taken off the black polar fleece she usually wore in the office. Being a redhead and petite, she tended to feel the cold more than most people, so if she felt uncomfortably warm, it was hot. "Are you cold, Susan?" she asked, trying to hide her surprise.

"I just can't get warm since the..." Her voice died as if unable to name the thing that had left her perpetually chilled.

"Trauma can upset everything, even your body temperature," said Tom. From any other man, Lucy might consider the unsolicited science lesson "mansplaining," but she knew Tom was only trying to help. He gallantly took off his sports coat and draped it around Susan's shoulders.

"Thank you, Tom. That's so kind," said Susan, clutching his cashmere jacket tighter.

Tom smiled and mouthed, "You're welcome."

"Now that we're all comfortable," said Lucy, "let's look at the schedule I sent out earlier."

"Excuse me, Mother Lucy," Reshma interrupted, "but can we pray first? Mother Susan is not the only one chilled by this event. I feel like we could all use God's comfort."

"Of course, Reshma," said Lucy. "Please pray us into the meeting."

Reshma never had to search for the words of a spontaneous prayer. They were usually brief but always exactly on point. "Oh, God, please comfort all those who grieve, especially the parents who lost their children, the students who lost their classmates, and all those who mourn. Strengthen those you have spared to grace our lives. Comfort the first responders who saw sights they can never forget. Encourage all who minister to the bodies and souls of those who have survived and hold in us your grace, through Jesus Christ, our Lord."

"Amen," they all said in unison. Susan reverently crossed herself.

"Thank you, Reshma, that was perfect," Lucy said and smiled approvingly in her direction. "And thank you for reminding us to ask for God's help as we struggle to understand this horrible situation." She scanned the faces of the others at the table. "The funerals will begin this week. Only four of the victims' families are Episcopalians, but some of the unchurched have asked for us to perform services or to use our sanctuary. One victim's family is Jewish. Rebecca Morgenstern will hold the funeral service in our parish hall. In addition to funerals, wakes, and burials, we may be called upon to assist other clergy as needed. If you have the schedule I sent out, let's look at it together." Reshma opened her tablet. Tom pulled it up on his phone. Susan laid a paper printout on the table.

"I heard a rumor that Kamala Harris and Jill Biden might come to Hobbs this week," said Reshma. "It would be so exciting to meet the vice president...and Dr. Biden."

"It's kind of the White House to send representatives," said Lucy, "but let's stay focused on our own community."

Susan said, "It's hard with so many people coming to Hobbs to offer sympathy. Buses arriving from places with mass shootings. The comfort dogs. People with no special connection, just a wish to comfort us. I know they mean well, but don't you sometimes wish they would let us mourn in peace?" They all turned to her, realizing she'd revealed a painful truth. All the condolences, no matter how well-intended, were a distraction and an invasion of families' privacy.

"Unfortunately, it's like any funeral," Tom said. "The families are held captive by the ritual. Friends and relatives show up to offer their condolences, and then they go home. The grieving are left with nothing but an empty hole in their hearts. That's why Lucy runs her bereavement group."

"The shooting hurt everyone in Hobbs," said Reshma. "There's not a single person who wasn't touched by it. What we need is a bereavement group for the whole town." She was right, of course, but Lucy's mind was overburdened with near-term obligations.

"Let's get through the funerals," she said, "and then we'll make plans for the long term. Now, if you can take a look at your assignments and tell me if you have any conflicts."

They went through the list of scheduled wakes, funerals, and burials. The funeral for the gym teacher would be held in the gymnasium of the high school. Since the shooting, only the police and the company hired to clean up had been allowed in the elementary school, where sympathy "gifts" from people continued to pile up faster than the sanitation department could remove them.

"Maggie Fitzgerald and I are planning the music for the funerals," said Lucy. "There are so many, but we want them to be individualized."

"Music is so important to grieving," said Tom, nodding. "It helps people channel difficult emotions like nothing else can."

"I've been asked to sing at the interfaith prayer service," Lucy said, "but I haven't decided yet. Bishop Greene will be attending and specifically requested it."

"Oh, Lucy, I think you should sing," said Susan. "You heard what Tom said. Nothing helps people express their grief like music. Sometimes, it helps bring up deep emotions you didn't even know you had."

Lucy turned to Reshma, but she shook her head. "I'm sorry, Mother Lucy, but she's right. And it will make the bishop happy. He loves to show you off."

"We have nine people dead. Others are fighting for their lives, and we still have to worry about politics," said Lucy, shaking her head.

"Always," said Tom.

There were a few schedule conflicts, but the individuals involved quickly traded places. Lucy congratulated herself on a quick and relatively stress-free meeting.

"Tom, I hate to give up your beautiful coat. It's so warm," said Susan, handing his jacket back to him with obvious reluctance. "Thank you so much."

"Susan, do you want me to turn up the heat?" asked Lucy. She tried to be a good steward of the parish resources, but she couldn't have the clergy in her church trembling with cold.

"No need. Reshma gave me her little quartz heater. It heats the room right up."

Lucy looked at Reshma for an explanation. "I'm not from here. I'm always cold, but now that you've raised the thermostat, I'm toasty warm, so I was happy to lend my heater to Susan."

The two exchanged a conspiratorial look. She was glad to see that their friendship had grown since Susan had mentored Reshma through her ordination. Lucy had hoped it would spare her some of

Reshma's hero worship, which could be cloying at times. Lucy had never enjoyed being on a pedestal, not even when she was an opera diva.

Tom put on his overcoat, as stylish and expensive as his jacket. Living with a wealthy husband obviously had benefits.

"Tom, can you stay for a minute?" Lucy asked. She nodded to Susan and Reshma to let them know their presence was no longer needed, and they left.

"Should I take off my coat?" asked Tom.

"No, we won't be long."

"Before you ask, yes, Liz called me this morning. I promised to tell you." It was so like Liz to make him promise to confirm it.

"Maybe you should take off your coat, Tom. It's so hot in here."

"I hope all that extra oil Susan is burning is helping her," said Tom, laying his coat over the back of the neighboring chair. "The price has come down, but I know how expensive it is now." Prior to coming to Hobbs, Tom had been the rector of a large historic church in Connecticut and would know the cost of heating an old building like the rectory. "Susan looks well, considering what she's been through."

"I doubt it's sunk in yet," said Lucy, sitting down. "I know that's true for Liz."

"It will take time, Lucy. I'm no expert on trauma, but it's hard to imagine something worse than being shot at."

"I don't know. Liz hasn't said much. She says she doesn't want me to 'shrink' her."

"I'm afraid that goes way back. When Maggie left her in college, Liz was afraid to get professional help, thinking it would go on her record and prevent her from getting into medical school. She was probably right. In those days, there was a real stigma attached to doctors who have mental health issues."

"But it's changed."

"We'd like to think it has, but we still think less of anyone in a position of responsibility who admits to having any mental illness. It's getting better, but we're not there yet."

Lucy hated to admit that Tom was right, but he was. "I'm hoping she'll open up to you. She trusts you."

"Liz and I have a different kind of relationship. We've known each other for forty years, so she doesn't have to waste time backfilling the story. Lucy, I know this sounds ridiculous, but I think it's a guy thing. Women threaten her too much, especially you."

Stunned, Lucy sat back. "Me? I'm her wife."

"Yes, and a very feminine woman." Tom gave Lucy's breasts a brief glance. "I don't know how many times Liz has told me how baffling she finds women. She chooses them as romantic partners but prefers the company of men, which makes perfect sense when you remember she grew up with brothers, and her profession, until recently, was dominated by men. Even now, medicine adheres to a male code. She expects me, a man, to honor her boundaries in a way that you won't."

"But I respect her boundaries!" protested Lucy.

"Oh, Lucy, don't take offense. It's nothing you're *doing*. It's who you are. As a gay man, I can look at this from both sides, or, at least, without the hetero bias. Interactions between men are more reserved. There are definite rules of what can be talked about and what can't. She expects me to follow them, but not you."

"Why not me?" asked Lucy, realizing she was prickling with indignation.

"She reacts to you emotionally and sexually *because* you are a woman. Like other women, you are dangerous and unpredictable. She's vulnerable right now. If her feelings are too scary, she'll withdraw from you. Don't worry. I'm sure it's not permanent. She adores you."

"But Tom, I *want* to help her."

"I know, dear, but be patient. Liz is used to processing her feelings alone. Knowing her, she's making herself crazy about this whole thing. Her brain is analyzing it to death."

"You mean she's not just sitting out there drinking scotch and staring into space? It's not just shock?"

Tom raised his bushy brows. "Seriously? Lucy, while she's staring into space, her mind is rehashing what happened. She's trying to figure out what she did wrong, and what she could have done differently. She's desperately trying to justify her actions against accepted principles of self-defense. She's blaming herself for what she considers a failure. Liz Stolz doesn't do failure. Don't you know that?"

Humbled by Tom's insights, Lucy stared at the table. "I thought I knew her, but I'm finding out how much I don't."

"You're a new couple. It will take time. This is your first big test, but I'm confident you'll both pass with flying colors." Tom's kind smile made Lucy feel a little better. Then he sat up and widened his eyes in a mock threat. "You'd better! I married you!"

"I'm grateful you're here to help her."

Tom sighed. "I'll do my best, but as you know, Liz is a hard case. And we have so many other fires burning. All these families who need ministering. As Reshma says, the whole town will need bereavement counseling. Where do we even start?"

*** 

Courtney tried to stay out of the way of the Morgenstern women while they set up the dining room for *Shabbat*. With her entire family gathered for the ritual dinner, Ruth was going all out. She'd put out her wedding silver, crystal wine glasses, and her best china (not kosher, Melissa had explained, but very significant). Ruth had inherited the wine glasses from her mother-in-law. The candlesticks were a family heirloom, brought from Poland by her grandmother.

"*Shabbat* is like having a holiday every weekend," Melissa had explained. "Usually, Mom doesn't make such a big fuss, but you and Kaylee are here, so she thinks she's doing ecumenical outreach."

Melissa rolled her eyes at the idea, but she'd added in a whisper, "at least she's stopped complaining that you're not Jewish." Melissa wasn't religious, but her sister, Rebecca, was a rabbi. Out of loyalty, Melissa usually showed up for Sabbath dinner.

All the other women were in the kitchen preparing the special meal. Courtney's daughter, Kaylee, and Rebecca's twins had been put to work cutting vegetables. Every time Courtney volunteered to help, Ruth sternly ordered her back to the couch to rest. Being catered to and fussed over was nice for a few days, but now that Courtney was feeling better, she wanted to get up and do something.

Rebecca put a tray of glasses on the table and smiled in her direction. She glanced furtively at the kitchen door and pretended to sneak away, taking exaggerated steps like a cartoon thief. "How are you doing?" she asked, sitting down beside Courtney.

"I feel useless. Your mother won't even let me get up."

Rebecca nodded knowingly. "Ruth is one of those Jewish mothers you read about in books." Courtney didn't have time to read fiction and had never read any featuring a Jewish mother, so that explanation didn't help. "It's hard enough being her daughter," said Rebecca. "I can't imagine what it's like having her for a mother-in-law. I'm so glad Judith's mother is in Israel." She rolled her eyes. "Don't get me wrong. I love the woman, but I'm glad she lives on the other side of the world." Rebecca took Courtney's hand. "Really, how are you doing?"

"I'm okay during the day, but the nightmares! I'm afraid to turn off the light."

Rebecca nodded sympathetically. "I bet. That was quite an experience. You might have bad dreams for a while. Have you talked to your doctor?"

Courtney shook her head. "They're overwhelmed with Dr. Stolz out on leave."

"You deserve care, especially now. Call them. They might be able to give you something to help you sleep. Seriously, self-care is really important now."

"I still can't believe it happened. We hear about a shooting at other schools. But here? In Hobbs?"

Rebecca fixed her dark eyes on Courtney's. "No one can believe it will happen to them because it's inconceivable that someone would shoot children. As women, it goes against all our instincts and everything we're taught. Our job is to protect children because they're the future."

"When mine came home that day, I hugged her so hard she said, 'Mom, please stop. You're hurting me,' but I never wanted to let her go."

"Did she know that you'd been one of the hostages?"

"Yes, but they wouldn't release the high school because they were busy dealing with the kids at mine. Thank God other people organized getting them back with their parents. I was such a mess I would have been useless."

"How long will they let you stay out of work?"

Courtney shrugged. "Right now, the plan is to send the kids to the other schools in the district until they can clean up mine. In other school shootings, they closed the school permanently. In Sandy Hook, they tore it down and built a new one. But Hobbs just built that new elementary school on a big bond issue and can't afford to tear it down. I'll know more in a few days after the school board meets. We have to get through the funerals first. Poor Mrs. Lavoie. Her husband is recovering from prostate cancer."

"That was the gym teacher?"

"She had a grandchild in the school." Courtney dreaded facing the girl at the wake, but she'd be expected to give the family special attention, maybe even sit beside them. She wondered what she would say to them.

Rebecca seemed to sense that Courtney retreated into her own thoughts and squeezed her hand. "Are you okay?"

"I'm fine. Thinking of the funerals. There will be so many."

Rebecca sighed. "This is only the second time I'll do a funeral for a child. The first one died of cancer. It was so sad, but the boy suffered. His parents admitted they were glad it was over. These deaths are senseless and only cause more pain."

Melissa came out of the kitchen looking for her sister. "Hands off, Becca. She's taken." She was teasing, of course. Apart from the usual sisterly spats, Melissa and her sister were each other's best friend. "Mom wants to get started. Jack's already walking around with his yarmulke on."

Rebecca lowered her voice to a confidential level. "When Jack first moved in, Mom tried to get him to stand in for Dad. He was smart enough to defer to me because, well...I'm an actual rabbi."

"Plus, he's not our father. Just her boyfriend," said Melissa. The Morgenstern sisters seemed to like Jack, but they were fiercely protective of their mother.

Kaylee came out of the kitchen and sat down practically on top of Courtney. Her daughter usually ignored her, especially around kids her own age. Since the shooting, she wouldn't let her mother out of her sight. Courtney remembered her own terror of losing her parents. Her grandmother often stayed with her after school until her parents came home from the hardware store they'd inherited from Courtney's grandfather. On stormy nights, her grandmother would anxiously watch for the headlights of her son's car coming into the driveway. "I hope they make it," she'd whisper, mostly to herself, unaware that she was planting the idea that Courtney's parents might never come home.

Ruth stuck her head out of the kitchen. "Girls, it's almost sundown. The twins are going to light the candles."

Rebecca got up and put on a cap brightly embroidered with colorful flowers and a multicolored shawl. Everyone came out of the kitchen to watch the candle lighting. "Blessed is the Oneness Who commands us to kindle the light of the *Shabbat*," Rebecca prayed. After a moment of silence, the women returned to the kitchen and a parade of covered dishes came out. Ruth directed their artful arrangement around the table. Rebecca put her hands on the heads of her daughters and said, "May God make you like Sarah, Rebekah, Rachel, and Leah. May God bless you and keep you. May God's light shine upon you and be gracious to you." After Rebecca blessed the others, her mother poured wine into an ornate silver cup. "Blessed is the Oneness who creates the fruit of the vine." Rebecca handed the ritual cup to Jack, who passed it on to Ruth. It went around the table, followed by a cup of grape juice for the girls. After a ritual washing, Rebecca took one of the challahs that Melissa had driven down to Webhanet to pick up that morning. "Blessed is the Oneness Who brings forth bread from the earth." She broke off a piece and sent it around the table.

Rebecca removed her shawl but kept on her little cap. Jack continued to wear his too, but otherwise it was like any other big family dinner. Ruth's pot roast was meltingly delicious, and the baked noodle dish called Kugel went with it perfectly. She carefully watched everyone at the table to make sure her food was being eaten with appropriate enthusiasm. Feeling her eyes on her through the meal, Courtney sensed that Ruth was still not completely sold on the idea of this new, inclusive family.

Kaylee and the twins were having their own sidebar, while the adults enjoyed a lively political conversation. Mercifully, there was no talk about the event that had transfixed Hobbs for days. Courtney knew she was the reason they were avoiding the subject, and felt like a ghost, listening to them talk around it. Then, Jack asked what Rebecca intended to say in her sermon at the boy's funeral.

"I'm going to read a couple of passages from *When Bad Things Happen to Good People*. I can't project myself into the tragedy of losing a child, so I've asked Olivia Enright to speak. She lost her son, you know."

"He killed himself after being caught with kiddie porn," said Ruth, making a face. "That's not the same."

"Some people would say his death was justified," said Melissa.

"Same with the shooter. After a murderer is convicted, the families always say they're glad for justice, but it doesn't bring back their loved one. Vindication is not the same as justice."

Jack said, "An 'eye-for-an-eye' has a long tradition."

"Doesn't matter," Rebecca said. "That kind of cheap transactionalism leads to a vicious cycle that never ends. That young man shot a teacher to get revenge for abuse, even though she wasn't the one responsible. And that wasn't enough. He killed eight little boys and could have killed more people. Instead of getting back, we should focus on healing."

"I'm glad Olivia agreed to speak," said Melissa. Courtney knew she'd developed a deep respect for the town manager since working with her on some local projects.

"I hope it's not just another campaign speech," said her mother, looking sour. Clearly, she was not an Olivia Enright fan.

After dinner, Courtney refused to be confined to the couch. She loaded the dishwasher while Melissa wrapped up the leftovers. The others were out clearing the table, which afforded them a rare moment of privacy.

"I had a great time tonight," Courtney whispered when Melissa stood close enough to hear. "I really appreciate your mother's hospitality, but I think it's time for us to go home."

Melissa looked up when the chattering women all returned at once, like a flock of birds landing. Naturally, Melissa felt at home here among her family and was reluctant to leave, but Courtney needed time to think without the constant distraction. "Please," she added in an urgent whisper when the noisy crew left again.

"All right," Melissa whispered back. "We'll go home tomorrow morning after breakfast."

\*\*\*

Maggie sat on the bed while Sam packed her bags. With a foot of snow outside, it was strange to see shorts and T-shirts going into her duffle bag, but in California, the temperatures would be much warmer. Sam had hung up some suits to take for formal meetings with the museum board. Maggie was pleased that she'd included the one she'd helped Sam pick out for Liz's wedding. The others were expensive and beautifully tailored, but the olive linen suit had softer lines and some flair.

When Maggie made suggestions about what to wear, Sam still bristled, saying her advice felt too much like when her mother tried to pretty her up and turn her into a lady. But Maggie didn't want to change Sam. She loved Sam's easy laughter. She liked her strength in bed, effortlessly moving her into any position she chose. She enjoyed the sensitivity of her fingers, playing played her body like an instrument and finding every erotic note.

Most of all, she enjoyed their conversations. Sam was quieter than Liz, but she paid attention. While they were married, Maggie had often wondered if Liz even heard her when she shared about her students' antics or a ridiculous faculty meeting. Maggie used to tell herself that Liz was a doctor and had more important things on her mind. Finally, she'd realized that her wife spent a lot of time in her head. Sam was a thinker too, but she *listened*. Maybe that would change. In the beginning, Liz had listened too.

"You might have to send me some stuff if I'm not home soon," said Sam, counting out her sports bras, "but I guess if I need something, I can buy it out there."

"I can bring you clothes when I visit. Just let me know what you need."

Sam tucked the neat stack of underwear into the corner of the bag. "I'll hate being away from you."

"You got the commission. That's the important thing."

Sam shook her head. "I don't usually trash other architects, but my competitors' designs were pathetic. I don't know what they're teaching in architecture school nowadays." For a moment, Sam sounded like Liz, complaining about the young doctors learning to do robotic surgery by playing video games. Maybe they all sounded like that now, looking at the younger generation and wondering what planet these aliens had come from.

Sam added socks to the bag and zipped it closed. She flopped down beside Maggie on the bed. "I just hope people don't think I'm running away."

"Sam, you're an architect. How can people fault you for doing your job? Your renovation business was just something to keep you busy while you waited for the next commission, right?"

"That's a nice story, Maggie. But I never thought I'd design a large-scale project again. My renovation business was how I planned to keep myself going until retirement."

"You have your trust fund money, or you could have drawn on your savings."

"Yes, but that's not me. You know how I hate sitting around doing nothing."

"As my mother would say, 'you have ants in the pants.'"

"Wow, that's an expression I haven't heard in a million years."

"What can I say? I'm old. You're just a baby." Maggie leaned over Sam and gave her a kiss before getting up. "I want to get the salad made before Alina gets here."

"She's coming for dinner?"

"No, I took out a casserole from the freezer for their dinner. She's been down here covering the shooting and doesn't have time to cook."

"Not that she did before. You did all the cooking. Will you go back to Scarborough after I leave?"

"Maybe for a few days."

"If you plan to be away longer, make sure you ask Liz to shut off the water. If the power goes out, we don't want the pipes to burst." Maggie instantly decided she'd keep her visits to Scarborough short to avoid getting Liz involved.

When the doorbell rang, Maggie went to answer it. At Liz's house, Alina always felt comfortable coming in after ringing the bell. Obviously, she wasn't sure how she fit into this new domestic arrangement.

"Hey, Mom," said the tiny, dark-haired woman, reaching up for a hug. Maggie waited for Alina to let go first because she'd been sensitive to rejection since childhood.

"You're late tonight," said Maggie lightly.

"Had to run some interference with the news agencies. I don't know why the networks can't stream broadcasts from the affiliates. The national reporters are so pushy. It's all about getting their faces in front of the camera, not the story." Maggie knew Alina still resented giving up a lucrative job in a large Florida market to get away from her abusive husband.

"Can you stay for a cup of tea?"

"A quick one."

Maggie turned on the electric tea kettle and dropped a tea bag into a mug. "You might as well take off your coat or you'll be cold when you go back outside." It had been frigid for the last week. At night, Maggie could hear the ice groaning as it expanded and thickened on the pond.

Alina hung her coat on the back of a chair. "Thanks for sending us dinner. The kids miss your cooking."

"With Sam gone, I might come up to Scarborough for a few nights." Maggie glanced at her daughter to see her reaction, but there wasn't any. Like a doctor, a reporter had to wear a poker face. "I can cook extra while I'm up there and stock the freezer for you," Maggie added with a smile.

"You don't need to do that. We appreciate the frozen dinners, but we manage." Alina probably thought she was reassuring her mother, but it hurt to hear that she was no longer needed.

"I wouldn't stay long," Maggie quickly added. "Sam's worried about the pipes freezing."

"You could always ask Liz to come over and turn off the water."

*Why does everyone assume I'm incompetent!* Bristling, Maggie changed the subject. "Who's been minding your newsroom while you're down here?"

"I have a new assistant, a Somali woman, whose parents came as refugees. She went to Husson for journalism. Wicked smart." She laughed. "Listen to me. I sound like a Mainer." Alina dunked her tea bag up and down to make it brew faster. "Part of the reason I'm hanging around is to see if I can land an interview with Liz. So far, she won't talk to anyone in the media."

"Can you blame her? She's been through a lot and news people can be obnoxious." Alina's long stare indicated she expected her mother to intervene. "Oh, no, Alina, I'm not helping you get the interview. You're on your own."

"But, Mom, you know how to handle her. Even if you just mention how it would boost my career."

"Sorry, but you probably have more leverage with Liz than I do."

"She still loves you." That landed hard. Maggie knew Liz still loved her. And she'd been Liz's first, which meant the feeling ran deep.

"I know, but that doesn't mean she listens to me."

Her daughter's face stiffened with disappointment. She started talking about the background information the police had just released to the press. She was convinced that Peter Langdon wasn't one of those school shooters who'd been planning his move for months. He'd had a stash of guns, but there was no evidence he was a second amendment fanatic. They'd found nothing in his computer or social media accounts that indicated that he'd admired other shooters or was looking for attention.

"This shooting was personal," Alina concluded. She'd finished the tea and got up to put on her coat. "Just give me a heads up when you plan to come up to the house." Maggie knew her daughter wasn't the best housekeeper and would need time to pick up after the kids before her mother arrived.

After her daughter left, Maggie started assembling the dinner ingredients. The doorbell rang again, and she assumed Alina had forgotten something, but when she went to the door, she found Liz peering through the glass.

"How nice to see you," said Maggie, smiling to cover her shock at Liz's changed appearance. She had a young face for a woman in her late sixties, but she'd visibly aged. Her eyes were glassy, probably from lack of sleep, which could make anyone look old and worn.

"Come in out of the cold," Maggie said, tugging on Liz's arm. She closed the door. Liz looked around like she'd never been there before. That was odd because Liz often visited and had helped Sam renovate the old cabin. "What are you doing here?" Maggie asked.

"I was out getting groceries. I shop at night because I don't want to be harassed in the supermarket. Lucy says I'm turning into a vampire because I'll only go out after dark." Even Liz's off-centered grin looked sad.

Any animosity Maggie still felt for her ex-wife instantly vanished. She pulled her into a hug. "Oh, Liz, you look absolutely exhausted!"

"Not sleeping well," Liz murmured into Maggie's ear. "My shoulder still aches. Don't tell Lucy." She had no reason to worry. Apart from choir business, Maggie didn't have much conversation with Lucy.

"Take off your coat, and I'll make you some tea."

"I don't plan to stay long."

"Take it off anyway."

Liz didn't argue, which surprised Maggie. Since the divorce, any subject could spark an argument. Liz hung up her parka but kept on the scarf Maggie had once knitted for her. She'd found the naturally dyed wool at a craft fair and thought the subtle tones would complement Liz's coloring. She was touched to see that Liz still wore it.

"I heard Sam is leaving tomorrow," Liz explained, sitting down at the kitchen table. "I'm here to say goodbye and wish her luck on the project."

"I think she's in her office getting her papers together. You just missed Alina."

"I know. I saw her car drive by. I'm glad she didn't see me. I've been trying to avoid her."

Maggie made a sad face. "Don't hold it against her. It's her job."

"I know she wants an interview. You can tell her she has first dibs when I'm ready."

"That will make her happy."

"I hope so. She left me an angry message the other day."

"She's under a lot of stress. Don't read into it."

"It's not just the reporters. People come up to me in the supermarket and thank me. They tell me I'm a hero. Maggie, I never wanted to kill that boy."

"I know, Liz," said Maggie. She raised her hand to stroke Liz's hair before remembering they no longer had that kind of relationship.

Sam walked into the room. "I thought I heard your voice!" she said with delight. Liz got up and suddenly they were a tangle of long arms.

"Hey, you, how are you doing?" asked Liz, enthusiastically returning the hug.

"Better than you. You look like shit."

"Thanks, so do you." Liz smacked Sam on the back a few times before she let her go. "I hear you're flying out tomorrow."

"I had to put it off because Brenda wanted me for another round of questioning. But they're done with me now."

"I hope so," said Liz in an uncertain tone that made Maggie uneasy.

"Hey, stay for a beer. Maggie's not going to drink it while I'm away, and if I take the bottles out of the fridge, the beer will get skunky."

"Well, skunky beer is not allowed. I'll stay for one, but then I need to get home. Don't want my lettuce freezing in my truck."

Sam took a couple of beers out of the refrigerator and led Liz into the living room. Maggie listened to the comforting sound of their voices and tried to calculate how long to delay dinner.

# Chapter 10

Cherie sat across from the woman whose son had killed a teacher and nine kids. Many people thought he'd gotten what he deserved, but like the parents of the victims, Renee Langdon had also lost a child.

She looked like any other worn-out single mother you might meet on the checkout line at the supermarket or filling up her car with gas on her way to work. Her diminutive stature made her seem fragile. She had warm brown eyes, but there were dark circles around them from worry or lack of sleep. There was nothing special about her to suggest she could raise a killer.

"Mother Lucy said I had to see you, Mrs. Harrison, because she's married to Dr. Stolz."

"Please call me Cherie, and yes, it's probably better that you talk to me than Lucy. She's too close to the situation."

"I hope Mother Lucy doesn't hate me now."

"Why should she hate you?" asked Cherie with surprise.

"Pete made Dr. Stolz shoot him."

Cherie hadn't expected that answer. "Are you angry that she shot him?"

"Honestly, I don't know how I feel," admitted Renee, inspecting her open palms as if they held the answer. It seemed strange that she wouldn't be angry and full of hate. Cherie still hated the trooper who'd killed her sister.

"Trauma can take a while to sink in," Cherie said gently.

"I'm sure Dr. Stolz never wanted to hurt him. She really liked Pete. She kept in touch after that gun class. She'd call him. They'd sit on the porch and drink a beer. She really tried to help him, got him that job with Sam McKinnon. They all tried to help him. They didn't know he was beyond help."

"Did you?"

Renee shook her head. "How much did Mother Lucy tell you about my situation?"

"Not much. She passed along her notes to me. I read that Pete had uncontrollable anger."

Renee frowned and reflected, as if she wasn't sure. "He once ripped the door off a kitchen cabinet because it bounced back and hit him. When he was high, he'd scream and smash dishes if he didn't like what I cooked. He had a bad temper like his father."

"Is your husband still in the picture?"

"God, no. He's been gone for years. I don't even know where he is. I think he's still alive...just dropped out of sight, so he doesn't have to pay child support for the younger kids."

Cherie scribbled some notes into her tablet with the stylus: "absent father...uncontrolled rages...possible domestic abuse."

"Did you know Peter was being abused by a teacher?"

"I knew he hated gym. Made up any excuse to get out of that class."

"Do you remember the night your husband threw Peter out?"

Mrs. Langdon sighed and nodded. "Bill was so drunk. I was afraid to go near him, but I knew Pete was smart and would find someplace safe to hide until morning. My second son was just a baby. I couldn't leave him."

"How are *you* doing? Do you feel safe? No thoughts of self-harm?" Asking about suicidal ideation was tricky. Cherie knew how important it was, but she didn't want to plant the idea, either.

"I can't think that way. I still have two kids at home. Pete wasn't my only child, although he'd be a lot for any mother."

"What about your children? How are they handling this?"

Renee shrugged. "They're sad, of course. He was their brother, but until his girlfriend threw him out, Pete hadn't lived at home for a while. When he lived with us, he'd be holed up in his room down in the basement. No one would see him unless he showed up for dinner.

"So, he's much older than the others."

"Yes, he was. My husband took off for a while. When he came back, he said he'd reformed and wanted to start again."

"Were things better?"

"No, worse."

Cherie entered some quick notes in the file.

"My kids say the other kids are making comments in school," said Renee.

"What kind of comments?"

"They say they come from a crazy family...that Pete deserved to die."

"Kids say all kinds of things. School can be a mean place."

"It can be, but most kids don't have to defend a brother who's a school shooter."

"Sounds like your children could use some counseling."

"We'll see. It will have to wait until after the funeral."

"How are the plans for the service going?"

"I'm having him cremated...now that they've released the body. The service will be private. Father Tom will say the prayers."

"I love Father Tom," said Cherie, nodding. "I really miss him."

"Me too," Renee agreed. "I wish he'd come back permanently. Mother Lucy could use the help."

"Well, she has Mother Susan and Mother Reshma. That's a lot of clergy for a small parish."

"Maybe, but Reshma was just ordained. I miss Father Tom," Renee insisted.

"How can we best support you right now, Renee?" Cherie asked, to change the subject.

"I don't know. My sister's coming up from Florida for the funeral. She wants me to move down there to be near her, and maybe I should. After the funeral, we'll figure it out," said Renee, sounding exhausted. "I can't think about it now."

"Of course. Take your time."

"I think it might be better to make a fresh start. I went to work yesterday because I was afraid to stay out longer. I've been working for that bank for twelve years, but these days, they'll fire you for anything. When I looked out my office door, I could see the tellers huddled together, looking in my direction and whispering. I can imagine what they were saying: 'Look at her. Her boy killed all those kids.'"

"Maybe they weren't saying that. Maybe they don't know what to say."

"Oh, you know how people can be, especially in a small town. Everyone is in everyone else's business. There's no place to hide."

Living and working in the same town wasn't easy. Cherie often felt like she was in a fishbowl.

For the next forty minutes, she tried to draw out her client. It was such a common tale that Cherie could practically document the case without asking any questions. What struck her was the underlying current of relief Renee Langdon felt, as if a huge burden had been lifted from her shoulders. It chilled Cherie to think any mother could feel that way about a child.

"I can see on the clock that our session is almost over," said Renee with a sly look.

"It is. Is there anything you'd like me to know before you leave?"

Renee thought for a moment. "I really tried with him. He was my first, so I didn't always know what I was doing. They always blame the mother. I swear to you I did not make him a killer."

"Of course not. I'm sure you did your best." Cherie opened her schedule. "I have this time available next week. Does that work for you?"

Renee nodded. "I don't know if I'll continue, but I appreciate what you're trying to do."

"There's no charge for these sessions. They're funded by the state."

"It's not the money," said Renee. "I just don't know what to say.

I'm sorry it happened. Really sorry. I wish I could have stopped him, but he never talked to me. I hardly ever saw him." She stood up and picked up her bag from the floor. "Can I say hello to Mother Lucy before I leave?"

"If she's not with someone. Sure." Cherie got up. "Let me go see."

Cherie went down the hall to Lucy's office. It was her day to write her sermon, and her fingers were busily typing when Cherie knocked on the open door.

When Lucy looked up, her smile wasn't as shiny as usual. "Hey, Cherie," she said softly. "What's up?" Cherie could hear the distraction and fatigue in her voice.

"Mrs. Langdon is here for her session. She'd like to say hello."

Lucy's green eyes widened with alarm.

"If it's not convenient, I can say you're busy," Cherie added quickly.

"No, I can't hide from her. I'm her priest, and she's suffering. How did she say she was doing?"

"She didn't say much. I think she's numb."

Lucy drew a long breath and let it out slowly. "Aren't we all?"

❋❋❋

Amy took off her glasses and gazed into the air thoughtfully. Olivia, who'd been cutting vegetables for dinner, had been anxiously waiting for her to finish. "It's just a draft," she said preemptively. "I'm open to suggestions."

"Give me a minute. I'm absorbing it." Amy delicately wiped the corners of her eye with her fingertip. "It's beautifully written and extremely moving. There won't be a dry eye in the room." Olivia had heard Lucy say making people cry at a funeral was good, so she considered Amy's comment an endorsement.

Amy got up and refilled her glass from the wine bottle on the counter. "Why didn't you tell me any of this? I thought you hated your son."

"How can you hate someone you've carried inside your body for nine months? And before you ask, yes, I did breastfeed him, but he was a hungry devil, and I could never give him enough."

"Strange." Amy sipped her wine reflectively. "I've seen you with your grandchildren, but I never think of you as a mother."

"I know. How could a cold thing like me be a mother?" asked Olivia, her acid tone dripping with sarcasm. "Unimaginable!" She poured oil into the skillet and turned on the burner. When she looked up, Amy was staring at her. "Well? Isn't that what you were thinking?"

"No, not at all." Amy gave her a tentative look. "Whenever you talk about your son, you tell me how angry you are that he wrecked your business and abused your granddaughters. I just read how much you loved him."

"Of course, I loved him! Everyone thinks I don't have any feelings! Well, I do!" Olivia forcefully threw the vegetables into the skillet. When some oil spattered onto the counter, she regretted her fit of temper. "Amy, you've spent more time with me than most people. I would expect you to know better." She picked up a sponge to wipe away the grease spray, but Amy nudged her aside and began to clean it up.

"Why don't you sit down and let me finish cooking? You've already done all the work. I can do the rest." Amy moved to take the spatula, but Olivia held it out of reach.

"No, I always finish what I start," she insisted stubbornly.

"See? You won't accept help."

"I don't expect help. That's different. I could never depend on people. That's why I don't bother with my family. Nothing but druggies and alcoholics ruining their lives. Well, I didn't let them ruin mine."

Amy retreated to the table and neatly stacked the papers she'd been reading. "I found a couple of typos. Do you want me to mark them?"

"Yes, thank you."

Amy took a pen out of her bag and flicked it over the paper. "Olivia, this speech revealed a side of you I never knew existed. If we're going to have a relationship, I want to know more about you."

Olivia looked up from the skillet. Amy had said the R-word. Whenever it had come up before, Amy had changed the subject. The aggressive sizzle from the pan meant the vegetables needed to be stirred. Olivia had been so focused on the conversation she'd forgotten the burner was on high. "You should talk, Amy. I have to *pull* things out of you," Olivia said, hurrying to rescue dinner.

"I'm a private person. That's how I was raised. My parents were doctors, trained to keep their feelings to themselves. I never once heard them raise their voices."

"Lucky you. Growing up, there was always screaming and throwing things in my house."

"You must have found that very frightening."

"I did, but I coped."

Olivia filled two plates. Amy got up to help. "Sit down," Olivia ordered. "I've got it." Amy dutifully sat while Olivia brought the plates to the table. "Eat," she commanded as she sat down.

Amy picked up her fork and took a mouthful. "Delicious as always."

"Thank you." Olivia took special pleasure in guests enjoying her cooking, especially Amy. "I'm sorry I jumped on you about the motherhood comment. The truth is, I was a lousy mother, although very attentive because I wanted to prove I could be good at it."

Amy looked up from her plate. "Unfortunately, many educated women fell into that trap. We were told we could and must excel at everything."

"After Jason became a toddler, I quickly lost interest in proving I was the perfect mother. When he was seven, we sent him to boarding school. He told me that a teacher was 'bothering' him."

Amy stopped eating to look at her. "You think he was molested? That's horrible!"

"He wasn't more specific and never mentioned it again. I was in the thick of divorce negotiations with Michael, so I didn't pay much attention. Now, it weighs on my conscience, especially because they say that children who are abused often become abusers themselves."

"That's never been conclusively proven, but there's a large body of anecdotal evidence, and the data is statistically significant." Amy was always full of facts and figures. Olivia respected people who knew what they were talking about instead of spouting off opinions with no evidence.

"I used to believe it was hereditary," said Olivia, cautiously watching for a reaction. Amy was quick, so it wouldn't take long.

Oh my God! Not you!"

Olivia focused on her plate because Amy's sympathetic look was unnerving. "On a camping trip. One of my father's friends came into the tent where my brother and I were sleeping. You're only the second person I've ever told...well, third, counting my therapist. I told Sam."

"Oh, Liv, I'm so, so sorry."

"Now you can see why this tragedy knocked me off balance. I know the pain of the mothers who have lost children, including the mother of the boy who shot them. When he said he'd been abused, I thought of my son, who tried to tell me something very important, but I was too busy to hear. I thought of myself, lying in a pup tent in my little child-sized sleeping bag from the Sears catalog, my little brother snoring beside me while a man stinking of beer stuck his big fingers inside me. I bled all the next day." Olivia put down her fork, knowing if she tried to swallow, the food would stick in her throat.

Across the table, Amy had stopped eating too. "Take a deep breath, Olivia. It's a difficult memory. I'm upset just listening to you."

"I'm sorry," said Olivia. "I didn't mean to spoil your dinner."

"You didn't," said Amy, picking up her fork. "You know, we don't have to go to this prayer service tonight. You've gone to every town event since the shooting. You have a heart condition, which is a perfect excuse. You could take a break."

Olivia shook her head. "No, I can't. It's my job as town manager to be there. That's what it means to be a leader. Show up and set a good example." When she reached for her fork, she noticed some grease on her sleeve. "But first, I'll need to change my top. I hate grease stains. They're so hard to get out."

***

Amy surveyed the seating options and debated whether she was spry enough to climb the bleachers. The high school gym, which doubled as the school's auditorium, was filling up quickly. Student ushers, wearing looped black ribbons pinned at the center with an enameled school logo, directed the younger and able-bodied people to the bleachers. The folding chairs lined up on the gym floor were reserved for the elderly and disabled, except for the front rows where the town leaders and officials would sit. As town manager, Olivia would sit on the stage with the clergy.

"Good luck," Amy said at the point where she and Olivia had to part. When she gave her a quick kiss on the cheek, Olivia's perfectly arched brows rose, and her face turned pink. To Amy's surprise, she was blushing.

"Olivia!" called a man wearing a magenta shirt and collar. Amy resented the intrusion into their tender moment, but Olivia instantly slipped into her public persona.

"Bishop Greene!" she said, radiating charm and status as she accepted the short man's embrace. "How good of you to come."

"Of course, I would come," he said, earnestly looking into her eyes. "I'm devastated by this horror. I had to come down to pray with the families."

"That's so kind of you, bishop. Your presence will be such a comfort."

Of course, his participation had been carefully planned, so this conversation was absurd. Amy fought the temptation to roll her eyes.

"Bishop, do you know Dr. Amy Hsu? She's a partner at Hobbs Family Practice."

His smile broadened. "You must work with Dr. Stolz," he said, reaching out his hand. "One of my favorite people." His unctuous tone made Amy want to wipe her hand on her skirt after she shook his, but she acknowledged the implied question with a nod. She was grateful when the man moved away to greet other well-wishers.

"Let's see if the Catholic bishop shows up," whispered Olivia near Amy's ear. "Since Maine eliminated the statute of limitations on sexual abuse, the RCs have been hit by one lawsuit after another. I hope they sue the bastards into oblivion!" The vehemence of her statement shocked Amy, but given their earlier conversation, it had new significance. "This is where I leave you," said Olivia. She reached down and gave Amy's hand a last squeeze.

Amy resumed her search for a place to sit. The bleachers were filled at the lower levels, so she had to climb the narrow steps to find a seat. She took off her down coat and sat on it because the aluminum benches were uncomfortable. This was one situation where a trim backside was not an asset.

She watched the crowd mill into the gym. The faces of people, stopping to chat with friends and neighbors, were grave. The somber atmosphere made it feel like a church, appropriate for a prayer service. The flags of the various denominations were lined up on the stage behind the stars and stripes. Because it was a Friday night, the Jewish community wouldn't have a representative, but its flag stood along with the others.

In a few days, this space would host the first lady and Vice-President Harris. Admission to the event was by ticket only. The families with children in the elementary school got preference, but most of the remaining tickets had gone to the press. People were griping about the unfairness. Even Ginny, the practice manager, who never complained, was resentful to be left out.

Amy watched her boss come in with Lucy Bartlett. Liz was

cutting a path for her wife. The Episcopal rector was so popular in town she couldn't get down the aisle without accepting handshakes and hugs. After they parted, Liz stood there, looking around for a place to sit. She considered the row where the town officials were sitting. As the town doctor and the leader of so many community organizations, she would certainly be entitled to sit with the dignitaries. Amy watched as Liz looked around for an alternative.

"Liz!" called Amy. Liz scanned the crowd, finally locating Amy, waving high in the bleachers. She nimbly climbed to where Amy sat, arriving just as Olivia was calling for silence.

"Thank you all for coming out on this bitterly cold night. Your presence tonight is a great support to the families who have lost so much. In the coming days, they'll need you even more. Don't forget to check on your neighbors. Call your friends. Just a friendly voice can mean so much at a time like this, and so can prayer." She paused and gestured to the people sitting on the stage. "I want to extend a warm welcome to all the faith leaders joining us tonight." She went down the row and introduced each of them. "And now, Bishop Greene will open tonight's service with an invocation."

When Liz audibly groaned, Amy smiled to herself. At least she wasn't the only one who didn't like the bishop. After he prayed, another minister rose to read Psalm 46, followed by a choral setting of Psalm 23 sung by the high school choir. Pastors of the other Hobbs churches offered prayers. The children's choir of the Baptist church sang "I am Jesus' Little Lamb." The cheerful melody struck Amy as dissonant with the sadness of the occasion, but Maggie Fitzgerald's "Amazing Grace" with St. Margaret's choir righted the tone. Tom Simmons read a New Testament passage. Monsignor O'Brien's homily about tragedies involving children made Amy grit her teeth. She knew that it was wrong to lump in all Catholic priests with the pedophiles, but the man's words sounded so off-key.

Finally, Lucy, wearing a beautiful white stole, rose and went to the microphone. "This tragedy has left us all numb. How can we take in the horror without it consuming us? How can we even imagine it, this thing that happens elsewhere, but not here? But it has happened here, where we live with our families, where we work, where our children go to school. I wasn't going to sing today, but my colleagues reminded me that music can help us grieve. During those times when our emotions are so painful that we think we can't face them, music opens us up. Tonight, I'm going to sing a passage from *Faure's Requiem* that always helps me release grief." There was a loud thud as Lucy turned off the microphone. When her powerful voice filled the room, Amy understood why.

Beside her, Liz's body moved subtly with the music. A tear fell from her closed eyes, followed by another and then another. Amy quietly searched in her bag for tissues.

***

Lucy finally located Liz sitting beside Amy in the bleachers. Amy was a calming influence on Liz, so Lucy felt confident leaving her wife in her competent hands. Other faith leaders had remained behind to talk to people after the service, but Monsignor O'Brien had made a hasty exit. Lucy had seen the audience shut down during his sermon. The same with the hymn the Baptist children's choir sang. How could some ministers be so tone deaf to people's feelings?

As Lucy chatted with an elderly woman who'd come up to compliment her singing, she noticed Bishop Greene heading in her direction. "I'm sorry, but my boss is coming over. I have to talk to him." Lucy's wink brought a conspiratorial twinkle to the woman's eyes.

"Before I go, what was that piece you sang, Dr. Bartlett?"

"The '*Pie Jesu*' from the *Fauré Requiem*."

"It was absolutely exquisite!"

By now, the bishop was at Lucy's side. "I'm so glad to hear you enjoyed Mother Lucy's singing," he said, extending his hand. "Hello, I'm Bishop Greene."

"I don't go to your church, Bishop, but I love to hear Dr. Bartlett sing."

"Mother Lucy is a treasure," he agreed. "We're encouraging her to sing another concert at the cathedral. Please join us."

After the old woman had moved away, the bishop leaned toward Lucy to speak confidentially. "I was hoping to have an opportunity to speak to your wife. Being forced to take the life of that sad young man must be devastating!"

Lucy nodded in the direction of where Liz and Amy were sitting in the bleachers. "She's not in good shape. She only came tonight to support me. She's hiding from the reporters."

"As much as I appreciate the publicity they give the diocese, they can be cruel and dangerous."

"It's not just the press, it's the townspeople too. They want to thank her for her bravery, but she doesn't see herself as a hero."

"I doubt she would. As a doctor, she's sworn an oath to do no harm." The bishop squinted while he studied Liz, sucked up into her hoodie like a belligerent gamer. "Would it help if I talked to her?"

Lucy stared at him, amazed that he hadn't picked up by now that Liz loathed him. She scrambled to think of a tactful way to deflect the suggestion. "She just needs time," she said. "But I'll let you know if calling her would help."

"Thanks, Lucy. You have excellent judgment when it comes to pastoral intervention, so I'll leave it to you." He smiled amiably. When he turned to shake the hand of the Baptist minister, Lucy saw her opportunity to escape. She used the backstage exit to get out of the auditorium. She was congratulating herself on evading the people waiting to talk to her, when she turned around to see Maggie behind her.

"Hi Lucy, you sang beautifully." Lucy's ear detected the little note of jealousy always present when Maggie complimented her performances.

"So did you," Lucy said with complete sincerity. "No one sings 'Amazing Grace' like you do."

Maggie looked up into the stands. "I see Liz up there, sitting with Amy. I was going to say hello to her, but it doesn't look like she wants company."

Lucy sighed. "She's been holed up in her workshop all week. She barely talks to me."

"Sam tried to call her. She never answers her phone." That worried Lucy. Liz never refused Sam's calls.

"How's Sam doing?"

"Okay. Glad to be away from all the suspicion. She's in her element talking to people about designing buildings, but I really miss her."

"I bet you do. When you talk to her, ask her to call me, please."

"I will," said Maggie, giving the bleachers another worried look.

Lucy was glad she'd taken off her pumps and put on her boots as she climbed to where her wife sat. Amy moved over to make room for her to sit down.

"Thanks for taking care of my wife. I hope she was on good behavior." Lucy saw Liz roll her eyes.

Amy smiled. Her sense of humor was subtle, but she was quick. "Mostly. Your performance brought her to tears, but she seems okay now."

Looking annoyed to be spoken about in the third person, Liz folded her arms on her chest.

"She doesn't look happy," said Lucy. "I'll take her off your hands now."

Amy patted Liz's knee. "Take care of yourself, Liz. We expect you back at work soon." She got up, and Lucy moved into her seat.

"You doing okay?" she asked, reaching for Liz's hand.

"We should go. I don't want to run into any reporters." Liz got up, which meant Lucy was leaving too.

The full moon illuminated the path to the parking area like a ghostly spotlight. When Lucy offered to drive, Liz surprised her by agreeing. Usually, she insisted on driving. She was silent, watching out the window, as Lucy drove. The countryside was bright in the moonlight, and the salt on the roads glistened. It looked so peaceful, almost magical.

"Your '*Pie Jesus*' was perfect," Liz finally said. "You weren't singing sharp, and if there was ever a piece to make you sing sharp, that's it." Then she was silent again.

When they came in from the garage, Liz hung up her parka and went into the kitchen. From the sound of glass clinking, Lucy guessed that Liz was reaching for her single-malt scotch. Leaning in the doorway, Lucy said, "Could you pass on the scotch tonight? I'd like to cuddle without you falling asleep on me. And you snore when you drink."

"Age will do that. All the structures in the throat become loose and flabby...like the rest of our bodies," Liz said in an annoyingly pedantic tone. To Lucy's relief, she replaced the cork and put the bottle back in the cabinet.

Lucy left her reading on her tablet while she took off her makeup, more than usual because of the stage lighting at the prayer service. No amount of foundation could hide the dark circles around her eyes. Just one good night's sleep was all she asked for, yet it was so far out of reach. Liz was still restless because she couldn't sleep on her bad arm. Lucy's nightmares about the dead children had persisted.

As much as sleep, she missed making love. This was the longest time they had gone without sex. Lucy craved the intimacy, the deep connection she always felt when they made love, a bond so close it sometimes felt like they were one body.

When Lucy turned off the light, Liz put her tablet aside, sighing as she pulled up the covers. She lay rigid and silent on the other side of the bed, which suddenly felt like a vast desert they didn't know how to cross.

"Liz, please hold me," said Lucy. After a long moment, Liz moved closer. She draped her arm across Lucy's body, not exactly a hug, but at least it was contact. "That's better. I've missed you." Liz's T-shirt smelled of laundry detergent and clean sweat. She liked to have her tummy rubbed like a puppy, so Lucy slid her hand under her shirt. "Can we make love?"

"We can try," said Liz but sounded doubtful.

When they kissed, Liz's mouth tasted minty. Eventually, she found some enthusiasm. Her passionate kisses were exciting until they became aggressive. She yanked down Lucy's nightgown and sucked her nipple until it ached. A little pain could be exciting, but this felt like it was meant to hurt. With guarded teeth, Liz bit her shoulder like she was trying to gnaw the flesh off her bones. She parted Lucy's legs with her knee and began to rub her hard.

"Liz, stop! You're hurting me!" said Lucy, pulling away.

Liz stared at her before retreating to the other side of the bed.

"What is *wrong* with you! Why are you so rough? You're scaring me!" Lucy pulled down her nightgown and rearranged it to cover her breasts. When she felt more together, she asked in a softer tone, "Liz, what's going on?"

"I don't know," said Liz sullenly.

"Too much aggression reminds me of the rape. You know that. Did you want me to push you away?"

The dark was silent for a long moment before Liz finally answered in a choked voice, "Yes."

Lucy reached out, but Liz only looked at her hand. "Liz, please. How can I help you?"

"Give me absolution."

"What?" More than surprised, Lucy was confused. Liz openly ridiculed the beliefs of the Church and its rituals. Why would she ask for something she routinely dismissed as 'bankrupt and absurd'?

"Please," Liz begged in a hoarse whisper. That's when Lucy realized she was not just serious, but desperate.

"Put on some clothes," said Lucy, getting up. "I'm not going to confess you naked."

"Isn't it good for a penitent to be naked before God?" The glimpse of the old Liz, full of spite for the Church, almost came as a relief, but Lucy was not going to let her make a mockery of a solemn ritual.

"Liz, do you want to do this or not?"

"Yes, I need absolution."

"Why? You killed in self-defense, and you saved two lives in the process, yours and Susan's."

"The commandment says, 'thou shalt not kill. I killed Peter Langdon."

"Oh baby, I know you must feel terrible. You loved Peter. You were so happy when he said he'd take your gun class. I was so happy because it looked like we were getting somewhere with him."

"Lucy, I *need* absolution," Liz insisted. When she became stubborn, there was no dissuading her.

"Wait here," said Lucy. She put on her bathrobe and went downstairs to the seashore room to get her sick call kit. She took out the miniature stole she wore for giving last rites and the compact *Book of Common Prayer*.

When she returned, Liz was shaking with cold. "I told you to get dressed," Lucy hissed. Liz looked at her but made no move to get up. With a sigh, Lucy went into the bathroom and took Liz's sweatshirt off the hook on the back of the door. After Liz put it on, she continued to hug herself. The heat was set to go down at bedtime, and it was a frigid night. Lucy imagined herself snug and warm in Liz's arms instead of preparing for an ancient ritual that few Episcopalians practiced anymore. Private confession was reserved for difficult situations when a penitent couldn't find peace any other way. Liz's case certainly met that standard. Lucy kissed the cross on the stole and put it on. She opened the *Book of Common Prayer*. "You're sure about this?" she asked, looking in the index for the penance rite.

"Is it like a Catholic confession? Do I say, 'Bless me, Mother, for I have sinned?"

"Yes, something like that. After that I say, 'The Lord be in your heart and upon your lips that you may truly and humbly confess your sins: In the Name of the Father, and of the Son, and of the Holy Spirit. Amen.'" Lucy put down the book. "All right, Liz. Tell me why you think you need absolution."

"I should have left talking to Peter to the negotiator. I was arrogant to think I could get him to let the hostages go. It's not the first time I've been arrogant. As a surgeon, I often tried things I knew were dangerous."

"You probably thought they might work, and that the benefits could outweigh the risks."

"Most of the time, but I also performed procedures to see what would happen. In some situations, the only way to discover the outcome was to operate. The results were not always what I expected."

"You probably hoped to make things better."

"I did. I hoped what I did might prolong a life or improve the quality of life, or if not, advance science. Sometimes, I did it for selfish reasons: to perfect a new technique because it could make it into the journals. Other times, I did it for the thrill of trying something new. I was something of a cowboy when I was young."

Lucy smiled because Liz thought she was telling her something she didn't already know. "So, are you confessing the sin of pride? You know that confidence is a positive thing. There's nothing wrong with being proud of your accomplishments. Taking considered risks can result in many benefits. You took one when you went into that school. You thought you could get the hostages released and help Peter."

"But I failed. He died."

"Have you considered that he intended to die?"

"I think he knew he might not get out of there alive. That's why he didn't negotiate for a way to escape."

"Maybe he didn't want to escape. Maybe all he wanted was someone to listen to his story. He invited you because you'd listened to him before."

"I wish he had told me about the abuse. Maybe I could have helped him."

"He probably couldn't tell you. What that teacher did to him was a dark secret he'd been hiding for years. Only a combination of extreme circumstances could force him to reveal it. His girlfriend leaving him brought back the humiliation of the abuse and his pain. When he tried to tell his teacher, she ridiculed him and called him a liar. He tried to tell his parents. One punished him, the other turned away. He turned to the people who should have helped, but no one believed him."

"I would have believed him."

"You weren't there, Liz!"

"We spent hours talking on his mother's porch over beers. Why didn't he tell me?" Liz threw out her hands in frustration.

"He couldn't. He wasn't ready. He'd suffered in silence all those years. The longer he held it in, the harder it became to tell anyone."

"If only he'd put a gun in his mouth like Jason Enright instead of killing all those innocent people!"

"He wanted to punish the perpetrators by proxy and 'save' the children from dying slowly like he did, but what he wanted most was to be seen and heard. This time, he made sure everyone heard and believed him."

Liz studied her for a long time. "You understood all this. Why couldn't you tell me before?"

"You wouldn't let me. You wanted to sit on the porch and drink that disgusting whiskey. You wanted its company more than mine." Lucy patted Liz's thigh. "You weren't ready to hear me."

"I'm sorry," said Liz. "I was trying to figure it out. I'm still trying to figure it out. I'm not done yet."

"You made a good start tonight. Give yourself time. It's a lot to process. Do you have anything else to confess?"

Liz thought for a moment. "I tried to hurt you tonight. I love you with all my heart, and I never want to hurt you. I am so sorry."

"I love you with all my heart, and I forgive you."

"That's it?" asked Liz, looking surprised.

"No, now you say this." Lucy handed Liz her prayer book and pointed out the text Liz was to read. She recited it reverently. Lucy read the words of absolution and closed the book. "There. You are absolved. Do you feel better?"

Liz frowned, but she nodded. Lucy carefully folded the stole and put it on her nightstand with the prayer book. "Now, do you think you can fall asleep?"

"Will you sing to me?" asked Liz in a tiny, hopeful voice.

Lucy sighed. She was exhausted and certainly didn't feel like singing. "What would you like me to sing?" she asked wearily.

"The '*Pie Jesu*' you sang tonight."

"If that's what you want, but I can't sing it lying down. It requires too much breath control."

"I can sit here and listen."

Lucy found her phone and turned on the same canned accompaniment she'd streamed through the speaker system at the high school. While she sang, tears streamed down Liz's face, a trickle at first, but then a flood. By the conclusion, she was sobbing as bitterly as when she'd knelt over Peter's body.

"Come on, sweetie," said Lucy, gathering her up. "Let's go to sleep." When she lifted Liz's arms and tugged the sweatshirt over her head, it was like undressing a child. "Come here," she whispered after they lay down. Holding Liz's face against her breasts, Lucy stroked her hair. She prayed that the tears dampening her nightgown meant the dam had finally broken.

# Chapter 11

From a table in the faculty room, Maggie watched the head of the English department root around in her mail cubby like a burrowing animal. "Nothing but junk today," said Maggie, to make conversation. "Just like the mailbox at home."

The woman turned around and stared at her before quickly exiting the room. She was the second person today to give Maggie the cold shoulder. She didn't understand what she'd done. She'd thought that once the other teachers at the community college had gotten past her Yale PhD and professorship at NYU, they'd accepted her as one of their own. She considered herself good at dealing with other women. She could read their body language and adjust her demeanor, allowing her to blend seamlessly into any female social group.

She gazed at the remnants of the sandwich she'd been eating. She always left the last bite, part of her portion-control strategy, and collected the wrappings—butcher paper to cut down on plastic waste.

The door opened, and this time, a friendly face greeted her. "Hey, Maggie," said Lise Boucher, one of the younger teachers on the humanities faculty. Young, these days, meant more than thirty years Maggie's junior.

Lise went to the refrigerator to take out a bottle of flavored water and sat down at Maggie's table. "How's it going?" she asked, grimacing as she tried to unscrew the plastic cap. "They make everything so hard to get into so some nut doesn't poison people, but they won't take away the guns," she muttered.

Lise was the first faculty member to mention the shooting. Maggie was relieved someone wanted to talk about it. "It makes no sense, does it?"

"None. Whatsoever." Lise took a few gulps of water. "How are you dealing with the bitches? Everyone is being so judgy. Drives me crazy."

"What do you mean?" Then it dawned on Maggie why her colleagues were so standoffish. "You've got to be kidding me."

Lise shook her head. "Nope. I heard them talking."

"But I did nothing wrong," said Maggie, stunned that educated adults would judge her guilty by association. With all her knowledge of human behavior, how did she miss that possibility? "Sam didn't do anything wrong either."

Lise assumed a patient expression. "Maggie, it was stupid to leave the door open."

"How could she have known that kid would sneak into the school?"

"She couldn't, but she should have thought it through better. There's a reason the school entrance has bullet-proof glass and automatic locks."

"She didn't want to drag the dirty water through the school." Maggie stopped. Why was she making excuses for what was, basically, a stupid mistake?

"If it makes you feel any better, I've defended you," said Lise. "Not that it made any difference. People always need someone to blame. It doesn't matter who, as long as there's a bad guy and a good guy. Pretty amazing that your ex took down the shooter. She's a real hero."

Maggie thought of Liz at the prayer service, hiding behind her hoodie, way up in the bleachers instead of sitting with the town officials where she belonged. "I don't think she sees it that way."

"She should. What she did was very brave." Lise's eyes rose to check the clock over the door. "Gotta go, Maggie. I have a class. Stay strong. Like they say, don't let the turkeys get you down." She gave Maggie an encouraging pat on the shoulder before she left.

With Sam in California, there was no incentive to rush home. On another day, Maggie might have lingered in the faculty room to grade papers. Now that she knew she was a pariah, she couldn't wait to get out of there.

***

Sam was still in her pajamas, or rather the T-shirt and men's knit boxers she wore when she slept. In Maine, it was already lunchtime, which meant Maggie might be on her break. Sam tried to remember her class schedule. She'd written it down, but then left it at home.

Before she sat down to call, Sam poured herself a cup of coffee. She appreciated that the apartment the museum committee had leased for her had a full-sized kitchen, even though she didn't cook much. Feeling lucky, she tapped open Maggie's number. The phone rang and rang until the sound finally changed. "I wondered if I'd hear from you this morning," said the sexy voice on the other end.

"I wrote down your schedule, but I didn't bring it."

"I'll send it when I get home."

"You're driving?"

"Heading back after my morning classes. I'm done for today. I was going to do a little shopping, but I changed my mind. Looks like snow again."

Sam glanced outside at the beautiful, sunny day. It was hard to imagine snow when it was sixty-five degrees outside. She could get used to this.

"Miss me yet?" asked Maggie.

"Of course, I do." Now that Sam had finally gotten used to Maggie's constant presence, it felt strange to be apart. The phone calls and video visits helped a little, but not as much as she'd hoped. "Is it strange in the house without me there?" asked Sam, hoping to hear she'd been missed too.

"It is. That's why I'm going to Scarborough this weekend. It's lonely in the house without you. Alina and Steve are going skiing at Haystack, so I'm watching the kids."

"That's good. I'm sure the girls will enjoy some grandma time."

"I'm sure they will, but I can't wait to get out of Hobbs. It's no fun here."

Sam frowned at the thought of what she'd left behind. She'd deliberately avoided reading the news or watching TV so she could stay focused on the reason she'd come to California. "Is it bad?" asked Sam, afraid of what she might hear.

"You can't go out during the day without getting stuck in traffic. It's like the middle of August with the tourists here, except the town is full of journalists and people who are here for God knows what reason. The first lady and Kamala Harris are coming to town. It will be a zoo."

"Are you going?"

"I'd like to, but all the tickets were gone before I could even get on the website!"

"You can always watch it on TV, if you want to," Sam said.

"Will you?"

"No, I'm trying to stay as far away from it as I can. It's a distraction, and I want to get this job moving so I can come home again."

There was a long silence before Maggie said, "If I were you, I'd look for opportunities to extend my trip."

A cold finger of anxiety stroked the back of Sam's neck. It made the close-cropped hair on the back of her head prickle. "Why? What have you heard? They told me I wasn't to blame. They said I was free to go."

"This has nothing to do with the police. You know how it is in a small town. People need something to talk about."

Sam's fists clenched as a spark of anger flashed through her. "Tell me what they're saying!"

"Believe me, Sam. You don't want to know."

"Maggie, tell me!"

"They're saying you're at fault because you left the door open."

"I swear to you, I never thought this would happen. I knew Pete was a pothead, but I never imagined he would sneak into the school and start shooting kids. Who thinks such things?"

"No one...until it happens. Oh, Sam, I shouldn't have told you. Now, you're going to be out of sorts all day."

"And I have a big meeting this morning."

"Have you had breakfast yet?"

"No, I'm just having my first cup of coffee."

"Take a long, hot shower and get dressed," Maggie said in a soothing voice. "Take yourself out for breakfast. While you're eating it, imagine I cooked it for you, and we're sitting at our kitchen table."

"Oh, I wish," said Sam mournfully.

"Me too." Maggie's long sigh was audible. "I saw Lucy last night at the prayer service. She said she'd ask Liz to call you."

"She called and left a message this morning while I was still asleep. I guess she forgot about the time difference. I do. One time, I got a client out of bed. She wasn't happy."

"I bet. All right, gorgeous. I'm home. Call me tonight when you're free."

Maggie sounded breezy and cheerful, but when Sam ended the call, she felt a distinct sense of dread.

***

Brenda was glad this was the last official meeting of the investigation team. The colonel of the state police had already gone back to Augusta. The crime scene unit had wrapped up its investigation. The FBI vans stood in the parking lot, packed and ready to depart for Boston.

Now that outside law enforcement was leaving, Brenda could finally focus on getting the town ready for their VIP guests. She needed this "compassionate visit" from the White House like she needed another asshole. The Hobbs police were already struggling with the traffic from the funerals and the frigging news people who parked anywhere they felt like it. There had been another mass shooting in the Midwest, and some of the news organizations had left to chase the new story. Brenda couldn't say that she would miss them.

*God, how can I even think this way? How can I be glad that carnage in another part of the country is solving my traffic problems?*

"Chief Harrison, do you have anything to add?" asked the FBI team leader, interrupting Brenda's thoughts.

"Uh, no. I think that does it."

"Good. Let's adjourn until further notice. Feel free to reach out with any questions."

Everyone got up at once. The attendees were mostly field officers, who hated to sit for long meetings. So did Brenda, but as chief, she couldn't avoid them. There was a buzz of conversation as people said goodbye to one another.

Jen Morin, the chief of state investigations, was obviously hanging back, waiting to talk to Brenda. She liked the woman, who listened more than she talked. Her questions showed she was 'wicked smart.' Most of the state police special units were headed by women. In the NYPD, men still held all the top jobs, but it had been years since Brenda had worn the blue, so maybe things had changed there too.

She waved to Inspector Morin across the meeting room and pointed in the direction of her office.

"Coffee?" she asked when Morin found the way to her door.

"Any more coffee, and I'll be visiting every rest stop between here and Augusta."

"Have a seat," said Brenda, taking hers. She leaned back in her chair while she waited for Morin to collect her thoughts.

"Are you in touch with Sam McKinnon?" she asked.

Brenda shook her head. "She's the architect of a new museum in California. I haven't spoken to her since before she left."

"I could see that you went out of your way to be impartial, which is good for you, and good for her." Brenda hadn't meant it to be so obvious, but of course, she would be impartial. She'd been trained to be a good cop. She wondered what Morin was trying to say. Finally, she showed her cards. "People know you're friends. You should continue to keep your distance until things settle down.

I don't recommend you reach out to her directly, but maybe you can find a way to get word to her. As you know, the standard for criminal negligence is high. While we're not charging her, she can probably expect some civil suits."

"Seriously? What have you heard?"

"Nothing, but I saw a damages lawyer who likes to try big cases hanging around. You know how those people are. I heard your friend has some money."

"She's a trust fund baby."

"In that case, she can pretty much expect a suit, and it wouldn't hurt to be prepared. Is there a discreet way to let her know?"

"We have many friends in common," said Brenda, thinking of Liz.

"Perfect."

"I suppose I should thank you for the heads up," said Brenda, frowning.

"Thought you'd want to know," said Morin, rising. She reached out her hand. "I'll let you know when they finish testing the lock we took out of the back door. It might be a couple of weeks. The lab is backed up, and they're very picky. Pun intended." Morin chuckled at her own joke, but Brenda wasn't laughing. She was worried about Sam. "Nice working with you, Chief Harrison. Until next time."

"Please God, let it not be another school shooting."

Morin mocked a shudder. "No, please, not that. I hope to never see one again."

After she left, Brenda wondered how to tell Sam that her nightmare wasn't over.

❉❉❉

Courtney arranged her things on the desk in the small office she shared with the assistant principal of the middle school. Now that her students had been divided up between the other schools in the district, she didn't understand what her role was supposed to be. Her return to work probably had less to do with the need for her services than with her contract. When they'd offered her more leave, Courtney had decided not to take it. She needed the money and to keep this job. If she and Melissa wanted to buy a house, they both needed a steady income.

She'd decided to come in today because there was no one at home. Kaylee was back at school. Melissa had returned to Boston to finish the deal with the clients she'd abandoned on the day of the shooting. The firm hadn't taken any time out of Melissa's billings, so she'd still make her quota for the quarter, which was a huge relief.

"Settling in, I see," said Courtney's office mate. Michelle Stevers, a large woman whose breasts preceded her when she walked into a room. As Melissa's mother liked to say, "they grow 'em big in Maine."

"I don't want to get too settled in," said Courtney. "I hope to be back in my own school soon."

"Oh, I bet you do," Michelle said with the exaggerated sympathy she might use with a child whose pet rabbit had died. "Did they tell you when they'll be finished cleaning up?"

Courtney shook her head. "I heard it's mostly done. They're still working on the gym. They had to replace the drywall in my office because it was shot up and covered in blood. Fortunately, these things survived." She pointed to the pictures of her daughter on the desk, the pen set her old school had given her, and her framed diplomas and certificates leaning against the bookcase.

"I'm sure your office needed a sprucing up before this happened. Now, it will be all fresh and new."

Courtney sighed. "It will never be the same again." She expected Michelle would understand she was talking about more than her office.

This time, the assistant principal's sympathy was genuine. "Are you afraid to go back there?"

Courtney scrutinized the woman's kind face to see if she could trust her. Gossips thrived in school districts. Courtney decided she had nothing to lose by telling the truth. "A little," she finally admitted.

"I would be too," said Michelle in a barely audible tone.

"I can't even imagine how Susan Gedney will get through this," said Courtney. "The poor woman had a gun to her head. The shooter's blood sprayed all over her. How can you forget something like that? I wonder if she has nightmares."

"She's a minister, isn't she?" asked Michelle.

"Yes, an Episcopal priest."

"Maybe that helps her cope."

"I don't know. She doesn't talk much about her other job. When she's in school, she's a teacher, not one bit religious."

"Good that she honors the separation of church and state. Not all teachers do. I feel bad for her, but I really feel sorry for the kids." Michelle lowered her voice. "Honestly, if I had kids in that school, I'd move to another town and never look back."

"That might happen," said Courtney. "People might leave town."

"How's your daughter handling it?"

"Kaylee is really into the news. She tells me what's going on. I can't watch TV. It's like reliving the whole thing all over again."

"I know exactly what you mean. I wish they would just stop talking about it. And I wish all these people would leave town. I'm sick of them. They come right up to you in the supermarket and stick a microphone in your face. And all the junk people sent. I feel like saying, 'Hey, we're hurting here. Just leave us alone!'"

"I wish they would all go. My voicemail is full of messages asking for interviews."

"It's against school policy to give interviews without the superintendent's permission."

"Hah! I wouldn't talk to them anyway. I don't even know how they got my number."

"The press can find out anything." Michelle sighed. "I hope you feel safe here."

Courtney stared at her. "I thought I was safe in my school with that state-of-the-art security system. Bullet-proof windows. Hardened steel barriers. When the time came, what did it do for us? Do you feel safe?"

Michelle looked uneasy. "Not really."

"I'll tell you the truth. I'll never feel safe again."

***

Liz opened the front door and found a very tall woman wearing a faux fur scarf around her neck, an elegant black coat, and stiletto-heeled boots that went up to her knees.

"Denise! I thought you were in Prague."

"I finished my gig there. I was heading to the Mediterranean to take some time off when I heard what happened here."

"Emily's not home."

"Not yet. She'll be here soon. I just arrived before she did. I was hoping you'd let me in next door."

"There's no heat over there. I'll have to turn it on. Nice of Emily to tell me she was coming home," Liz grumbled, looking around outside.

"I think she called her mother to let her know."

Liz hadn't talked to Lucy since she'd left that morning. Usually, she texted when something important came up, but between funerals and grief counseling, she was swamped. Liz opened the door wider, but Denise looked reluctant to come in. "Come on, Denise. It's too cold to wait for Emily outside." Denise glanced over her shoulder at the luggage piled by the garage door. "Don't worry. It's safe there. No one will take it. Before I leave, I'll go over there to turn on the heat and bring it through the bay door. You can take it upstairs later."

Denise finally stepped inside. "You're sure it's okay?"

"Just because I wouldn't let you move in doesn't mean you're not welcome. It's fine for you to be here as Emily's guest. I'm on the way out the door. I'm meeting Tom Simmons in..." Liz glanced at her watch. "...fifteen minutes. And it takes twenty minutes to get there. I'm sorry, but you're on your own until Emily gets here. Now, take off your coat and make yourself comfortable. You're welcome to anything you find in the kitchen. There's chicken salad I made this morning and bread in the drawer. Help yourself."

"Thanks, Liz. I do appreciate it," said Denise, slipping off her coat.

On the way to Webhanet, Liz carefully observed the speed limit in the areas where she knew the police might be lurking, but leaned on the gas pedal everywhere else. As she raced down the back roads to avoid the traffic, she planned what she would say to Tom. With shrinks, she usually found it helpful to get her story straight ahead of time. Lucy would probably say it was self-defeating, but she didn't care. She was only talking to Tom because Lucy had insisted.

When she arrived at Tom's house, she had to park right behind his car. The driveway had been hastily cleared by hand and was still partially blocked. Between the non-stop snowstorms and the press vehicles and buses parked everywhere, the plow trucks couldn't find time for their residential customers.

Tom came to the door, looking relaxed in jeans and a Fair Isle sweater. "Come in," he encouraged with a warm hug. "Jeff is making us a pot of tea. He brought home some delightful scones from the bakery. I know it's a professional visit, but we might as well be civilized."

"Sorry to be late, Tom. I was just about to leave when Denise Chantal showed up on my doorstep."

"I thought she was living in Boston. What brings her back to Hobbs?"

"She was heading for a warm vacation between engagements when she heard about the shooting. Emily's coming home too."

"That's what people do when there's a family tragedy. They come home to be with their people. You can decline a baptism or a wedding, but not a funeral. Nothing brings us together like death."

Tom ushered her into the room overlooking the ocean. "We could meet in my office, but I like the light in here. Jeff promised to hide on the other side of the house to give us privacy. You don't mind?"

Liz looked down at the surf crashing loudly on the rocky beach at the foot of the cliff. "How could I mind? It's beautiful and inspiring."

"Good. That's what I'd hoped you'd say. I'll be right back." He left and returned with a tray bearing an artisan tea pot, two mugs, and a plate of scones.

"Thanks for giving me something to eat. I rushed out without having lunch."

Tom looked at his watch. "Late for that, isn't it?"

"I was doing telehealth visits. Some of my patients refuse to be seen by one of my partners. I guess I lost track of time." Liz frowned. "I've been doing that a lot lately. Awake at night and napping during the day."

"I don't need to tell you that's a symptom."

"No, you don't," agreed Liz, already feeling uncomfortable.

"It was clever of Lucy to blackmail you into coming to see me," said Tom, pouring the tea. He handed Liz a cup.

"She knows I hate dealing with shrinks."

Tom clucked his tongue. "Still hasn't cured you of using that word. You're incorrigible."

Liz shrugged. "It's been said."

Tom sat back with his teacup and crossed his legs. "Let's not waste time. Knowing you, you've been trying to figure out what went wrong. Have you come up with any answers?"

"I should have left the negotiations for the FBI agent. Maybe he could have gotten Peter to release the hostages without me getting into the room with him."

"Do you really believe that?"

"No," Liz admitted. "The man was an idiot."

Tom thoughtfully stirred his tea. "I've read the transcripts, and it sounds to me like Peter Langdon had decided to kill Susan before you got there. After taking down the gym teacher, she was the one he was after."

"Maybe I could have talked him out of it. I thought I was getting somewhere."

"I don't think so," said Tom conclusively. He raised his cup to his lips and took a sip. "I think he'd decided to kill her, and there was nothing you could have said to stop him."

"I didn't want to kill him. I shot to disarm him instead. That's against police protocol, you know."

"It's clear that you only killed him because you had no other choice. How do you feel about that?"

"I killed someone. How do you think I feel?"

"I don't know, Liz. That's why I asked." His blue eyes peered at her over his teacup. "You still haven't figured out how you feel, have you?"

"I feel terrible."

"Terrible is not an emotion, Liz."

"No, it's not. All right, I feel guilty. That's why I asked Lucy to give me absolution."

Tom looked more amused than surprised. "You did?"

"What can I say?" said Liz, looking out the window. "I was desperate."

"Desperate enough to retreat to childhood magical thinking. You Catholics always end up back there as a last resort. I hear lots of deathbed confessions."

Liz stared disapprovingly. "Tom, you're a priest. Don't you believe in your own magic?"

"Private confession is rare in the Episcopal Church, as I'm sure Lucy already told you. It's a holdover from our Catholic roots, and it's remained for a reason. There are situations where a person is so consumed with guilt they think only God can forgive the sin. The real magic of penance is not the absolution, but the confession. The act of admitting the terrible deed, unburdening oneself of it by telling another, is what makes someone feel better. Did it work that way for you?"

"It helped a little. What helped more were the questions Lucy asked me."

Tom's white beard almost hid the fact that he was compressing his lips. "She was doing a little therapy with you, such as she can do as your wife."

"She made me cry."

"Ah, that's good. I bet it's hard for you to cry."

"When I was training to be a surgeon, we were told to suck it up. 'Lost a patient on the table? Tough, but all in a day's work.'"

"I bet they don't say that anymore."

"No, now they sit around and talk about it."

"Which is the healthy way to deal with it. Just out of curiosity, what did Lucy say to make you cry?"

"It wasn't what she said. She sang for me after an abortive attempt at sex."

"Oh, Liz, music gets you every time. But I'm glad something helped you process your emotions." He studied her. "Why do you say your sex was abortive?"

"Lucy pushed me away because I was too rough."

"Oh, dear. I bet that brought up memories of her rape."

"That's what she said."

"So why did you do it?"

"Lucy figured out that I wanted her to push me away."

Tom shook his head. "That rape nearly destroyed her. Think of how your behavior frightened her. No matter how bad you feel about yourself, never do that again."

Liz deadpanned, but she knew Tom was right.

# Chapter 12

Although Susan understood the rationale for getting the children back to school, especially after the setbacks from all the COVID interruptions, she thought it was too soon. She knew because she wasn't ready to go back. Recurring nightmares woke her nearly every night. Flashbacks came at the strangest times—at an intersection, in the supermarket, at morning prayer. She trembled for no reason, no matter how high they raised the thermostat in the rectory. When she washed her hair, she imagined feeling Peter Langdon's sticky blood matting the strands.

No one had forced her to come back. The district had offered her extended leave. She'd declined because her students had already been through so much. She wanted them to feel the security of seeing their regular teacher when they returned.

While she might be familiar to her students, she didn't recognize her class. Of the six boys who had survived the shooting, only two had returned to school. One of the critically wounded had died, and three boys were still in the hospital, one in intensive care. He'd been a bright child, interested in maps. Susan liked maps too. In the closet, they'd found an old globe from the 1950s. The African countries had their colonial names: Belgian Congo, Rhodesia, French Guinea, Gold Coast… James had listened attentively while Susan traced the new boundaries and told him the countries' modern names. He'd been shot in the head and suffered brain damage. When he awoke from his medically induced coma, the doctors expected him to be mentally disabled.

Susan glanced at the clock. There wasn't enough time to start a new lesson, so she would read aloud from *Little Women*. She'd been introducing the classics because they'd given her so much comfort in her grandparents' crazy house when she was young. She'd gotten through two chapters by the time the bell rang. The boys instantly jumped up, noisily throwing their books into their backpacks. The girls packed up too, but more quietly. Susan lined them up at the door to head out to the buses.

They left, but her day wasn't done. Lucy had assigned her to afternoon calling hours at the funeral home. She'd asked if Susan wanted to be excused, especially because the dead children had been her students. Trying to assure her that she was able to do *all* her pastoral duties, Susan had insisted.

The truth was, she dreaded this wake. In her years as a priest, none of the rituals of death had repulsed her, not even anointing the dying with the cloying smell of the sickroom in the background. This was different. All the caskets would be closed because the bodies had been damaged beyond recognition.

Susan didn't have to see the dark-haired boy, who'd sat in the third row, to imagine him lying pale and still on a satin pillow. She'd met his parents earlier in the school year at the parent-teacher conference. They were affable, salt-of-the-earth people. The mother ran a four-chair beauty salon. The father worked the service counter at the local Ford dealership. She'd liked them instantly, especially the mother with her platinum blond hair highlighted with bubblegum-pink strands.

Because she had this after-school duty, Susan had worn a classic charcoal-gray wool suit she'd found in a thrift store. In a tight stall in the faculty bathroom, she put on a clerical stock with the collar attached over her black shirt. Without good light and a close inspection, no one would notice it wasn't a real linen collar.

The funeral director had texted Susan instructions to park in the space reserved for clergy. When she approached the funeral home, she could see why. The street was lined with cars all the way back to the intersection. Every space in the parking area was taken. Trucks and SUVs had climbed ice banks for a place to park. Despite the extreme cold, the line of mourners looped twice around the parking lot. It was as if the entire town had shown up.

Susan took a deep breath to calm herself before getting out of her car. Students from the elementary school, their parents, and parishioners waved as she passed. When she entered the building, an usher, wearing an impeccably pressed dark suit, directed her toward the viewing room. She'd never seen so many young children in a funeral home. Usually, parents spared them this awful duty until they were older.

"Ms. Gedney," called a small voice. "Hi, Ms. Gedney." The girl's huge brown eyes, staring at her collar, made her stop.

"Hello, Charlotte," she said, bending so her face was at the same level as the girl's. "How are you? Okay?" Susan nodded to encourage a positive response. She patted the girl's cheek. "I'll see you inside." The girl flung her arms around Susan's neck and hung on. Her dead weight felt like it was dragging Susan deeper into the abyss of her own sorrow. Humbled, she gently returned the girl's desperate embrace. She'd come to comfort these children and their families with her prayers, but what she had to give them seemed so meager and useless. *Thoughts and prayers.*

"Susan," called a voice behind her. She gently disentangled herself from the girl's arms so she could stand up and saw Reshma effortlessly flowing through the crowd. "Susan!" Her lips curved slightly, but she didn't quite smile because it was a sad occasion. Susan wondered if suppressing a smile was as hard as forcing one. "I came to help," Reshma explained.

"Does Lucy know you're here?" asked Susan suspiciously.

Reshma's smooth brow puckered into a frown. "I don't think so. I didn't tell her I was coming. Does she need to know?"

"I thought she might have sent you. In case I couldn't manage by myself."

Reshma bent to look directly into Susan's eyes. "This was my idea. I had last night's service. What a scene! Children screaming, parents breaking down. I've never seen anything like this. Have you?"

Susan shook her head.

"The lines get longer every day. People bring food to eat in line because they think they'll be waiting past dinnertime."

"But it's so cold."

"It doesn't seem to matter. A woman told me she just couldn't stay away. When you talk to them, some tell you they don't have kids in the school or even know the families. Some are from other towns, other states. One family came all the way from Connecticut, from the town where all the children were shot."

"Susan!" called a female voice. She turned around to greet Nathalie Griffin, the other third-grade teacher. She knew that Susan was a priest, but stared at her collar. With all the scrutiny it was getting, Susan worried that someone might notice that it was just a stock with a fake collar attached.

"Come on," said Reshma, tugging on Susan's arm. "I found the best place to stand is with the family. We can help keep the line moving. Otherwise, the people waiting outside will never get in."

Listening to the visitors, Susan learned that many had grown up in Hobbs and been pupils in Hobbs Elementary, as had their parents and grandparents. This tragedy was washing over not just them, but generations. When children approached the small casket, some of them asked loud questions. Others began to cry. Susan wondered about the wisdom of bringing infants and toddlers until she realized their parents probably had no childcare at home.

People hugged Susan as if she was one of the family. They praised her for her bravery while she was a hostage. Some wondered how she could be there, comforting others when the experience was still so fresh. She wondered too.

Usually during a viewing, all the mourners gathered respectfully to listen to the prayers, but the line still wound around the parking lot, so the family had set an arbitrary time for the service. Susan had chosen some scriptural passages from the burial rite. She excelled at extemporaneous sermons, easily riffing on a Bible passage or a related current event. Because this occasion was so personal, she worried that she wouldn't remember her thoughts, so she'd written them down. At the end, she led the group in "The Lord's Prayer." Wondering if she could quietly slip away, she glanced at Reshma, who showed no sign of leaving.

"I need to go," Susan whispered in Reshma's ear. "Are you coming?"

"I can't. I have the evening service, and it looks like the break they planned for the family isn't going to happen. There are still people outside. I'll stay, so the parents can get away for a few minutes. They must be exhausted."

"I would stay with you, but I just can't."

"I understand. You worked all day, and this must be so hard for you." Reshma turned to her. "I thought Lucy shouldn't assign you to these services, but it was a wise decision, as always."

A young woman reached up to hug Susan. Feeling the warmth of the embrace, she finally realized why Lucy had sent her to do this service. She needed the comfort of these people more than they needed hers.

***

"After all this warm weather, I never thought the lake would freeze hard enough for ice fishing," said Brenda, relieved to be talking about something besides the shooting.

"I know, but do you think it's worth pulling out the ice shack?" asked Liz.

"Sure. Why not? If the ice is thick enough. Can't let the winter go by without getting in some fishing," Brenda agreed, refilling her glass with beer. "Maybe when Sam comes back, we can all go out together."

"Maybe," said Liz, but looked doubtful. "Nothing is the same, is it?"

"Nope," said Brenda. "Nothing." She knew they were no longer talking about fishing. She thought of Cherie at home with the kids.

She'd insisted that Brenda take a night off from childcare to do something 'normal.' "Go hang with Liz and drink some beer. We can't let this evil thing steal our lives, like a mugger that beats you up and takes everything you have. Don't let that happen, Brenda. Take it back!"

Brenda stretched out on the wicker settee and wiggled her woolly toes. She'd worn her thermal socks in case she got a call. "I'm glad all the agencies pulled up stakes and left. They were annoying the shit out of me. The FBI particularly. Feds always act like they know everything."

"Nothing like interference by people who think they know how to do your job better than you do. That's why I left Yale. When the accountants took over, it stopped being about patients. Oh, and the marketing people. They posed me every which way for publicity photos. I felt like a department store mannequin." Liz grinned. "Remember when they'd leave them naked before dressing them for the new season? Barbie Doll figures with pointy tits and no nipples. Just a blank between their legs. Could be any sex or neuter, or 'non-binary,' as they say now, but they were fully made-up, like women were in those days. Blue eyeshadow, thick black liner, dark mascara, the works!"

"I remember," said Brenda, thinking of how she'd stared at the naked dummies while her mother tried on dresses. She'd seen her mother's pendulous breasts and doughy belly after five kids and knew real women didn't look like that.

"When women were women," said Liz, raising her glass. "Not like us."

"What do you mean, not like us?" asked Brenda, taking her legs down from the settee.

"Well, you know. Cherie and Lucy and Maggie are that kind of woman. The kind men like."

"I tried to fit in," said Brenda. "Hell, I bleached my hair for thirty years!"

"It looks better now," said Liz. "But it does make you look older."

"Fuck, I should look older. I've earned every one of these grays. I've done plenty in my life. So have you. Who cares if we don't fit in?"

Liz sighed. "God knows my mother tried, but when I came out, first, she threw me out, then she disowned me. Best thing that ever happened to me. Made me grow up fast."

"I bet. Did you know I almost married a man?"

"No way!" Liz sat up and gave her a penetrating look. "How come you never told me?"

Brenda shrugged. "I probably didn't think you'd be interested. I gave back the ring. My mother was so disappointed."

"Our mothers were more brainwashed than we were. Sam's mother was Junior League. She went to a finishing school. She was raised to marry money. She wanted Sam to get the same advantages...by marrying a man."

"Speaking of Sam," said Brenda, seeing the perfect segue into the topic she'd been wanting to bring up. "I had a little chat the other day with the head of the state investigations unit."

"Don't tell me they're still thinking of charging her."

"No, no. Nothing like that. She didn't do anything wrong except leave the door open. She could have left that door open a hundred times and nothing would have ever happened. This one time, because she fired that kid, it ended in tragedy. Just one of those things."

"Do you really believe that, Brenda? Bad luck?" Obviously, Liz was in one of her philosophical moods.

"Well, she did have that strange feeling. Maybe that should have told her to go back inside, lock the door, and go around the other way."

"She was afraid of slopping grout water on the floor. See? This is where our mothers' training screws us. A guy would have just stomped through that atrium without a second thought!"

Brenda thought about it. "Maybe so."

"What did the investigator say?"

"She saw that ambulance chaser, the one who advertises on late-night TV. She was hanging around the families. Morin thinks there could be a lawsuit."

Liz put her legs up on the settee again. "Well, that would not surprise me."

"Really?" Brenda was afraid Liz would say that, and it worried her because she was good at guessing what would happen next. She'd correctly predicted the COVID pandemic when it was just a blip in the financial markets. "What do you think we should do?"

"We should warn her, of course. I'm sure she won't see it coming. She's not the suspicious type. Or cynical like me." Liz gulped down some beer.

"People sue for anything," Brenda said, shaking her head.

"Hell, some slick lawyer tells you that you might make a lot of money. What would you do? Remember that actress who brought the malpractice suit against me? She died a few months back. The breast cancer spread until it was everywhere. At the end, they did chemo, radiation, clinical trials, juice cures, everything."

"That's too bad, but don't you feel vindicated? Like she got what was coming to her?"

"No."

"No?" asked Brenda, surprised.

"Hell no! I feel sad. If she had only listened to me and done radiation when I told her to, she might still be alive. It's my job to keep people alive. That's why I became a doctor."

They were both silent for a long moment, but Brenda knew what Liz was thinking. "I'm glad that's why you became a doctor. Seems like many people go into it for the money."

"I also did it to impress Maggie. Even though she'd already married a man. The bitch."

"Liz, you need to get over that."

Liz crossed her arms, meaning she had no intention of getting over it.

"Will you call Sam?" Brenda asked. "I can't get involved because I may be called to testify."

Liz pursed her lips and thought for a minute. "Sure, I can call her, but first, we should ask Melissa's advice."

"Good idea." Brenda finished her beer and looked at her watch. Cherie would be putting the kids to bed about now, and she wanted to be home to kiss them good night. She got up and stretched, arching her back, which had begun to hurt whenever she sat too long. "I gotta go, Liz. Thanks for the beers."

"You're welcome. I'll let you know what Melissa says."

Brenda was rinsing out her glass when Lucy came into the kitchen. "How do you think she's doing?" she whispered, glancing through the window in the direction of the porch.

"Considering everything, she's okay." Brenda could tell from Lucy's worried look that she didn't agree.

"Tell the truth, Brenda."

"She's being Liz. What can I say? You're the expert. What do you think?"

Lucy's green eyes studied her for a long moment. "She's a little better now that she's been talking to Tom. Killing Peter really upset her. Have you ever had to kill someone?"

Brenda turned around and leaned against the counter, mirroring Lucy's position. "A perp threatened my partner, and I had no choice."

Lucy reached up to rub Brenda's shoulder. "I'm so sorry. How did you deal with it?"

"I took leave. The department provided counseling. I ended up leaving the homicide unit and going into community relations. Best thing I ever did." Brenda put her arm around Lucy's narrow shoulders. "I know you want to help, Lucy, but Liz has her own way of solving problems, and it usually works."

Lucy still looked doubtful. "I hope so."

\*\*\*

Bobbie completely trusted Teresa, a nurse with many years of experience. She'd confirmed Bobbie's suspicion that it might be RSV, the virus that was surging among small children and the elderly. Now that COVID was mostly under control, people forgot that there were other deadly respiratory viruses, like influenza and this old virus that had suddenly become virulent.

"Wouldn't she be better off in a hospital?" asked Teresa. It was an obvious question, but Bobbie was torn. Joyce's advanced directives specifically ruled out any extraordinary measures, including intubation.

"You know they'll put her on a vent. She doesn't want that."

"Perhaps a stronger decongestant and oxygen?" suggested Teresa. "I can set it up."

*What if this is the end?* There had been false alarms before. Despite everyone's best efforts and careful masking around Joyce, she'd come down with a cold that went into pneumonia. Bobbie and the others had done everything they could to keep her out of the hospital and off a ventilator, nursing her around the clock. To everyone's surprise, she'd pulled through.

After Teresa left to get the tank, Bobbie adjusted Joyce's pillows and tried to lift her, hoping it would help her breathe more easily. Even though they fed her nourishing high-calorie foods, Joyce was pitifully thin. She looked like it would be easy to move her, but the disease had left her rigid. She fought Bobbie's attempts to reposition her.

Bobbie studied Joyce's pale face. Her skin was so thin it was almost transparent. The lacy network of blue veins was clearly visible at her temples. Her prominent cheekbones had become sharp. *This is what a beautiful woman looks like at the end, a shadow of what she'd once been.*

Bobbie's phone vibrated in her pocket. The screen showed Susan's photo and phone number.

"Hey," said Bobbie softly, moving away from the bed for privacy, although Joyce was nonverbal now and probably couldn't understand the conversation. "How are you doing?"

"I just got back from doing a prayer service at a viewing. One of my students."

Susan didn't have to say more. Her tone indicated how difficult it had been, but Bobbie asked anyway. "How did it go?"

"The service went fine. I wish I could say I'm fine, too."

"I'm sorry." Bobbie watched Teresa wheel in the oxygen and took her conversation into another room. "Knowing it was your student in that casket must have been doubly hard."

"That wasn't the worst of it. Hundreds of people showed up. Everyone was sobbing. It was heartbreaking."

Bobbie could imagine the scene and the toll it had taken on Susan. "I'm sorry," she repeated.

"Bobbie, I'm struggling. Ordinarily, I'd ask Reshma to sit with me for a while, but she's still at the funeral home. Lucy is meeting with her bereavement group. I don't want to bother you, but I need to talk to someone."

"Did you call your sponsor?"

"We were on the phone for over an hour. That's why I'm calling so late."

Bobbie looked at her watch. It was a quarter past nine, not terribly late. "I'm sorry, Susan, but I'm in a bind. Joyce is having trouble breathing, and we're trying to stabilize her. Can I call you back?"

"No, don't bother," said Susan. "I'll be fine."

Bobbie recognized that brave tone women use to dismiss their crises. Susan had so much practice she sounded more convincing than most. Teresa came out of Joyce's room and waved to her, leaving Bobbie torn between her past and her future. She knew that this situation could be a real threat to Susan's sobriety. But Joyce might be dying. She couldn't leave her. "Susan, I have to go. I'll call you back in a few minutes."

***

Liz listened to Bobbie describe Joyce's condition in the precise medical terms that told her everything she needed to know. "Yes, it sounds like it could be RSV," she agreed. She'd read Joyce's advance directives, so she could guess why Bobbie was calling her instead of an ambulance. "Do you want me to come over?"

"No, I think we have it handled. Honestly, I don't want to get you involved because of the DNR, but I appreciate the offer."

"Okay. So, what can I do to help?"

"It's Susan I'm worried about. That wake tonight really got to her. And the convenience store down the street is a little too convenient, if you know what I mean."

"I do," said Liz, glancing at the thermometer by the kitchen window that showed both the inside and outside temperature. Inside, it was a pleasantly warm sixty-eight degrees. Outside, it was twelve. She really didn't look forward to going out into the cold, but she heard the desperation in Bobbie's voice.

She quickly calculated the benefit of getting involved in a problem that wasn't hers. If Susan fell off the wagon, it would cause an unnecessary crisis that would impact everyone. With everything else going on, they didn't need that too. "All right. I'll go to the rectory and see what I can do."

"Thanks, Liz. I'll call her and tell her you're coming."

Liz tapped off the call and berated herself for volunteering. This was how she always ended up in charge of everything. It was also how she'd ended up in the principal's office with Peter Langdon. Wanting to help was dangerous. She composed a text to Lucy to tell her where she was going.

It was snowing lightly when Liz pulled the truck out of the garage. She made a sharp turn in the driveway to avoid hitting Denise's car. The property service they'd hired to clear the driveway hadn't pushed the snow back far enough. Anticipating she'd get the commission in California, Sam had warned Liz that she might not be able to plow that season. It was strange how things were the same for a long time, and then suddenly weren't. While they were the same, you hardly thought about them until they changed and required attention.

Only the back door light was on at the rectory. Although Liz had a key from working on the wiring and plumbing in the building, walking in unannounced didn't feel right, so she rang the bell. The light came on in the hallway, and a moment later, Susan's pale face was visible through the glass. She unlocked the dead bolt and opened the door.

"Liz, thank you so much for coming. I must be in bad shape for Bobbie to call the doctor."

"She didn't call me as a doctor. She called me as your friend." Liz wouldn't ordinarily say something like that to Susan, but tonight, she looked like she needed a friend. Liz tapped the snow off her boots before stepping inside. She pulled off her cap and slapped it against her thigh a few times.

"You didn't have to come all the way over here in the snow," said Susan, locking the door behind her. "You could have called."

"Well, because I'm a doctor, I like to see people to judge how they're doing. That's why I'm not wild about this telehealth thing."

"I doubt you would be. You're a traditionalist like me."

Liz raised Susan's face by the chin and scrutinized it.

"How do I look?"

"Like hell." Liz grinned, but she wasn't kidding.

Susan shook her head. "That's one thing I can always count on, Liz. You always tell the truth."

The wet soles of Liz's boots squeaked as they made their way down the tiled hall and up the polished steps. When Susan opened the door to the rector's apartment, warm air blasted out. Liz's eyes quickly located the source of the heat, a small quartz heater. Although it was probably eighty-five degrees in that room, Susan was wearing a heavy sweater.

"Nice and warm in here, Susan. Still having chills?"

"So Lucy told you I'm running up the heating bill. I'm not actually cold, but I keep trembling."

"PTSD will do that." Liz peeled off her parka. Susan took it and hung it on the old-fashioned coat tree by the door.

"Would you like a cup of tea?"

"If you have decaf or I'll be up all night. It's bad enough I keep Lucy up with my nightmares."

"You have them too?"

"And flashbacks. I keep seeing the look in Peter's eyes when I shot him in the arm."

Susan blinked, probably feeling the blood spray on her face the way Liz did when she'd described shooting Peter. "What did he look like?" Susan asked. Unfortunately, that meant Liz had to relive the scene again.

"Shocked that I had a gun. Surprised that I'd shot him. For a split second, he looked sad. Like I'd betrayed him...because I had. Then his eyes were full of fury. That's when I knew I had to decide."

"Dear God," Susan breathed. "What I remember is bad enough. Sit down while I put the kettle on to boil."

"You should get an electric teapot. They're faster. I think we have an extra. I can give it to you."

"Thanks, but I like the old-fashioned way. The whistle is so cheerful. Except I worry about disturbing Reshma."

"Not a chance," said Liz, sitting down. "These old walls are way too thick. You're fine."

While Susan was in the kitchen fixing the tea, Liz looked around. The walls were covered with bookcases. In one corner, there was an antique roll-top desk with an old-fashioned desk blotter on the surface. Liz wondered where they still sold blotting paper. She browsed Susan's books, finding Bible exegeses and Gospel commentaries by the dozens. Lucy had them too. One bookcase was devoted to literary classics, including a complete "Modern Library." She hadn't known that Susan was so well read. She rose a notch in Liz's estimation.

Susan brought in the tea and set it down on the table near the matching club chairs.

"I hope you don't mind me looking at your books," said Liz.

"Please, go ahead. If you see anything you'd like to read, I'd be happy to lend it to you."

Lending someone a real book felt so neighborly and old-fashioned. "Thanks. It was bad enough I had to read Lucy's theology books when she was getting her degree."

"Yes, they can be a heavy slog. I didn't know how you like your tea, but I brought out half and half and sugar. That's how Lucy takes hers." Liz looked at her, not with any specific emotion, but Susan hurried to add. "Don't worry, Liz. That's all in the past."

"I'm not worried," Liz said truthfully.

Susan gestured to one of the club chairs. "Have a seat." Liz sat down while Susan poured the tea. "Reshma often comes over and we have what she calls a 'tea party.' They used to have high tea at her boarding school to teach the girls manners."

"I didn't know she went to boarding school."

"A group of churches in Maine adopted her and another refugee girl and sent them to an Episcopal school in New Hampshire." Susan handed Liz a china cup on a saucer. It felt so delicate and fragile, an alien thing from another time. "I'm surprised Lucy didn't tell you."

"Lucy is close-mouthed about people. She mostly lets them tell their own stories."

"A good practice. I should follow it," said Susan with a decisive nod and took a sip of tea.

Liz didn't understand. This visit felt like dropping in on a neighbor for tea, not a five-alarm emergency requiring a doctor's presence. "Susan, why did Bobbie think I needed to come here tonight? You seem fine."

"I wished out loud that the convenience store wasn't within walking distance. Maybe she got the wrong idea. You don't know me very well, and you've seen me at my worst, but ordinarily, drama isn't my style." Liz nodded, only to acknowledge she'd heard. "Before I called her, I'd bent my sponsor's ear for over an hour."

"Bobbie told me you found the service at the funeral home difficult."

"It was an unnerving experience. No sugar coating that."

"Lucy looked like a ghost when she came home from the wake last night. She said the lines go around the parking lot. People are coming from everywhere." Liz took a sip of tea and found it comforting. Back in college, Maggie used to make her strong, sweet tea when she was stressed about an exam. "What do all these people want?"

"To express their sympathy...their shock...their sorrow for all those dead children. They want to let us know that we're not alone." Susan sighed. "Did you know I lost almost half my class in that shooting?"

"No. That's terrible. Why would Lucy send you to do that prayer service?"

"Actually, it was the right thing to do. She's forcing me to get back into the community. I thought I was consoling people, but they were consoling me." Susan reached out a plate of shortbread cookies, but Liz shook her head. Sweets didn't usually appeal to her. "Reshma likes these," Susan explained. "That's the reason I buy them. I certainly don't need the extra calories."

"Neither do I."

Susan bit into a cookie and chewed thoughtfully. "I've been wanting to talk to you."

"Lucy told me." Watching Susan eat the cookie, Liz changed her mind and took one. "I'm sorry, but I haven't been up to it."

Susan's calculated look reminded Liz of when Lucy slipped into her therapist's role. She hoped Susan wasn't going to try to counsel her. "I understand, but I wanted to thank you for saving my life. I will be forever grateful for your bravery."

"Everyone keeps telling me how brave I was. The truth is, I was scared shitless." She grimaced at the obscenity.

"It's all right, Liz. I've heard that word before."

"I went in to talk to Peter because everyone expected me to solve the problem. That's what I do...most of the time."

"Yes, you do. As a doctor, and an important member of this community. But you risked your life to save mine. You saved several lives that day. Maybe many more."

"But not Peter's. I'd hoped we'd all get out of there alive, but we didn't." Liz took another bite of the cookie and decided it was good. She might have another. "Were you praying the whole time?"

"Actually, yes. I made a good act of contrition and prayed for all of us, but especially for you."

"Why me?"

"I knew that you might have to make a terrible choice between me and that young man. I sensed that he cared for you, and you cared for him. I can't imagine how you feel, but I know you'll always regret killing him."

"No one knows what it's like to kill until you've done it. Brenda tells me it breaks cops. After they kill someone, some quit or ask to be reassigned, so they never have to be in that position again. Soldiers returning from war are driven crazy by the killing. Once you've killed, you're never the same again. Never innocent. There's always blood on your hands."

"I'm sure it will haunt you for the rest of your life. But Peter is at peace now. Imagine the terrible guilt he'd suffered over being touched by his teacher, his pain at being betrayed by his parents. You released him from that misery. He asked for you to listen to his story. He trusted you to listen to it with compassion and understanding. In the end, he trusted you to take his life."

Liz's eyes had filled while Susan was talking. She tried to blink them away. When they refused to stop, she stared at her feet. "I don't see it that way."

Susan put down her teacup. She waited until Liz had composed herself before speaking. "I know you don't, but I pray that someday you can."

# PART III

# Chapter 13

Soaring above the clouds was the one aspect of long-distance flying that Maggie still enjoyed. Otherwise, flying had become a nightmare of delays, cancellations, missed connections, and unannounced schedule changes. She'd arrived in California to find the airline had lost her luggage. She always packed a carry-on with a day's worth of clothes, but her bags had shown up by nightfall. Today, her departure from Oakland had been delayed for almost an hour by storms in the Midwest. She hoped her driver in Boston had checked the status updates.

The annoyances confirmed that a long-distance relationship wouldn't be easy. Then Sam had thrown her completely off balance by saying how much she liked Berkeley and wouldn't mind living there. Maggie had dismissed the comment as wishful thinking, like people looking at the local real estate offerings on vacation. But now that she'd seen Sam in her little Airbnb apartment with a pool and vividly colored flowers outside her back door, she could picture her living there. She seemed so alive working on this museum, happier than Maggie had ever seen her.

When they'd first met, shortly after Liz had proposed, Sam's career as prize-winning architect was already in the rear-view mirror. Sam was still doing small jobs, mostly renovations, but no major construction, and she'd seemed content. Now, Maggie was seeing a different Sam, a more engaged, confident woman. She'd even accepted an invitation from the UCB architecture faculty to teach a seminar on modern design aesthetics.

"I couldn't have done this without you, Maggie," Sam said humbly when Maggie mentioned the change. "You made me feel good about myself again." Maggie didn't know what she had done, and Sam, who was a woman of few words, couldn't articulate it more clearly, but whatever it was, it was working.

Gazing at the gauzy clouds through the plane window, Maggie wondered if she could take another big move. When she'd left New York to live with Liz, she'd been younger. Now, she was almost seventy. Moving to Scarborough after the divorce hadn't felt like a big dislocation. At the beach, she was still stepping into the same ocean. When Sam had invited Maggie to move in, she'd been delighted to be back in the town where she had friends and knew the layout of the supermarket. She'd finally felt settled again.

Early in her marriage to Barry Krusick, his engineering job had taken them here, there, and everywhere. Maggie had blamed their vagabond life for her inability to conceive. To mollify his wife, Barry took a pay cut to work in the corporate office, but their center-hall colonial in a suburb of Stamford had provided the perfect address and a sense of security that Maggie had lacked as a child. The divorce settlement gave her the Connecticut house, which she'd sold after the girls had gone off to college. By then, she was teaching in New York, and the commute was too long. Her coop in the Village, within walking distance to NYU, was the first home completely in her name. Cramped as it was, she'd felt at home there. Moving to Maine to be with Liz had literally been a sea change. Could she uproot herself again?

*You're getting ahead of yourself,* Maggie told herself. *One step at a time.* Sam hadn't specifically said that she wanted to move, but she was anxious about what was going on at home, especially after receiving a  check from the town for the balance owed on her work in the school bathroom along with her invoice marked "paid in full."

Last night's Zoom meeting with Melissa and Liz had given them an uncomfortable preview of what Sam might face on her return. While Liz had summarized her conversation with Brenda in that annoyingly dispassionate doctor's voice, the set of Sam's jaw had revealed her growing anxiety.

"Melissa, do they even have a case?" she'd asked.

"I don't think so, but a personal injury lawyer usually works on contingency. They only get paid if they can get a settlement, so they usually don't take the case unless they think they can win it."

"Is there *anything* I can do?"

"You might try heading off a suit by making a gesture of support for the families, such as a contribution to the funeral expenses. Liz tells me you have a trust fund."

"But I don't get it until my mother dies, and she's very much alive. Until then, I only get an allowance." It was strange to think of a woman in her sixties getting an allowance, but Maggie knew it was enough for Sam to live on without having to work.

"I know the funeral director," Liz had said. "Maybe we can work out a deal."

"You mean like a quantity discount?" Sam's tone had sounded more angry than cynical. "Yeah, Liz, you know all about lawsuits."

"Don't go by me, Sam. When my attorney suggested I prepare for a malpractice suit, I thought she was kidding. Obviously, the case was frivolous, but the patient started talking up her intentions to the tabloids. After that, it was like a runaway train. I think Melissa is giving you good advice."

At the end of the meeting, Sam had stabbed the red button to leave it so hard that Maggie was surprised the screen didn't break. When she'd tried to bring it up later, Sam had snapped at her, "It's my problem, and I'll handle it." But she didn't sleep that night. The next day, it was like the meeting had never happened.

Maggie was glad that Liz was looking out for her friend, but that's what she did. What Sam would do was another question.

Despite the blower blasting in Maggie's face, the stagnant air on the plane made her drowsy. The dull roar of the engines was ironically soothing. She glanced at the time on her tablet. Three hours until they reached Boston. There was plenty of time to take a little nap, so she slid down the plastic window shade and released her seatback.

\*\*\*

Lucy was pleased to see Liz getting along so well with Denise. She'd invited her and Emily for dinner. Now the three of them were deeply involved in one of those brainy conversations that could make Lucy's eyes cross. At least, they were talking about music, which Lucy knew something about. When Erika was still alive, she and Liz would go down some philosophical rabbit hole, leaving Lucy stranded.

Fortunately, no one had asked her to contribute to the conversation because she was spent. So many services, one right after the other, had drained her emotionally. Her online bereavement group had grown so large she'd decided to break it in two, so everyone had a chance to speak. Tom had volunteered to take over the second group. "Since you're doing it on Zoom, I can continue even if I'm not in Hobbs." Lucy secretly panicked whenever he talked about leaving, but when she asked how long he planned to stay, he always gave the same answer: "As long as I'm needed."

Someone's cell phone played loud music. "Excuse me, but that's mine," said Denise. "It's probably my travel agent."

While Denise was on the phone in the other room, Emily turned to Liz. "Thank you for inviting Denise and being so nice to her."

Liz frowned. "Emily, I like Denise. Why wouldn't I be nice? She's always welcome...*as your guest.*" Apart from the little edge in her voice, Liz was hiding her frustration well. No doubt she thought the question of where Denise would live had been settled. So did Lucy.

"Don't worry," said Emily with the hint of a pout. "She promised to leave when I go back to school next week."

"Good," said Liz. "I'm glad we all understand each other."

Emily raised her eyebrows, which Lucy guessed was really a frown. Since heading to Yale, Emily had made progress in emoting successfully, but intense situations still challenged her. "She says she came back here because she misses her family. That's us, isn't it?"

"I think she also means Reshma, and her friends at St.

Margaret's," sid Lucy. "Denise made lots of friends when she was music director there."

"She told me her mother won't speak to her since she transitioned," said Emily, looking appropriately sad. "We're her only family now."

Across the table, Liz engaged Lucy's eyes. She was waiting for her to handle the situation because Emily was her daughter, but Lucy didn't know what to say. Liz had clearly explained why she didn't want a permanent tenant in the garage apartment. She'd only allowed Emily to occupy the place during school breaks to give her a place to entertain her friends.

Denise returned to the kitchen. "Well, I'm glad that's settled. My travel agent got me a full refund for the vacation I canceled. Once she'd told them I had to come home because of the shooting, they agreed without question."

"I'm sure that's a relief," said Lucy."

"I'm finally making decent money, but I can't just throw it away. It's bad enough I pay rent for an apartment where I never stay." Lucy was sympathetic. During her singing career, she'd paid for an expensive apartment in New York because she'd needed a legal address and a place to keep her belongings. "I've been renting month to month," said Denise, "but the landlord is pushing me to sign a lease, for a rent I can't afford. I guess I need to start looking for another place."

When Emily and Denise came to dinner, they were on cleanup, but Liz suddenly jumped up and began clearing the table. She hated housekeeping chores, so she was only dealing with the dishes because the conversation was making her fidgety.

"Boston is high on the list of the most expensive cities," said Lucy, keeping an eye on Liz. The clatter of the dishes in the sink was louder than usual. "Unfortunately, rents in any big city will be expensive. Have you considered living in Europe?"

"Oh!" Denise cried dramatically. "It's even worse there!"

"I've heard there are cities in Italy and Spain where rents are still reasonable."

"Believe me, Lucy. I've looked into it."

Liz spun around. "All right, Denise, you can live in Emily's apartment," she said in an exasperated tone. "But she's family, and we don't charge her rent. If you move in, I expect you to pay for the utilities and give me some notice when you blow into town, so I can turn on the heat."

Everyone turned to her in surprise.

"Wow," said Denise. "I wasn't expecting that. Thank you."

Despite Emily's impaired ability to show emotion, she pumped her fists in a silent cheer.

Liz squeezed the water out of the sponge like she intended to kill it.

Lucy said, "Honey, Emily and Denise are supposed to do the dishes."

"Yes, Liz, I wish you'd sit down," said Denise. "I have an idea I want to run by you."

"Well, in that case," said Liz, returning to her seat.

"Denise wants to do a concert to raise money for the victims' families," Emily blurted out.

Lucy looked at Denise to see if she was disappointed to have her big announcement preempted, but she smiled at Emily affectionately. Their on-and-off romance was clearly on again.

"Lucy, I heard that your '*Pie Jesu*' at the prayer service brought everyone to tears," said Denise. "In November, I sang the *Duruflé Requiem* in Nice. What do you think about a concert like the one we did at the Cathedral? We could sing selections from modern requiems—Fauré, Duruflé, Rutter, Lloyd Webber...Britten has interesting moments. Maybe we can even dip into the nineteenth century a teensy bit and do some Verdi or Brahms. But nothing too loud. It should be soothing for the children." She anxiously leaned forward to read Lucy's face. "What do you think?"

"Hmm," intoned Lucy. Since the shooting, she hadn't felt much like singing. She'd continued her relentless practice for the new production of *Lohengrin* because she'd made the deal with Liz.

Liz, who'd been listening with her arms crossed on her chest, said, "It sounds like a good idea, but don't count on Lucy. She's rehearsing day and night for the Met performance. Plus, she's swamped with counseling." Lucy appreciated how Liz always defended her from demands on her time, but she liked the idea of a fund-raising concert.

"Most people had to put the funeral costs on credit cards that were already maxed out. Many of the parents lost time from work. Plus, there are medical expenses for the children in the hospital. There's so much need. I'll do what I can, Denise."

"Even if you sing one number. You know, dueling '*Pie Jesu*'s'. The one that gets the most tears wins." Denise grinned. Lucy laughed, but it was a clever idea. "Lucy, we need you as the headliner. You have the name recognition. I can bring friends from Boston and some of the people I've met in Europe, but no one has the box-office draw you do."

"I bet Olivia would help organize it," Liz suggested. "She has a talent for squeezing money out of people and she's buddies with that asshole, the bishop." Lucy shot Liz a disapproving look, but it was true that Olivia had the bishop wrapped around her finger, and no one could raise money like she could.

"Denise, are you sure you have time for this?" Lucy asked. "Aren't you booked?"

"I am. But I have a break in my schedule at the end of March. If someone could organize the event from here, and we can settle on the program, I could work it in."

"We could talk to Melissa about setting up a foundation," Liz said with a faint note of enthusiasm. She was warming to the idea. "That would be a perfect way for Sam to funnel money to help pay for the funerals."

"Sam McKinnon?" asked Denise, raising a perfectly tweezed eyebrow. "What does she have to do with it?"

"You weren't here, and the police have been trying to keep it quiet," Liz explained. "The shooter got into the school through the back door. Sam left it open while she was cleaning her tools."

Denise's blue eyes grew wide. "Shit," she said under her breath.

"Yes, shit. The police cleared Sam of criminal negligence, but there are rumors of civil lawsuits," Liz said. "Melissa Morgenstern suggested Sam donate money to the families to head them off."

Lucy always enjoyed watching Liz's mind work. The whole thing had come together in her mind as a full-blown plan, but she patiently answered questions and listened while they worked out the details.

At the end of the discussion, Denise raised her palm for a high-five. "Let's do this!"

❊❊❊

Olivia sat at the kitchen table to keep Amy company while she washed the dishes. She loved the familiarity of this ritual because it implied a settled domesticity that felt comfortable. In her marriage to Michael Enright, she'd felt strangled by the lopsided division of labor. They'd had a maid to cook and clean and a nanny for baby Jason, but dealing with the help and doing their tasks on their days off always fell to Olivia. It didn't matter that she put in as many hours on the stock exchange as her husband. He'd been raised by his socialite mother to think that other people, especially his wife, existed to serve him. His imperious attitude was as much a factor in the divorce as his affairs.

With women, achieving balance wasn't a struggle. Complete parity was too much to expect, but the allocation of duties was more equitable. Olivia had never asked Amy to help clean up the kitchen. She'd volunteered. Even Sam, who had strong opinions about roles, got up to clear the table after a meal and wash the dishes.

Besides the homey feeling of watching Amy standing at the sink,

Olivia liked the view of her shapely buttocks in the tight skirt. Olivia had only glimpsed Amy's naked body when they were in a store, trying on clothes. Modestly, Amy had turned away, but she couldn't hide in a dressing room walled by mirrors. Olivia took the opportunity to admire her trim figure and perfectly proportioned breasts.

Amy interrupted Olivia's pleasant memory by asking, "How did your tour of the school go today?" Olivia appreciated that she always paid attention to the things she said. Her questions were curious and interested, but never invasive. Olivia wondered if her tact came from her training as a doctor, but when Liz took a medical history, it often felt like an interrogation. "The inspection was today, wasn't it?" Amy prodded without a hint of impatience.

"Yes, this morning. My God, what a nightmare!"

"Why? Isn't that company you hired doing a good job?"

"They did a beautiful job in the principal's office. When they put it back together, I suggested a rearrangement of the furniture so poor Courtney won't have flashbacks every time she walks in."

Amy sighed. "Unfortunately, she may still have flashbacks."

"Maybe the new arrangement can help her make new memories."

"That's insightful of you, Olivia," said Amy with a nod. "I didn't realize you thought about such things." From anyone but else, Olivia would have heard the comment as sarcasm, but not from Amy, who seemed constitutionally sincere.

"See? I'm more complicated than you thought."

"Oh, I know you're complicated. Why do you think I keep coming back for more?" She brought her wineglass to the table and sat down. "So what made the inspection such a nightmare?"

"The gym is a disaster. The company did a great job replacing the old bleachers, but the flooring people! Amy, if you saw this, you would die. They replaced all the boards with bullet holes, but the wood of the old floor had a nice amber patina. Wherever they replaced a board, there are obvious light patches. Every time anyone goes into that gym, they'd have to see exactly where those poor children and their teacher died."

"Oh, that's horrible! What were they thinking?"

Olivia shrugged. "They probably thought they were saving us money by patching it so precisely, but when poor Courtney saw it, she almost lost it. She managed to hold it together long enough to excuse herself. I assume she went to the ladies' room to throw up."

"That's too bad. What can you do?"

"The contractor needs to strip those sections and dye the wood to match or we're not paying him. I tell you, Amy, once I saw that, I understood why other towns tore down their schools after a shooting. Our elementary school is only a few years old. We're still paying it off, so we can't do that. But can you imagine the students going back to that place?"

Amy drew a long breath. "I haven't told you, but we've had many of the parents asking for sedatives or tranquilizers for their kids. They can't sleep or they wake up with nightmares. And these are the children who *didn't* witness the shooting. God help the ones who did!"

"Poor babies. They'll never be the same again." Olivia swallowed hard to get rid of the lump in her throat and blinked back the tears. She still wasn't comfortable crying in front of other people, not even Amy.

"On a happier note," Olivia said, getting up. She took her laptop from the sideboard and brought it to the table. "I'm trying to finalize my hotel reservations for Lucy's performance at the Met."

"I forgot that it's coming up soon."

"Just a few weeks away. I'm assuming you'd like to go."

Amy looked at her cautiously. "With Liz out of the office, I don't know if I'll be able to get away."

"But I already bought you a ticket." Amy's brows went up, but clearly not from surprise. Olivia quickly tried to explain. "I had to reserve tickets before they sold out. You'd be more upset if you wanted to go and didn't have a ticket." She switched to a deliberately casual tone. "But if you're not interested, I'm sure I can sell it at a profit. They're in high demand." Amy's brows rose higher.

"I want to go, Olivia. Of course, I want to go. Lucy is enormously talented, and I'm a big fan of hers, especially after she spoke out about her sexual assault." Amy's brows returned to their usual position. "I'll speak to Liz to make sure she's okay with both of us being out of the office. Please don't sell my ticket before I can talk to her."

Olivia smiled. *That was easy.* "Now, we need to figure out the accommodations. I found a great hotel deal. We only have to figure out if we want one room or two." When they'd traveled before, they'd taken two rooms. Olivia held her breath.

"Is it expensive?" Amy asked.

"It's New York. What do you think? But I'm paying, so it doesn't matter. We need to decide today because the offer is expiring."

"It might be fun having a roommate...like in college."

That wasn't what Olivia had in mind, but she pretended to take it in stride. "So I'll ask for a standard room with two beds, not a king."

"Probably the best plan." Amy leaned on her hand and studied her for a long moment. "Olivia, I really enjoy spending time with you. We have a great friendship. If we become involved, it will be unethical for me to treat you. You'll have to look for another doctor."

"So? I'll find another cardiologist." She studied Amy. "Why don't you want to sleep with me? Don't you like sex?"

"I love sex, but I'm still not over my bad marriage, and I'm not sure I'm ready for a relationship. Can you understand?"

Of course, Olivia understood. She was an intelligent woman, used to reading people and figuring out how they worked, mostly for her own devious purposes, but she still hadn't determined why Amy wouldn't sleep with her. They'd been seeing one another for more than a year. Olivia had never waited this long to bed a woman. "No one can ever be completely sure when they start a relationship," said Olivia in the reasonable tone she used during high stakes-negotiations. "I never told you, but the morning of the shooting, I'd decided I'd ask you to spend the night. Then...well, you know what happened."

The look in Amy's eyes softened. She reached across the table with an open palm. Cautiously, Olivia covered Amy's hand with hers. "Why is having sex so important?"

"Sex makes me feel alive...young. Since my heart attack, I feel like an invalid, a dried-out old woman."

Amy nodded sympathetically. "We all have doubts as we age and our bodies change. But you're not old, and you're very much alive. I want to keep you that way."

"You said I'm healthy enough for sex."

Amy grinned wickedly. "Maybe not for sex with me." She wiggled her eyebrows suggestively.

Surprised, Olivia sat back. This was a side of Amy she'd never seen before, but she liked it. "Tonight?" she asked in a small, hopeful voice.

"Not tonight. I'm tired. It's so busy with Liz out of the office. Fortunately, she's coming back this week. Maybe when we're in New York, but no promises. Let me hook you up with a new cardiologist and let her check you out. If she agrees your heart is strong enough for sex, we'll see what happens. Okay?"

Olivia's phone on the sideboard began to chime. Interrupting such an important conversation annoyed her, but as town manager, she was always on duty. She fished her phone out of her bag.

"Liz Stolz," she said, looking at the screen. "I wonder what she wants."

Amy gestured, urging her to answer.

"I know this is short notice," Liz said when Olivia opened the call, "but can you jump on a Zoom call with me, Melissa, and Sam? It's important."

"Amy's here."

"Oh, good," Liz said. "She can listen in if she wants."

Olivia looked across the room to where Amy sat. "Liz wants us to join a Zoom meeting," she said with a shrug. "Okay with you?"

Amy nodded her agreement.

***

While Melissa waited for Liz to admit her to the online meeting, she looked around the office. The previous owners had used it for significant work. Lucy had written her doctoral dissertation there. Erika Bultmann had finished her last book, the definitive work on the German political philosopher Jürgen Habermas. Melissa was illiterate when it came to philosophy, but Liz, who knew something about it, said it was brilliant.

The circumstances of Erika's death made Melissa anxious whenever Courtney went to bed with a migraine, as she had tonight. She'd had migraines since high school, and it was no surprise they'd increased since the shooting. After what Courtney had seen in the gym during the walk-through to inspect the cleanup, a painful episode was almost inevitable.

When Melissa had suggested they swap rooms with Kaylee, Courtney had dismissed her concerns as superstitious. She reminded her that Erika hadn't died in the master bedroom they were giving up. Technically, her life had ended in the hospital after they'd harvested her organs. But weren't the spirits of those who died suddenly more likely to haunt the spaces they'd inhabited in life? Melissa still expected to see Erika's ghost roaming the house at night and tended to turn on lights even when she didn't need them.

Curious about the former owner, she'd gone to see her grave in the old cemetery next to Lucy's church. It was easy to find. The modern, Germanic headstone stuck out among the worn colonial-era markers and ornate Victorian monuments around it. Erika's father had insisted that his daughter be buried, not cremated. He'd survived the bombing of Berlin, and fire terrified him.

Beside the grave was a stone bench erected in Erika Bultmann's memory by her Colby students. Melissa had sat there, contemplating the life of their beloved professor. Erika had grown up behind what used to be called the "iron curtain." Her heroic escape from the GDR in the trunk of a car belonging to a sympathetic East German policeman was like something out of a spy novel. Before her death, she'd become well known for her political commentary on radio and TV. She'd left a legacy of respected writings and enlightened students. Compared to what Erika had done with her life, making a lot of money writing trusts didn't seem like much of a contribution, especially because Melissa's reason for going into law had been to make a difference. Erika was an inspiration, not a ghost to be feared. Before leaving the cemetery, Melissa had placed a pretty pebble on top of the granite headstone.

The twirling circle on Melissa's laptop indicated the Zoom meeting was about to begin. While she waited to be connected, she used the screen reflection as a mirror while she tried to rein in her bushy hair.

"Hey, Melissa," said Liz. "Thanks for joining us." The town manager, the transgender singer, and the rector of the Episcopal Church occupied the other squares. "Sam's having some technical difficulties, but I can see her trying to get in. Let's give her a minute. Oh, there she is!" Sam's face appeared. She looked tanned and rested, but humorless. No one was smiling these days. Another window opened and Maggie Fitzgerald's carefully made-up face came into focus. "Okay," said Liz in an upbeat tone. "We're all here. Thanks for taking time out of your evening."

Melissa was pleased to hear Liz's upbeat tone. When they'd met that morning to discuss Chief Harrison's concerns about a potential lawsuit, she'd sounded so discouraged. Melissa recognized the change in Liz's energy. When she was trying to ensure the independence of her medical practice, she had that same determined look.

She quickly summarized the potential for a civil lawsuit and explained why Melissa had suggested doing damage control. "Specifically, she recommended Sam make a gesture showing she wants to make amends, like contributing to the funeral expenses. Tonight, Denise gave me an idea. Why not create an organization to support the families and fund it with donations and charity events?

Denise suggested a benefit concert, but there are lots of ways to raise funds, including private donations. We'll need seed money. I'm willing to contribute. I hope Olivia will, too."

Olivia didn't look one bit surprised at being volunteered. "You can count on me, Liz, and I know people who do development work."

"Great," said Liz. "Melissa, can you figure out the best kind of financial structure for this venture?"

"Yes, probably a trust held by a non-profit. Let me think about it."

"Olivia, you have an in with the bishop. Can you ask if we can use the cathedral as the venue for a concert?"

"Leave it to me," said Olivia.

"Denise is still on tour," Liz continued. "Lucy's too busy getting ready for her Met performance and her pastoral duties. They'll pitch in and perform, but we need someone to select the concert program and recruit the talent. Maggie, I was thinking of you. Can you ask Tony Roselli to help?"

"I'm sure he'd be happy to join us. Too bad it's the middle of winter and the playhouse is closed. That would be the perfect venue."

"We could do another concert in the spring right before the season opens," said Liz. "We need to think of this as a long-term venture. We're going to need money for counseling after the state ends its funding, college scholarships for the elementary school kids. We'll probably want to create a memorial, and—"

"Melissa," interrupted Sam. "Will this stop them from bringing a suit against me?"

"No, of course not. You may still get sued, but any effort that shows goodwill on your part will work in your favor, even if it gets to trial. The initial endowment must come from you. It doesn't need to be big, but substantial. We'll need to generate publicity and hold a press conference to announce it."

"My daughter can arrange it through her station," said Maggie. "She loves Sam. She'll be glad to help."

"Melissa, once you figure out the best financial entity for this project, how long will it take you to get it together? I'm guessing timing is critical."

"It is," Melissa agreed. "We don't want to give the damages attorney time to talk to too many of the families. Give me a couple of days to put it together."

The meeting concluded within ten minutes. Melissa sat in her office, trying to absorb all the information that had been exchanged. She'd been in many planning meetings before, but she'd never experienced anything like this. She felt like she'd been hit by a speeding truck. A notification pinged, indicating a new email—Liz sending a list of action items and the assignments for each task. She was a woman on a mission.

# Chapter 14

As much as Sam had enjoyed the exchange with the student, she was glad for the quiet after she left. The young woman was full of passion for sustainable housing for the homeless and saw tiny houses as the solution. Sam had been surprised by the number of female students. At Princeton, she'd been one of three women in her class. And the scale of projects had changed. When she was in school, the dream of every architect was to build taller skyscrapers and huge public buildings that made a big statement. Now, architecture couldn't be too small, which made sense. Fully functional structures with a smaller footprint were more efficient and kinder to the planet.

Sam felt as if she'd awakened from a long sleep. While she'd been doing renovations, the world had changed. She wondered what she could teach this next generation of architects, yet some of her students looked up to her like she could walk on water.

Maggie was always complaining about how disrespectful her students were. They talked out of turn and interrupted one another. They asked questions designed to trip her up and ended up revealing their own ignorance. Like every generation before them, *they* knew better. It was *their* time. Sam hadn't found that among the young people she taught. She enjoyed being challenged by their questions.

The dean wanted her to stay on, but she'd made no promises beyond the end of the semester. They would soon break ground for the new museum. Once construction started, she'd have to monitor the progress and might be called back for questions, but she was already thinking of the next project. She'd submitted designs for a senior housing project in Chicago and a corporate headquarters outside of Boston.

As much as Sam liked teaching, design work made her feel alive. The sketches that started from a few pencil lines had been stiff at first. Her mind and fingers were rusty, but now her strokes on the pad were graceful and fluid again. Samantha McKinnon, prize-winning architect, was back.

She gazed into the courtyard, where vivid flowers brightened the landscape. At home, the February scene outside her window would be desolate and cold. The pond would be frozen solid and covered with a thick layer of snow.

On a call about the foundation, Liz had mentioned ice fishing. Sam imagined herself sitting in Liz's ice shack around the augered holes in the ice where they dropped their lines. Brenda would make hot tea on the tiny stove. Liz would add a slug of whiskey to each cup, but not the good stuff that should never be watered down.

The fantasy made Sam ache to be in Maine with Maggie and their friends, but could she ever go back? Would she always be the stupid woman who'd left the door open so a killer could get in and shoot children? Was it too much to hope that people might someday forgive her? As beautiful as California was, Sam wanted to go home. She desperately hoped Liz's scheme worked.

❖❖❖

"It was so good to see you on the Zoom call the other night. I've been worried about you," said Amy, her eyes automatically giving her friend a quick evaluation. Sam had wanted to make a bold statement on turning sixty and had her head shaved on one side. She'd since grown it out again because asymmetrical hairstyles were out of fashion. *Butch women and their haircuts!* thought Amy. Liz still wore her hair in a deliberately messy grunge style, her gray waves as wild as a stormy surf. That was out of style too, but it perfectly expressed Liz's defiant repudiation of corporate medicine.

"It still makes me angry that I need to defend myself," said Sam. "I feel bad enough about the whole thing, and now I might be sued?" She sounded so discouraged. Amy wished she could reach through the screen and give her a hug.

"Olivia went to the meeting about setting up the trust. Sounds like Melissa thinks a lawsuit doesn't have much merit."

"That's what Liz told me." Sam didn't look like she believed it, and Amy's reassurances weren't working, so she changed the subject.

"How's the project going?"

Sam's face instantly brightened. "Great! We've finalized the plans and started interviewing construction companies."

"Vincent told me you've been applying for new projects."

"I sent in some preliminary sketches to get a sense of what people are looking for."

"My brother says your new work is the best you've ever done."

"Coming from Vincent Hsu, that's a real compliment. Thanks for getting us together. He's so much like you, it's almost like having you here. Plus, he's a big fan of mine and keeps telling me how great I am. Does a lot for my self-esteem, which, as you might guess, isn't high right now."

"He loved meeting you and wants to invite you for dinner soon." Amy's hand flew to her mouth. "Oops. I should have let him tell you."

"It doesn't matter," said Sam with a quick laugh. "I'll act surprised when he asks me."

"Oh, Sam, you're such a bad liar. He'll see right through it, but it doesn't matter. He's in awe that he got to meet you. And if he says he's going to invite you, he will." Amy glanced at the clock to see how much longer she had for the call. "When you get home, let's do lunch."

"Sure Olivia won't mind? Sounds like you two are getting hot and heavy."

Amy ignored the insinuation, but it surprised her. Sam had never seemed like the jealous type. "You know how Olivia is. She compartmentalizes everything. What she had with you is finished and she's moved on. Holding a grudge would be handing over control to someone else, and Olivia will *not* stand for that. I'm more worried about Maggie."

"Now, there's a woman who holds a grudge! You know, that was the real reason her marriage broke up. If Maggie hadn't slept with that actor to punish Liz for kissing Lucy on the boat, they might still be together. But don't worry. I told Maggie I won't tolerate any interference in my friendships, not with you and not with Liz. I need my friends, especially now."

"I'm here for you, Sam," said Amy.

"I know you are."

The light on Amy's desk phone lit—the medical assistant, announcing that her patient was ready. "Have to go, Sam. Have a good flight. Call me when you get back, and we'll set a lunch date. Meanwhile, hugs."

"Hugs back."

The video chat window closed. Amy looped her stethoscope around her neck and headed down the hall. She was relieved to hear Liz's voice floating out of the staff room. Since the town had revived from its stupor after the shooting, the practice had been swamped with appointments. In Liz's absence, most of her duties as senior partner had fallen to Amy, doubling her workload.

Amy literally bumped into Liz in the hall, apologized and laughed. "Liz, I need to talk to you," said Amy, hanging on to her arm to steady herself.

"Lunch today? You can tell me what's been going on around here."

"Great idea!"

"Let's go to Billy's Chowder House. I need a lobster roll." Amy smiled because whenever they went out to lunch, Liz *needed* a lobster roll. She blamed global warming, which, supposedly, would make all the lobsters move to Canada. Before they did, Liz intended to eat as many as she could.

Exactly at noon, Liz was knocking on Amy's door. They headed to Billy's and settled into a booth overlooking the salt marsh. Where the sea grass wasn't covered with snow, it was brown and matted.

"Winter in Maine is so bleak," said Liz, gazing out the window. Amy gave her the kind of critical look she would give any patient who'd expressed dark thoughts. She saw that the lines in Liz's face were more than sun damage from boating. The creases in her forehead had grown deeper.

Liz returned from her long inspection of the scene outside the window and smiled. "The winter marsh has a stark beauty, like a Japanese watercolor, don't you think?"

Amy looked outside and could see exactly what she meant. She would never have expected an ex-surgeon to have such a sensitive eye, but Liz, with her mini lectures on philosophy and every other subject under the sun, didn't fit any of the stereotypes.

"What kind of music did you play in your OR?"

"Opera mostly, but I bet you could have guessed that," said Liz with an endearing off-center grin.

"Didn't you find it too distracting?"

"Nah, I listen to opera when I do woodworking. So far, I've managed to avoid cutting off my digits."

"That's good. We need those hands. It was incredibly busy while you were out."

"I'm sorry, but I needed some time off."

"You could have taken more," Amy said. "We would have managed."

"I have no doubt, but I knew it was time to come back." Amy guessed that Liz had been bored, which was reassuring. It meant that she wouldn't retire soon. When Amy was young and ambitious, she would have been eager to take on more responsibility. Now, she was glad to have someone more experienced answer her questions, make the hard calls, and deal with the personnel problems. Liz seemed to love doing it. Amy could see her aging into one of those old doctors everyone talked about, still practicing medicine well into her eighties.

Liz smiled at the waitress, who'd suddenly appeared to take their drinks order. At Billy's, Liz always drank the brew of the week. After the drinks arrived, she tasted it. Amy wasn't a beer drinker, but Liz's puzzled expression made her curious. "Not good?"

"It's okay. I've had better," she said, regarding the glass with a critical eye. "Every guy in Maine thinks he's a brewer." Liz moved the glass to the end of the table. "Tell me what's going on in the office. When's Bobbie coming back?"

"Joyce is holding her own, so soon. Teresa came back last week. She's such a good nurse. I wish we could pay her at that level."

Liz shook her head. "Until she gets her license, we can't. If one of the other assistants finds out, there would be resentment." Liz thought for a moment. "But we could give her a merit raise."

"Good idea," agreed Amy. "She's so impressed with Bobbie that she's talking about going to school to become a nurse practitioner."

"See? That's why we need immigrants. They work hard and have ambition that puts the rest of us to shame. Good for her."

"Will you hire her as a nurse when she gets her license?" asked Amy.

"What do you think?" asked Liz, peering into her eyes.

Amy knew this was one of those trick questions meant to test her readiness to become the managing partner. "I think she'd make a great addition to the staff," said Amy in a confident tone. Anything less and the interrogation would continue.

Liz apparently liked that answer because she smiled. "Let's see where we are when she passes her exams. What else is going on?"

"Parents are bringing in the kids who were traumatized. They can't sleep. They have flashbacks and nightmares. But I don't feel comfortable prescribing psychotropics. So many have paradoxical effects in children."

Liz nodded. "I know. I asked Lucy to recommend a psychiatrist to review the cases and give us some advice." Amy wasn't surprised that Liz had already thought of that.

The waitress came to take their order. Liz ordered a different beer and two lobster roll specials with melted butter. Amy was glad Sam had confided the preferred way to dress a lobster roll. "Mayonnaise is for tourists," she'd explained.

While they were waiting for their food, Liz asked, "Now, what did you want to discuss?"

Amy sized up Liz's mood, which seemed positive. A long pre-amble would be unnecessary. "Olivia invited me to your wife's opening-night performance."

"I know," said Liz, sitting back, so the waitress could serve their lunch. "She asked where I'd reserved seats because she wanted to buy tickets near where we're sitting. I assume you accepted the invitation."

"Not yet. I wanted to check with you first. It means we'll both be out of the office at the same time."

The waitress returned with Liz's beer. "Well," said Liz, pro-longing the suspense by taking a sip. That one pleased her. She acknowledged the glass with a nod. "Since I've been out so much, I've decided to stay in the city only two nights. Lucy is a pro and doesn't need me parked there during rehearsals. But I am curious about this new music director."

"Nézet-Séguin? He's gay, isn't he?"

"Levine was gay too, but this guy is out on a whole new level—bleach blond hair, conducting outfits with a colorful Harlequin pat-tern. I got Olivia tickets to the cast reception on opening night. One for you too. You'll get to meet the new wunderkind."

"So you're okay with my being out of the office while you are?"

Liz shrugged. "I expected it. You and Olivia have been seeing a lot of one another lately." Amy wasn't sure how she felt about people assuming they were a couple. It seemed to make a relation-ship a foregone conclusion. But Liz was right. They were seeing a lot of one another. "Ask Bill to take your patients on the days you plan to take off," Liz suggested. "If he gives you any trouble, let me know.

By that time, Bobbie will be back. If necessary, we can ask Cherie to work some extra hours. Don't worry. We'll work it out."

Their sandwiches arrived. Liz opened her mouth wide to avoid spilling the mountain of lobster as she took a bite. She closed her eyes and smiled while she chewed. Amy smiled too, watching her enjoyment. For all her complexity, Liz was basically a simple person. Little things made her happy.

❋❋❋

Despite the demands on their time, Lucy had decided to continue the pastoral team meetings. As Tom had pointed out, they needed to get together to compare notes, get feedback, and bring everyone up to date. "Most of all, we need to look one another in the eye to remember why we're doing this," he'd said. Lately, Lucy had really needed a reminder. Attempting to bind up the emotional and spiritual wounds of Hobbs had been overwhelming.

After they ended the meeting, Lucy asked Reshma for a concluding prayer. She'd come to see her curate's short invocations as liturgical gems. Reshma bowed her head. "Gracious God, let us draw strength from you and one another as we go forth to help heal your people." There were murmured amens around the table. Everyone got up and passed around an embrace. Talking about their dinner plans. Susan and Reshma left. Denise was flying back to Europe the next day, and they'd invited her and Emily for dinner.

Tom hung back after the others left. "Lucy, do you have a few minutes for me?"

Lucy glanced at her watch. Maggie and Alina were coming for dinner to discuss the media launch of the new foundation. "Is this going to take long?"

Tom grimaced. "It could, Lucy, but I promise it's important."

Lucy remembered that Maggie still had a set of keys to the house. She'd only need a reminder to bring them. "Fine, Tom. Just give me a minute to let people know I'm going to be late." She composed a quick text message while she explained, "We're having some people over to plan the announcement of the Hobbs Promise Foundation."

Tom looked contrite. "I'm sorry. I should have scheduled some time with you instead of springing this on you."

"It doesn't matter now. Sit down." Lucy pulled a chair out from the table.

"I probably should have come to you with this sooner," said Tom, taking a seat, "but I've been struggling with telling you because it means breaking professional confidence. I've prayed over it and decided I have an obligation to tell you, especially because I'm going away for the weekend."

Lucy leaned forward to encourage him to get to the point. "Go on. I'm listening."

"Liz is one of my oldest friends. Technically, we're talking as friends, but you know how it is. Everything can get confused in cases where friendships and professional relationships cross."

"Did she specifically ask you to keep what you're going to share with me confidential?"

"No, but I'm sure she assumes that I won't share what she tells me."

"Then maybe you shouldn't." Lucy was getting annoyed with Tom for playing this cat-and-mouse game.

"You need to know."

Lucy finally lost patience. "Tom, if it's that important, just tell me!"

He looked directly into her eyes. "Liz considered taking her life."

Stunned, Lucy sat back. "No! Not Liz. She's the strongest person I know."

"Yes, she has enormous ego strength, but when I asked about self-harm, she admitted that she'd considered it."

"No!" Her mind refused to believe what her ears had clearly heard. Tears sprang to her eyes. Tom reached across the table for her hand.

"Lucy, I'm so sorry, but it's true, and it sounds like the ideation was fairly developed, not just a ho-hum wish."

"Was this recently?"

"No, a couple of weeks ago, but not right after the shooting. At first, she sounded relieved to still be alive, almost giddy that she'd survived. Then she seemed to slide into a dark place. She's been up and down. Right now, she's up because this scheme to help Sam has given her something positive to do."

"I thought we'd gotten through the worst. Lately, she seems like her old self. Our life finally seems like it's getting back to normal. She's back to work. She's building a project in her workshop."

"That does sound positive."

"After the shooting, she wouldn't even let me touch her. Now, she can't get enough sex." Although Lucy had always been candid with Tom, he blushed a little. "I know sex can be a way to blot out pain, but this feels genuine and loving."

"Maybe I shouldn't have said anything. The suicidal thoughts might have been a fleeting moment of weakness."

"You said the ideation was well developed. Tell me what you mean."

Tom rubbed his hand over the bristly white hair at the back of his head. "She told me that after you went to bed, she'd drink whiskey on your porch with her loaded pistol in her lap, the same gun she used to shoot Peter Langdon."

Lucy's hand flew to her mouth. "Oh my God!" Liz had been just downstairs from where Lucy had been sleeping. How could she be so completely unaware that the woman she loved had thought of killing herself?

"Should I go on?" Tom asked quietly.

Reluctantly, Lucy nodded. "Yes, I need to know. Tell me everything...from the beginning."

"After I asked about self-harm, she started talking about the gun she'd used to kill Peter Langdon. How special it is, some Czech make—a CZ, I think she called it. She pulled it out of her bag and showed it to me. For ten minutes, she went on about the gun's virtues—how it has the lowest misfire rate, the highest accuracy rate, and lots of gun stuff I don't understand. I finally asked her to put the horrible thing away because it frightened me, and she did."

"Did you feel threatened?"

"No, not at all. She talked about the gun like one of her performance cars, going on and on about its engineering virtues. You know how Liz loves mechanical things. But then things took a darker turn. She described the various places where she could shoot herself...in the mouth, the temple, the throat." Lucy felt a sympathetic twinge in the same places in her own body.

"Was she serious?"

"Hard to tell. She enjoys shocking people, but it was chilling to listen to her discuss it so dispassionately." While Lucy imagined Liz's neutral doctor's voice describing her plan to kill herself, the hair stood up on the back of her neck. "I'm sorry, Lucy, I probably shouldn't have gone into such detail. This must be causing you so much pain."

"Yes, but I need to know. Did she say why she didn't go through with it?"

"She knew her death would be instant, but she was afraid of the pain. She said she kept trying to get drunk enough to work up the courage to pull the trigger, but her tolerance for alcohol is too high." Lucy thought about all the empty bottles she'd seen in the recycling bin. "She was very worried about leaving a mess for you to see. She considered doing it outside, but you'd see the blood spray on the snow and the exit wound when you found her."

"That's what worried her? How she would look?" Lucy stared at him incredulously.

"You know what I mean. She wouldn't want you to see her afterwards because it would hurt you. She spent a lot of time explaining that you were the only reason she didn't go through with it. How she loved you and never wanted to hurt you. She told me again and again that she could never bear to hurt you. Then the circle of people got larger. She mentioned her friends and how they needed her. Her niece and her family. Maggie and her granddaughters. Emily. She told me how she loves you all. She told me she loves me too. She said that only love stopped her from pulling the trigger."

That finally broke Lucy, and she burst into tears. Tom jumped up and yanked tissues out of the box in the middle of the table. He held them out to her with both hands.

"Thanks," sobbed Lucy. "Sorry, I'm such a mess."

"Don't apologize," Tom said, soothingly rubbing her shoulder. "You didn't expect this, and it's a shock."

"I'm okay," Lucy said when she could finally breathe. She mopped up the streaked mascara as best she could. "Go on, Tom. Tell me the rest."

Tom handed over another fistful of the tissues and sat down. "She was thinking of giving her guns to Brenda until she felt stronger. I told her I thought that was an excellent idea and encouraged it. At our next session, she said she didn't think it was necessary. She'd gotten past the crisis."

"Do you think she has?"

"For now, yes. We had more conversations about what to do about the guns. She said she'd considered selling them, donating them to her gun club. When I asked in another meeting what she intended to do, she said she still hadn't decided."

"Do you think there's still a danger she'd harm herself? Should I ask Brenda to take her guns?"

"I think you need to encourage Liz to give them to someone she trusts for safekeeping, but don't involve others. Let her decide. Don't you agree?"

Lucy imagined Liz's fury if the police showed up asking for her guns. "It breaks my heart that she would even think of hurting herself. She knows that Erika's death almost killed me. I don't know if I can survive losing Liz, too. I was terrified when she went into that school to talk to Peter Langdon."

"I'm sure."

"Doesn't she know how much I love her?" Lucy asked desperately.

"I think she knows, Lucy, but she's so full of guilt and self-loathing she doesn't feel worthy of your love. She can't forgive herself for killing that poor young man. She said she asked you for absolution. She asked me too."

"Oh, Tom! How could she even think of killing herself and leaving me alone?" The tears came again, but this time, Lucy couldn't keep up with them. Tom handed her more tissues.

"Lucy, I think her love for you is the only thing that stopped her. She deeply loves you and doesn't want to cause you pain. She knows that many people need her—her patients, her friends, the townspeople, but especially you. Fortunately, her hyper-developed sense of responsibility and concern for others stopped her."

"I'll take whatever she tells herself that keeps her from pulling that trigger."

"I made her swear to me she would call if the suicidal ideation returns. But I'll be away for the weekend, which is why I'm telling you now. I trust Liz to keep her word, but you're here if something goes wrong..."

Lucy was glad Tom had left it deliberately vague. She took a deep breath and stared at the tissues full of makeup. She must be a sight, but when she saw herself reflected in Tom's kind eyes, she realized it didn't matter.

"I only wish you had told me sooner. All this time, I could have been watching for signs."

Tom hung his head. "I was caught between my loyalty to Liz and my obligation to tell you. Then I tied myself into knots over the professional confidence issue. At least, now you know." Tom looked directly into her eyes. "Jeff is going to stay in Florida."

"But you're coming back?" she asked anxiously.

"Yes, on Tuesday."

"Tom, I really appreciate you coming up to help us, but you and Jeff have your life in Florida."

"And we'll get back to it in due time. I came out of friendship for you and my love for this town that has given me so much. I'll stay as long as I'm needed."

When Lucy got up, Tom enfolded her in his arms and gave her a sturdy hug. "Don't worry. I'll be back in a few days." That seemed so far away. Lucy hugged him harder, wanting to hold him here as long as she could.

***

Liz came home to find Lucy and Maggie huddled around the kitchen island. They were speaking in hushed tones and didn't notice her at first. She stood in the doorway to admire them. These were the women she'd loved enough to marry. Maggie, with her thick white braid and careful makeup, proved every day that a woman at seventy could be glamorous and sexy. Lucy's red hair wasn't as fiery anymore, but the mere sight of her was exciting. Both women were beautiful, but looks alone couldn't explain why Liz found them so attractive. Sometimes, she loved them so fiercely she felt like her heart would break.

She listened carefully, but she couldn't make out the words they spoke. She guessed they were talking about her. They were always conspiring to reform her or save her from herself, but their faces were grave, Lucy's particularly. Something was wrong.

"What's going on?" asked Liz, stepping into the room. "Did something happen? Another kid die?"

"No," said Maggie, coming to meet Liz at the door. In the moment, Liz forgot and kissed her on the mouth like a wife. She looked over Maggie's head to see Lucy staring at her. After their talks about inclusive relationships, she hoped there wouldn't be repercussions from the kiss.

"Hey, Lucy," said Liz, approaching her with a weak smile. "Did you have a good day?"

Lucy's lips were taut when Liz kissed her. "Liz, we need to

talk," she said in a firm voice. Her fingers gripped Liz's arm tightly. "Excuse us, please, Maggie."

"Sure. I'll get dinner started." Maggie's hazel eyes were wide as she watched them head to the door.

"Come with me," ordered Lucy, pulling Liz down the hall to her office. Once inside, she pointed to a chair. "Sit," she ordered and closed the door. She was still wearing her collar, which made her look even more forbidding.

"Lucy, I'm sorry," said Liz, sitting down. "I was distracted. I forgot."

"Forgot what?"

"I kissed Maggie on the lips..."

"I don't care about that." Lucy waved dismissively. "Just don't make a habit of it."

"Okay," said Liz cautiously, realizing that wasn't the problem. "What's going on?"

"You told Tom that you were having suicidal thoughts. Why didn't you tell me?"

"He told you? Fuck him!" Liz jumped up and began to pace. "He said our talks were confidential. You priests and your 'privileged information.' It's only privileged as long as it's convenient for you!"

"Liz, he was ethically obligated to tell me. I'm your wife. I needed to know. Were you serious or just playing one of your games? I know how you like to manipulate therapists to show you're smarter than they are."

Liz took a deep breath to calm herself. "It crossed my mind, but believe me, if I really wanted to kill myself, I would have done it."

"But you *thought* about it...in detail, from what Tom told me. You were making concrete plans."

"It was a thought experiment. I'm good at visualizing procedures. It's how I used to prepare for surgeries. I'd rehearse the entire process in my mind."

Lucy didn't look like she completely believed her, but she nodded.

"Fuck! I never should have trusted that bastard! Did you know he tried to come on to me when he was dating Erika?"

"Liz, that was over forty years ago! He's a married gay man and an ordained priest. You can certainly trust him. But what I want to know is why don't you trust *me*? I'm your wife!"

"Of course, I trust you, Lucy, but I didn't want to worry you. You were under so much pressure with the services and counseling people. I didn't want to add to your burdens."

"Not good enough! I'm your wife. I love you. *Nothing* is more important than you!"

The fire in Lucy's eyes made Liz stop pacing. "I'm sorry," she said lamely.

Lucy pointed to the chair and Liz sat down. "I knew I shouldn't leave you alone out there with your damned scotch. And you were sitting there with a loaded gun, the one you used to kill Peter!"

"Lucy, I wasn't serious."

"But I am!" The shrillness of Lucy's voice underscored her message. "Get rid of that thing. Sell it. Give it away. I don't care what you do with it but get it out of this house."

"Lucy, it's my favorite carry pistol."

"I don't give a damn. It goes, or I do."

The threat instantly ignited Liz's anger. "No, you blackmailed me before. You can't seriously think I'm falling for that trick again?"

"Okay," said Lucy, getting up. "Try me." She headed to the door.

"Lucy, wait. Okay. I'll get rid of the gun. Tomorrow, I'll call the Kittery Trading Post and ask for a price."

"No, it can't wait. After we talk, you're going to call Brenda and ask her to come and get your guns...all of them!"

"Lucy..."

"I mean it, Liz. When you're in better shape, she can give them back. But they need to be gone. Tonight!"

"I can lock them up in the gun safe at the fish and game."

"Where you have the key to the building and know the combination? What do you think, Liz? I'm stupid?"

"No, Lucy, I absolutely know you're *not* stupid."

"Liz, please! I love you with all my heart. If you hurt yourself, it would kill me!" When Lucy burst into tears, Liz realized what effort it had taken to maintain the tough act. She got up and tried to put her arms around her.

"No, don't," Lucy said, pushing her away. "I don't want your hugs. I want those guns gone!"

Liz sighed when she saw there was no alternative. "Okay. I'll call Brenda after dinner."

"Now, Liz!" Lucy yanked on Liz's arms for emphasis. "Now!"

Liz reached into her pocket and took out her phone. When Brenda answered in a cheerful voice, Liz was tempted to engage in their usual banter, but Lucy's unflinching stare made her get right to the point. "Brenda, I need you to do something for me."

"Sure, Liz, if I can. What is it?"

"Come and get my guns."

"Okay," said Brenda, sounding suddenly alert. "I'll be right there."

***

"Mom, what's going on?" asked Alina, leaning closer to speak confidentially. "When I passed Liz's office, I heard raised voices."

Maggie shrugged. "None of our business," she said, although she knew exactly what Lucy and Liz were arguing about.

"I see you're making dinner," said Alina, glancing in the direction of Liz's office, "so I guess you expect them to be awhile."

"When I accepted Liz's invitation to this meeting, I told her I'd make dinner. She said she misses my cooking. Gives her a break from her own."

"I bet Lucy doesn't cook like you do. I'm sure she misses yours." Alina looked sympathetic. During long talks over many glasses of wine, Maggie had confessed to her daughter that she regretted ending the marriage. She hoped Alina didn't say anything about that now. She was relieved when she asked, "Can I do something to help?"

Maggie selected a chef's knife from the knife block and found a cutting board in the rack in the pantry. She pointed to an onion on the counter. "Peel and dice that for me," she said, handing her a paring knife. Alina got to work. "What are your kids eating tonight?" Maggie asked.

"The sitter is heating up one of the casseroles you left."

"I bet they'll be glad when things get back to normal. You too."

"You can say that again. But the pace of this reporting has been stimulating. And guess what?"

"What?" asked Maggie, playing along. Alina had always loved guessing games, even as a hyperactive toddler.

"What could be the best outcome for me from my coverage of the shooting?"

"You get recognition on national news," Maggie guessed.

"Better."

"Better? Come on, Alina, don't keep me in suspense."

"Steve told someone at network operations that Liz is going to let me interview her. They're going to give me ten minutes on *Sixty Minutes*."

"No!"

"Yes!"

They jumped up and down like delighted children. When they'd finished their little victory dance, Alina said, "I feel a little guilty that I blackmailed Liz into doing it, but she really wanted the coverage for the foundation. I know that's the only reason she agreed."

"It's not the *only* reason. Liz loves you and wants to help you boost your career. She just needed to figure out what she wanted to say. You know how she is."

Alina snatched a piece of carrot out of the salad Maggie had prepared. "I still can't believe my own stepmother took down a shooter. That a gray-haired grandmother is a real-life badass."

"Proves little old ladies will one day rule the world."

"Mom, Liz is anything but little. I'm little. Compared to me, she's a giant."

*In many ways*, thought Maggie, but she continued to smile at her daughter, because she always needed her approval.

Lucy came into the kitchen. She gave Alina a hug. "How long until dinner?" she asked. Maggie glanced at the clock over the stove. "About half an hour. Is that okay?"

Lucy snatched a piece of carrot from the salad. "That's fine. Brenda's coming over."

"Oh? Should I set another place at the table?"

"I don't think so. They usually eat early. Cherie tries to get the kids to bed on time."

Maggie glanced at Lucy's collar. "Look at you. You're still in uniform. Why don't you change?"

"Good idea. Liz is upstairs, changing out of her work clothes. After that, she's going to get her guns together."

Alina, who never missed a news lead, jumped on the information. "Is Liz giving up her guns?"

"Temporarily," said Lucy, fishing another piece of carrot out of the salad. "Excuse me while I put on my civvies. Maggie, I think you can tell her why Liz is handing over her guns, but, Alina, this is *family business*, not to be shared with anyone, and certainly not for broadcast. Understood?"

"Absolutely," said Alina, covering her heart with her hand. "I would never say anything that would embarrass Liz."

"Good," said Lucy. She grabbed another slice of carrot out of the bowl and left.

Maggie looked into the salad bowl. "Between you two, all my carrots have disappeared. If you don't mind peeling more, I'd appreciate it."

"In the vegetable bin?" said Alina, opening the refrigerator.

"Yes, that was one of the few things Liz wasn't able to move after I left."

"Is Lucy invoking the yellow flag law?" Alina asked into the refrigerator as she rooted around in the bin for the bag of carrots.

"Not formally. Brenda and Liz are friends. It's like everything in Hobbs. A lot goes on behind the scenes." Alina returned to the cutting board to scrape the carrots. "Alina, swear to me this will never come out in public." Maggie gave her daughter a penetrating look.

"You don't need to make me swear. I love Liz and would never do anything to hurt her."

"Not even to get ahead in your career?"

"Mom, Liz has been like a second mother to me. My kids consider her their grandmother. You might be divorced, but Liz is still family."

The doorbell chimed. "I bet that's Brenda." Maggie dried her hands on a dish towel and headed to the door. Opening it brought in a blast of cold. It was snowing again.

"Whew! Seriously chilly tonight," said Brenda, scraping her boots on the doormat and shaking out her Hobbs PD watch cap on the porch before stepping inside. "Hey, Maggie," said Brenda, bending to kiss her. She smelled of cold, clean air.

After Brenda unlaced her boots and hung up her parka, she stopped at the living room door. "Wow, that's *a lot* of guns," she said, looking at the neat row of cases and carrying sleeves. "I guess she needs them for her safety classes." She turned to Maggie as if she expected an explanation, but she'd tried to ignore Liz's gun obsession and didn't know.

Coming down the stairs, Lucy looked calmer. She thanked Brenda and kissed her on the cheek. Liz came into the living room with more gun cases.

"I had no idea you had so many guns," said Brenda.

"Neither did I, but then I never counted them. I have an inventory in my safe, with the serial numbers. I can get it if you need proof that you got them all."

"Nah, that's not necessary. You might try to fool me, but you'd never lie to Lucy." Brenda glanced in Lucy's direction for confirmation, then studied the plastic cases lined up by the door. "I was going to lock them at the station in the room where we store our firearms, but that's a lot of guns. Doesn't your gun safe have a programmable lock?"

"Actually, it does. I paid extra for that."

"So, why don't we put the guns back in the safe, and I can change the combination? When everyone thinks it's safe, I'll give it to you. Meanwhile, Lucy can have it....for insurance."

Lucy shook her head. "I don't want it. You know how convincing Liz can be."

"I'd feel better if someone had the combination besides me," said Brenda uneasily.

"I'll keep it," Maggie volunteered. Afterwards, she didn't know why. They all turned to stare at her.

"Maggie, that's a lot of responsibility," said Brenda, looking skeptical.

"If Liz is okay with it, I am." Maggie looked at Liz, who shrugged and nodded. Maggie wanted to hug her for trusting her with something so important.

"Brenda, I just wish you had come up with this plan before I had to look for all those gun cases," Liz said. "Now, I have to put them all back!"

"Oh, stop bellyaching. I'll help you carry them to the basement. But you'll have to stay in your office while I change the combination."

"Please don't fuck it up. It's one of those explosive-proof safes. If you don't do it right, the company has to come down to reset the combination."

"Don't worry. I'll take Maggie down with me to read the directions."

Liz opened her gun purse and took out her pistol. "I want you to take this one, Brenda. Lucy wants it gone."

Brenda gazed admiringly at the pistol. "Isn't this the gun you used to take down Peter Langdon?" Liz nodded. "It's a hero's gun. You should sell that one at auction. I bet you'd get a mint for it. People are ghoulish. They love stories like that."

"I'm not trying to make money off it, and I don't want to give it up, but Lucy says she doesn't want it here."

"You could destroy it," Brenda said. "I can arrange it."

Liz shook her head. "That would be like shooting a racehorse in its prime. It needs to go to a good home. To someone who doesn't know its sad history."

"It's a beauty, all right," Brenda agreed. "Why don't you lock it up with the others and think about it?"

Lucy's sharp look indicated that having the gun anywhere in the house was not an option. With a sigh, Liz stowed the gun in the French-fitted foam case. "Brenda, please take it home until I figure out what to do with it."

Brenda reached for the case. "Okay. I'll put it in my car."

✻✻✻

Cherie tried to avoid arguments in front of the children because their home with their birth parents had been a place of shouting and tears. That was one reason Cherie kept their marital disagreements private. She could see Brenda wanted to continue the conversation about Liz's gun, but it would have to wait until later. It was dinner-time, and Cherie had to leave soon for her therapy appointments.

Instead of talking about it, she sent little darts of anger across the dinner table. She knew the silent treatment was petty and ju-venile, but guns set off a reaction in Cherie that knew no words. When she was first dating Brenda, Liz had tried to cure Cherie of her gun phobia by taking her to the range to shoot her favorite gun, the same one Brenda had brought home last night. In Cherie's small hands, that pistol had felt so big and scary. Liz wouldn't let her quit until she'd fired all the rounds from an extended capacity magazine that seemed endless. The exposure therapy had allowed Cherie to tolerate her wife's service pistol and backup revolver...barely.

Now Brenda wanted to own this fancy gun because it was "beautiful." How could an instrument of death be *beautiful*! Cherie had never understood that part of gun culture. When Liz got a new gun, she and Brenda would go into another room and ooh and aah and carry on about its technical features. Cherie shivered just thinking about it.

She gazed at her wife innocently eating her dinner. She wasn't really mad at Brenda for wanting to help out a friend. She just didn't want any more guns in the house.

"Honey, I think you need to leave soon," Brenda said, glancing at the clock over the sink.

"I know," Cherie replied in a grumpy voice that made Keith stare at her curiously. She was aware of the time, barely enough to scarf down her dinner before facing three hours of evening appointments. After she put her plate in the sink, she kissed the kids. Brenda raised her cheek for a kiss. Cherie remembered how much she loved this woman and stuffed down her anger over the gun. "See you later, alligator," she said with a wink to the kids. "In a while, crocodile," they answered in unison.

"Be careful. It's icy out there," said Brenda, hanging on to Cherie's arm after the kiss.

"I will. I don't want to embarrass the police chief."

"No, don't do that. I'll never hear the end of it."

"Don't worry, I'll be careful."

Since the big snow, a melt-freeze cycle had left the roads treacherous. Otherwise, Cherie would have pushed the speed limit a little. The Hobbs cops knew her car and left her alone, but she didn't want to get killed, either.

Cherie hated to be late for any clients, but especially for Renee Langdon. It seemed like she'd given up, resigned to everything that had happened—her son's death, the rejection by her coworkers, the bullying by her children's schoolmates. She struck Cherie as the ultimate victim, a woman who'd stayed too long in an abusive marriage, where she'd taken both her husband's complaints and his hard fists. So far, Cherie hadn't been able to rouse a reaction from her about her son's death—no anger, no horror at the losses, not even a murmured complaint. She'd completely shut down.

Lucy was leaving when Cherie arrived. She waved on her way through the parking lot. Under the blue light of the mercury lamp, her breath hung in the frigid air like a ghost.

The rectory hall was nice and warm when Cherie came in. Her client was sitting on the bench across from the admin's desk. Renee was so still that she could have been a performance artist pretending to be a statue. Until Cherie was nearly on top of her, she didn't even turn her head.

"Sorry, I'm late," said Cherie, unlocking her office door.

"Don't worry. I was enjoying the peace and quiet. Sometimes, it's so noisy at home."

"Your kids play loud music?" asked Cherie, turning on the lights.

"Sometimes, and the TV is always on. Or my son is playing loud video games. That's how Pete got so interested in guns. I just hope Billy doesn't grow up to be like his brother."

"Come in and let's get started." Cherie hung her coat on the ancient coat tree by the door. Renee found a hook for hers.

"Before we get in too deep, I want to tell you this will be our last session," Renee announced as she sat down on the old sofa.

Cherie tried not to show surprise, but the statement had blindsided her. "Usually, we talk about ending therapy and then wind down gradually," she managed to say in an even voice.

"I'm sorry for the short notice, but I sold my house. I was going to fix it up before I put it on the market, but there's such a shortage of homes for sale, the real estate lady said not to bother. Sure enough, I listed it and got full price in two days. I promise I didn't intend for things to go so fast."

"You talked about going to live near your sister. Is that still the plan?"

"She talked to the manager of her bank in Florida, and he said they'd be glad to have me. I'd have to start as an assistant manager, but I could work my way up." She leaned forward and engaged Cherie's eyes. "I have to get my kids out of this town," she said in a desperate whisper. "They don't deserve this."

"Are the other students still picking on them?"

"In school, on social media, in town. It's just awful."

"I'm so sorry. Kids can be so mean."

"Like chickens in a barnyard going after the old, sick hen until they peck her to death. My kids need a fresh start in a place where no one knows them."

"The story has been all over the national news. Is there any place where people won't know them?"

"People have short memories, and if it's not in their own back-yard, they don't pay attention. They get wrapped up in their own problems and forget. And I have other reasons to leave Maine. I'm sick of the winters. Tired of shoveling, raking the roof, paying the plow guy money I need to pay for oil. I just can't do it anymore."

Cherie, who'd grown up in Louisiana, knew that a warm climate had its own challenges. If the air conditioning didn't run full time, mold would grow on the walls.

"I'm not usually one to advocate the geographical cure, but in your case, it might be good to make a new start. When you get settled with your next therapist, I'll be happy to transfer my notes."

Renee stared. "Oh, I'm not doing therapy where I'm going. Health insurance in Florida isn't like it is here. I mean, I probably won't have any for a while."

Cherie opened her mouth to speak, but Renee put up her hand.

"I know what you're going to say, Cherie. You think I need more counseling."

"Especially after what you've been through, losing a child like that, enduring the blame for what he did even though it's not your fault."

"Isn't it? I raised him. I couldn't keep him from being hurt by his father or that teacher. I knew something was wrong, but I was afraid to ask. We had so many other troubles. Putting food on the table was hard. No money to pay the taxes. We almost lost the house. I didn't have time to pay attention to what Pete was doing in school. Now, it's too late to pay attention. He's gone, and I need to take care of the children I have."

The barrage of compelling reasons left Cherie momentarily speechless. "I understand, but please consider getting some help after you move. I really think you can benefit from talking to someone."

"Mother Lucy said she will contact the rector there to find out if she can arrange for counseling. Like it will change anything." She stared at the floor. "Why does it even matter?"

The poor woman sounded so utterly hopeless that Cherie had no idea what to say.

✳✳✳

Liz sat in the back of the media room with the soprano score of the opera on her lap and a bottle of cabernet franc at her feet. The premiere of the new production of *Lohengrin* was quickly approaching. She wondered how long Lucy could keep working all day and practicing for hours every night. She still got up at dawn to sing exercises, returned from their morning walk, now cut to a half hour, and sang even more.

Sometimes, she whimpered in her sleep from a pain that went beyond the physical, like a puppy having a bad dream. Liz was glad the performances at the Met would soon be over. Afterward, their life could return to normal. Maybe normal was too much to hope for. At least, they could go back to their routine.

This second debut should have been a happy occasion, but all the demands on Lucy's time had turned the preparation into a grind. In the process, Lucy's high-wattage smile had noticeably dimmed. If her singing career hadn't been interrupted, one performance wouldn't be so important, but Lucy was at the age when other singers were retiring or winding down. In the twilight of their careers, they might do special projects like premiering new works by modern composers or giving master classes.

When Lucy's voice broke on a note, Liz clapped her hands loudly. "Okay, that's enough for today," she called from the back of the media room. She cut the stage lights and sound system with the remote while Lucy trudged up the aisle to the last row of home theater seats. "You need a break. There's always tomorrow."

"Tomorrow is the press conference for the foundation," Lucy reminded her.

Liz had almost forgotten that Alina was coming to the high school auditorium with her news crew to video the announcement for the evening news. It meant Liz would have to dress for the occasion. Weeks away from work had accustomed her to living in jeans and sweatshirts. Just the thought of putting on a power suit made her tired, but she was one of the officers of Hobbs Promise, so she had to be there.

"I'll come home at lunchtime and practice," said Lucy, flopping into the seat next to Liz's.

"I think you should take tomorrow off. We'll go out to dinner after the press conference," said Liz, handing her a glass of wine.

"I can't, Liz. I need the practice."

"Lucy, as a doctor, I can hear the stress you're putting on your voice. Even star athletes take a night off when they're preparing for a big game. They know pushing beyond their limits can cause injuries. You need a break, Lucy. You can't keep on like this."

"All those years when I desperately wished I could sing at the Met. Now, I can, and...I'm terrified."

"Why? You're prepared, maybe over-prepared. You sound better than ever."

"I just wish I had more time to practice," said Lucy. "All this pastoral care has been so exhausting." She leaned into Liz's body and gently stroked the inside of her thigh. "And I've missed you."

"It's almost nine. We could go to bed," said Liz hopefully. "In your book, you say that couples should never get so busy that they don't connect. You say that intimacy is even more important during stressful times."

"I wrote that, didn't I?"

"Yes, you did."

"I'm pretty smart."

"Yes, you are."

Lucy's smile brightened. "Put a cork in that bottle. Let's finish our wine upstairs."

# Chapter 15

While Maggie waited in the choir office for Simone, she thought about the pot roast she'd left in the enameled pot on the enclosed porch. She'd learned the trick of using the porch as an extra refrigerator from Liz. Maggie briefly wondered if she should have transferred the pot to the refrigerator. The temperature was supposed to be a little warmer today, but it wasn't supposed to break forty.

Her plan to welcome Sam home with her favorite meal had been scuttled by Liz's invitation to a family dinner at La Scala after the meeting. Maggie had braised the pot roast in the stove the old-fashioned way. Sam might love her slow cooker, but Maggie would never think of using it to cook a serious meal. She didn't care if Sam called her a food snob. At least, Olivia, another trained chef, understood. She'd told Maggie she didn't even own a slow cooker.

Olivia had been growing on her. Maggie had been surprised to hear that she'd intended to contribute such a large amount to the Hobbs Promise Foundation, especially given her history with Sam. Olivia's generosity had shamed Maggie into making a modest donation. Money was flowing in from surprising sources. The fire and police departments had taken up a collection. The Episcopal diocese had given money. Melissa's mother, Ruth Morgenstern and her boyfriend, Liz's surgeon friend, had given a sizeable amount. The fund already totaled close to a half-million dollars. After years of fundraising for off-Broadway theater and the Webhanet Playhouse, Maggie knew that a big initial endowment attracted more donors. The professional fundraiser Olivia had recruited said the forecast was encouraging.

The committee had nixed Liz's suggestion to allocating funds to gun safety as too political. "There are already plenty of organizations for that purpose. Give money to them," Olivia had flatly said. Unlike Maggie, she had no trouble standing up to Liz.

But Maggie's relationship with Liz had been changing. After the shooting and Liz's close call, they were painfully aware that life was short. The stupid things they'd done to break the trust between them now seemed trivial. Trusting Maggie with the combination to her gun safe showed Liz was feeling that way too. They were finally getting past their petty resentments.

Maggie had never believed for a minute that Liz would kill herself. She was too damned reasonable. She'd talk herself out of it before it ever got that far, but how could anyone know another person's limits? She was glad that Brenda had locked up the guns, but now she wanted Maggie to take Liz's favorite pistol off her hands. "You're all alone out there on the pond, and it's so isolated," she'd said. "Liz taught you how to shoot. It's a perfect gun for home defense." Brenda's motives and rationale were so transparent. Understandably, Cherie wanted the gun out of the house. It was true that Maggie felt vulnerable being alone, but she couldn't imagine fending off an intruder with a gun. Before taking Liz's pistol as a favor, she'd ask Sam. After all, it was *her* house.

Sam kept insisting that it was Maggie's house, too. Now that Alina and her boyfriend wanted to buy the place in Scarborough, Maggie had to decide if she trusted Sam's generous words. If not, Alina had assured her mother that she always had a home in the basement apartment. There was only one problem. Maggie no longer felt like she belonged there.

"Hello, Maggie," said Simone cheerfully as she came into the room. She glanced at the watercolors of seascapes that Maggie had hung on the walls. "How nice to bring a little beach into the room, especially since there are no windows."

"Glad I don't have to spend a lot of time down here," said Maggie. "I had those up when I was music director. Glad to be back."

"You don't think Denise's return will upset things?" Simone asked cautiously.

Maggie looked right into Simone's eyes. They were an amber

color, like the eyes of a fox. "Denise resigned, and I'm in charge now. Besides, she won't be here much. She has her career to worry about and she'll be traveling. I say we welcome her when she's here and otherwise, wish her the best."

"Sounds like a plan," agreed Simone with a warm smile.

St. Margaret's children's choir would be performing in the big fundraising concert. After they reviewed the music Lucy and Denise had selected, they discussed who should sing the solos. They needed a boy soprano for Lloyd-Webber's "*Pie Jesu.*"

"I think it should be Keith Harrison," said Simone. "I know he's my grandnephew, but he has a beautiful voice and perfect pitch. For all the mischief he gets into, he has a lot of poise for a little boy."

"Are you sure it won't be too much for him?"

"Keith survived a shooting not once, but twice. He's like a miracle boy, and that has significance for this concert."

Maggie trusted Simone's perceptions, but given all the grief in the community, she wanted to make sure the selection of soloists appeared unbiased. "I think we should still hold auditions."

"I agree. We need to be fair, but my instincts tell me he's the one."

"Okay, then. We'll find out tomorrow at practice."

\*\*\*

Olivia moved through the maze of tables set up in the atrium of the town hall. The head librarian had curated an exhibit that would soon be open to the public. She'd taken on the task of culling the herd of stuffed animals, picking a classic teddy and a few plush toys that represented popular cartoon characters. She'd thinned the forest of angel lawn ornaments and decorated crosses, carefully preserving all the photographs. Like artifacts from an ancient society given new life in a museum, the grave lanterns were illuminated with electric candles.

With the help of the town historian, the librarian had carefully arranged the notes in albums. Handwritten notes crowded some of the plastic sleeves; others held only a single card, like the one from the president and first lady, elegant and official. Olivia had been impressed by the speeches Vice President Harris and the first lady gave when they'd visited. Unfortunately, they'd done compassionate visits for shootings too many times before.

"God needed another angel, so he took you to heaven," read one card, a sentiment that had always struck Olivia as silly and crass. She considered herself a good Episcopalian, but she didn't believe in heaven or hell. She knew that even the worst people had a backstory, and good people always had an agenda. She wasn't a theologian like Lucy, but she was a woman of faith. That's why she understood how harm to children could break it.

Under Olivia's watch, nine little boys had died. *Where was God that day, and why wasn't he watching over them? Where was he when Jason molested his daughters, or when that long-ago gym teacher touched Peter Langdon?* Olivia wanted to spit in the eye of people who talked about God's will and lessons to be learned. When it came to children, there was only one lesson to learn—adults kept failing them.

"What do you think, Mrs. Enright?" the head librarian asked anxiously. Her contract was expiring soon, and she was obviously hoping Olivia would put in a good word for her.

"I think you've done an amazing job," said Olivia honestly. To arrive at this collection, the librarian had needed to sift through tons of stuff, most of which had already been carted to the transfer station for disposal. This display would be winnowed again. What remained would have a permanent home in the library's basement.

"Are you going to the press conference?" Olivia asked.

"Yes, I wouldn't miss it." Of course, she wouldn't, not with all the selectmen and the library board attending.

When Olivia emerged from the library, she decided to walk to the school. The parking lot was already filling up. The auditorium of the high school was the only place in town large enough to hold the crowd they were expecting. When the first lady and vice president had come, they'd had to put on a winter trolley to ferry people from parking areas around town. Olivia was still hearing complaints about how the press had snapped up all the tickets, shutting out the townspeople, but you can't please everyone.

After she hung up her coat backstage, she stepped out to mingle with the others. Liz was a knockout in a designer suit. Maggie's influence showed in the outfit Sam had chosen, an olive wool suit that flattered her angular figure. Olivia brushed aside her jealousy that Maggie could influence Sam. When they were involved, Sam had resisted Olivia's suggestions.

The loud tapping of the microphone signified they were ready to begin. Olivia took her seat on the stage, along with the other founding donors.

"Could everyone please take their seats so we can begin?" Liz waited patiently for the crowd to settle down. She had a naturally commanding speaking voice, so it didn't take long. "Thank you all for coming. Today, we are pleased to announce a fund founded to support the students of Hobbs elementary, their families, and anyone in Hobbs impacted by the shooting. Although some of us were more directly affected, we all need to heal." Olivia looked around and saw that people were listening attentively. Liz was a good speaker. "As a physician, I've always believed that the best way to help yourself is to help others, and that's why we founded Hobbs Promise. Now, I'm going to hand over the microphone to Samantha McKinnon, our founding donor."

There was silence as Sam crossed the stage to the podium. She looked nervous. Considering the animus coming her way, Olivia couldn't blame her.

"Thank you, Dr. Stolz. My friends and I came up with this idea because I wanted to do something to help the people who lost children in the shooting." Liz discreetly raised her hand on her thigh. Sam noticed and added, "And the family of the teacher, too. So, I've decided to help pay for the funerals."

"YOU left the door open!" shouted a woman in the crowd.

Sam stared at her but didn't get ruffled. Obviously, someone had prepared her. "I did, and I'm sorry."

"He only got in because of you! Those kids died because of *you!*"

Sam looked at Melissa, who got up and headed toward the podium. Before she could speak, another voice from the audience calmly said, "He would have gotten in anyway."

Everyone turned to look at Brenda, who wasn't wearing her uniform, just a polar fleece with the Hobbs PD logo. "The lock on the back door was old and useless. You could have opened it with a credit card." There was a collective intake of breath in the room, followed by a buzz of confusion.

Frowning, Liz turned to Olivia. "Did you know about this?"

"Before my time. I had no idea."

"Leaving the door open made it easier for the shooter to get in," Brenda continued, "but anyone who wanted access to the school that day could have easily gotten in. During the investigation, we tested both back-door locks. They were never changed or upgraded."

"Why?" asked a loud voice.

"Because the town spent all the money on the front doors—bulletproof glass, the automatic locks for the classrooms, locks you'd need a grenade to break. They only bought stuff that you can see. For some reason, the back-door locks and hardening access to the administrative office were put on the back burner."

The murmur of the crowd turned from surprise to anger. "That's outrageous!" someone cried. "Who's responsible for this?"

The head of the school board reluctantly stood. "It was on the list of improvements, but with COVID, we needed technology upgrades to deal with remote learning, and it fell by the wayside."

"Damn," muttered Olivia under her breath, "Now they're going to sue the town!"

"No, they won't." Liz got up and gently nudged Melissa away from the podium.

"After the funerals and the medical bills for the victims, the first thing the fund will pay for is upgrading the school security. Now, will everyone please sit down and let us speak?" Liz's voice had the kind of quiet authority you'd hope to hear when all hell is breaking loose, but the crowd, still talking about the old locks, wouldn't settle down.

Finally, a man stood up and said in a loud voice. "Let her speak! Let Dr. Stolz speak!"

"Thank you, Dan," said Liz, saluting the man. "And thank you, Chief Harrison, for that important piece of information. Clearly, we have work to do. But the fact is, no matter how well prepared we are, these mass shootings will continue to happen, and we must be prepared. We will use some of the foundation money for the schools, but also to help young people suffering from mental illness. Unfortunately, Peter Langdon is not an exception. As you all heard, he was a victim too. We can't keep sweeping child abuse under the rug. Abused children grow up to be angry adults who hurt others."

"All the money in the world won't bring back our kids," a woman said.

"No, it can't," said Liz evenly, "but it can help the living. Sam McKinnon, our founding donor, just wants to help. Others want to help too. Now, I'm going to ask our legal counsel, Melissa Morgenstern, to read the names of the donors and how much each of them has pledged."

Melissa read the list. Olivia was surprised to hear names she hadn't expected, including Fire Chief Duvaney and Amy Hsu. The amounts weren't as large as the founding donors, but they all added up.

Olivia noticed someone in the back making a hasty exit. Although the woman looked familiar, Olivia struggled to place her. Then she recognized her as the face of the personal injury law firm that advertised on late-night TV.

Melissa finished reading the names. "Our goal is to raise one million dollars this year. Each family who has lost someone in the shooting will receive a check for ten thousand dollars to defray funeral expenses. We will contact the families whose children are still recovering to see how we can help with medical expenses. Harriet Keene is the point person for receiving claims." The town lawyer, sitting on the stage, waved to identify herself.

Even before the Q&A part of the conference ended, reporters were rushing out to post their stories. It was time to wind this conference down. Melissa gestured to Olivia. "And now for some final words from our town manager, Olivia Enright."

"Thank you all for coming to listen to our plan. Maybe we could have done better in preventing this tragedy, but we could only do our best. Hindsight is twenty-twenty, as they say. I hope you'll forgive Sam McKinnon. She has done a lot of good for Hobbs."

"Sam's a good person," said a woman in the front row. "She installed the shower rails for my old mother and wouldn't take a dime."

"She fixed my parents' rotting deck for nothing," another person said. Many more people stood to vouch for Sam's character. It was becoming a contest to see who had the best story about Sam's generosity. Olivia finally cut off the testimonies so she could bring the meeting to a close.

"Thank you all for sharing your stories. They show that Samantha McKinnon is a kind, decent woman. Let's not forget that she's one of us, and in Hobbs, we take care of our own."

# Chapter 16

Sam's duffle bag sat in the front hall while she made a last stop in the bathroom. Watching through the window for the airport limo, Maggie couldn't believe it was already time for Sam to leave. The week had gone by so fast. Sam needed to be back in Berkeley to teach her class, and the construction manager had been calling constantly with questions. Sam's body might be in Maine, but her mind was back in California.

As much as Maggie wanted to have Sam's focused attention, especially because she'd been home for such a short time, she was glad something could distract her. Despite everyone's efforts, two of the victim's families had filed wrongful death lawsuits. Melissa and Sam's attorney kept telling her the case was weak and not to worry, but Sam was a worrier.

She returned from the bathroom just as the black town car pulled into the driveway. When she hugged Maggie, Sam's long arms wrapped around her until they reached the other side. Feeling so completely enfolded was reassuring, especially because Maggie wouldn't see Sam for weeks. The inconveniences of transcontinental air travel had discouraged more frequent visits. Besides, Maggie didn't want Sam to get too comfortable on the West Coast.

After Sam won the Chicago commission, she knew she could make a living as an architect and could live anywhere. She'd started talking about moving again until Maggie had said, "All our friends live here, and there's no way I'm living in California." That had put a stop to the conversation about moving, but Maggie sensed that Sam wasn't done with it.

"I'll call you before we take off and when we land," Sam whispered into Maggie's ear. "Don't worry. I'll be home again soon." As much as Maggie enjoyed the protracted last hug, her ear delighted in hearing the word *home*.

***

"If I'd only known we'd end up together, I'd have gotten you a ticket, too. I had to order them months ago. Now, they're all sold out."

Bobbie listened to Susan's continued apologies while she drove her to the rectory to pick up her car. Most of the parish already knew they were a couple, so the attempt to deceive anyone was getting ridiculous. Susan almost seemed disappointed that there hadn't been more outrage.

"It would have been fun to go with you to New York, but with Amy and Liz both out of the office, I need to be here. Next time." Bobbie wished she could go. It had been years since she'd gone into the city to have dinner and see a show. After Joyce's diagnosis, the visits to New York had tapered off until they stopped. Joyce wasn't an opera fan, so Bobbie had never been inside the Metropolitan Opera House, where Lucille Bartlett would be singing for the first time in almost twenty years. To get a sense of what Susan would experience, Bobbie had searched the internet for online photos of the crimson-and-gold interior, the Chagall murals, and the crystal chandeliers designed to look like galaxies of stars.

"I need to be there," said Susan. "I was with Lucy during those awful years when she was trying to save her career. I remember the day when she finally gave up. Her return to the Met has been so long in coming."

"Susan, I understand, and I want you to go. You should support your friend. You support me. You read to Joyce and listen to music with her."

Bobbie felt Susan's eyes on the side of her face. "I'm glad you're not still worried about Lucy."

"I never was," Bobbie honestly replied.

"You weren't?" Susan didn't even try to hide her disappointment.

Bobbie tried to think of a way to let her down gently. "I know Liz. She's not going to share Lucy with anyone. Must be nice to be so in love."

After a long moment, Susan said, "I think I'm falling in love with you."

"I'm glad...because I feel the same."

"Do you think Joyce is still upset about us getting together?

Bobbie shrugged. Now that Joyce couldn't speak, Bobbie couldn't ask. "I think she was more upset when she thought I might leave her because you were in the picture. Now she knows, as far as she can still understand, that I'd never abandon her."

"I truly admire what you're doing," said Susan. "Love can be expressed in many ways."

"Yes, it can," said Bobbie, pleased that Susan understood.

They'd arrived at the rectory. Instead of a goodbye kiss, they held hands for a moment before Bobbie handed Susan the soft cooler with the tuna sandwich she'd made for her lunch. "Have a great day at school," she said. "Will I see you tonight?"

"I have to pack for my trip."

"So I won't see you again before you leave?"

Susan shook her head.

"I'll miss you," Bobbie said.

"Me too, but I'll call you later and every night while I'm in New York. Reshma taught me how to video chat. Maybe we could try it!"

As she drove to the practice, Bobbie pondered the subtle obligations that went along with being in a relationship—telling someone where you were going, when you would return, asking if they minded if you did something. It felt strange to be there again, but right.

✳✳✳

When Liz had invited her to ride with her into New York, Susan had wondered if the five hours in the car would be tense, but they were almost in Manhattan and hadn't stopped talking yet.

"Are you nervous about the TV interview?" Susan asked.

Liz shrugged. "I've been interviewed on TV before, and I had to give a lot of press conferences when I was head of surgery at Yale.

But this is different. What I have to say about guns won't make anyone happy."

"Why?"

"Because I see both sides."

Susan nodded as she absorbed it. "Would you like to preview your comments with me?"

"No," said Liz bluntly. Then she seemed to realize she'd been abrupt and added, "Not that I wouldn't share it with you, Susan, but I don't want to talk about it until I have to. I'm sure you understand why better than most people."

"I certainly do. Bobbie often asks me if I'd like to share my feelings. She thinks it's important to talk about them. Usually, I'd agree, but I'm not ready to talk about it. When I do, I'm back there in Courtney's office, thinking the next moment will be my last."

"Were you praying the whole time?" asked Liz, briefly turning to face her.

"Of course. I prayed that God would forgive that poor, tortured boy. I prayed for you because you were risking your life and you don't believe."

Liz faced forward. "You know that's an urban myth."

"I thought so," said Susan, smiling. She wondered if Lucy knew Liz's secret.

"But I appreciate your prayers, Susan, and what you said the night I came over for tea. I've been thinking about what you said."

"And...?"

"I hate the idea that Pete chose me to put him out of his misery. Why not step up to the window and let one of the snipers take a shot at him? Or turn the gun on himself?"

"Because he trusted you. You're probably the only adult he could count on. He knew you cared about him."

"But he gave me this terrible burden!"

"Yes, he did."

Susan knew Liz was fighting back tears when she audibly

swallowed. After that, she became more attentive to the traffic. There was silence until they reached their hotel.

***

Amy looked at the clothes she'd laid out on the bed. It had been a long time since she'd attended a dressy occasion like a night at the opera. When her marriage with Jill was ending, she became a hermit. She'd looked for excuses to refuse invitations, even from well-meaning friends. In the tiny, sterile apartment where she'd lived after she'd moved out, she'd barely cooked enough food to sustain herself. She'd subscribed to one of those ridiculously expensive meal services, so she didn't have to go to the grocery store or think about what she was eating. The first time that food had any taste again was a meal that Olivia had cooked for her. That's when Amy had decided their friendship had potential.

But now it might change. The report from Olivia's new cardiologist concurred with Amy's prognosis. Olivia had completely recovered from her heart event and was tolerating her medication well. That meant Amy had to face the real question: was she ready for an intimate relationship?

She carefully folded the pretty nightgown and matching negligee she'd bought online. If she was going to wear a classy dress and jewelry to the opera, shouldn't her sleepwear be elegant too? Amy told herself she was dressing to please herself, except it wasn't true. She wanted the first time she shared a room with Olivia to be special. She wanted to be beautiful in her eyes.

She'd imagined their first night together many times, never letting on to Olivia how much she desired her. She imagined Olivia would be a bold lover who took what she wanted, and the idea excited her. But how to find the delicate balance between submission and becoming a victim again? Amy also liked to take the lead, but would Olivia allow it? She always wanted to be in control. There was only one way to find out, but once they crossed that bridge, things would never be the same again.

\*\*\*

Olivia's nerves buzzed with excitement as they waited for the performance to begin. During her cultural enrichment campaign after she'd married Michael Enright, she'd bought a subscription to the Met. To her surprise, she'd discovered she loved opera. After the hedge fund started making money, she'd given millions to New York arts institutions and enjoyed rubbing elbows with the senior management and the perks of being listed in the top category of donors. Since she'd left New York, she hadn't shown her face at the Met.

Beside her, Amy sat studiously reading the program notes. Her outfit tonight was the epitome of understated elegance. Olivia had been proud to sit across from her at the trendy downtown restaurant Liz had suggested. The food was excellent. Liz loved to eat, so Olivia always trusted her recommendations. They couldn't join them because Lucy never ate before a performance. Olivia didn't mind the opportunity for a private dinner with Amy, which made dining in the upscale restaurant feel more like a date.

Olivia glanced at her watch. Ten minutes until curtain.

She leaned closer to speak into Amy's ear. "I raised tons of money for this place when I was into that kind of thing," she said casually.

"I bet you did," said Amy, raising her eyes from the program. Olivia was disappointed that she didn't look more impressed.

"Do you like opera?" Olivia asked, trying to make conversation. She'd never thought to ask.

"Some of it. Italian opera appeals to me more than Wagner. My parents insisted I have a well-rounded education, even though I was always destined to become a doctor. Did I ever tell you I wanted to be a professional tennis player?"

"No," said Olivia, drawing back for a better view. "Were you good enough?"

"My father thought so. He was my first coach. I made state championships."

"Why didn't you continue?"

"My mother thought tennis was good exercise, but I should focus on getting into a good college, so I could get into medical school and become a doctor like them."

"How did your brother escape from joining the family business?"

"Vincent has always been a rebel. I envy his ability to resist my parents."

"He's a man. That makes a difference." Olivia studied Amy. She seldom talked about her family and never negatively. "What else did your 'well-rounded' education include? Music lessons?"

"Yes, I played the violin."

"Do you still play?"

"Occasionally. It soothes me when I'm upset."

"Will you play for me sometime?"

"I'm not very good."

"Knowing you, you're just being modest."

"In fact, I was in the New York State youth orchestra, which impressed college admissions officers. Got me into Barnard."

"You'll have to share your resume with me," said Olivia, although she'd already done a background search on Amy.

"Why? Are you thinking of hiring me?"

"Maybe," Olivia replied with a wink.

The chandeliers rose and the house lights dimmed. The murmur of the audience grew softer. A man with bleach-blond hair bounded to the conductor's podium to a round of applause. He bowed but didn't launch into the overture as expected. Instead, the massive gold curtain waved, and a man in a tuxedo came out from behind it.

"Good evening, ladies and gentlemen. Welcome to the debut of our new production of *Lohengrin*. Before we begin, Lucille Bartlett, our Elsa this evening, has an announcement to make." He extended his hand. "Ladies and gentlemen, Madame Bartlett." Lucy, in full costume, a white gown and a long blond wig, emerged from behind the curtain. The applause, accompanied by shrill whistles and shouts of "brava," was wild. The audience rose to its feet, including Liz and Emily, three rows ahead.

Lucy crossed her hands over her heart and gracefully lowered herself into an old-fashioned diva's curtsey. "Thank you," she said when the applause finally faded. "I'd like to dedicate my performance this evening to the victims of the Hobbs shooting. Some of you may know that I live in the town in Maine where this tragedy took place. We've created a foundation to support the students of Hobbs Elementary and their families and help heal the community. If you would like to contribute to Hobbs Promise, the web address and telephone number will appear in the subtitles screen on your seatback and on the screens to the right and left of the stage," she said, gesturing in both directions. "Thank you in advance for your generosity. I hope you enjoy the performance." Vigorous clapping accompanied Lucy's exit behind the curtain.

The house lights faded into darkness. Finally, the overture began.

Amy leaned over to whisper into Olivia's ear. "Thank you for this," she said, taking Olivia's hand. "It's so exciting!" Olivia gazed at Amy's face and admired the perfection of her profile.

***

Brenda sat down in the living room and twisted open a bottle of beer. She'd only brought along a glass because Cherie was trying to teach the kids manners. Brenda's mother had tried to turn her into a lady, even though she'd had a different standard for her sons. They could swill beer from the bottle and fart without apology, but a lady, Brenda's mother had explained, must always observe the rules.

Cherie wasn't even here to witness Brenda's adherence to a bygone standard of social convention. She was upstairs getting the kids to bed, but she'd made Brenda promise to set up the DVR so she could watch Liz's interview on *Sixty Minutes*.

The lights flickered again. Outside, the wind was howling. Brenda hoped the power wouldn't fail. She hated pulling the heavy generator out of the garage, and she didn't want to miss the broadcast. She glanced at the time on the cable box. Maggie had said it would probably air after the first segment. While the secretary of transportation talked about the train wreck in Ohio, Brenda drank her beer and took a mental vacation. The show broke for a commercial. Then a petite, dark-haired woman appeared on the screen: Alina Krusick in the starring role of her career.

"Tonight, I'm talking to Dr. Elizabeth Stolz of Hobbs, Maine. Dr. Stolz bravely entered a hostage situation, hoping to talk an active shooter into handing over his guns." The camera focused on Liz, who wore more makeup than Brenda was used to seeing. She knew from her stint as a regular guest on Fox News that TV lights flooded out details, so makeup artists laid it on thick.

"Dr. Stolz, I understand you knew the shooter, Peter Langdon, pretty well," Alina began. "Please tell us how you met."

"The rector of the Episcopal church told me that Peter's mother had expressed concerns about the number of guns he had in the house. Dr. Bartlett turned to me for advice."

"And how did you respond?"

"It's always tricky when a concern comes through professional channels. Neither of us could directly intervene because there wasn't a credible threat. We couldn't officially report it to the police without breaking professional confidence. Fortunately, Peter was my patient. I routinely ask about firearms in the home to evaluate threats, so during an exam, I talked about my safety class and convinced him to sign up."

"Why did you think taking your class would make a difference?"

"It's been my experience that when people see first-hand how loud and destructive firearms can be, they develop a new respect for them. That's one reason I offer classes."

"What are the other reasons?"

"I want everyone who owns or uses a gun to handle it safely. Most gun accidents involving children occur because people don't know how to store guns correctly."

"You own guns."

"Yes, I do."

"Including assault weapons?"

"I have several tactical weapons. An AK-47, an AR-15 and another rifle made in that style."

"Why do you have these weapons, which are intended for war?"

"Only the AK-47 is an actual military grade weapon. The others were designed for the consumer market. Gun manufacturers make them specifically for non-military use."

"Such as?"

"Well, they don't make good hunting rifles because the flesh would be shredded beyond being edible. Mostly, people buy them because they're fun to shoot and very accurate. But Stephen King got it right when he said, 'Semi-automatics have only two purposes. One is so owners can take them to the shooting range once in a while, yell yeehaw, and get all horny at the rapid fire and the burning vapor spurting from the end of the barrel. Their other use—their only other use—is to kill people.' To be clear, pistols are also semi-automatic weapons."

"If there were a ban on assault weapons, would you surrender yours?"

"If there were a ban on any guns, I would be the first in line."

"Why don't you just do it?"

"That's a good question. Until there is a ban, it's an arms race. I have guns because other people do. With the polarization in this country, I'm concerned about political violence. Like any woman in our society, I face a threat of sexual violence, which is one reason I carry a handgun wherever I go. I own assault rifles because I use them in my classes to make a point. They are destructive beyond our wildest imagination. Once you fire one, its danger becomes something real."

"You've let me fire yours at the range, and it's a terrifying experience. Do you think violent video games contribute to gun violence?"

"In other countries, people play the same games and don't turn into killers. But video games dehumanize the targets. Despite all the realistic blood and gore made possible by computer graphics, the 'enemy' is never represented as human beings."

"But Peter Langdon was a human being, someone you knew quite well. How could you kill him? Aren't doctors sworn to do no harm?"

Brenda could actually hear Liz gulp. "That's part of the Hippocratic oath, but I went to the scene as a physician and ended up being a deputy. I thought that if I talked to him, he would release the hostages. I tried everything to avoid killing him. I even went against police protocol and shot him in the arm so he wouldn't kill a hostage. When I shot him, it was only because he'd turned his gun on me."

"So, it was self-defense."

"Yes, but that hasn't made his death any easier." Liz cleared her throat. "Excuse me."

"It's okay," said Alina. "I understand this is an emotional subject."

"Thanks for your sympathy, but I don't think anyone can understand. People come up to me in the supermarket and thank me for killing Peter. They call me a hero for making myself a hostage. I'm not a hero."

"Why not take credit for saving lives that day?"

"I'm glad those women are alive, but if I had handled it differently, there might have been a different outcome."

"We'll never know, will we?"

"No, we won't," said Liz in a regretful tone.

While the segment cut to commercial, Cherie came into the room and sat down next to Brenda on the couch. "How's she doing?"

"Amazing."

"Sorry I missed the beginning," said Cherie. "The kids are anxious about the storm and needed some TLC."

"I'll play it back when it's done." Brenda raised her finger to her lips because the commercial was ending.

"I'm here with Dr. Elizabeth Stolz," Alina reminded the audience. "We're talking about the recent shooting in Hobbs, Maine." She turned to Liz. "People say you're proof that 'a good guy with a gun' can make a difference in a shooting. What do you say to that?"

"Red states think gun reform means making it *easier* to carry guns. That's crazy. Having more guns means more danger. Arming teachers won't keep kids safe. Most teachers with guns only attend a few hours of training before bringing a gun into a classroom. When you're faced with an active shooter, you need to be so well-trained you act by instinct."

"Apparently, most gun owners think they could perform."

Liz shook her head. "When I was considering buying my first handgun, I told a friend of mine, a Vietnam vet and ex-marine who'd won awards for marksmanship. At the time, he was the same age I am now, namely, late sixties. He said, 'Liz, when I was in 'Nam and shooting every day, I could take down a shooter in a school or shopping mall, no problem, but I don't practice enough now. My eyesight's not what it was in my twenties. My reflexes are slower. When I'm stressed, my hands shake. There's no guarantee that if I were in a shooting situation, that I could even hit the target!'"

"That's a compelling observation," Alina agreed.

"And that's what's wrong with the 'good guy with a gun' theory. Most gun owners couldn't perform if faced with a real shooter."

"But these people are walking around with guns."

"Yes, they are."

"So, they're more of a danger than a defense."

"And consider this, when the police arrive at the scene, how do they know who's the 'good' guy? Faced with gunfire, they have to make a choice. Sometimes, they shoot the 'good guy.'"

"That's unsettling."

Liz nodded. "Very."

"The NRA has been criticized in recent years for its violent rhetoric, but you're still a member."

"My father belonged to the NRA when it was still an organization to promote shooting sports and gun safety. When I got my hunting license as a teenager, I joined too. I resigned my membership, around the same time as George W. Bush did in 1995. I joined again when I became a safety instructor. Being affiliated with the NRA allows me to train more people in more situations. It's a trade-off, but one that I'm willing to make for now."

"Liz, we're almost out of time. What's the one thing you'd like to tell our viewers tonight?"

Liz frowned and thought for a long moment. Then she looked directly into the camera and said, "It's the guns."

# Chapter 17

Olivia drank her first cup of coffee while Amy finished dressing. The ocean was angry after the storm. All night long, the wind had roared outside. The calendar might say they were heading into spring, but this backloaded winter weather wouldn't quit.

The scuff of Amy's heels instantly drew Olivia's attention. Wearing a sleek suit, her hair coiffed, and her face tastefully made up, Amy cut the perfect image of a professional woman. She gave Olivia a soft kiss before she headed to the coffeemaker.

Amy had turned out to be a generous and tender lover with a wild side Olivia hadn't expected, but certainly didn't mind. She liked surprises. It kept things interesting.

"I'll make you some breakfast," said Olivia. "A cheese omelet okay?"

"If you can be quick. I can't be late this morning. Liz is off today."

"I am the most efficient chef you'll ever meet," said Olivia, reaching into the cabinet for her favorite omelet skillet.

"Of that I have no doubt," replied Amy dryly. She checked her phone while Olivia vigorously beat the eggs.

"After Lucy's stunning performance, has Liz made any more noises about retirement?" Olivia asked to get her attention. Amy merely smiled. Maybe she thought it was none of Olivia's business. "Just curious. If Lucy starts traveling more for her career, I wonder if Liz will go with her. Naturally, we're all glad to have her back full time."

"Especially me, because it gives me more time to be with you." Amy raised a sexy brow. "To answer your question, I think Liz is weighing her options, but I doubt she'll retire. That's fine with me because I'm not ready to be the senior partner. I'm good at the business side, but it's not my favorite part of medical practice. Fortunately, Liz loves it."

"Yes, she does, and she's quite good at it." Olivia deftly flipped the omelet in the pan. "Will you be back for dinner? I was thinking of making scallops."

"Is that an invitation?"

Olivia made a prissy face to show Amy that her understated humor hadn't flown under the radar.

"I seem to be here all the time," Amy said. "Won't you get bored seeing me?"

"I don't think there's a prayer of a chance of that happening." Amy's toast popped up right on time. Olivia slathered it with premium butter and brought the plate to the table. "There. How's that for a speedy breakfast?"

"You're hired," said Amy and bit into a piece of toast. "And yes, I'll be back for dinner."

❄❄❄

"I was so surprised that the foundation would even consider me," said Renee. "Considering what Pete did…"

"But you didn't do it, he did," said Lucy. As Renee Langdon's former rector, Lucy had called to see how she was settling into her new home in Florida. "You and your children are as worthy of support as any other family who lost a loved one that day."

"The funeral money helped a lot, and the contribution to the moving expenses. I had no idea it would cost that much. Please thank Dr. Stolz for sticking up for me with the committee." Lucy knew it had been a fight to get the foundation to include Renee in the grants, but Liz wouldn't back down.

Renee reported that the rector of the local church had been in touch to invite her to a bereavement group. "It didn't matter to her that Peter was the shooter," said Renee with surprise.

"Of course it didn't," said Lucy. "You're grieving too."

Lucy saw a message from her agent suddenly cross her screen. She'd been on the phone with Renee for almost an hour and she was curious to see what Roger wanted. His message only said to call him right away.

"Renee, I'm really sorry, but I have to go. I have another call. Please keep in touch."

After Renee assured her that she would, Lucy hung up and called Roger.

"Good morning, Lucy!" he said in a merry voice. "You're up and at it bright and early today."

"Yes, Roger, and I'm really busy this morning. What's so urgent that it can't wait?"

"How would you like to sing Senta in *Der Fliegende Holländer* this spring at the Met? Late May, early June. Two performances only. And they want you for *Tannhäuser* next season."

Lucy's heart did a few flip-flops. She'd told people she'd only returned to the Met to prove a point, but performing again on that stage had been exciting. The reviews had lavishly praised her. Only one had mentioned the forced apology and the sad history behind it.

"Well?" asked Roger when Lucy's prolonged silence grew unnatural.

"I'm thinking about it."

"Both roles are in your *Fach*. You've sung them before."

"Yes, in Stuttgart. Years ago."

"Well?"

"Let me think about it. I've had my hands full with pastoral work. I've got all those performances this summer. I don't want to spread myself too thin."

"Lucy, let me be frank. You're going to be fifty-nine this June. You're getting to the age when many sopranos retire. You don't have much time left."

"Gee, thanks, Roger, for reminding me how old I am." Lucy wasn't generally snippy with Roger unless he pushed too hard. This was different. He was reminding her of an uncomfortable truth. Kiri Te Kanawa had quit singing because she could no longer stand to hear her own voice. Maybe Lucy would get to that point too.

"You know I'm right, Lucy," said Roger.

"But I don't want to be typecast as a Wagnerian. How about some Verdi or Puccini?"

"Everybody sings those. You're special, Lucy."

"When do they need to know?"

"By tomorrow morning."

"All right. Let me think about it. I want to talk to Liz."

"You know she'll agree with me."

Of course, she would. It annoyed Lucy that he was right about that too.

***

"Do it," Liz said. "I'll be in the audience every night."

"I love you to pieces!" Lucy declared.

"I love you too. Now, get back to work!" Liz could hear Lucy chuckling as she hung up the call.

Liz watched from the kitchen window as Denise and a friend moved more boxes into the barn. She'd offered the storage space over her workshop, but she was surprised to see that Denise had so much stuff. It still made no sense to Liz that someone who needed regular access to an airport would want to live so far from it.

Something about Hobbs kept drawing Denise back, and Tom. He and Jeff had come back early from Florida and intended to stay until next winter. Hopefully, Sam would come home, too.

They'd all come to Hobbs for a reason. Liz had come because corporate medicine had destroyed the profession she'd once loved. Maggie came, hoping to relaunch her acting career. Brenda just wanted to keep being a cop. Cherie had brought her father home to die. Olivia was seeking atonement for her son's sins. Amy wanted to forget a bad marriage. They'd left their storied pasts behind and come "from away." In Hobbs, they'd found a safe harbor, a place where people accepted them for who they were. It might have taken a while for the townspeople to adjust to them, but eventually, they did.

Liz pulled her phone out of her pocket and looked up Denise's number in her contacts. "When you take a break, bring your friend, and I'll make you some lunch," she said after Denise answered. "Nothing fancy. Just soup and sandwiches."

"Sounds wonderful!" replied the enthusiastic voice on the other end. "We'll be right in!" Liz heard the excited conversation in the background before Denise ended the call.

Liz took two containers of tomato soup out of the basement freezer. Last summer's weather had been perfect for tomatoes, but since Maggie had moved out, Liz hadn't put up as much of her harvest. Instead, she'd given what she couldn't use to her friends or the church food pantry. She could have grown fewer plants, but starting them under grow lights in the basement had become a tradition, and she could never resist trying new varieties.

Impatiently, she watched the soup defrost in the microwave and wished she'd thought of taking it out earlier. Instead of counting down the seconds, she went back to the basement and brought up a jar of bread and butter pickles. Her grandmother's pickles had always won blue ribbons at the Grange fair. Liz's version followed her recipe to the letter, but her pickles never tasted the same. Maybe it was the water, or the vinegar...or her imagination.

Denise and her friend brought the cold in with them. "This is Ryan," said Denise, nudging forward a spindly young man with a sparse beard. Liz wondered why she would choose someone so slight to help with moving. When he shyly took her hand, his felt delicate and cool. "He plays cello with the BSO," Denise explained.

"Can I use your bathroom?" Ryan asked. "I'd like to wash up." Liz directed him down the hall.

Denise curiously studied her. Liz seldom invited her to the main house unless Emily was home, but she'd gone back to Yale to prep for her thesis defense. "Thanks for having us," Denise finally said.

"I was making myself something to eat and thought you might be hungry." Liz felt Denise's eyes watching her as she ladled out tomato soup into oversized mugs. "Tomato soup seems to go with grilled cheese, don't you think?"

Denise murmured something that sounded like 'yes.' Liz scooped the sandwiches out of the pan and cut them on the diagonal. She arranged the triangles on plates with the mugs and pickles. The scene reminded Liz of the ads she used to see in her mother's old issues of *Good Housekeeping*.

She looked up and saw that Denise's eyes had filled. "What's the matter? Don't you like grilled cheese?"

"I love grilled cheese. It's my favorite comfort food. When my parents weren't getting along, I'd go to my grandmother's house across the street, and she'd make me grilled cheese and tomato soup."

"Mine too. I tell people, if it weren't for my grandmother, I'd have grown up to be a serial killer." Liz grinned, but the joke that used to be funny fell flat. Denise nodded, apparently understanding.

Ryan returned from washing his hands. "Bread and butter pickles! I love them!"

Liz handed out the plates and led them to the table in the breakfast nook. "Did you find enough room for your boxes in the loft?" she asked, sitting down on the bench opposite them. "I moved some things around to make more space."

"Yes, thank you," said Denise. "Those are boxes I never unpacked. I've been on the move for a long time." She closed her eyes and smiled when she bit into her sandwich.

The gooey cheese made Liz think of her grandmother. Whenever her granddaughter showed up, she'd stop what she was doing, even interrupt her "stories" as she called the afternoon TV soaps. She never asked why Liz had come, or what was wrong in the big house. She'd look in her cupboard and the old refrigerator moved up from Brooklyn and find something to cook.

Liz imagined Denise as a little boy taking refuge in her grandmother's kitchen. Did she know then that she wanted to be a girl instead? Maybe Liz would ask her when they were alone.

"Ryan is trans too," Denise suddenly volunteered, which caused him to look up sharply. His pale eyes were wide with trepidation. "It's okay," Denise assured him. "Liz is cool."

Ryan regarded Liz cautiously. He nodded and bit into his sandwich. "Good," he murmured with his mouth full. "Real good."

Liz watched the young people enjoying her food and listened to them carry on about the ridiculously simple meal.

*I've become my grandmother*, she thought. *I'm feeding the dislocated children.*

***

Bobbie tried not to listen with a clinician's ear to Susan's heart, but it was a deeply ingrained habit that she couldn't turn on and off at will. She remembered the day Susan had shown up at the practice complaining of palpitations. Luckily, the scare had turned out to be nothing but anxiety. Listening now to Susan's strong, steady heartbeat, she hoped it portended a long life together. Then she reminded herself that she'd imagined a happy future when she'd met Joyce. Maybe she should have known better after caring for Joyce's mother, who'd had Alzheimer's too.

Joyce was still asleep in her room in the main house. The baby monitor picked up her breathing. Like a baby, Joyce couldn't say what she needed. She hadn't spoken a single word since the respiratory infection. As a specialist in geriatrics, Bobbie knew that cognitive decline wasn't steady. The plateaus and dips in function were like descending stairs. A big health setback, like the RSV infection Joyce had, could be like falling off a cliff. At the thought, Bobbie snuggled closer to Susan's body for comfort.

"Did I tell you Lucy asked me to take on a new ministry?" asked Susan, the sound of her voice hollow because Bobbie was listening with one ear. She sat up so she could hear better. "She thinks I should get more involved in parish life. She's worried brooding over the incident puts too much temptation in my path."

"Does it?"

"Sometimes when I'm alone. When I'm with other people, I hardly ever think about alcohol unless others are drinking."

Bobbie felt guilty. She'd stopped drinking in Susan's presence in a gesture of support, but she'd stopped hiding all the alcohol. One thing had never made sense to her. Why didn't drinking the altar wine break Susan's sobriety? "I barely touch it to my lips and tell myself it's no longer wine, but the Eucharist, and it works. I don't know why."

Bobbie still didn't believe in religion and probably never would, but she felt a strange sense of awe seeing Susan at services. The vestments seemed to transform her so that she was no longer Susan, her best friend, or the woman who made the sweetest love to her, but a priest. Bobbie couldn't explain it any more than Susan could tell her why the communion wine didn't make her fall off the wagon.

"What is this new *ministry*?" Bobbie asked, saying the word with hesitation. Church terms still felt strange on her tongue, so she had to pronounce them distinctly to make sure they sounded right. When Susan looked puzzled over some medical term Bobbie used, she always took time to explain it. They were teaching each other a whole new vocabulary.

"Lucy asked if I would take over her bereavement group. Besides pastoral counseling, I have group experience from AA, so it would be a good fit."

"But you're still dealing with your own issues. Won't it be too hard to take on other people's problems?"

"That's the whole idea behind group therapy. By sharing each other's burdens, we lighten the load for everyone. I'd benefit too."

Bobbie groped around in the dim light and found her nightshirt. Susan's gaze instantly dropped when Bobbie caught her admiring her. "Hey, it's okay to look at me. Makes me feel sexy." But no matter how often they were naked together, or how many times Bobbie murmured worshipful compliments, Susan was still shy about her body. They'd just been naked making love, but she had the bedsheet pulled up into her armpits.

Bobbie got back into bed. "Will you get a raise for taking on this new *ministry*?"

"Not likely. It's part of my job. They pay me as half-time clergy and provide housing, so I really should be doing more."

"Susan, you suffered a big trauma. Are you sure you're ready to take on more?"

"No. I still have nightmares. Loud noises make me jump. The bell at school makes my ears ring."

"You should let me take a look."

"It's not physical!"

"It could be. Loud noises like gunshots can damage your hearing."

Susan sighed. "All right, Bobbie, examine my ears...if it makes you feel better."

"I feel better when I help other people feel better."

"That's exactly why I want to do the bereavement group. And Lucy's right. It's important to be in the community. We all need each other right now."

Bobbie admired Susan's handsome profile in the amber glow of the bedside lamp. "You're a good woman, Susan Gedney."

"So are you, Bobbie Lantry."

"Turn off that light and let me hold you."

"I'd like that." Susan reached over and switched off the lamp.

# Chapter 18

"Liz, we don't have time this morning," Lucy said, but she wanted to stay under the duvet, enjoying Liz's warm hand on her breast and her fingers gently teasing between her legs. She sighed as the caresses became more insistent. Distantly, she heard her mother calling. "Lulu, get up now. Time to practice, honeybunch."

*Later, Mommy. I'll practice later.* Liz disappeared under the covers like a child hiding in a blanket fort. Her lips on Lucy's nipple were causing the sweetest sensations. Her fingers were inside her now. The touch of her tongue on that most sensitive place made Lucy's breath catch.

"Get up, Lulu. It's time to sing your exercises. Be a good girl."

*No, Mommy, not now.*

Lucy wound her fingers into Liz's hair. She tried not to pull too hard as the orgasm began. It flowed over her, enveloping her like a warm bath, moving up from her crotch to her chest. The space between her breasts flashed with heat and tingled.

After the climax reached its peak, Liz slowed her pace. She knew Lucy became sensitive after she came, but she always teasingly kissed her one last time to make her jump. A moment later, Liz was grinning against Lucy's cheek, obviously pleased with herself.

Now that the excitement had passed, Lucy could no longer silence her mother's calls. The vocal exercises she'd been doing every day since she was a girl played in her head. Torn between getting up to practice and satisfying her lover, Lucy chose Liz. She was easily excited and always came quickly. Today was no exception.

"You're off today. Go back to sleep," Lucy whispered, smoothing Liz's hair, wild from her visit to the blanket fort.

"No, I'm getting up with you. I promised we're in this together, and we are." Liz reached under Lucy's nightgown and gave her a last, teasing touch that made her flinch.

"You're bad," Lucy said.

"That's why you love me."

It wasn't true. Lucy loved the little naughty child in Liz, always testing limits, but she loved the woman who pulled herself from their warm bed to listen to her practice even more.

Liz made a detour to the kitchen to fill her thermal cup with coffee. Lucy only sipped water before practice. She used the concert grand near the tiny stage to find her first note and then launched into her scales.

"Lulu, don't strain," said her mother's voice in her head. "Ease into the top notes."

Lucy smiled. *Yes, Mommy*, she said in her mind.

❋❋❋

Sam got off the red eye from Oakland and headed to the limo depot. Her mouth tasted like dirt, but when she reached into her pocket for the tin of Trader Joe's tea mints, she found it empty. *Shit*, she thought. She felt so grungy after the long flight, even though she'd taken a shower before she left. With everyone coughing and sneezing on the plane, she was glad she'd worn a mask. People looked at her funny, but she didn't care. Liz told her she should wear a mask if she didn't want to bring home some bug to Maggie.

She spotted the elderly driver, the one who usually came for her, holding up a sign with her name on it. He reached for her duffle bag, but she said, "It's okay. I'll carry it." She trudged behind him until they came to the town car and finally handed over her bag so he could put it in the trunk. He reminded her of the blanket and pillow on the backseat.

"Thank you," said Sam. "I'll probably sleep all the way home." She wound herself in the polar fleece with the wolf face on it and punched up the little paper-covered pillow. She intended to close her eyes, forget everything, and embrace oblivion, but her mind had other plans.

She remembered Maggie's red mouth offering a pouty kiss

before they ended their video chat last night. She couldn't wait to take her to bed and show her how much she'd missed her. That was the good part of coming home. The bad part was appearing for depositions at the lawyer's office tomorrow. One of the lawsuits had already been dropped. Melissa said the other probably wouldn't make it to court either. Under the blanket, Sam crossed her fingers.

"Would you like me to turn on some music?" asked the driver through the electronic speakers. "Something soothing to help you sleep?"

"That would be nice. As long as it doesn't make you go to sleep!"

"No, don't worry. I'm the one who always meets the red eye. You'll be fine."

He played a song by that reedy Irish singer, what they used to call "new age." Not that new anymore. Trying to remember exactly when the song was popular, Sam fell asleep.

***

The March wind was shaking the trees outside, so Courtney had decided to wait inside the atrium. As the children passed on their way to their classrooms, she listened to the chorus of small voices: "Good morning, Ms. Barnes," "Hello, Ms. Barnes," and an enthusiastic "Hiyah, Ms. Barnes!" The small girl grinned and waved vigorously. Courtney waved back.

She saw Brenda Harrison approaching with her children. "Good morning, Ms. Barnes," said Brenda, touching her fingers to her hat.

"Good morning, Chief Harrison," replied Courtney, with equal formality.

Brenda bent to kiss her little ones goodbye. "Have a great day," she said. "Enjoy your classes. Bring home something you learned that you can teach me and Mama C."

"Mama B, you already know everything!" said Keith, swinging his book bag.

"No, I don't. I can always learn, and so can you!"

She touched the boy's rosy cheek with her hand. "Try to behave." Megan reached up for another hug.

When the children were out of earshot, Brenda said. "We've scheduled another drill for next week."

Terror instantly gripped Courtney. She couldn't go back to that day. No matter how they cleaned up the place or changed her office, she still saw Peter Langdon standing there with his gun. If she didn't need this job, she would have already quit. "Please, no. It's too soon. The kids are still traumatized."

"I know, but it's important. We learned a lot from that incident, and we don't want anyone to forget."

"They won't forget," said Courtney. "They'll never forget. I won't either."

Brenda looked reflective. "No, I suppose you won't." She gave Courtney a long, measuring look. "Maybe we can skip the drill this month." She touched the brim of her hat. "Have a good day, Ms. Barnes."

***

Susan anxiously waited for the swirling circle to stop moving. Reshma and Lucy made it seem so easy, but Susan found technology a continuing challenge. She tried to remember all the instructions Reshma had given her, which was why she'd stuck notes all over her screen. "Smile during the count-down," read one. "You're live before you know it." A large post-it at the top said, "LOOK AT THE CAMERA!"

In exchange for helping Reshma get the Sunday School running, Susan had gotten lessons on how to use Facebook Live. When Susan volunteered to take morning prayers during school break, Lucy had looked skeptical, but she'd agreed, saying, "People no longer come to church, so we need to be wherever they are."

Once Susan realized her image and words were being broadcast, she momentarily froze. Even though she couldn't see her listeners, she greeted them as warmly as she would during a live service. After that, she began to relax into the rhythm of the prayers. She read the scripture appointed for the day and gave a brief homily. She prayed for those on the church prayer list. Besides the sick and dying in the parish, Susan always added those struggling with addiction or mental illness and the families of the shooting victims. After delivering a blessing, she remembered to keep smiling until the circle ended its rotation. When it stopped, she sighed in relief.

The knock on her door meant Reshma was outside. She opened the door and found herself scooped into Reshma's arms. "I am so proud! In a few minutes, Facebook will post the recording and we can watch it together."

"I'm not sure I want to see how bad I was."

"You weren't bad. You were nervous, but you did great!"

Susan's phone was dancing on her desk. She'd forgotten she'd put it on vibrate after Bobbie showed her how. Now, she couldn't get enough of it.

"Congratulations!" said Bobbie when Susan answered the call. "You were brilliant! Beautiful! Sexy!"

"Sexy? Bobbie, it was a prayer service."

"I know, but you were sexy."

"I didn't know you'd be watching."

"Cherie and I put it on the TV in the staff room. Other people watched on their phones. You had a big audience at Hobbs Family Practice. Should be good for your ratings."

Susan laughed. "My ratings," she repeated, shaking her head. "That's a good one."

❈❈❈

Maggie came into the faculty lounge to check her mail. "Good morning," said a voice. Maggie turned around to see Lise Boucher sitting with other teachers from the humanities department.

"Like to join us?" one of them asked.

Maggie wondered what this was about, but she smiled warmly. "Sure. I have a few minutes. Let me get myself a cup of coffee."

While Maggie sorted her mail, she felt their eyes on her back. She tossed the junk mail into the bin by the counter and headed to pour herself a cup of coffee.

"Did you settle on the end-of-the-semester play yet?" asked one of the women as Maggie sat down.

"I picked three plays. I'm running a survey online. I figure, let them vote on it."

"You narrow it down to what you think is within the range of their abilities, but you let them choose. I like that idea."

Maggie couldn't miss the flattery, but she didn't know what was motivating it. She glanced at Lise for clues, but her friend's smile revealed nothing.

"And how are midterms going for you?" Maggie asked, to show interest. She mostly taught performance arts and rarely gave written exams. She politely listened to the other teachers' answers.

"Maggie, we want you to know how much we like working with you," Lise finally said.

Maggie kept her face neutral as she studied them. "I like working with you too," she said cautiously.

"We know, but we want you to see that you're welcome here. If it didn't seem that way after the shooting, we're sorry."

"Thank you, but I didn't need an apology."

"We...well, let me speak for myself. The others say what they want." Lise paused to collect her thoughts. "We weren't always fair. I know that Sam didn't mean any harm. My cousin's a volunteer fireman, and he said she was at the scene, directing traffic. I think what you and Sam are doing for the victims and the school is amazing."

Maggie looked at each of them in turn. "One thing I know is that scapegoating never leads to anything good. We all do stupid things. Sam never intended to hurt anyone. She feels bad enough."

Some of the women stared at the table or their coffee cups. The silence became unnerving. Maggie was glad when one of them asked, "Which play do you think your students will pick?"

"You know, that's a damn good question. I have no idea."

\*\*\*

Cherie saw Liz in a pew near the back and decided to sit with her. "Nice to see you," Cherie whispered as she sat down. The singers were on break, but being in a church always inclined her to keep her voice down.

Liz replied at her normal volume. "I'm very curious to hear what Maggie and Denise have cooked up for this concert."

"I hear that Denise moved in with you."

Liz looked at her with a raised brow, then went back to watching the activity in the front of the church. "Not quite," she said. "She's living in the apartment over the garage."

"I bet Emily's happy about that."

Liz shrugged. "That's not why I did it. Emily's never there. Denise needed a place to live and rents are expensive. I look at it as an investment in the career of a promising singer." Despite the perfectly reasonable explanation, Cherie could tell Liz had other motives. Her boss wasn't as hard to read as some people thought.

"Keith's very anxious for me to hear him sing this duet in a church," Cherie said, "even though St. Margaret's isn't as big as the cathedral. Simone explained acoustics to him. To my surprise, he taught me a few things I didn't know."

"Bring him over sometime. I'll show him the sound system in my media room."

"He'd like that. He's into that techy stuff. But we should move down a little. Brenda will be here soon." Liz moved down in the pew. "How's the fundraising going for the foundation?" asked Cherie.

"We got a huge haul from Lucy announcing it at the Met. If this keeps up, we'll hit our goal before the concert."

"It can't hurt to have more than you planned. The need for counseling isn't going away anytime soon."

"Nope," said Liz, still watching Denise and company work things out in the front.

"Brenda said at breakfast that she thought things were getting back to normal. I bit off the poor woman's head. Things will never be the same again."

"No, they won't. And people will never forget. Ten, twenty years from now, we'll still be talking about it." Liz looked reflective. "Well, you might be. I don't know if I'll still be around then." Cherie looked at Liz, trying to calculate how old she'd be in twenty years. Close to ninety wasn't as old as it used to be.

Brenda showed up in her police uniform. "Did I miss anything?" she asked anxiously, taking the empty space they'd left for her.

"Just the adult choir rehearsing," said Liz. "Some of Denise's friends sang. Don't worry. Your son hasn't sung yet."

Susan and Reshma came into the church and headed down the aisle to where the others were sitting. "What are you doing way back here?" asked Susan.

"The sound is better," Liz explained. "Sit down." She slid deeper into the pew, suggesting with a nod that Cherie and Brenda should do the same.

At the front, Denise clapped to round up her troops. "Everyone! Please take your seats. We're going to get started again." The organist returned to her bench. The chamber musicians picked up their instruments. Denise and Lucy moved into position to sing the "*Recordare*" from *Verdi's Requiem*. Out of the corner of her eye, Cherie could see Liz smiling with pride. Next, Denise sang the "*Pie Jesu*" from the *Duruflé Requiem*, sounding divinely anguished. Lucy followed with the piece that had brought everyone to tears at the prayer service, the "*Pie Jesu*" from the *Fauré Requiem*.

When Lucy finished singing, Liz whispered close to Cherie's ear, "What do you think of this dueling '*Pie Jesu*'s idea? Not too gimmicky?"

"No, it's very moving. I think it will make people cry, and that's good. We need to cry. Better to cry over beauty than ugliness."

Liz nodded thoughtfully. "Yes, it is."

Maggie came out of the sacristy, holding Keith's hand. He looked around, blinking at the spotlights overhead. When he noticed his parents, he waved enthusiastically. Cherie blew him a kiss. He looked so small up on the raised steps of the sanctuary, but there he was, safe and whole, while so many of his classmates weren't. A lump formed in Cherie's throat, but despite her sadness, she smiled for her son's sake.

The familiar melody of the Lloyd-Webber "Pie Jesu" began to play. Maggie, holding Keith's hand, sang. Keith entered, right on cue, his pure, young voice blending perfectly with Maggie's adult soprano. A few tears of pride escaped Cherie's eyes. Beside her, Brenda was beaming.

Cherie listened to the plaintive music with a heavy heart. They were so lucky to have their child, but what about the others? And those victims yet to come? Lucy would say that God never promised to fix everything, and neither could they.

*But we need to try*, thought Cherie, and wiped away her tears. *We need to try.*

When the others began to applaud, she clapped as hard as she could

# Author's Note

If I were programming the concert described in this book, I would end it with the *"Pie Jesu"* from *Rutter's Requiem* because it is so healing and restful. Having lived through the school shooting in Newtown, Connecticut in 2012, I know how much a community needs privacy, calm, and peace after the news crews depart. I no longer live in Newtown, but I know many people who do.

The town is still grieving, and like Hobbs, it will never be the same. There is a real Sandy Hook Promise dedicated to promoting gun reform and protecting children from gun violence. You can visit their website at www.sandyhookpromise.org.

Full disclosure: I am a gun owner. Like Liz, I have a concealed carry weapon permit and carry a pistol every day. I support commonsense gun laws, a ban on assault weapons, and mandatory safety training for all gun owners.

# Also by Elena Graf

## HOBBS SERIES

### HIGH OCTOBER

Liz Stolz and Maggie Fitzgerald were college roommates until Maggie confessed their affair to her parents. When Maggie breaks her leg in a summer stock stage accident, she lands in Dr. Stolz's office. Is forty years too long to wait for the one you love?

### THE MORE THE MERRIER

Maggie and Liz's plans of sitting by the fire, drinking mulled wine, and watching old Christmas movies get scuttled by surprise visits from friends and family.

### THIS IS MY BODY

Professor Erika Bultmann, a confirmed agnostic, is fascinated by Mother Lucy, the new rector of the Episcopal Church, especially when she discovers Lucille Bartlett was a rising opera star before mysteriously disappearing from the stage.

### LOVE IN THE TIME OF CORONA

Police Chief Brenda Harrison shows an interest in Liz's biracial PA, but first Cherie needs to get past her loathing for all law enforcement since a state trooper shot and killed her sister.

### THIRSTY THURSDAYS

Liz Stolz initiates Thirsty Thursdays, a weekly cocktail party on her deck, so her friends can socialize safely during the pandemic. Pretentious, overbearing Olivia Enright pursues Liz's friend, architect Sam McKinnon, and tries to push her way into the tight-knit group.

### THE DARK WINTER

Erika hires Sam to build a soundproof practice room for Lucy. Fortunately, the early Christmas gift is ready before tragedy strikes. As the women of Hobbs pull together to help a beloved friend deal with her loss, the dark winter brings tension and realignment in their small community.

## SUMMER PEOPLE

Melissa Morgenstern, a high-profile lawyer from Boston, is spending the summer with her widowed mother. She's doing some trust work for Liz who introduces her to the attractive Courtney Barnes, Hobbs Elementary's new assistant principal. The arrival of Susan, Lucy's ex, complicates her deepening relationship with Liz.

## STRANDS

Cherie hears her biological clock ticking and would like to start a family. When a shocking tragedy creates an opportunity for her and Brenda to become parents, their friends need to step up to make it happen.

## THE RECTOR'S WEDDING

The sudden opportunity for Lucy to return to her singing career throws everything in her life into doubt—her vocation as a priest, her settled life in Hobbs, even her upcoming marriage to the woman she loves.

## THE VANISHING BRIDGE

Rev. Susan Gedney tries to rebuild trust after her humiliating exit from Hobbs. Bobbie Lantry always needs to rush away to take care of a mysterious elderly woman. They need to share their secrets, but do they dare?

## PASSING RITES SERIES

## THE IMPERATIVE OF DESIRE

A coming-of-age story that takes a brilliant aristocratic woman from La Belle époque through a world war, a revolution that outlawed the German nobility, and the roaring twenties to the decadent demi-monde of Weimar Berlin.

## OCCASIONS OF SIN

For seven centuries, the German convent of Obberoth has been hiding the nuns' secrets—forbidden passions, scandalous manuscripts locked away, a ruined medical career, and perhaps even a murder.

## LIES OF OMISSION

In 1938, the Nazis are imposing their doctrine of "racial hygiene" on hospitals and universities. Margarethe von Stahle has always avoided politics, but now she must decide whether to remain on the sidelines or act on her convictions.

## ACTS OF CONTRITION

After the fall of Berlin, Margarethe is brutally assaulted by occupying Russian soldiers. Her former protégée, Sarah Weber, returns to Berlin with the American Army and tries to heal her mentor's physical and psychological wounds.

# About the Author

In addition to the Hobbs series of contemporary novels set in a small town in Maine, Elena Graf has published four historical novels set in twentieth-century Europe. Two of the titles in the Passing Rites series have won Golden Crown Literary Society and Rainbow awards for best historical fiction. She pursued a Ph.D. in philosophy but ended up in the "accidental profession" of publishing, where she worked for almost four decades. She lives in coastal Maine.

Find out about events and new books at her website, www. elenagraf.com. You can write to Elena at elena.m.graf@gmail.com. Or find her on Facebook.

Elena is a member of iReadIndies, a collective of self-published independent authors of Sapphic literature. Please visit our website at www.iReadIndies.com for more information and to find links to the books published by our authors.

Printed in the USA
CPSIA information can be obtained
at www.ICGtesting.com
BVHW051859240823
668850BV00005B/60